FULL THROTTLE ATTACK

"Three closing on you. Eight miles dead ahead. Scramble now!"

McEntire's guidelights went off and he went into a fast vertical climb. Hauling the stick back, Gander eased his throttle and concentrated on trying to stay on his leader's wing, chasing a shadow.

"Data feeds are in. Weapons free. Arm 'em up. Infrared says Mirages."

And then, they were into it. McEntire launched two missiles, but the lead Mirage dodged them, diving beneath them. Gander pushed his nose down, had him in the gunsight for a half a second, and fired off thirty cannon rounds. The tracers all fell behind the target.

McEntire rolled right and went into a tight right turn. Gander stayed with him.

"One, Hawkeye. You've got a Mirage tight on your six. Pull G's!"

"He's got a radar lock on you, One."

"Break left!" McEntire ordered, checked his CRT, then launched two Sidewinders.

The hot exhaust stung Gander's night vision as he watched both missiles slam into the Mirage. It blew apart in streaks of yellow and blue.

"Thanks, Irish," Kimball called.

"Anytime, buddy."

ALPHA KAT

WILLIAM H. LOVEJOY

ZEBRA BOOKS
KENSINGTON PUBLISHING CORP.

*For Jane, Jodi, and David,
and for my friend and technical advisor,
Terry Keating*

ZEBRA BOOKS

are published by

Kensington Publishing Corp.
475 Park Avenue South
New York, NY 10016

First Printing: November, 1992

Printed in the United States of America

CHARACTERS

Kimball Aero Technology:

Bryce Kimball, "Cheetah," President
Sam Eddy McEntire, "Irish Eyes," Executive Vice
  President
A.J. Soames, "Papa," Vice President, Administration
Susan McEntire, Comptroller

Pilot/Engineers:

Conrad Billingsly, "Frog"
Howard Cadwell, "Cardsharp"
Phillipe Contrarez, "Speedy"
James Alan Gander, "Gandy Dancer"
Gaston Greer, "Gray Ghost"
Jay Halek, "Barnfire"
Alex Hamilton, "Flamethrower"
Thomas Keeper, "Miner"
Warren Mabry, "Dingbat"
Ito Makura, "Falcon"
Dave Metger, "Uncle Pete"
Sam Miller, "Dart"
Frederick Nackerman, "Flapjack"
Mel Vrdlicka, "Downhill"
George Wagers, "Gambler"

Mechanics:

Tex Brabham, chief mechanic
Carl Dent
Paul Diamond
Luke Frale
Zack Freeman
Walt Hammond

Wes Overly
Elliott Stott
Virgil Thomas
Perry Vance
Mark Westergood
Darrell Williams

Washington, D.C.:

Benjamin Wilcox, Deputy Director of Intelligence, CIA
Ted Simonson, Deputy Director of Operations, CIA
Brock Dixon, Major General, USAF Intelligence
Jack Ailesworth, Lieutenant General, USAF Weapons
    Procurement

Mercenary Force:

Derek Crider, Mission Leader
Wheeler, sniper, medic
Alan Adage, sniper
Emilio Lujan, pilot
Del Gart, munitions
Corey O'Brian, munitions

Lon Pot Organization:

Lon Pot, Prince of Southeast Asia

Henry Loh, Air Force Chief
Dao Van Luong, Finance Chief
Vol Soon, Army Chief
Micah Chao, Police Chief

PRE-FLIGHT CHECK

One

The earth was upside down.

As it should be.

When Kimball glanced to his right, he saw the foothills of the Rockies descending to their rugged and majestic peaks. Far away, there were still a few snowcapped pinnacles backed by low cumulus clouds. On his left were cultivated green fields, creamy squares of wheat, the twin ribbons of Interstate 25 clogged with Saturday drivers, and Sam Eddy McEntire.

Half a mile ahead, and above him, was the landing strip, starkly dark gray next to weed-cluttered fields and white and tan industrial buildings. The July sun glinted off the Plexiglas and the aluminum skins of thirty parked aircraft. A flight of six F-16 Falcons were lined up on the taxiway, waiting for their chance at the runway.

A gravel road passed over him, a hundred feet away. He continued to lose altitude. The earth pulled him closer. His engine screamed pleasantly, and the wind streaming past the open cockpit whistled at the edges of his helmet.

The two Pitt Special biplanes passed over the boundary markers and then the end of the runway with thirty feet of clearance between the asphalt and their stubby wings. Kimball concentrated on staying aligned with the western side of the strip. A touch of right rudder moved him to the left.

When he saw the crowd of tanned faces, sunglasses, and vibrant T-shirts in his peripheral vision, Kimball clicked the mike button on the stick once.

9

McEntire clicked back twice.

Kimball snap-rolled left at the same time McEntire rolled to the right. The wingtips cleared the runway surface by less than five feet. As soon as he came level, he neutralized the controls and pulled the throttle full back, and the engine roar died away.

The main gear touched down with a chirp of rubber on asphalt. McEntire was right beside him, a couple feet back.

The speed bled off quickly, and Kimball allowed the tail to settle. It bounced twice.

At the end of the runway, McEntire pulled off onto the taxi strip, and Kimball turned in behind him. In consort with McEntire, he goosed the throttle a tad, and the two biplanes raced back toward the aircraft park.

Two of the F-16s shot past him, their turbofans wailing, lifted off, and retracted gear immediately. Two more Falcons were right behind them. The biplanes bobbled in the turbulence of the passing fighters.

McEntire's voice sounded in his helmet, "Miss it, Kim?"

Kimball had once flown with the Air Force Thunderbirds. He keyed the mike, "Only difference, Sam, they go faster."

"You're so very damned good at answering a question."

"I don't miss it."

Maybe just a little. It was easily suppressed, however, when he tempered the longing with memories of mind-numbing regulations, social and career expectations, and brassy-voiced, narrow-minded commanders. Not all of them, he reminded himself. There were a few with wider minds.

The apron in front of the main hangar and the airport operator's office was roped off with orange nylon line and yellow flags to contain the spectators, and Kimball estimated the crowd size at around seven or eight thousand people. That would be enough to ensure their minimum cut of the gate receipts.

Tex Brabham waved Sam Eddy, then Kimball, into a line of parked airplanes and gave them a cut-throat signal.

Brabham was a scaled-down man, barely touching five feet four inches, weather-wrinkled and tanned the color of old brown boots. His boots were, in fact, old and brown and run-over at the heels, but polished to a high luster. He wore what Kimball called a seven-gallon hat to protect his completely bald head. He was the best all-around aircraft mechanic that Kimball had ever met.

Kimball switched off the ignition and killed the power to the radios. He disconnected the helmet's communication cord, removed the helmet, and placed it on the floor of the cockpit. Unbuckling his parachute and seat harness, he stood up, then stepped up on the seat and stretched. Bryce Kimball's six feet two inch height, broad chest, and wide shoulders made many of the cockpits he inhabited overly cramped.

"Nice routine, boss," Brabham said.

"That's because everything worked better than it was supposed to, Tex. The power plant sang happy tunes." He swung a leg outboard, found the step plate with his toe, and descended to the asphalt. It was hot, but the sun felt good on his face. He had come to prefer the warmer climes.

The announcer on the PA system turned it over to an Air Force major who introduced the crowd to the Thunderbird pilots in a soothing, public relations voice.

. . . the third aircraft is piloted by Captain Bryce Kimball of Tulsa, Oklahoma. His wingman, from Boston, Massachusetts. . . .

Kimball walked around the wing, patting it with affection. Both biplanes were finished in white with orange scallops topside and white with yellow on the underside. The color differentiation helped the spectators on the ground follow the attitude of the airplanes during acrobatic maneuvers.

Sam Eddy McEntire joined them at the nose of Kimball's plane. Kimball could hear the engine popping as it cooled, until a noisy Falcon shot down the length of the runway doing a four-point roll.

"Nice technique," McEntire said, his eyes following the

11

General Dynamics F-16. Perhaps with some longing.

"You talking about us or the Air Force?"

"Us."

"I agree with you."

"You guys ready for lunch?" McEntire asked. He was usually fond of food, no matter the origin or preparation.

"You two go on in," Brabham said. "I'm going to tie down the birds and prep 'em for morning, then drive on up to Cheyenne. I'll meet you there tomorrow."

"Ah, ah!" McEntire said. "Chickie-poo?"

"Knew a couple gals when I was stationed at Warren. Maybe they're still around and still single."

Tex Brabham was a dedicated bachelor close to sixty years old, but he kept looking for companionship. As far as Kimball had ever determined, he had a pretty fair success ratio.

"Okay, Tex. Be good to her."

"Or them," Brabham said, turning to walk over to his van parked off the asphalt.

The Chevy mini-van was cream-colored, with a pale blue stripe that expanded as it flowed back from the front end, then broke up into the stylized logo, "KAT." The van belonged to the company, but by reason of possession, it was Brabham's, and it was crammed with his own specialized tools.

Kimball and McEntire left the aircraft park, ducked under the orange nylon rope, and headed out to the field where the rented car was parked. The field was weedy and dry, and dust soon coated Kimball's Wellington boots. He unzipped and shrugged out of his flying jacket.

Sam Eddy drove. He drove or piloted whenever he was allowed. He hated getting his hands greasy under a car or in an engine compartment, but he loved being in control of anything mechanical. McEntire, like Kimball, had been a major in the Air Force when they both departed the service ten years before their retirement checks had been scheduled for printing. He was a couple inches shorter than Kimball, fair-skinned and dark-haired, and he wore a Boston Blackie moustache that was always carefully trimmed. Sam

Eddy said he had forgotten how many times he had been married, but Kimball was pretty sure the count was now at three. All three of them were exes.

He pulled out of the industrial park that was springing up around the Fort Collins-Loveland Airport, followed the frontage road north until he could cross over the interstate and join its northbound lanes. Traffic was heavy, which McEntire always took as a personal combat challenge, but he didn't push the rental Olds hard today.

"You suppose we're going to be hopping around to air shows the rest of our lives, Kim?"

The dream had been much grander when they had bailed out of the Air Force, and Kimball had begun to worry about the dream in earnest in the last six months.

He said, "Hell, no, Sam. Just to tide us over."

"Yeah. Maybe."

McEntire took the Harmony Road exit west and kept the speed at fifty-five as they passed the sprawling Hewlett-Packard plants. Kimball thought his friend was being very reserved today. Maybe thinking about his future, which he had never thought about before. Maybe he had lined up another job? That added to Kimball's worry. He didn't want to lose his chief pilot, primary propulsion engineer, company vice president, large stockholder, and most importantly, friend.

Five miles later, McEntire took Lemay Avenue over to Horsetooth Road, then continued west until he reached the Fort Collins Marriott and pulled into the lot. The foothills to the west were a brownish gray. The notched gap called Horsetooth Rock was clearly visible. There was a lot of nice greenage—cottonwoods and aspens and pines—to the south.

Kimball kept waiting for Sam Eddy to break the bad news, or some kind of news, to him, and Kimball certainly knew that he, himself, wasn't going to open the subject.

Twenty minutes later in the hotel's restaurant, with a club sandwich and a Michelob in front of him, McEntire's mood had not improved. That was contrary to his relationship with food.

Kimball used his fork to pick desultorily at a plate he had heaped high at the salad bar and wondered if he would get through half of it.

"Bryce Kimball?"

He looked up. The man standing next to the table was in his fifties, smooth-cheeked and a bit jowly, with graying hair and soft hazel eyes. To many of the younger people in the dining room, he'd have been an ideal daddy. Instinctively, Kimball felt the eyes and the easy smile on his face were deceptive. He wasn't dressed for the casual West. His blue suit was summer weight, dimly striped in silver, and expensive. He wore a brilliantly white shirt with a widespread collar and a dark red tie.

"Have we met?"

"No. But we were both in Bangkok at the same time once. The name's Ben Wilcox."

That introduction made Kimball immediately suspicious, but he didn't want to antagonize a potential client. "Have a seat, Mr. Wilcox."

Wilcox pulled out a chair and sat down. "You're a hard man to run down, Mr. Kimball. Your office in Phoenix led me in this direction, and I drove up from Denver this morning, but I missed you at the airport."

"You didn't see us fly?" McEntire asked with disbelief overriding his tone.

"Sorry, I missed it."

"Damn, you sure did," Sam Eddy said. "Would have made your whole day."

Was this something that couldn't be taken care of on the phone? Creditor?

Kimball lowered his fork to the plate. "Who do you represent, Mr. Wilcox?"

The man reached inside his jacket and withdrew a leather folder. He flipped it open, and Kimball saw the shield with the sunburst, the eagle head in profile. It was a familiar logo to Kimball.

Central Intelligence Agency.

"I don't want any part of this," Kimball said. "It was

14

nice meeting you, Mr. Wilcox. I'm truly sorry you couldn't stay around and talk."

"Now, hold on a minute, Kim," Sam Eddy McEntire said. "Let's not jump to any expensive conclusions."

Two

Major General Brock Dixon drummed his fingers on his desk top, thinking. It was an old, large, and solid walnut desk, and drumming his fingers was an ingrained habit; the varnish coat near the telephone was eroding after three years of Dixon's thinking.

Dixon was a big man, barrel-chested. His hair was blondish gray and clipped to near-baldness. There were Vietnam and Panama service ribbons among the six rows of ribbons above the breast pocket on his blue uniform coat. He wore the jacket at all times, even when at his desk thinking and drumming his fingers.

In his thirty-two years in the Air Force, whatever the geography might have been, Dixon's assignments had consisted of a country paying him to mull over difficult topics, to plan countermeasures, and to execute operations. He was not very active, and the sedentary life-style had gone to his waist, which is why he kept his coat on.

Finally, he gave up drumming and used his stubby forefinger to punch the private line on his telephone console and then hit one of the memory buttons.

"Weapons Procurement, this is Linda."

"Linda, Brock Dixon here. Let me talk to General Ailesworth."

Ailesworth came on the line a couple of minutes later. "What's up, Brock?"

"Wilcox."

"What about him?"

"He flew out to Denver early this morning, then rented a car and drove to Fort Collins."

Ailesworth laughed. "Goddamn, Brock. Doesn't Air Force Intelligence have anything better to do these days than spy on the CIA?"

"Jack, you know damned well that all the funny proposals showing up in the National Security Council meetings are coming off Wilcox's desk. The man's a menace."

"Hey, Brock. The Agency's in the same boat Defense is. With all of the bad guys in the world turning in their black hats, everyone's looking for new ways to justify their existence."

"You don't believe that, Jack."

"About the bad guys? Of course not. There's always going to be a few around. Check the Middle East, South America, and Asia. But the public thinks it's getting better, and they love it. Face it, we're cutting back, and so is the Agency. Wilcox wants to redirect some of his resources into new areas, just so he can hang onto the resources. He and his buddies over in operations have got a hell of a budget they don't want to lose. You blame him?"

"No, I guess not," Dixon said.

"Then why are you following him around? To see if he has a scheme you can steal?"

"You're going to be damned glad I had him watched."

"Why?"

"He went to Colorado to meet Bryce Kimball."

"Shit! He didn't."

"He did. Kimball and McEntire are flying acrobatics in some air show up there. My man called from the hotel where they're meeting."

"Ah, damn. I'm going to have to make some calls."

"Yeah, I thought you might."

"And Brock, you find out what they're talking about."

"I'll do that," Dixon said.

They went up to Kimball's room to talk, and McEntire brought along a six-pack of Michelob and a big bunch of

17

small bags of potato chips and Fritos. His appetite was returning.

Wilcox draped his suitcoat over the end of the bed and sat down next to it. McEntire twisted the caps off three bottles and passed them around, then sat in a chair at the small table next to Kimball. He tore off the top of a bag of chips and began to crunch them.

"I want to tell you about Kimball Aero Technology," Wilcox said.

"I know all about it," Kimball told him.

"You don't know my version of the story."

Kimball shrugged. He was going to have to sit through it because Sam Eddy was intrigued.

Wilcox put his bottle on the nightstand and leaned back on straightened arms. He appeared completely at ease, and Kimball wasn't happy with that appearance either. The man had a salesman's face, and Kimball wasn't in the mood to be sold, either up or down the river.

"Back in the beginning," the CIA man said, "Bryce Kimball got himself a degree in aeronautical engineering from the Air Force Academy down in the Springs, but that was just dressing. He was in it to fly, and fly he did. All kinds of airplanes. Top man at the Red Flag aggressor exercises. T-bird team. Instructor. Aviation advisor in Israel, Saudi Arabia, and Thailand."

"This is already getting boring," Kimball told him. "I've read the book."

"It gets better. For both of you, because McEntire has most of the same experiences."

Sam Eddy grinned and swigged from his bottle.

"Major Kimball had a bright, bright, soaring future in the Air Force. If he could just toe the line, he'd probably make general officer. But he fucked it up."

"How?" McEntire asked.

Wilcox paused to sip from his bottle, then leaned forward and reached across to the table for a bag of potato chips. "I missed lunch."

"Let's miss dinner next time. How about sometime next year?" Kimball asked.

18

Wilcox grinned. "This Kimball guy? He kept getting upset about Air Force procedures and inflexibility. He thought he could do it better than the Air Force could do it."

"I've shown that I can." Despite a desire to stay out of a debate, Kimball couldn't resist defending himself.

"To yourself, perhaps. You haven't proved a damned thing to anyone who counts, that is, the people who control the bucks. Can I finish my story?"

"Shoot," McEntire said. "I like a good story."

"So along the way, Kimball gets a file jacket full of letters of reprimand. Mild insubordination, ignoring the regulations, going around the chain of command. Bitching to some key congressional people, which is a real down-to-earth, glaring no-no. There's enough in the file to be irritating to promotion boards, and he's pretty sure he won't make lieutenant colonel, much less brigadier. He's young, and he's still got a chance to mend his ways, but do you think he'd do that?"

"Hell, no!" McEntire responded. "I can tell this guy's a real loser."

"In his spare time, he's been doodling little blueprints that don't interest his bosses or anyone else who hangs around the Pentagon. So Kimball gets fed up with the whole thing, resigns his commission and starts an airplane design and fabrication outfit."

"Good for him!" Sam Eddy shouted.

"I'll admit, Kimball, when I was researching this, you surprised the hell out of me. You raised forty-five million dollars in financing just like that." Wilcox snapped his fingers.

Kimball didn't say anything.

"But I looked around some, and I saw that your old man was in the oil business at one time, and I'll bet he had lots of friends with money just reeking of high-grade crude. I figure you took a few trips to Tulsa, Houston, and Denver, then stuffed your bank account. Good deal."

"My business is none of yours," Kimball said, regretting his need to spout the obvious.

"You did some other things. Fourteen highly trained and expensive pilots, not including Sam Eddy here, followed you out of the Air Force. You took along twenty-some damned good technical people, too. I'll bet Air Force Personnel was pissed at you for a long time. I'll also bet they didn't see the other angle, like I did. It takes some leadership qualities to talk forty people into giving up an assured pension."

"You getting to the end of this, Wilcox?"

"Easy up, Kim," McEntire said. "As a vice president of the company, I want to listen to the pitch."

"I'm getting to the best part now," Wilcox said. "You actually built eight airplanes. . . ."

"Seventeen."

"I'm only talking about the ones that you can actually get in the air," Wilcox grinned. "Personally, though I'm just a layman, you understand, they look pretty good to me. They met the specifications right down the line, and there's a very nice per-unit cost. Super-nice. But let's talk about cost. "All the high-tech materials were expensive as hell. Your legal expenses must have been a bitch, getting the licenses to buy classified electronics from the biggies in the defense industry, but they were happy to sell to you. They knew you were going under anyway."

"Now, goddamn it. . . ."

Wilcox held up a hand, palm out. "We're getting there. Besides the production and design overhead, you've had a hell of a salary load for the past three years. In fact, I happen to know that you might as well close your bank accounts. Any cash you have, you could carry in your hip pocket."

Kimball didn't think it was that bad. The cash flow would last for another few months.

"That's why you leased all of the aerobatic aircraft and put your pilots on the barnstorming trail. You're hunting for cash any way you can."

"Maybe we just like to fly," McEntire said, reaching for a fresh bottle of beer.

"Yeah, sure," Wilcox said, signalling for another bottle for himself.

"You ready, Kim?" McEntire asked.

"Not yet."

"In the last year, you've demonstrated your airplanes to the Air Force, Navy, and Marines," Wilcox continued. "And nobody was interested."

"You know why?" Kimball asked.

"Sure. First, the tactical organization is strange to them. Just because they've done it their way for so long, they think they like airplanes that can go independent. Second, they don't like the idea of publicity that suggests their planning has been all wrong. Third, if the public found out that the Air Force could buy one of your Alpha Kats for half the cost. . . ."

"One-sixth," Kimball corrected.

". . . of an F-15, John Q. Public would start climbing the Pentagon walls. The good old boys who've been leading the defense effort sure as hell don't want anyone to think they've been leading it in the wrong direction."

"You're aware of what the US and AF is now doing, I take it?" Kimball asked.

"Sure. They're reorganizing. Hanging onto all of their old assets, but managing it in a different way. Big damned deal."

"That's what I thought," McEntire said.

"What's this got to do with us?" Kimball asked, not really wanting to know. His curiosity level didn't run as high as McEntire's.

"How would the Central Intelligence Agency like to buy some airplanes?" Sam Eddy asked. "We could work out a favorable discount, maybe. If there's a real national security angle."

"I've got one more point to make, then I'll buy the airplanes."

That made Kimball sit up. He finished his beer and slapped the bottle down on the table.

"You've got more lines in your face than the last picture I saw of you, Kimball. High stress, you think?"

21

The pilot's squint lines at the corners of Kimball's blue eyes had deepened in the past couple of years, and the flecks of gray in his umber hair were spreading fast. Back in the old Air Force days, he had been accustomed to smiling a lot, too, but the smiles were less frequent now. The go-to-hell attitude had evaporated.

"That's your point? Come on. Let's get to it."

"Okay. Let's see. You can't sell your fighter aircraft and its required AWACS to the Pentagon, so naturally you take aim at some of the friendly third world and developing nation markets. And what happened there?"

"You've done the research," Kimball said.

"State, Commerce, and Transportation all denied permission to either export the aircraft or to take them out of the country for demonstrations. Apparently, they don't have as much faith in your little airplanes as you do."

"Bullshit," Kimball said. "They were pressured by our competition."

"Aw, you don't mean there's a conspiracy to run you out of business?"

"You're damned right there is. Like you said, the military services don't want to be proven wrong, and they're in bed with the aerospace conglomerates who don't want to lose their markets, even the downsized markets that are going to be left after the end of the Cold War. If Kimball Aero makes one good sale, we'll undermine what Lockheed, Boeing, Rockwell, McDonnell Douglas and everybody else has been doing. They'll be forced to redesign and retool in order to compete. That's damned expensive for outfits the size of Lockheed. Hell, they're already trying to contract their size."

"I don't think there's a conspiracy," Wilcox said, smiling a little smile.

"And you're the Deputy Director of Intelligence?" Sam Eddy asked. "That confirms an opinion I've always held about the Agency."

"I don't think there's a conspiracy that I want to try to prove. Or could prove. Try it that way."

"That's the point?" McEntire asked. "Okay, good point. Now buy the airplanes."

"Actually, I don't want to buy your planes. I want to lease them."

"For what?" Kimball asked.

"For how much?" McEntire asked.

"I like the way Vice President McEntire thinks," Wilcox said, shifting his position on the edge of the bed. "He's a bottom-line man."

"So am I. But my bottom line doesn't necessarily revolve around dollars."

"I'm well aware that your principles are high, Kimball, and I don't doubt your patriotism for one tiny minute. But what if it's more than dollars?"

"If it's a covert operation, it's probably not worth talking about," Kimball said.

"Let's talk about what I'll do for you. I'll give you three million dollars. The three million buys you a few more months more of cash flow and it underwrites a foreign demonstration tour."

Sam Eddy stuffed potato chips into his mouth.

"We can't. . . ."

"And additionally, I'll arrange all of the permits you need to take the aircraft out of the country."

McEntire grinned. "That's worth more than the three mil, Kim."

Kimball waited.

Wilcox stood up and began to pace. He said, "Now let's talk about what you'll do for me."

Three

Down in the wide corridor off the lobby of the Marriott, Benjamin Wilcox picked up a phone, dialed the number at Langley, then punched in his credit card number.

Ted Simonson answered his own private line. Simonson was the Deputy Director of Operations, and Wilcox had known him for over twenty-five years, most of them as a friend as well as a colleague.

"This is Ben."

"Where in the hell are you? You didn't even tell your secretary you were leaving."

"It was a spur of the moment thing, Ted." Wilcox turned and leaned against the wall. The guy in the black suit and blue tie was still sitting in the lobby. He was a patient type, probably suited to intelligence work.

"You know that idea we were kicking around a couple of weeks ago?"

"Which idea? You've got too many plots going, Ben."

"Well, I'm not going to mention it on the phone. I've got a friend sitting close by."

"Good friend?" Simonson asked.

"No."

"What day did you mention this?"

"It was a Thursday evening. We went to the Sans Souci. You had the lobster."

"Oh, yeah. I remember."

"I just talked to Kimball."

"No lie? And what did Kimball say?"

"He hasn't yet, but he'll go for it."

"You're sure?"

"Positive. I looked deep into his background and his business, and he's out of choices. The main thing I'm calling about, I want you to tag the dollars in your contingency fund. Don't go spending them elsewhere." Wilcox looked back toward the lobby at the man in the black suit, and the name finally came to him.

"How many dollars?"

"Three big ones."

"You're going to have to come up with some of your own."

"Yeah, I can take part of it, I guess," Wilcox agreed. "Even though it's rightly in your directorate, rather than mine. For my contribution, I want to control it."

"Missing the good old days, are you, Ben?"

"Not so you'd notice. I've just got a vested interest in this project. It's also damned important."

"Have you forgotten, Ben, that we don't have approval for this? Hell, I haven't even mentioned it to the DCI."

"You told me you would."

"Yes, but it slipped my mind."

"The White House is fully aware of the problem," Wilcox said. "We've been highlighting it in the intelligence estimates."

"I read them."

"We're running out of time, Ted. It used to be months. Now it's weeks."

"I'm well aware of it, Ben."

"So you don't think it's worth the gray matter I printed it on?"

"No, that's not it. I can buy it. My question: does Kimball buy it?"

"He will because it's got a national interest ring to it. The Secretary of Defense himself said that drug interdiction was a priority defense consideration," Wilcox said. "Kimball doesn't say it out loud, but he's a patriot at heart."

"You didn't tell him the whole story, then?"

"If I told him the whole story, it wouldn't sound so demanding of his patriotic fervor, would it?"

"Are you going to? Tell him?"

"Maybe. We'll just have to see how it goes."

"Well, hell, as long as he's in, I don't see how we can pass on this project."

"Damn right," Wilcox said. "Where else are we going to find a private air force?"

"Is it a capable air force?" Simonson asked.

"I'll be damned if I know about that, Ted. It looks good on paper, but I don't know how it performs. We're talking both hardware, which appears up to snuff, and people. My office is checking out his people, now. I tried to flatter him without being too obvious about it. Negative persuasion, you might call it."

"If the airplane doesn't perform as promoted?"

"I have a feeling the aircraft will be all right. But the pilots have been too long away from the discipline."

"So if they don't fit together?"

"Then we have us a sacrificial lamb, Ted. But we may still accomplish the goal. We do still have the same goal?"

After a long pause, Simonson said, "Yeah, you're right."

"Get hopping, then. We're going to have to ram it through back channels and try to keep it out of the NSC. We can have an okay before anyone even thinks about the ramifications."

"And the Senate and House Oversight Committees? I can already count the votes."

"Use a Presidential Finding. Tell the committees after it's all over," Wilcox suggested.

"The backlash on the Agency could be devastating."

"I don't think so. I think we might pass some of our secret medals around."

"You're getting awfully damned optimistic in your old age, Ben."

"Are we going to worry about the way the liberals vote, or are we going to take one little step for the country? For the world, for that matter."

"I'll go up and see the Director."

26

"Hey, Ted, you want to call Melinda for me?" Melinda Mears was Wilcox's secretary.

"You're saving on long-distance calls, right?"

"Tell her I'll be in Cheyenne, somewhere."

Wilcox hung up the phone and headed for the sunlit glass doors of the entrance. As he passed the man in the black suit, he stopped and bent over the back of the couch to tap him on the shoulder.

"Enjoying your vacation, Major Nash?"

Kimball stood at the window, swirling the beer in the bottom of his bottle. There was a lake on the other side of Horsetooth Road, and he saw a small flight of Canadian geese approach from the south, passing over residential homes, to settle on its surface. A lone eagle presided over the lake, circling high to the east.

He felt pretty much like the eagle. All alone, searching for a decision that wouldn't endanger the geese in his pond.

"There's a risk factor," he said.

"Since the day you and I went down to Lackland and started playing airplane jocks, there's always been a risk factor," Sam Eddy said. "There's always been high stakes, too, but never higher than they are now."

"We'd be committing a lot of good people we haven't talked to, yet."

"Name me some names."

"What names?"

"Of anyone who won't go where you go."

Kimball couldn't think of anyone. The trouble was that his life, or his outlook on it, had changed considerably in the last three years. In the Air Force, he had worried about his wingman, and to a slightly lesser extent, the men in his squadron. As President of Kimball Aero Tech, he worried about a great deal more. The people were the most important to him. He had enticed many of them away from the security of the service, and they depended upon him making the right decisions. Except for a few people they had

27

hired locally to work in fabrication and assembly, they were almost family. A hell of a lot of brothers and sisters replacing his biological family.

Then, beyond his company family were the investors who had trusted him. They deserved the best he had to give, and they didn't deserve the condemnation that might come out of this soiree.

As Wilcox had figured out, his father had provided him with the list of investment contacts to make. Even today, he felt guilty about not calling or visiting his parents when he had had the chance.

Wilcox had probably figured out some other things also.

"The company people all have a stake, too," McEntire reminded him. "Not only in their jobs, but in their investments of time, money, expertise, and trust."

All of the KAT employees were shareholders in the company to some degree. Kimball owned the biggest block (thirty percent) because the designs were his and had been fleshed out while he was still in the service. But he had passed out stock to those who had joined him.

He turned around, went to the bed, and stretched out on it. "I don't like government contracts."

"You mean, like the ones we've been trying to sell?"

"No, damn it. Like working for Washington. Jesus Christ! The CIA! No one works for the CIA, Sam Eddy."

"Betcha we never see anything in writing," McEntire said as he walked to the nightstand and picked up the phone. "Room Service? This is Mr. Kimball in 312. I could sure use a six-pack of Michelob and maybe some nachos. You have nachos? Great! Send up two orders."

"I don't want anything," Kimball said as Sam Eddy replaced the receiver.

"I didn't order you anything. Look, Kim, this is just what we need to get us out of this great big hole we dug for ourselves."

"It's a big carrot, yes. Wilcox knew it would be."

"You bothered by the mission?"

Kimball thought about the briefing Wilcox had given them. After listening to the man for awhile, it had not been

28

as farfetched as it had sounded in the beginning. "No, no I'm not. The objective is all right. Hell, the objective is fine."

It was better than Sam Eddy would ever know.

"All we have to do is blow this Wop Bop. . . ."

"Lon Pot."

"Lon Pot guy out of existence."

"And work for the CIA," Kimball reminded him.

"And take their bucks and licenses and visas and transport permits."

"And expect that Lon Pot won't fight back? You heard what Wilcox said about the guy's defensive posture. He won't go easy."

"Fuck him. Can the Alpha Kat do it or not? What the hell do we think we're selling?"

"Throw me the damned phone."

Grinning, McEntire dialed the number, then handed the phone to Kimball.

Susan McEntire answered promptly in Phoenix. She was Sam Eddy's third ex-wife.

"Hi, Susie."

"Kim? Anything wrong?"

"Should there be?"

"Is Sam Eddy all right?"

"Everybody's fine. Quit worrying. We've got some schedule changes to make."

He heard paper rustling. "Okay, tell me."

"Sam Eddy and I will make the show in Cheyenne tomorrow, but we'll return to Phoenix just as soon as it's over. I want you to call around and cancel the rest of our tour."

"What!"

"And then start tracking everyone else down and call them back to Phoenix. I want pilots at nine o'clock in the morning, the day after tomorrow. We'll need to call around and cancel their schedules, also."

"Damn it, Kim! You're talking about cutting off a lot of income."

"We're finalizing another contract."

"It better be out of this world." Susan McEntire handled all of the accounting for Kimball Aero.

"Three million."

"Hurry back," she said.

There was a knock on the door, and McEntire got up to open it and take the tray from the waiter. Kimball watched him sign the tab and figured he had added a big tip, then signed Kimball's name.

He sat up and said, "Let me have my nachos while they're hot."

"You didn't order any."

"I changed my mind."

They were accompanied with a dirty look from McEntire.

Jimmy Gander figured he was the first one back. He had only gone down to Tucson for a one-day show, and he landed his Beechcraft Staggerwing at Sky Harbor International Airport at three o'clock on Sunday afternoon.

The big radial engine purred as he turned off the runway used by the noncommercial air traffic onto the taxiway leading to the general aviation section. Some of the Air National Guard guys were getting their flying hours in, he could tell, since there were gaps in the rows of parked ANG aircraft.

"Beech one nine, you're purtier than any seven-sixty-seven," Phoenix Tower told him.

The big passenger-cabined biplane was a full restoration, finished in yellow, with every detail crafted to match the original. Even the more modern Nav/Com radios were mounted in a temporary rack on the floor so they could be removed for air shows.

Gander grabbed the mike resting in his lap. "Thank you, Phoenix, I feel purty. One nine out."

James Alan Gander was an Arizona boy, born and raised in Phoenix. He loved the hot, dry environment, and he even liked Barry Goldwater. KAT's decision to locate in the capital city was one of the reasons he had given up his captaincy after seven years in the Air Force. He was twenty-nine years old and lanky: body, face, and limp brown hair. He had held at 166 pounds since his junior year of high school, when he was on the chubby side, but his height had climbed from five foot two inches to six foot two inches by the time he took his master's in electrical engineering from the University of Arizona in Tucson.

He rolled the Staggerwing off the taxiway toward the big hangar leased by KAT. It was painted cream, and "Kimball Aero Tech" was lettered in blue above the big doors. Because of the size of the lettering, there hadn't been room for the "nology" part of the company name.

Gander turned into the aisle behind the second row of aircraft in front of the hangar, then turned again to aim the nose toward the runway and park the Beech next to one of the three Kappa Kats. Only two of the Kappa Kats were operational; the third was just a shell without engines, instrumentation, or avionics. The eight Alpha Kats parked in the first row were also shells awaiting power and electronic components, but they were parked out in front for advertising reasons. The six operational Alphas were tied down in the third row.

Those airplanes were the second, and higher, reason Gander had left the service. Gander thought that, like Ford had once claimed, Bryce Kimball had a better idea.

They looked like a private air force parked there, identified only by the small "KAT" logo on the rudders, the FX-41 or CX-41 model number below the canopies, and the Federal Aviation Administration-assigned N-numbers on the fuselages. All of them were finished in a matte midnight blue which made them difficult to see at night or on clear days, but then, they weren't designed to be seen.

Gander shut down the Beechcraft, popped open the door, and got out with his flight bag. He dropped the bag on the tarmac and spent some time chocking the wheels and tying the airplane down. He liked the Staggerwing almost as well as he liked the Alpha Kat and wished that he, or the company, owned it, rather than leased it.

Flying the Beech or the Alpha Kat was a pilot's dream.

31

He was totally in control of his aircraft. It was back to the basics, and there was nothing wrong with the basics. Gander had flown F-15 Eagles for the Air Force, which was kind of like supervising an automated roller coaster. There were lots of times, of course, when he had been allowed to do his own thing, but mostly the Eagle's computers ran the show: *do this, do that, turn here, lock on target, let go and let me fly it, you jerk.*

Looking between the wings of the Beechcraft at the row of Alpha Kats, Gander was very aware of sixty years of evolution. The Alpha Kat was small. At twenty-six feet, the wingspan was five feet less than an F-16 Falcon. It was a semi-delta wing, each wing deprived of being a full right-angled triangle by the forward sweep of the wing from the tail to the wingtip. The wings were thin and, from this distance, looked like razor blades. The four weapons pylons could handle a wide variety of missiles, and the tandem centerline hardpoints were designed to accept external fuel storage, electronics pods, ordnance, or a mix of the three.

The fuel bladders were mounted inside the fuselage with the single Kimball/McEntire turbofan engine. The KM-121 developed 38,000 pounds of thrust, 14,000 pounds more than either of the engines in McDonnell Douglas's F-15. The KM-121 had no afterburner to promote an infra-red signature and high fuel consumption, though the lack did cut into its acceleration. The engine casing was primarily a ceramic casting to reduce the RCS (radar cross section). Even the turbine blades were manufactured from carbon-impregnated plastic for the same reason. Elongated and variable engine intakes were mounted to either side of the fuselage, slightly forward of the wing. Intake air was channeled internally in a slight inward curve toward the centerline-mounted engine. That prevented radar signals from "seeing" the spinning turbine blades through the intakes. To drastically reduce the infrared exhaust signature, the tail pipe was longer than normal.

The wide, squat fuselage was mostly fuel storage, and the Alpha Kat had a ferry range, in a straight line, of 3,700 miles, one hundred more than an Eagle and nearly 1,400 more than a Falcon at the Alpha Kat's economy cruise speed of Mach 1.2. It wasn't as fast as the Eagle or Falcon, but Gander didn't think the top end of Mach 1.9 was a crawl.

The twin rudders, mounted close to the wide fuselage, were canted inward at the top, designed to also camouflage any heat from the engine that might create an infrared signature. The single small canopy, barely a bulge over the down-sloping nose, was tinted a dark bronze to eliminate sun glint and infrared return.

Every leading or trailing edge had a slight curve to it, again to foil searching radars.

It looked tiny, lean, mean, agile, and quite deadly. And it was.

And parked beside him, the Alpha Kat's bigger sister, the Kappa Kat command craft had a similar appearance. The wingspan was fifteen feet greater, and the fuselage was longer and wider in order to accommodate twin turbofan engines and four ejection seats. The Kappa Kat seated a pilot and a navigator/copilot side by side and two air controllers at matching consoles behind them.

At Lockheed's famous "Skunk Works" design center in Burbank, now phased out, such aircraft would have been cloaked in secrecy. At Sky Harbor International Airport in Phoenix, Arizona, Kim Kimball parked them in the open for the world, and the competition to see. He wanted to advertise, and besides, the hangar would only accommodate two aircraft simultaneously because it was also crammed with alignment jigs, casting machines, calibration equipment, machine tools, and stored airframe and turbofan parts.

Gander picked up his flight bag, with "Gandy Dancer" stenciled on the side of it, and started walking toward the hangar.

An optimistic Kimball had taken lease options on the three hangars to the east for expansion.

Jimmy Gander knew Kimball was less optimistic now. In fact, the main reason Gander had given up the security of the Air Force was Bryce Kimball, but he had changed dramatically in the last six or seven months.

He dragged. There was less spring in his step. The smiles were forced. His normally spontaneous good humor had vanished. Kimball had never been married, and he carried something of a subdued reputation as a ladies' man. *Had carried.* Gander didn't think his boss had dated anyone in four months. Mollie Gander, his wife, had mentioned it, too.

It was going bad.

Gander figured tomorrow morning's meeting had been scheduled to tell them that loans had been called, that Federal Aviation Administration airworthiness certificates had been withdrawn, that test flights were to be further curtailed to cut the fuel bills, that. . . .

. . . that something, anything, everything was wrong.

He could feel it in his bones. The company was peering over the edge.

The outlook for himself wasn't great, either. The Air Force and the other services were cutting back, dumping pilots on the job market. And subsequently, the defense contractors were also reducing their payrolls.

As a pilot and an electrical engineer, Gander might have to look for work in a restaurant.

The security guard, who was stationed in a small corner office looking out on the tarmac and a few million dollars' worth of aircraft, let him into the building. They exchanged pleasantries, and Gander went on down the hall toward the front door and the parking lot. The east side of the hangar had been subdivided into a hallway with small offices, restrooms, a dressing room, and a front office sectioned against the outer wall.

A complete aerospace defense industry in sixty thousand square feet. It felt empty and forlorn.

Sometimes, Jimmy Gander wished he was back in an Eagle, looking for something to shoot down.

Four

Kimball and McEntire had landed their Pitts Specials at Sky Harbor late on Sunday night. Judging by the wide variety of aircraft parked on the apron in front of the Kimball Aero hangar (Staggerwing, P-51 Mustang, P-38 Lightning, Stearmans), Kimball thought most of the pilots had already made it back. The ground crews who had accompanied them in vans, both owned and rented, would be dragging in throughout the night and Monday morning.

Kimball drove his restored '68 Camaro convertible north on 32nd Street to his small condo off Camelback Road. He was almost eagerly prepared for deep sleep, but after he had showered, found himself wide awake. He pulled on a pair of faded jeans, opened a bottle of *Dos Equis,* and went out onto his balcony. The night was warm, but the stars were crisp, even with the glow of downtown Phoenix interfering with vision. The lamps along the sidewalk between the rows of condominiums spilled soft light on the yellowing grass and the gravelled sections containing several varieties of cacti. There were two mammoth saguaros, the familiar sentinel of Arizona. They were becoming an endangered species, with people sneaking out into the desert to steal them for home improvement projects.

Kimball wasn't sure how he felt. Much as he hated the CIA, and didn't much care for Ben Wilcox, he was looking forward to the tour they were funding. Action of any kind was better than beating himself to death trying to reach Defense Department weapons procurement people or

Transportation and State Department bureaucrats. He had been fighting that battle for over a year and had almost reached the last resort, which was going to court. Even then, the odds of forcing the government to pay attention to him were barely fifty-fifty. On top of which, he couldn't afford the justice system, for both financial and publicity reasons. It wouldn't help to publicize in the media the fact that the United States government didn't think his airplanes should fly overseas.

He decided he felt alive again.

Or maybe just restless.

After an hour of jumbled thoughts, Kimball finished his beer and went back inside. It was after midnight, but he toyed with the idea of calling Cathy before deciding to skip it. He had not talked to her in so long, she would probably hang up on him. And she had to go to work in the morning, anyway.

He went to bed, woke at 4:30 A.M., and showered again, then shaved. He thought his eyes looked brighter, bluer, in the mirror. His face, with its flat planes and high cheekbones and deep tan, appeared healthier. The skeletal substructure was there for a purpose, rather than just to keep his skin from sinking farther. He needed to get a haircut.

At five o'clock in the morning, he called Wilcox and found him already in his office.

"Well?"

"You on your office phone?" the DDI asked.

"No, home."

"That should be all right for now. We'll meet personally in the future. The Director and the National Security Advisor met with the man at Camp David yesterday afternoon. He signed off, and it's a go."

Kimball breathed a sigh of relief or anxiety. He wasn't certain which. "The money?"

"The money will be transferred to your Phoenix account this afternoon. It will be followed in the overnight mail by a consultation contract for you to sign."

"I'm not signing shit," Kimball said.

36

"Hey, Kimball, this is cover. It just says that a Kimball Tech team will advise some company or another out of Atlanta, I think, on aviation matters. I don't know what company they picked, but it isn't the Agency. That clears you on your income. Be sure and set aside enough for your taxes."

"Are you my financial advisor now?"

"No."

"Okay. Did you find my aircraft for me?"

"Yup. There are two C-141Bs currently on reserve status, and they will be leased to you for three months. One's at Homestead Air Base in Florida, and the other is at Charleston Air Force Base. This is shaping up like a real travelling circus," Wilcox told him.

"What about the paperwork?"

"First, I'm going to have to have you fill out all the applications."

"No damned way. The applications are already completed and sitting in offices all over your fair city. I'm not doing it again."

"That's all right. That's good, in fact. I'll start making the rounds this morning."

"And you think you can swing it?" Kimball asked.

Wilcox laughed. "If I can't, I have this short letter signed by the big boss. What about on your end?"

"I've already made contact with the appropriate defense ministers and officers in the countries we want. Hell, I did that over a year ago. There was a lot of interest at the time, and I suspect that I can revive it. But it's still going to take about a week to put together."

"Timeline?"

"We can be wheels-up in ten days. Make it July fifteenth."

"Good by me. I'll have a package together for you before the twelfth. Let's meet in Denver."

"You're running this?" Kimball asked. Wilcox belonged to the Intelligence side of the CIA.

"Well, it'd normally fall in the operations directorate, yeah, but I'm doing some temporary duty."

"Is that a good idea?" Kimball was leery of people operating out of their specialties. He wouldn't put a transport pilot in an FB-111 fighter bomber.

"I was in the field for seventeen years, Kimball."

"Just checking."

"You have a fax machine?" Wilcox asked.

"In the office."

"All right. You'll get a picture on it sometime this morning."

"Picture of what?"

"Picture of a who. Guy named Nash, a major. He's an AFI snoop who was following me for awhile, but now he's on your tail."

"What the hell? What's going on?"

"Hey, Kimball, you think there's a conspiracy mounted against you? We've got our own going, too. It's all part of the game, so don't sweat it."

The meeting started at nine o'clock.

Kimball kicked everyone out of the front office except for the sixteen pilots and closed the doors. Susan McEntire put up a fuss about the exclusion of women, and he had to promise a briefing for her later.

The room wasn't really big enough for all of them. It was cramped already with Susie's and the receptionist/secretary Andrea Deacon's desks, two computer credenzas, an eight-foot couch, and several potted plants. Five oversized color prints of the Alpha Kat and the Kappa Kat in flight were mounted on the walnut-panelled walls.

There were a few fights for possession of chairs. Most of the pilots leaned against the walls, and Sam Eddy McEntire sat in the middle of Andrea's desk blotter, his legs crossed Indian-fashion.

Kimball stood by the glass front door. "No problems with any of the air shows?"

Sixteen negative responses.

"Good."

McEntire grinned at him, but it was a sarcastic grin.

38

Sam Eddy had never cared for Air Force briefings, and this was shaping up like one.

"You guys each own five thousand shares of stock in the company," Kimball said. That was about two percent each. McEntire owned twelve percent because of his rather dedicated and brilliant involvement with the engine designs. "It's worth maybe a thousand dollars, if you could find anyone who wanted to buy it."

The morose faces told him they had been expecting something like this.

"It's not particularly undervalued because we're showing about thirty-nine million dollars in assets and forty-five million in debt. If we could find someone willing to buy the assets."

By all that was true and fair, they should have been many more millions in debt. Nothing was cheap in this world, and a shoestring operation in aerospace technology just didn't survive on less than a hundred million dollars. They had gotten this far only because everyone contributed heavily in expertise and reduced salaries.

Jimmy Gander, sitting on the floor against the far wall, next to Mel Vrdlicka, looked halfway sick.

Kimball grinned at them. "I think that, within the next couple of months, each of your five thousand-share holdings are going to be worth at least fifty thousand dollars, maybe more than that."

Clothing rustled as they sat up. Backs straightened. Shoulders rose from slumps. Howard Cadwell stuck his two clenched fists in the air and shook them. Warren Mabry's teeth splashed white against his ebony skin.

McEntire said, "At least."

"We're getting our clearances for a foreign demonstration tour."

"Hot damn! . . . 'bout fuckin' time . . . ah, mother . . . where to, boss?"

"Tentatively, I'm scheduling demonstrations in Chad, Saudi Arabia, Pakistan, India, and Thailand. Those will all have to be confirmed, and there may be a couple more."

The grins told him they were ready. They had been ready

since the first Alpha Kat fighter rolled out of the hangar, eighteen months before.

Kimball slipped the eight-by-twelve photograph from the file folder Wilcox had given him in Cheyenne. He held it up, the face toward them, and said, "There's one little hitch."

"Who the hell's that ugly son of a bitch?" Jay Halek demanded.

The picture was fuzzy, blown up from a telephoto shot, but the man's features were clear enough. He had thick black hair piled high on his head, heavy brows over narrowed dark eyes, a broad and squashed nose, and a grim gash for a mouth. The visible teeth were jagged. His skin was heavily pocked with smallpox scars.

"This is the hitch. He's one of Southeast Asia's leading entrepreneurs and billionaires."

"You got to be kidding, Cheetah," Vrdlicka said. "Cheetah" was Kimball's old Air Force call sign.

"I'm not. His name is Lon Pot, and he's Cambodian, or Kampuchean as they call it now, though he lives in the Shan State of Burma."

"I call him 'Pothead,' " McEntire said.

"That's the Golden Triangle," Mabry said. "Heroin billionaire."

"You got it, Warren."

"Hang on a minute," Gander said. "Where's this going? What hitch?"

"Let me tell you about Lon Pot and his farming venture first, Jimmy. This guy is a major export center for heroin. His collection teams roam the mountains and jungles of Burma, Cambodia, and northern Thailand where the local farmers grow a lot of pretty red and purple flowers. They don't have to do much cultivation; the flowers grow wild, and they have seed pods full of alkaloid. The sides of the pods are full of thick, sappy, stuff that the farmers dig out. The alkaloid is raw morphine, and the sap is opium gum. Some Liu or Hsong tribe member will get himself a few hundred *baht* per kilo every April, that's maybe eighty bucks, just enough to tide him over until the next harvest.

"Lon Pot's collectors haul packages of the gum to one of his five refining and distribution centers. After the gum is refined into heroin powder, a kilo can bring close to a thousand dollars. That's a hell of a profit margin."

"Better than the aerospace industry at the moment," McEntire said.

"Thanks for the observation, Sam Eddy. Anyway, out there in the jungle, Pot doesn't have a hell of a lot to spend his money on, so he buys himself an army. He's got to have it, anyway, to maintain his power."

"How good an army?" Halek asked.

"I don't know, and it doesn't affect us."

"What does affect us?" Gander asked.

"His air force," McEntire said.

"Shit," Gander said. "You getting to this little hitch, now?"

"Yes. Sam Eddy and I struck a deal with . . . a government agency we'll call Mr. Washington. In exchange for our clearances and some operating cash, we take out Lon Pot as a sideline to our demonstration tour."

"You might call it an operational demonstration," Sam Eddy told them.

There were a few moments of silence, though not really stunned silence, Kimball thought.

Finally, Warren Mabry asked, "How big an air force?"

"We'll have better intelligence later, but right now it looks like he's got a half-dozen MiGs, four HAL HF-24 Maruts which were built in India, several helicopters, and a bunch of elderly transport aircraft. Anything from DC-3s to C-130s. They're based at three small and two large fields in northern Burma, Thailand, and Kampuchea. Pot thinks they're pretty well-hidden, but we're getting satellite photos of them."

"Piloted by?" Mabry probed.

"My information is that he's trying to build up a cadre of his own pilots, Kampuchean or Burmese probably, but that he still relies heavily on mercenaries."

"That could mean Americans," Mabry said.

"Yes. Or French, or Aussie, or Vietnamese, or Chinese.

41

Who knows?"

"And who gives a shit?" McEntire said. "Whoever is flying for Pothead, as far as I'm concerned, he's peddling horse on 42nd Street in New York or Sunset in L.A. or Van Buren in Phoenix. If I down him, I'm not going to grieve. Hell, I'm not even going to think about it."

Not one of them had ever killed. They had been too young for Vietnam. Two of them had Persian Gulf experience before leaving the Air Force, but the sorties they had participated in had never run into hostile aircraft. Anything they ever shot down had been a remote-controlled target drone or computer-simulated in war games.

"No one here has to go along," Kimball said.

"Oh, hell, boss," Gander said. "I'm not worried about going along. I *want* a shot at these assholes. I want to show off our airplanes. It's just going to take me a few minutes, or even a few hours, to absorb it."

Halek rotated his shoulders, stretching. "Kim, are we supposed to assume this will all be covert? I mean, we're not going to go in blasting in broad daylight?"

"It's covert, Jay. We've got the planes for it."

"US and AF has the 117s," Tom Keeper said. "They could make a stealth strike, too."

McEntire responded. "First, they don't have any cover, any reason for being in the area, Jay. Second, the US hasn't yet set a policy that allows the military to take direct action against drug targets."

"Not without the host country's cooperation," Kimball added, "and they're not getting that in Burma. With the tour, we've got a reason to be in Burma, and in the next ten days, we'll have to plan our tactics."

"What's the fallout if it goes public?" Mabry asked.

"It would be similar to Hiroshima, I expect. The liberals will blow up, and the conservatives will dig in for a long siege."

"Keep in mind that we could be the patsies in this whole thing," McEntire said. "Kim and I don't have an abiding faith in Mr. Washington. If we fuck it up, everybody we know, and don't know, will disown us."

42

"That's the risk," Kimball said. "Beyond the chance to get shot down or have to eject over some Burmese jungle. We might save the company, or we could blow the whole thing. In addition to the people, we're also risking most of the prototypes."

"I'm for saving the company," McEntire said. "Just so you know my position."

"We've got enough cash to give everyone a combat bonus," Kimball said. "It's not much. Ten thousand for pilots, three thousand for ground crewmen."

"We rescue the company, that's my bonus," Mel Vrdlicka said. "I don't mind being a capitalist."

"Sam Eddy and I will take a walk in the sun and give you guys a chance to talk it over," Kimball offered.

"To hell with that!" Gander said. "I'm voting."

He stuck his arm straight up and was immediately copied by fifteen more arms.

"Damn, I love you guys," Kimball told them. He didn't often express an emotion, but when he did, he meant it.

"Just don't get too close to me," Sam Eddy said.

"Okay, let's kick it off. First, no one mentions a word to anyone. Not wives, not kids, not girlfriends. We're simply touring the airplanes. Questions on that?

"Good. I'm going to have Soames set up a flying schedule. Everyone gets time in on the Alpha Kats and the Kappa Kats so we can back each other up. Everyone does time as an air controller. Later, I'll make seat assignments, both for the demonstrations and the combat sorties."

"Don't lock in the seats, Kim," Halek said. "Let us rotate, will you? I want my shot."

"I'll keep that in mind, Jay. We've got a hell of a lot to accomplish by the fifteenth. Mel, you and Jimmy are leaving by commercial air for Homestead first thing in the morning. Sam Eddy and Howard, you're headed to South Carolina. We've leased ourselves two C-141 Starlifters to haul our act around."

"First class," Gander said.

"I've got a minor point," Howard Cadwell said. "What about ordnance?"

43

"We've got the dummy Phoenix and Sidewinder missiles we were going to use for demonstrations. We'll practice with those until they're gone. Sam Eddy will pick up more training missiles on his way back from Charleston. We can't get Phoenix, but we're supposed to have AIM-9 and the new AMRAAM. For air-to-ground, Mr. Washington's trying to get us the Rockwell Hellfire."

"We'll get to use the laser designators finally," Conrad Billingsly said.

"Let's hope so, Connie. We also get some five-hundred pound iron bombs. That gives us a wide range of defensive and strike ordnance for the demonstrations. The arrangement is that we'll get live missiles and ammo on the other side of the Atlantic."

The mood was definitely up-tempo when the group broke up, everyone headed back to their particular duties. Kimball Aero Tech's pilots were not only pilots. Bryce Kimball had selected them for expertise in engineering, ordnance, electronics, controls, and the like. Everyone had a job within the company beyond flying aircraft. Different people were qualified in different types of aircraft, and all of them carried instructor's ratings.

Kimball had to repress a shudder when he realized he was not only risking his pilots, but also the core of the company's engineering life.

"Okay," Susan McEntire said, entering the office, "my turn. Lay it out for me."

She would be eternally cute, Kimball thought, like Connie Stevens. Big, big green eyes in an open, clear face, and an uptilted nose. Lots of dark red hair framing her face. She was slim and pert and given to short white cotton skirts and blouses stamped with Southwestern prints. Better, she had a mind that could follow intricate engineering blueprints and a maze of financial transactions. She had only been there three weeks before he had named her the company's comptroller.

"Why'd you give up on Sam Eddy?" he asked.

"Because."

"Because why?"

44

"Just because."

"Want to go to lunch?"

"Nope. I'm not having anything to do with pilots in particular anymore. Just pilots in general."

"I'll tell you how you can find three million dollars."

"Just a hamburger, then."

TAXI

Five

On Tuesday morning, A.J. Soames hit the ground running, feeling better about himself and the choices he had made than he had felt in some time. Kimball's announcement on Monday had made the difference.

Soames was one of two pilots at Kimball Aero Tech who had retired from the Air Force before following Bryce Kimball out to Phoenix. He was forty-five and something of a father or uncle figure to many of the younger men. His last assignment on active duty as a lieutenant colonel had been as a deputy wing commander in the Tactical Air Command, at Langley Air Force Base. In fact, Kimball and McEntire had flown for him.

Soames's love of flight had been tempered in his later years by enforced desk duty and slowed reflexes. He was not as idealistic as he had been in his earlier years, or as some of his younger colleagues still were. Experience had taught him many things, the chief one being that one doesn't often or successfully buck the establishment.

Kimball had spoken to him frequently about his disenchantments and frustrations with the Air Force's traditions and expectations, and when Kimball actually carried through with his threat to resign, Soames had taken a close look at himself. His hair was already graying at the temples, his green eyes had taken on a washed-out appearance and weren't nearly as sharp as they had once been, his face was fuller and more mature, and his body was following suit. Having been passed over once for promotion to full colonel, the odds in a downsizing organization were increasingly likely that he would be passed over again. He put in his papers, and he and Miriam left verdant Virginia for beige Arizona.

Soames had less to worry about than most of KAT's employees. He was drawing his military retirement check, and his only son had already completed college and entered the arcane world of computer systems analysis. Like others in the company, though, Soames wore several hats. He was a pilot, though he put in less air time than the others. Because of his background, Kimball had installed him as Vice President of Administration. In that position, he supervised all of KAT's logistics—supplies and materiel flow, the physical plant, and personnel—and oversaw the front office, which included Andrea Deacon and Susan McEntire, who was the comptroller.

Under his third hat, Soames had come to learn that he was a damned good airborne air controller. His reflexes didn't matter, someone else was at the controls of the Kappa Kat. But in the backseat at his radar console, his mind could grasp the entire theater of combat, read the radar screen efficiently, and make the necessary snap decisions. It helped, too, that his experience and command presence brought instant trust and respect from the pilots who relied on his decisions. They had given him the code name "Papa," somewhat different from the "Bronco Rider" he had carried in his Air Force fighter days.

In the tactical simulations they had run hundreds of times, with one Kappa Kat controlling six Alpha Kats, Soames found he could steadily visualize the three-dimensional arena of combat, separate in his mind the dozens of radio calls coming in, and still create order out of chaos.

It didn't surprise him that Conrad Billingsly, also an older veteran and retiree, and a former Strategic Air Command B-52 pilot, had also gravitated toward the air controller position.

All of the pilots did time in air control, but few had

the discipline and calm which would be necessary in a time of moving, jumbled, erratic confusion.

Soames was righteously, and quietly, proud of the fact that he had found a niche for himself outside of his academic and military training.

He parked his Volvo in the lot outside the KAT hangar and unlocked the front door to let himself in. There were always early birds, and he heard their voices coming from the coffee room just behind the front office.

He walked back to find Tex Brabham and Alex Hamilton, a pilot and air frame engineer, sitting in two of the four chairs at the single small table. The coffee pot gurgled in the corner, and one of the two had brought in a foot-high heap of breakfast rolls.

Hamilton would be the guilty party. He was barely over thirty, but fighting an expanding waist. Bland-faced, with blond hair, he had a professorial appearance. With a mind as keen as he had, and with his penchant for getting along with people, he should probably have been teaching physics and stress engineering over at Arizona State in Tempe.

"Mornin', A.J." Very few people knew the A.J. stood for Albert Johann, and Soames intended to keep it that way.

"Hello, Alex. You made it back all right, Tex?"

"Damned sight earlier than I planned on. Had me a nice thing going in Cheyenne."

Soames got himself a mug of coffee, and after delicate deliberation, picked up a chocolate donut. "Miriam will kill you for this, Alex."

"Only if she finds out," Hamilton assured him.

"Anybody going to tell me what's going on?" Brabham asked. "Alex tells me his lips are locked."

"Sealed, I said."

"What-the-hell-ever."

Soames was the personnel manager, and he knew that whatever else Kimball might have in mind about ground crew, Brabham would be his first choice. There was no sense in holding back with the old veteran, and after cautioning him about the confidentiality required, laid out the whole plan.

"No shit?"

"No shit, Tex. What do you think?"

"I think me and my boys got a hell of a lot of prepping to do in the next ten days. My birds got neglected while we were traipsing all over hell, playing barnstormer."

"Keep in mind, Tex, that all of the Alphas have to be flying in the meantime, while we bring everyone up on their time."

Brabham got up and refilled his mug. "I'm going to go over time logs now, and set up a schedule."

He hadn't reacted verbally, one way or the other, to the news, but the light in his eyes and the lively movement of his booted feet told the story.

Soames watched him leave, sipped from his mug, and said, "It's a changing world, isn't it, Alex?"

"Sure enough. I'm glad I got out when I did."

"Me, too. I talked to my old wing commander a few days ago. I don't think he likes the new organization much."

"Where's he at now?"

"Still at Langley, which is headquarters for the new Air Combat Command," Soames said.

Langley previously headquartered the Tactical Air Command, while Offutt AFB in Omaha headquartered the SAC. In the reorganization of the Air Force, much of it still under way, TAC evaporated, becoming part of the old Strategic Air Command under the new unified command. The new titles and acronyms replaced organizations that had been around for over forty years, and most of the good old boys didn't like it.

"I was at Scott in Illinois when I got out," Hamilton said. "It's now the base for the Air Mobility Command."

"I heard Offutt lost twenty-five percent of its personnel," Soames said. "That has to have a hell of an impact on the local economy. Omaha will be reeling for years."

The number of operational aircraft was being reduced also, with different reductions assigned to different types of aircraft, and as a result, the pilot corps was going through a planned attrition.

"Hurts a lot of people."

"A reduction in force affects everyone, civilians included," Soames said.

"That's another reason I'm glad I got out on my own. With my luck, I'd have been fired."

"I doubt that, Alex."

"That was my luck before KAT, A.J. It's changed now."

"It's changed for all of us," Soames agreed.

"What I can't believe is the way the Pentagon is covering its ass. You see the quotes. 'Air power should be treated as a unified whole,' the Air Force Chief of Staff said. 'Desert Storm taught us what Air Force leaders have believed for years.' "

"And spent most of their time resisting," Soames added. "Still, I can't fault the Billy Mitchells and Curtis LeMays." Lemay had shaped the Strategic Air Command. "They did the right thing for their time."

"It's a new time, A.J. Wait'll we show them what the Alpha Kat can do. She'll be something else they've believed in for years."

Jimmy Gander and Mel Vrdlicka arrived at Miami International Airport at noon and went down to the baggage carousel to retrieve their flight gear. They ate hamburgers and French fries in a concourse lounge before hauling their duffle bags outside and flagging a cab.

The cabbie, probably Cuban, liked the size of the fare, and cheerfully catapulted his wheeled wreck out of the terminal area, heading for Coral Gables and then Homestead.

"Jesus, Jimmy, I didn't know I'd become so acclimated

to the desert. This humidity's going to do me in."

Vrdlicka was originally from Montana. Gander wouldn't guess at the nationality of the name, but the man sported neat, clipped hair that was brick red and eyes green as unripened apples. He was fit, of medium stature, and had well-developed shoulders and arms. Gander thought he had taken to lifting weights. He had been a first lieutenant, overdue for captain, when he got out. Like himself, Vrdlicka had both jet ratings and multi-engine ratings. He was the communications specialist for KAT, and Gander had always thought that appropriate. Anyone lacking a necessary vowel in their name ought to be a communications specialist.

"You're almost thirty, Mel. You don't notice the climate until you're thirty."

"I'm aging fast, in that case."

In the Operations Office at Homestead, they ran into the bureaucratic wall that Gander had expected.

The duty officer was a major named Blankenship. When Gander finally got him to the counter, he said, "I'm here to pick up a C-141."

The major looked him over, almost leaning over the counter to take in the jeans and cowboy boots. He took a long, not appreciative, look at the Stetson hat. "You're an Air Force pilot?"

"Not any longer, Major. You should have orders that were forwarded to you yesterday. A copy went to your flight line people, and the airplane should be ready to go."

"We don't allow civilians to fly our aircraft," the major said.

Gander was struggling to be polite. "First time for everything, Major. Maybe the Air Force needs the rental income, huh?"

Blankenship took ten minutes to search through in-baskets before he found the orders, and despite their origination in the office of the Chief of Staff, had difficulty believing them. He called in a colonel who was the

54

operations officer.

The colonel called in a general, who wound up calling the Pentagon.

The orders verified, another carnival ensued in which Gander's and Vrdlicka's licenses and flying logs had to be confirmed through the FAA and which, after forty-five minutes of phone calls, were.

"Insurance," Blankenship said. "You don't have insurance for that bird."

Gander produced the quickly purchased policy. A damned expensive one, too.

"This doesn't have a tail number," the colonel said. "It just says a C-141B."

A half-hour of phone calls and faxing around with the insurance carrier produced an insert for the policy which had the correct tail number. The major photocopied the policy.

With extremely obvious misgivings, Major Blankenship allowed them to file a flight plan and leave his office for the flight line.

Walking across the hot tarmac, Vrdlicka said, "Just like the old days, hey?"

"The good old days."

Their C-141 Starlifter had a gaggle of ground crewmen surrounding it, and Gander located a master sergeant who spent twenty minutes with him, going over the logs and paperwork, then touring the monster for a visual inspection.

The wingspan was 159 feet, supporting four 21,000-pound thrust Pratt and Whitney turbofans. At 168 feet, the B-model's extended fuselage seemed to go on forever. The cargo bay could accept loads up to seventy feet long and ten feet wide, and the second model of the airplane had been the primary transport for the Minuteman ICBM.

Gander climbed through the entry hatch just aft of the cockpit and took a look through the doorway back into the cargo bay and found it empty. The compartment behind the cockpit had a few bunks in it for extended flights that required relief crews, and Vrdlicka was sitting on one of the bunks, changing into his flight gear. His duffle bag was open on the deck at his feet, his personal oxygen mask and helmet on top. The helmet was silver blue, with "Downhill" handpainted in red script across the front of it. Vrdlicka was an avid skier.

"You want to drive, or should I?" Vrdlicka asked.

"You go ahead. Bus-driving bores the hell out of me."

Gander didn't bother donning his flight overalls. He did change out of his high-heeled cowboy boots and retrieved his helmet and mask from his duffle bag.

He climbed the ladder and settled himself into the co-pilot's seat, pulled his helmet on, and plugged the communications cable into its receptacle. He hooked up the oxygen line, also. The transport was pressurized, but emergencies were always possible.

The checklist was on a clipboard hanging from the center pedestal, and he called it off as Vrdlicka scanned the instrument and switch settings. They were operating without a flight engineer, and Gander handled those duties also. Finally, communicating with the crew chief hooked in by cable to an exterior connector, Vrdlicka fired up the turbofans.

"How do they look, Jimmy?"

Gander checked the pertinent pressure and temperature gauges. "Four's lagging a little, still cold. All of them are in the green, though."

"Go ahead and call us in."

Gander dialed in the Nav/Coms for ground control. "Homestead Ground, this is Starlifter six nine."

"Six nine, Homestead."

"Six nine, requesting permission to taxi."

"Six nine, you may proceed to runway two seven left and hold. Go to Air Control now."

"Thank you, Homestead Ground. Six nine changing to Air Control."

Vrdlicka waved to the ground crew, then advanced the

inboard throttles. The huge plane began to roll.

Gander watched the gauges on number four, but by the time they reached the runway and braked short of it, the exhaust temperatures and pressures, as well as the oil pressure, had risen to match the other three jet engines.

He called Air Control, and after a C-130 Hercules landed, they were given permission to take off.

"Can I have some flaps?" Vrdlicka asked.

"Whatever your little heart desires." He lowered the flaps and checked the warning light panel for open hatches, clamshell doors, and the like. "Okay by me, Mel."

"Punching it."

Vrdlicka advanced the throttles to full ahead, and the RPMs came roaring up the scale. Without a load, they needed less than half the runway, and Vrdlicka rotated into a steep climb.

When the end of the runway passed several hundred feet below them, the pilot said, "Gear and flaps."

Gander retracted both and got green lights. He cleared with Homestead Control, then said, "She's all yours, Mel. I'm catching some Z's."

"So much for decent company," Vrdlicka complained.

Bryce Kimball sat in the right seat of CX-41, N17732, the second Kappa Kat off the assembly line. CX-41, N17668, the first Kappa Kat, had been selected by Tex Brabham as the tour craft, and it was undergoing a thorough maintenance checkup. Three Two would be used for the training sequences.

Kimball couldn't quite believe, as he was sure the others couldn't quite believe, that they were training for a combat mission. When they had formed KAT, the idea had been to create a better multi-role fighter and, personally for each of them, to keep up their flying skills in a hot fighter available to civilians. They had intended to train themselves for demonstrations and to utilize the secondary academic and engineering talents each of them professed to have.

The risk factors of engaging hostile aircraft had been left behind them, Kimball had thought. Now, those factors were back in place, and as far as he could tell, no one was unhappy about the change. They were as eager as dogs in heat.

In the left seat, as command pilot, was Sam Miller, a former captain and F-111 driver, and a current systems engineer. His undergraduate education had been accomplished at Dartmouth, the source of his nickname, "Dart." Beneath the raised visor of his helmet, his face was beefy and sported a Pancho Villa-shaped, utterly black moustache. He had the Kappa Kat at 32,000 feet over the desert floor south of Casa Grande. The Organ Pipe Cactus National Monument was thirty miles ahead, and beyond that was the Mexican border. The Papago Indian Reservation was directly below.

In the back, beneath a separately sectioned canopy, at the twin radar consoles, were Phillipe "Speedy" Contrarez and Conrad "Frog" Billingsly. Contrarez, an ex-major who had spent most of his time as a navigator on fuel tankers, was an hydraulics engineer who was so happy most of the time, it was ridiculous. His controller colleague on this flight had retired as a full colonel and was Director of Flight Operations for Kimball Aero Tech. Billingsly had gone prematurely gray in his mid-thirties, and now at forty-eight, featured fluffy, pure white hair. His eyes were warm and sincere, and he had a deep, throaty voice. He sang bass with a pick-up quartet on weekends. Billingsly was a widower and empty-nester, having had cancer strike both his wife and his daughter.

Kimball had already decided that Soames and Billingsly would be his air controllers, with Contrarez and Dave Metger as backups. The four of them would get the most rehearsal time in the backseat of the Kappa Kat.

The Airborne Warning and Control craft was a larger version of the Alpha Kat. The modified delta wing configuration was the same, though fifteen feet greater in span, and she had the same twin, inward-canted rudders. The fuselage was longer and wider, to accommodate twin turbofans, and the nose was wide and flattened, allowing for the four seats and the package of ultra high-tech avionics, electronic countermeasures gear, and radars. Except for her stealth characteristics and her decoys like chaff and flares, she was pretty much defenseless. The Kappa Kat carried no ordnance, and her centerline hardpoint was utilized for a conformal fuel tank that gave her two-and-a-half hours more endurance than the Alpha Kats. Her weight kept her top speed almost 400 knots slower than the fighters.

Since she mounted all of the high-cost electronics, the Kappa Kat was the most expensive craft in the KAT fleet, delivered to any purchaser for a mere twenty-four million dollars each. The basic configuration of an Alpha/ Kappa tactical unit called for one Kappa Kat and six Alpha Kats, though the Kappa Kat controllers could handle up to twenty-four fighters. The Kimball Aero Technology brochures recommended one backup Kappa Kat for each one to three tactical units since the Alpha Kats were pretty much useless without a controller craft available.

With the unit price of an Alpha set at 3.5 million dollars, one minimal tactical unit of six Alpha Kats and a Kappa Kat ran to a total of forty-five million dollars. That compared to seven F-15 Eagles for 140 million. Because of the sliding scale of manufacturing and raw material costs, Kimball could offer discounts on larger orders. The cost per tactical unit dropped substantially as more Alpha Kats were added to each Kappa Kat.

The cost efficiency on the more sobering side, of course, was that losing one Alpha Kat to hostile fire was considerably cheaper than losing one F-15.

One of the great selling points, or so Kimball had thought until making his pitch to the American air services, was that the odds of losing an Alpha Kat were considerably less than those of losing a conventional fighter. The stealth characteristics were responsible for that. One couldn't shoot down what one couldn't see.

Billingsly's voice sounded in his earphones. "Two and Three, go HICAP."

"Ah, Frog!" Jay "Barnfire" Halek came back.

"Maintain radio discipline, Two. Execute."

Kimball turned slightly sideways to look back at Billingsly. He had his eyes locked onto the screen of the AN/APG-67 radar as if it pictured his whole world, which Kimball was certain that it did. The advanced radar of the Kappa Kat was an all-digital pulse-Doppler and allowed the detection and tracking of targets at all altitudes. Each set, and there were two aboard the Kappa Kat, was capable of identifying and tracking sixty targets at up to 150 miles away. Unwanted targets and debris were filtered out, leaving the screen's display clearly defined.

Halek, who was something of a firebrand, was objecting to Billingsly's random selection of himself as one of the high-level Combat Air Patrol pilots. Billingsly was fond of shaking up the order of things, giving different pilots different assignments as CAP, as wingmen, and as flight leaders at any given time. Kimball agreed with him; he wanted all of his pilots capable in all roles.

He rotated his head back to the front, checked his Head-up Display, which repeated the same targets Billingsly had on his scope, and then leaned forward and sideways to peer through the canopy.

The six Alpha Kats were in a diamond formation, with two of the craft trailing in staggered echelon, two thousand feet below the Kappa Kat. As he watched, numbers two and three rose out of the diamond and climbed quickly. The trailing aircraft moved up and filled in the diamond.

Far below, the earth was beige and tan and barren. There was no welcome glint of sun reflecting off water.

Halek and Ito Makura, flying the second CAP aircraft, spread apart as they climbed and finally assumed stations a thousand feet above, and a half-mile off each side, of the Kappa Kat. They served as the defensive cover for the Kappa Kat and were also a reserve against unexpected emergencies.

"Hawkeye, Bengal Two on station," Halek reported. Kimball had assigned the codenames for the demonstration tour.

"Bengal Three ditto," Makura said.

"Roger that," Billingsly replied. "Four, take the lead. One, you're on his wing. Bengal Five, you have the second element."

A chorus of "rogers" replied on the radio.

"We have two intruders," the air controller said. "I designate them Tango and Sierra. Four, go to one-seven-four. Tango is on a heading of zero-zero-nine, speed four-five-zero knots, angels one-two, three-two miles. Five, your target is Sierra. He is heading three-one-five at four-two-five knots, altitude two-six-thousand, distance four-one miles. Hawkeye Four, take the second element."

"Roger, I have the second element. Five, go to Tac Three," Contrarez said.

Aboard the Kappa Kat, the pilot was Hawkeye One, the navigator (Kimball today) Hawkeye Two, and the controllers were Three and Four. Contrarez had just taken control of Bengals Five and Six and moved them to another scrambled radio channel in order to separate his and Billingsly's dialogue with the fighters.

Since he wanted to monitor both actions, Kimball keyed in a second receiver and listened to the conversations on both Tac Two and Tac Three.

On the Head-up Display (HUD), Kimball picked out the blips of Bengals Four and One turning to the left and accelerating. Next to the blips were numbers that kept decreasing—291 . . . 289 . . . 286. The numbers represented the altitude of the aircraft, 28,600 feet and falling off rapidly as the two Alpha Kats dove toward an interception with their target. The aggressors, Tango and Sierra, had not yet changed their courses.

Bengals Five and Six were also turning, to the right, and gaining speed, intent on Sierra. Their quarry was headed north, forty miles away.

"Four, turn left to one-seven-zero. Hold altitude," Billingsly ordered.

"Roger, Frog."

On Tac Three, Bengal Five, piloted by Thomas Keeper, asked, "Hey, Speedy, you sure I'm aimed right?"

"Right on, Miner Forty-niner. Intercept in four minutes."

"I trust you, guy."

The fighter pilots had to trust their controllers implicitly and totally for the fighters did not carry search and attack radar. The lack of radar aboard the attack craft served several purposes. It saved weight and cost, of course, but it also kept the stealth aircraft stealthy. One drawback to radar was that, when it was radiating energy, it was identifiable to hostile forces. Since they never transmitted search radar emissions, the Alpha Kats could move unseen into firing positions on their targets. All they needed was clear directions from the Kappa Kat controllers and active data links.

The tactic had presented two problems. The communications problem had been solved by Mel Vrdlicka's adaptation of existing radios with new technology. His black boxes for the tactical channels two through eight in both controller and fighter aircraft scrambled voice transmissions and changed radio frequencies every second. If the black boxes sensed electronic countermeasures in the form of jamming, the jammed frequencies were avoided as the radios leapt from one frequency to another.

The second problem was unavoidable. Though they were stealthy and undetectable on enemy radars, the Kappa Kats were required to utilize their search radars almost continuously if they were to direct the attack planes. The strategy was to keep them high, with more time to detect surface-to-air missile launches, and a suitable distance from the action of the fighters. An enemy aircraft or radar site which detected the Kappa Kat was not therefore guaranteed the location of the Alpha Kats.

"Dart, let's do a one-eighty," Billingsly said over the intercom.

"One-eighty coming up," Miller said, and banked the Kappa Kat into a right turn.

The maneuver not only sought to disrupt any tracking of them by hostile radars, but in this case was practical. They didn't want to enter the Mexican ADIZ (Air Defense Identification Zone).

"Frog, Sierra's picked up our emissions," Contrarez said on the intercom.

"Jolly good," Billingsly replied.

Both hostile aircraft were F-16 Falcons which belonged to the Arizona Air National Guard. They had been reluctantly loaned to KAT, after some telephone calls from Washington, to serve as aggressor aircraft.

"He's gone supersonic, thinks he can reach us," Contrarez reported.

"Just do your thing, Speedy," Billingsly told him.

On Tac Three, Contrarez said, "Five, Hawkeye."

"Five."

"Sierra's turning into you and climbing. He's at Mach one-point-three."

"Copy."

"Climb to angels two-zero, execute Immelmann, and come down on his six o'clock when he passes under you."

"Five."

"Six," George Wagers, Bengal Six, acknowledged.

A similar scenario was occurring on Tac Two, where the target aircraft had also established a contact on the Kappa Kat. Because he was listening to two channels at once, Kimball missed some of the dialogue which overlapped, but he had a sense of the action.

"Four?" Billingsly queried.

"Go Hawkeye."

"You should have a visual in thirty seconds. Tango is bearing two-eight-two, altitude two-one-thousand and climbing, velocity Mach one-point-four."

"Tally ho," the catchword for a visual sighting, came twenty seconds later.

"Weapons released, Four. Fire at will."

Tango, intent upon reaching the Kappa Kat, still had no idea where the Alpha Kats were, that they were swinging in behind him, coming up from below.

"Infrared lock-on," Bengal Four said.

Kimball switched to the Tac Five channel they were sharing with the aggressors and keyed the microphone built into his helmet, "Tango, bang, bang!"

"Shit!" Gaston Greer replied. "I'm taking my airplane and going home."

"Bye-bye," Kimball told him.

He switched back to Tac Three, where the intercept hadn't been as successful. Bengal Five reported that he and Six had lost too much speed on their climb out, and by the time they rolled upright at the top of their loop, they had been unable to catch the hostile plane.

"Okay, Hawkeye Four, I've got it. Barnfire, here's your chance," Billingsly said in his deep, unperturbable voice.

"Two."

"Sierra's closing on us at Mach one-point-five, your heading two-zero-four. Contact in forty seconds. Take him out."

"Two."

The Alpha Kat above them on the left raised its right wing and peeled off.

The HUD radar display in front of Kimball disappeared as Billingsly switched the radar to passive.

"Do something other than what we're doing, Dart," Billingsly suggested.

Sam Miller dropped his right wing, and the Kappa Kat rolled over, under Bengal Three, into a descending right turn, spiralling downward. Bengal Three rolled on her right wing and stayed with them. With their emissions

64

halted, the aggressor would lose track of them quickly.

"Tally ho!" Halek reported.

"Tell me, Two."

"I've got him head-on."

"Wrong," Billingsly said, but added, "Weapons released."

"Phoenix is gone," Halek said.

Kimball hoped fervently that it wasn't so. The propulsion systems on the missiles hadn't had their safeties removed.

"Hell, he shut down on me," Halek complained.

"Is it a hit, or not?" Billingsly asked.

"Wham! He just went by me," Halek reported. "I don't know about the hit."

"I give it fifty-fifty," Kimball said on the intercom.

"I agree," Billingsly said, then keyed in his tactical radio, "Go Three."

Bengal Three left them as Miller pulled the Kappa Kat out of its dive, now heading almost directly east at an altitude of 16,000 feet.

"Three. I've got a visual. Damn it!"

"That doesn't tell me anything," Billingsly said.

"I almost couldn't turn in on him, Hawkeye. Got him, now. Infrared lock-on. Released."

"We'll scratch that one, Three," Billingsly told him. "You didn't have weapons permission."

Kimball jotted the item on his clipboard. He had a full clipboard of errors and omissions for the debriefing session.

He switched to Tac Five and said, "Sierra, I'll give you fifteen seconds to spot us."

After the countdown ran out, Sierra reported, "Negative, Hawkeye. You people are gone."

"At least the stealth part works, Cheetah," Sam Miller said.

Ben Wilcox waited until the jet engines shut down,

65

then walked across the cooling concrete toward the C-141. Except for a few floodlights, it was dark, but to the northeast, the lights of San Antonio brightened the horizon. The headlights of traffic on Highway 90 and the 410 bypass were still tightly clustered at nine o'clock at night.

The big transport was parked with other aircraft, but was the only one with any activity around it. Ground crewmen swarmed over it, and a fuel tanker pulled up beneath the left wing.

As he watched, the big clamshell doors on the back end parted and the airplane's ramp lowered to the ground. The interior lighting seeped outward. Two figures descended the ramp.

Wilcox approached them, carrying his thin attaché case. "Good evening, Sam Eddy."

"Howdy there, Mr. Washington. This is Howard Cadwell."

Cadwell was a stocky, heavyset man who looked as if he might be a retired defensive lineman for the Dallas Cowboys. In the light spilling from the cargo bay, Wilcox saw thinning brown hair with a pronounced widow's peak, but couldn't see his eyes clearly.

"Mr. Cadwell." He offered a hand.

Cadwell shook it. "Mr. Washington."

He peered upward into the cavernous and empty cargo compartment. "Just the two of you?"

"We're the whole show," McEntire said.

Wilcox raised his arm and rotated his hand in a large circle. Close to a nearby hangar, the headlights of two semi-tractors illuminated, and one after the other, they shifted into gear and headed toward the plane.

"You didn't have any trouble in Charleston, did you?" Wilcox asked.

"Not after all of the right telephone calls were made," McEntire said. "Suspicious damned Air Force we got."

"With no Soviet Union, we've got to be careful about everyone else," Wilcox said.

66

McEntire patted the skin of the clamshell door next to him. "I'll bet you people didn't tell the Chief of Staff that these planes were going to KAT. Otherwise, we'd have payed hell getting them."

"Seemed an unnecessary admission at the time," Wilcox conceded.

The first semi-truck pulled up near the ramp. It was followed by a forklift.

"We got us two whole truckloads of dummy missiles?" McEntire asked. With an ear-to-ear grin, he said, "We can practice right into the next century."

Wilcox stepped away from the ramp, drawing McEntire and Cadwell with him. The back doors of the trailer were tugged open to reveal narrow crates stacked almost to the ceiling.

"Those crates are labeled 'Hughes/Raytheon AMRAAM, Simulated Warhead,' 'Ford Aerospace/Raytheon AIM-9L, Simulated Warhead,' and 'Rockwell Hellfire, Simulated Warhead,' " Wilcox said. "Same thing for the twenty millimeter rounds and five-hundred-pounders."

"Our active radar seeker and the Sidewinder infrared homing missile. Air-to-ground. Nice going," McEntire said. "I'm changing my mind about you."

"About half of those AMRAAM crates are tagged, 'Simulated Warhead, Model 2C.' For the Sidewinders, look for labeling that says 'Mark VI.' The Hellfires are 'System Two.' On the bombs, you'll want to watch for the Mark 84s that read Mk 84B. Half the cannon rounds are 'Blank Firing—Series Two.' " Wilcox told him.

"These are new training systems? If there's so many new dummies around, how come we haven't heard about them?"

"They're not so dumb," Wilcox said.

"Oh, shit! We're getting the live stuff here?"

"I wouldn't fly that airplane over heavily populated areas," Wilcox cautioned.

"What are they doing on a training base?"

"We brought them over from Randolph. Anything more, you don't want to know."

Wilcox unlatched his attaché case and gave McEntire a thick file folder. "That's the export and transportation licenses for your cargo, Sam Eddy. Be careful, will you?"

"On tippy toes."

"Anything more you need?"

"You going to buy us dinner?" McEntire asked.

Major General Brock Dixon was dressed in a nicely tailored civilian suit that had set him back seven hundred dollars, standing at the public telephone attached to the side wall of a 7-Eleven store in Alexandria.

"I talked to quite a few people," Jack Ailesworth told him.

"And they said?"

"They didn't have to say much. All of them were disappointed, to say the least."

Dixon drummed his fingernails against the small plastic shelf under the phone. "And what is Procurement's position?"

"Naturally, we hold the position we've always held. We want what's in the national interest."

Dixon mulled that very general statement for awhile. Every conversation tended to be abstract. No one was going to mention specifics, and the interpretations had to be exact. Then he asked, "How far do we want to go with this?"

"I believe the consensus is that the nth degree is out, is not desirable. But some kind of flanking action would be helpful."

"Jesus, Jack. That's pretty abstract."

"We, that is, they trust your judgment."

"Resources?"

"I can get you two million right away. More later, if required."

"I'll call you tomorrow," Dixon said and hung up.

From his inside coat pocket, he withdrew a small notebook. He thumbed through it until he found the right page, which he ripped out. It took him several minutes to memorize the number, then he used his cigarette lighter to burn the page. He would not be using this number again.

Placing a stack of quarters on the shelf, Dixon dialed the number, then fed quarters into the phone.

The phone rang three times before it was answered. "Crider."

"I've got a job for you, if you're interested."

"Who is this?"

"That will remain unknown."

"I'm not interested."

"There's a code," Dixon said. "Alligator meat."

"New phone number," Crider said. "Give me ten minutes to get there."

Dixon waited eleven minutes, smoking Marlboros, before he dialed the pre-arranged number, which was probably another public telephone. He deposited the required number of quarters.

"Tell me about the money," Crider said.

"A million up front, more if it's necessary."

"I'm interested."

Six

"I'm nervous as hell," Sam Eddy McEntire said. "You ever see me nervous before?"

No one had, so no one said anything.

Wednesday morning was bright outside the front windows of the office. The July heat wavered over the parking lots in mirage-like images. By noon, everyone and everything would be well-baked.

The pilots gathered in the room weren't as nervous as McEntire professed to be. Their faces reflected confidence and eagerness, Kimball thought. Tex Brabham, who had been invited to join them, only reflected Tex Brabham.

If he moved close to the side window and looked down the alleyway between hangars, Kimball could see the tall tail of the C-141 carrying the ordnance. He figured he was more nervous than McEntire. All that high explosive sitting out in the sun.

"You talk to the man from Washington yet?" Sam Eddy asked.

"He's not in his office. I'll be seeing him tomorrow, according to the message I got."

"I'm not absolutely fond of him changing the schedule on us. Jesus Christ, Kim! Traipsing around the country with a few tons of high explosives on board wasn't on the agenda."

"Probably illegal," Jimmy Gander observed.

"Tell you how nervous Sam Eddy was," Howard

70

Cadwell said, "he wouldn't let me touch the controls. The landing here was so soft, I didn't wake up until we were parked."

Kimball didn't like having Wilcox spring surprises on him, either. The missiles and bombs were safe enough, unless some errant airplane or pickup truck crashed into them, but his mind had been wrapped around picking up the live missiles in Saudi Arabia or Pakistan. Somewhere else, and overseas, anyway. Like McEntire, he was nervous, and also like McEntire, he suspected, less nervous about the ordnance than the unexpected change in plans.

"Well, we've got it, and we're stuck with it," he said. "Have you checked it out, Tex?"

"Yeah, Kim, I did. What I could see without unloading the damned plane. Looks all right."

"Who do you want to put on it?"

"Carl Dent should be in charge," Brabham said. "He was an F-15 weapons specialist."

"Fine by me. You pick out the rest of your crew?"

Brabham handed him a sheet of paper ripped out of a notebook, and Kimball looked it over:

Zack Freeman	Virgil Thomas
Wes Overly	Paul Diamond
Mark Westergood	Luke Frale
Darrell Williams	Elliot Stott
Walt Hammond	Perry Vance
Carl Dent	

"You haven't mentioned our secondary venture to any of them?"

Brabham snorted. "Hey, boss!"

"Sorry. Is this going to be enough manpower, Tex?"

Kimball Aero had about thirty top mechanics they could draw from, all of them with experience in the Air Force or one of the other services, and all of them serving in supervisory roles for the rest of the workforce. He passed the list around for the pilots to scan.

"They all have at least two specialties," Brabham said. "I'd put one man as chief on each plane, plus ordnance, electronics, communications, and computers. Everybody can shift around where help is needed. Thing is, boss, I don't even have to ask these guys to volunteer. They'll go, soon as I drop the hat."

"Plus," Sam Eddy said, "we've got you."

"Plus, we've got me," Brabham agreed matter-of-factly, inching his hat up a fraction on his forehead.

"You the loadmaster, too?" A.J. Soames asked.

"Yeah. What I'm going to do, I'm going to pull the dummy missiles off the plane that we need for the rest of the training mission here. Then I'm going to split up what's left between both transports. Tools, supplies, spare parts, and ground crew get spread between both planes, too."

In case one of the C-141s went down or was grounded for maintenance somewhere along the line, Kimball knew, but didn't say. No one else voiced the obvious, either.

"We got us one spare turbofan," Brabham added, "and if no one cares, I'm going to take it along, too."

"Do it," Kimball said.

The recommended list of mechanics had made its way around the room.

"Any objections?" Kimball asked.

No one complained, and Kimball said, "Okay, Tex. You can tell them now. Families and girlfriends have to stay in the dark. We'll ship out on the fifteenth. You've got my new training schedule?"

Brabham nodded and left the room, closing the door behind him.

"All right, next item. Have we got any problems with the transports?"

Gander and Vrdlicka both shook their heads negatively, as did McEntire.

"Next. Yesterday's exercise."

There were a couple of moans.

"I know we've been away from the discipline and the training for a long time, guys, but this was miserable."

Kimball moved across the room and leaned against Susan McEntire's desk. He scanned the clipboard he was holding.

"Jay."

Halek grimaced, crunching the unlit cigar in his mouth. He liked cigars, but never lit them.

"When the AC tells you to move somewhere, you move. No bitching about it."

"Gotcha, Kim."

"Warren," Kimball said.

The black pilot grinned at him. Mabry had been Bengal Four the day before.

"Nice engagement."

"Thanks, Kim."

"Fred."

Fred Nackerman, who had flown Bengal One, said, "Yo."

"Warren lost you on the final turn."

"Damn, Kim, he was pulling G's as if they were a dime a dozen."

"I know you've got a lot of time as a flight leader, but when you're the wingman, stay on the wing."

"Roger that, Kim."

Kimball went to his next note. "Tom and George."

Keeper and Wagers, Bengals Five and Six, sat straighter on the sofa. Tom Keeper was one of the two pilots who weren't ex-Air Force. He wasn't even a pilot, if service definitions were acknowledged. An ex-Navy lieutenant, he was an aviator, and his experience was in F-4 Phantoms. The fluorescent lights glinted off Wagers's balding head.

"My fault, there," Billingsly broke in. "I initiated the action too late, and they didn't have a chance to catch the Falcon."

"I may have carried my climb out for too long," Keeper said. "I wanted too much altitude, and I dropped the speed under three hundred knots."

"Let's keep working on that maneuver then," Kimball said. "Back to Jay."

"I know," Halek said, removing his cigar and rolling it between his thumb and fingers. "I took him head-on with an AMRAAM on attack data link and shouldn't have. He didn't present enough of a target for the missile, and I likely had a miss. With his closing rate on Hawkeye, I should have used active radar."

The Advanced Medium-Range Air-to-Air Missile, designated the AMRAAM-II for the model they were utilizing, was targeted in either of two modes. The Kappa Kat could illuminate the target and transfer the target information by data link to the missile aboard the Alpha Kat. When the fighter pilot heard the lock-on in his earphones, he released the missile, which would also home on the target's emitting radar. In the other mode, which might make the Alpha Kat a radar-visible target, the pilot initiated the missile's own radar and then fired it when the missile had contact. The AMRAAM's radar guided it to the target, whether or not the target radar was emitting.

"Correct," Conrad Billingsly said. "I shut down our radars to protect Hawkeye at the same time the Falcon radar went passive, and the missile had data that was out of date."

"Let's not be so eager to get into action, Jay, that we forget to think," Kimball said.

Halek stuck his cigar back in his teeth and clamped it tight.

"And Ito, we scratched your hit because you released weapons without permission."

Makura nodded. "I know. I am sorry, Bryce."

"When we get where we're going, there's a chance for a lot of traffic. If somebody fires without a positive ID or weapons permission from Hawkeye, we could down, say, an Air India 747. Anybody want to live with that?"

The silence was answer enough.

"Okay, I've got a final training schedule, and I've named the controllers. A.J. and Connie will be the lead controllers, backed up by Phillipe and Dave."

Except for Phillipe Contrarez and Dave Metger, the others appeared happy enough with that decision.

"Phillipe and Dave, you'll be on the Alpha Kat training schedule, also."

That revived half-smiles.

"We're going around the clock. Four fighters at a time, with two undergoing maintenance according to Tex's schedule. If anyone asks you about the intense schedule, we're preparing for our demonstration tour.

"During the day, the routine is the same one we'll actually use for demos. Night flights are different."

"You find a bombing range?" McEntire asked.

"We contributed ten thousand bucks to the Papago Indian Reservation Educational Fund, and they're letting us use some empty desert."

"You did that?" Sam Eddy asked.

"Susan worked it out. We rented a recreational vehicle, and Tex is sending two men south to camp out and set up ground targets for us."

"I could do that," McEntire volunteered.

"It's not a big RV, Sam Eddy. It won't carry a lot of beer."

"Maybe I won't, in that case."

"The schedule has your flight times and your sleep times listed. I want you to get used to sleeping during the day," Kimball told them.

"Alone?" Sam Eddy asked.

"There wasn't room on the schedule for recreation, Sam Eddy."

The group broke up, more somber than when they had assembled at nine o'clock. They were learning that, anywhere from three to four years out of military training, they weren't quite the hotshot pilots they remembered themselves as being.

Kimball was well aware of his own deficiencies. He had placed himself prominently in the training schedule.

Susan McEntire and Andrea Deacon returned as the last of the pilots filtered out. Andrea, a petite and pert blonde just out of her teens, with a refreshing dose of naivete, was in jeans and a boat-necked blue blouse that intrigued most of the men in the building. She was good on the phone, worming her way past receptionists, secretaries, and minor bureaucrats. Susan was wearing her customary short white skirt and a blouse that featured Indian motifs.

"Mornin', Susie," Sam Eddy said.

"Good morning," she replied formally.

"You want coffee later?"

"No. Goodbye, Sam Eddy."

McEntire looked across the room at Kimball, shrugged, and went out.

Kimball settled onto the sofa while the women reclaimed their desks.

"You're going to have to build a conference room, Kim," Andrea told him, "if you're going to have all these meetings that keep us away from work."

"I wouldn't think you'd complain about that. But it won't be for long, Andy. How are the reservations going?"

She picked up a legal tablet. "You gave me confirmed dates for Riyadh and New Delhi, and I've got tentative reservations for hotels in both cities. Landing fees, fuel, and aircraft parking are set. Until you set up the other stops, I can't do much more. And if you have to skip some country, I'll have to redo the whole thing."

"Got the message, Andy. I'll get on the phone."

Susan motioned toward the doorway with a shake of her head, and left the room.

Puzzled, Kimball followed and found her standing in the hallway.

"Something wrong, Susan?"

"I don't want to alarm anyone, but I think somebody's following me."

"What!"

"You go out in the parking lot and look for a white Oldsmobile. There's a man sitting in it."

"He followed you from home?"

"I don't know. I just saw him as I came to work, and he drove into the lot after I did."

Kimball studied her face. Susan McEntire didn't often get upset, but there was some fright showing in her big green eyes and a twitch at the corner of her mouth.

"I'll go take a look."

"Be careful, Kim."

"Give me a cigarette."

"You don't smoke," she reminded him.

"It's cover."

She frowned, but went back into the office and came back with her purse. She rummaged around in it and found him a cigarette and butane lighter.

Kimball took them, went down the corridor, and let himself out the front door.

He stood beside the door, on the narrow strip of grass someone had high hopes for, between the hangar and the parking lot sidewalk, and lit up.

Guy taking a break, right?

The sun beat on him, raising globules of perspiration on his forehead. The air was dry, and the reflections off chrome and glass in the lot hurt his eyes. He stood there, smoking and looking around.

He found the Oldsmobile five spaces back in the second row, but there was no one in it.

Susan was probably being a little paranoid.

Turning toward the east, he sauntered down the grass strip, passing the corner of his hangar. The space between it and the next hangar was blocked by an eight-foot-high chain link fence. He stared down the opening, but there was nothing between the two hangars except dirt and a few weeds the defoliant

77

hadn't been able to conquer.

The next hangar was vacant, the owners waiting out the period until his option expired before attempting to rent it. Kimball had about two months before he lost his option money. He almost reversed course then and headed back to his office, trying to come up with a gentle way to tell Susan she was hallucinating.

Something prodded him to take a look, and he kept sauntering until he reached the first door into the next hangar. He tried the door handle, and it turned.

It shouldn't have.

Shoving the heavy door inward, Kimball stepped inside.

The cavernous structure was empty, dimly lit by the sunlight forcing itself through the rows of grimy windows high overhead. The concrete floor had been swept, but was mottled with old oil, grease, and fuel stains. The far sidewall had several small office and storage spaces abutted to it.

The Oldsmobile man was at the far, runway end of the hangar, standing on an upturned wooden crate, snapping photographs rapidly through one window in the sliding hangar door.

The clicking of his camera shutter echoed across the concrete. Kimball could hear the tiny whir of the film advance motor after each click.

The man was so intent on his photography that he didn't hear the padded footfalls until Kimball was ten feet away.

Startled, he whirled around.

His face was wide, made wider by large ears, and there was a thin, white scar running across the right side of his forehead, disappearing into thick umber hair. The face was less grainy than the faxed photo Kimball had seen.

"Doctor Nash, I presume?"

He came off the crate in a rush, his camera swinging at the far end of its neck strap.

Kimball hadn't expected an attack.

He threw up his left arm.

His forearm blocked the strap, but the camera whipped around his arm and slapped him in the forehead.

Stunned, Kimball went to his knees, his arm reflexively jerking back against his shoulder, trapping the camera's strap and ripping it out of Nash's hand.

Nash didn't wait around.

He kept on running, heading for the door.

Kimball knelt on the concrete, shaking his head until the little black dots in his vision went away.

Henry Loh put the C-123 Provider into a gentle left bank and circled the airfield at a thousand feet of altitude.

The Provider had probably once belonged to the U.S. military, before it was left behind in their hurried flight from Vietnam. It had had a half-dozen owners since, but after a thorough overhaul of the twin 2500 horsepower Pratt and Whitney radial engines, the fuselage had been stenciled for Air Jungle Ltd., chartered as a cargo and occasional passenger hauler. Air Jungle owned one C-123, two old Douglas DC-3s, and a DC-6 that had once been an American Airways passenger liner.

Henry Loh was a match for the beat-up transport. He had been born and educated in Taiwan, but gotten his world reality drummed in as a mercenary, a Nung Guard, working for the Americans in Vietnam. Since his personal pullout from the war-torn nation in 1972, he had learned to fly practically anything with wings, and he too had had a half-dozen owners.

He was big for a Chinese. Weighing 170 pounds, he stood five feet, eleven inches tall. He had massive shoulders and a strong upper body and arms. His chest and face were laced with scars resulting from run-ins with shrapnel, broken beer bottles in bar brawls, and one long, long session at the hands of an avid Khmer Rouge torturer. His dark hair was lanky and long, and he had the habit of whipping his head to fling the hair away from his eyes.

His copilot was a Frenchman going by the current name of Jean Franc. He had a mean, red mouth and narrow yellowed eyes. Both physical traits were probably the legacy of many battles with malaria, dysentery, and other diseases common to Westerners stuck in Asian jungles.

Henry Loh saw nothing unusual taking place in the immediate vicinity of the airstrip. It was located sixty klicks south of the village of Keng Hkam on the Salween River, and was comprised of the short dirt runway, one tin-roofed shack, one canvas-roofed warehouse, and one stack of fifty-five-gallon drums.

"Do you see anything you do not like, Jean?"

"No. Still, we should prepare."

"Yes. Do that."

Franc crawled out of his seat, edged back to the hatchway, and lowered himself down the ladder to the cargo deck. He and the three Thai cargo handlers would arm themselves with Kalashnikov AK-47s and be ready for anything that appeared once the ramp was lowered.

The airstrip disappeared into the jungle canopy as Loh leveled his wings and headed east. He flew five miles, then turned back to recross the river. It was shallow and muddy in the broad curve it made through the jungle.

To the north and west, the high plateau country was spotted with jungle, hills rising above it. It was not a welcome landscape, but Henry Loh had never known a landscape that thrilled him particularly.

As the river passed under, he retarded his throttles, then reached down for the lever controlling the flaps and deployed them.

The Provider bounced upward with its new lift, and Loh eased the control column forward to counter it.

The airstrip appeared again, revealed as he approached the lip of the jungle clearing.

Loh lowered the landing gear, then idled the engines. The medium transport settled downward slowly, and the big tires grabbed the ground and bounced once. As soon as it settled the second time, he ran the engines into reverse thrust and felt himself shoved forward against his seat harness as the airplane slowed itself.

The two simple structures were at the far end of the runway. Loh taxied toward them, noting the ramp warning light come on. Franc had lowered it partially.

When he reached the end of the runway, he used the left brake and ran up the right engine. The plane turned quickly, almost 270 degrees, so that the ramp was aimed at the warehouse.

Speaking into his cantilevered microphone, he asked, "Jean?"

"Looks okay, Henry," Franc told him over the intercom.

Loh locked the brakes down, idled the engines, and unstrapped from his seat. Working his way back to the hatch, he watched the cargo handlers labor, shoving three goats down the ramp, untying crates marked Carnation Foods, General Mills, and Hong Kong Enterprises. Others were labeled in Chinese, Thai, Russian, and Laotian letters and phrases.

The men pushed and shoved the crates and cardboard boxes toward the rear of the plane, setting them down on the rollers of the ramp, letting them slide on out the back.

Nine people, all small men belonging to some tribe he did not care about, had appeared from nowhere, but probably from the shack. No one said anything, just began to pick up the crates and haul them toward the warehouse.

Franc stepped off the ramp to the ground, carrying

his assault rifle at port arms, and walked off toward the warehouse. He came back five minutes later, climbed the ramp, and worked his way around the cargo to reach Loh.

Loh raised an eyebrow.

"Syrup. Fifteen drums of it."

"Let's get it aboard and get the hell out of here."

Derek Crider had been a Green Beret major during the last years of the Vietnam circus. Closing on forty-eight years of age now, he did not show it. People would guess him for, maybe, his late thirties because of his wedge-shaped figure, shoulders that stretched to both sides of a doorway, and musculature that gave him a neck like that of Dick Butkus. He could have been bald, his fair hair was shorn so close to his skull. His skin was tanned the color of deer hide that had been stretched in the sun for three weeks. The gray eyes probing from deep-set eye sockets rendered the more meek speechless for a few seconds.

Two months after the fall of Saigon, in June, Crider had resigned his commission in disgust with the politicians and dedicated himself to helping people who really cared, like Angolans, Salvadorans, and Contra rebels. For a price, of course. Crider liked to take vacations in nice places.

He met Emilio Lujan in the lounge of the Airport Holiday Inn in Miami. It was gloomy in the lounge, and Lujan disappeared into the gloom. He was a short man with long, curly black hair and dark brown eyes. His complexion blended in with the brown Naugahyde covering the benches of the booth, and only the quick, nervous movement of his hands caught the light from the candle.

"Want a beer, Emilio?"

"Sure, man, why not?"

Crider signalled the waitress, who was not all that

busy in mid-afternoon, anyway, and they soon had *Carta Blancas* on the faked walnut Formica in front of them.

"Hey, man, I ain't heard from you in three years. What's up?"

Crider took a long pull at his beer, then asked, "Where you been working, Emilio?"

"Around. Here. There."

"Been flying out of Colombia?"

"No way, man. You can get locked in tight."

"No drugs at all?"

"Maybe a run or two. Panama, Mexico. Small-time dealers, you know?"

"I need a plane and a pilot," Crider said.

"Where, and how long?" Lujan asked, his eyes held steady on Crider's, though his hands continued to fondle nervously his icy bottle.

"Africa and maybe the subcontinent. Not over a month."

"Shit. I ain't flown that area in ten years."

Crider sipped and considered. Finally, he said, "You get 150 grand, flat, for you and the airplane. I want a business jet of some kind."

"United's cheaper."

"United's got a schedule to follow. I need mobility."

"What's the op?" the Mexican asked.

"Need to know basis only. You wouldn't be directly involved."

"For 150 big ones?"

"Something might come up. Call it contingency pay."

"You ain't calling it hostile fire pay?"

"Not right now."

"You going to be alone?"

"There'll be a few others, maybe six of us all together. The plane has to handle that."

"Heavy luggage?"

"Nothing that won't slide through customs like it was greased," Crider told him.

"My picture's been around, man."

"Part of the deal, you get a new passport."

"I need two, three days to find the plane."

"Call me when you've got it," Crider said and finished the last drops in his bottle.

Kimball had a lump the size of a walnut high on his left temple, but he owned a new Nikon 35-millimeter camera with automatic film advance. He had dropped the film off at Fotomat for developing on his way home.

He had come home early in the afternoon to dust and vacuum and take care of some chores that had fallen by the wayside during the month he and McEntire had been touring the Pitts Specials. Then he had showered, changed clothes to a light gray suit with a striped tie, and taken Cathy Colby over to Scottsdale for dinner.

They were back in his condo by eight o'clock. Kimball tossed his suitcoat on a chair in the living room, poured her a cognac, and fixed himself a soda water with a wedge of lime in it.

"You aren't drinking?" she asked.

"I'm flying at midnight."

He pulled open the sliding glass door to the balcony, and they went out to sit on the beige cushions of his wrought iron chairs. It was still warm out, but not uncomfortably so. The fiery highlights of sunset were just dying and the pathway lamps below began to flicker into life.

Cathy Colby placed her glass on the table between the chairs, and drew her legs up under her. She wore a pale aqua cocktail dress with a Chinese collar decorated with dark blue scrolling. Five years younger than Kimball, she had been married once, to a venture capitalist who lost a bundle in the Keating affair. Now she was doing well for herself as the publisher of a business magazine which her former husband had underwritten. They had first met when she did a feature story on the start-up Kimball Aero Technology.

She was tall and slim, with delicate facial features under styled platinum hair. Her china blue eyes were direct, always questioning. Her skin was smooth and gave the impression of being porcelainized. In the right light, Kimball had noted that he could practically see through her earlobes.

"Aren't you overdoing the training bit a little?"

"It's a stealth airplane, hon. The customers . . . potential customers . . . will want to see it operate at night."

"They can't see it at night."

"That's the point," he assured her.

She shook her head and the dim light from below reflected off her eyes.

"Are you going to be able to pull it out, Kim?"

She was a bright woman. Her magazine closely followed the rise and fall of business fortunes in the Phoenix area, and while she might not know the details, she knew KAT was faltering.

"Damned right," he said, though with less conviction than he had a year or two before.

"You need a big sale to the Air Force."

"Or a few small sales to the third world. It would be nice to have the Alpha Kats in an operational role for awhile. The Air Force would come around after watching it for a period of time."

"Isn't that being overly optimistic? This is the age of downsizing, Kim. And especially in the military. I don't see this Congress allocating big budget dollars for a new weapons package."

"That's the point, Cathy. They don't have to. We don't want new dollars. We want to be in the replacement schedule, using dollars that are already dedicated. Hell, why replace one F-16 or F-15 with the same aircraft, at an inflation-driven higher cost, when you can retire six old Eagles and replace them with six Alphas and a Kappa, and save the taxpayer fifty million dollars? We can replace the entire air superiority fighter fleet in ten years."

"You sound just like an aerospace CEO," she said with a smile.

"On top of that, they'd need fewer airplanes than they have now. The Alpha Kat has a limited ground attack role, and the Beta Kat" (then on the drawing-board) "even better serves the ground attack role. A hell of a lot cheaper than the F-117 or the A6, which is way, way past its prime, anyway. Christ, a dozen Beta Kats and a Kappa Kat can replace a whole wing of B-52s or B-1s. And the half-billion dollar B-2 Stealth bomber? Scratch that. Twenty years from now, the entire Air Force, Navy, and Marine fleets could be based on three aircraft types, all of them with interchangeable parts. Think of the savings in spare parts inventory alone."

"You don't have to be so fervent with me, Kim. I'm a believer."

"Sorry. I get damned angry when I think about what the military bureaucracy and the defense industry is foisting off on us."

"Plus, you'd like to keep KAT solvent," she said with customary practicality.

"It's a good concept," he defended.

Cathy picked up her snifter and swirled the liquid in it. "I just had another thought, Kim. Without new dollars from Congress, you wouldn't recover your research and development costs."

"We've built that into the per-unit pricing. It's identified, and we're not hiding anything. As the R&D costs are recovered, the price goes down."

"The plane gets cheaper?"

"Well," he admitted, "maybe not. It depends upon inflation rates. Still, as manufacturing costs go up, the R&D cost lowers. At worst estimate, the price stays the same for eight or nine years."

"I think your problem is that you're approaching the military without being devious. They don't know how to deal with that."

"Maybe."

She tilted the balloon glass and finished the last drops of cognac.

"You want another one of those, Cath?"

"No. I want to stop talking business, go inside with the air conditioning, and possibly shed this hot dress." She grinned impishly. "You still have your tie on, you know?"

Kimball tugged at the knot of his tie as he stood up. "That's how bad it's been. I hate ties."

He took her hand, pulled her out of the chair, and ushered her inside. As he slid the door shut, the phone rang.

"Damn it."

"Don't take it."

"I'd better."

He grabbed the phone from the counter between the dining room and the kitchenette.

"Kim, it's Susan."

"Hi. Problem? Are you still working?"

"Still here," she said.

"Are you alone?" he asked, thinking about Major Nash.

"No. There's fifteen or twenty people around."

"Don't go outside by yourself."

"I won't. Look, Kim, I've got all the numbers together, and we've got to spend some time on them."

"You sign all the checks, Susan. Go ahead."

"Not this time. I want your okay on them."

Kimball looked over at Cathy, who was toying with the buttons of her Chinese collar. She ran her tongue across her upper lip. He glanced at his watch. "All right. I'm flying at twelve, but I'll get out there an hour early."

"Good enough, boss," she said and hung up.

"That was Susan," he told Cathy.

"I picked up on that right away," she said, her slim fingers undoing the hooks of her collar. "She knew you were seeing me tonight."

It was a statement, not a question.

"What?"

"She took the message when I called you back this afternoon."

"What's that got to do with anything?" he asked.

"She's in love with you."

Kimball was dumbfounded. "That's nuts."

"Not so. I've seen her around you."

"Crazy."

"Uh huh. She's checking up on you."

Cathy led the way toward the bedroom, and Kimball followed, suddenly unsure of a lot of things.

Seven

"Why are you looking at me like that?" Susan McEntire asked.

"Like what?"

"Like that."

Kimball was searching her face and eyes for the tell-tale emotions that Cathy Colby had attributed to her.

Nothing.

He couldn't see anything in her eyes or face or manner that suggested she thought anything more of him than as a somewhat slipshod employer.

Women! They were super-sensitive to nuances that were undetectable to male radar. Talk about stealth.

"You look tired," he told her.

"I am tired. It's been a damned long day."

They were seated in the front office, Kimball in a straight chair pulled up alongside her desk. The chief executive officer of Kimball Aero Technology didn't have a desk or chair of his own.

There were lights on in the corridor and back in the hangar proper, and Kimball heard people barking at each other as they prepared the aircraft for the second round of night flights. Lack of sleep was making some tempers shorter than normal.

"Okay," Kimball said, "let's get it over with, so you can go home."

She shoved a small stack of financial spreadsheets toward him. He noticed a smudge of ink on her chin.

After a fifteen-hour day, her blouse was wilted, and her auburn hair was in some disarray. It put him in mind of Rita Hayworth for some reason. Some old bedroom scene, hair tousled, eyes inviting. There was a touch of redness around her green eyes, and the tiny silver flecks in them appeared dulled.

He hadn't really noticed the silver flecks radiating from the irises before.

"The first sheet is the overall view, and the rest of these outline the details of the impact of three million in revenues. We've never had three million in revenue before."

KAT did have some income, from various federal research grants, and from licensing some of their patented designs, but in the global scheme of things, the income was not significant.

"Let's just deal with the overview," Kimball said. "The details are up to you."

"That's just the way you and Sam Eddy approach everything."

"We get extremely involved in the design details," he defended. "We're engineers, not accountants."

"My degree's in history, remember?"

"Yeah, but you're so good at taking on new challenges."

"The last three years has certainly been a challenge, Kim. You're right about that."

With the tip of a ballpoint pen, she stabbed at a top number on her own spreadsheet. "There's the three million. Added to our cash on hand, it gave us three-point-five-five mil."

They had not quite been down to what was in their pockets, as Wilcox had insisted. Kimball found the number on his spreadsheet.

"I'm with you."

"With our tax loss carry-forward from last year, which is stupendous and our expected deductions for this year, our estimated corporate tax will be around two hundred thousand. I transferred that amount to our tax escrow account."

"Good girl."

She wrinkled her nose at him.

"Sounds better than good woman," he said.

"The estimated cost of the demonstration tour is now at four hundred and sixty thousand," she said.

"I thought it'd be more."

"Andrea booked you into cheaper hotels than you're used to," she grinned, "but I've set aside another forty thousand as a contingency fund."

"Don't use it, you mean?"

"You're the boss, Kim. It's your decision."

"Yeah, but I've got the recommendation from the comptroller, right?"

"Right."

"You know we'll be getting an Air Force billing for the dummy missiles?"

"Damn it!" she said. "How much?"

"Probably close to four hundred thou."

"Oh, shit!"

"It's a bargain, Susie. It really is. Probably a fourth of what we'd normally pay."

Susan knew that the C-141 parked on the tarmac was loaded for bear. She hadn't said a thing, one way or the other about it, to either Kimball or McEntire. She didn't mention it now, just moved her penpoint to the next line.

"The payroll coming up amounts to 246 thousand."

"That's with our half-time people?" Kimball asked. For the last four months, almost everyone in the manufacturing area had been working half-time. They were struggling with their monthly bills, and he knew it.

"When everyone's on full-time, the monthly payroll is 380 thousand, Kim."

"Let's take them back to full-time."

"To build airplanes we may not sell?"

"They need the money," he insisted.

91

"Three-quarter time."

"We'll do it your way. Just tell A.J."

She made a notation in the margin of her spreadsheet.

"Now, on our ninety-day credit accounts, we owe slightly over three hundred thousand. For the shorter-time accounts, it's around another two-eighty. We can satisfy them if we cover half of it."

"Do it all," Kimball said. "If we go under, I don't want to take a couple dozen subcontractors and suppliers with us. They've been straight with us, so let's reciprocate."

"God. And you thought you were tough enough to run a major corporation?"

He smiled at her. "They'll feel better about us, and A.J. can give them enough orders for materials to complete three more Alpha Kats. That'll keep our three-quarter time work force busy while we're gone."

Shaking her head, Susan worked her nimble fingers over the keys of a small calculator. She had very deft fingers, Kimball noticed. Her nails were coated with a pale cinnamon color. The nail of her right forefinger had a chip in it.

He found himself examining the tautness of her wilted blouse. Guiltily, he lifted his eyes back to her face. For some reason, he was just beginning really to notice her, and with his luck of late, he'd be slapped with sexual harassment charges.

"That'll leave us with enough to meet overhead and payroll for five months," she said.

Kimball saw a quick mental image of himself laying people off as Christmas presents. High-tech Scrooge.

"That's great! Last week, we could only last a month and a half," he said.

"So, this is progress?"

"Damned right."

She wrote the new numbers on her spreadsheet, then dated it. Spinning the page around, she shoved it toward him and handed him the pen.

"Sign it."

He did.

"Feel better?" he asked.

"Not particularly. But I want some protection from the shareholders on these kinds of decisions."

"The shareholders are all our friends."

"I'm a shareholder, and I question our ability to survive."

"Not me," he said, trying to be optimistic for her. "We've got 'em right where we want 'em. Just like Elway with ninety-eight yards and a couple minutes to go at Cleveland."

"Uh huh. This may be our last drive, Kim."

Tex Brabham stuck his head through the doorway. "You leading this picnic or not, boss?"

"Coming, Tex.

Kimball picked up his helmet from the floor and stood up. He was already in his flight suit and gravity suit and sweating a bit despite the air conditioning.

"I know I don't say this often enough, Susan. I appreciate what you do for us more than you know."

She rose from her chair, facing him. "I'm doomed to believing in what you're doing, Kim."

He grinned. "Doomed? Come on, honey, let's be optimistic. Think on the bright side."

She was six inches shorter than Kimball, and she looked up at him. Her eyes were large, and with the redness, somehow sad. The silver flecks were prominent at this range.

He still couldn't read any signals.

"Boss?"

"I'm coining, I'm coming."

Susan reached out and gripped his wrist, looked pointedly at the discolored lump on his forehead. "Be careful."

"It's a training mission."

"But for what?" she asked, then released his wrist

and turned back to her desk.

He studied the back of her head for a moment. The fluorescent lights put shiny streaks in the dark auburn. Several strands of hair stood out from static electricity.

Kimball left the office, and he and Brabham headed for the back of the hangar.

"How are the birds, Tex?"

"Tip-top. Hell, with the workout they've been getting, it only reinforces the claims we're making about maintenance. We haven't had a major systems malfunction yet."

"And minor?"

"You always get the minor stuff, boss. Trim tab solenoid. Left wing speed brake failure on two-one. We changed out a Nav/Com on one-five."

They passed through the brightly lit hangar on their way to the tarmac. One Alpha Kat was parked inside, with all of her access doors open. Seven technicians had their heads or hands tucked inside.

"We're going to get what we need to complete three more, Tex."

"Good fucking deal."

"You'll need to set up a work schedule before we go."

"No sweat. Full-time?"

"Three-quarter."

"That's better, anyway."

They stepped over the sill of the pedestrian door in the huge sliding hangar door and out onto the flood-lit apron. The four Alpha Kats were parked close by, in a single row. A Texaco tanker was just driving away.

"Keeper just took off in the Kappa Kat," Brabham said.

"A.J.'s the AC?"

"Right."

Standing in a group by the first aircraft were Mabry, Gander, and Greer. Mabry was juggling his helmet, the ebony skin of his shaved head shining under the lights.

He had sharp, sharp eyes; was as capable as they came; and like Kimball, had once flown with the Thunderbirds demonstration team. Gander always looked a little lost without his cowboy boots, but he was wearing his hat. Gaston Greer was a Floridian who had grown up around boats and kept a thirty-foot sailboat in San Diego. He was a bachelor who had said he admired Tex Brabham's ability to stay unhitched and intended to follow his fine example.

"I want you in ought-eight, boss."

Kimball checked the N-numbers on the fuselages. N17708 was third in line.

"There's a problem, Tex?"

"Sam Eddy complained about the response time on the air intakes. See what you think."

The large air inlets on the Alpha Kat changed their angles automatically, dependent on the attitude of the aircraft. At high angles of attack, the inlets aimed downward, to keep the flow of air uninterrupted, so the turbojet engine would not become starved for air and stall out.

Kimball joined the pilots. They had briefed together earlier, but he had not given assignments. "Okay, guys. I've got the squadron, and Warren, you're on my wing."

"Just try and lose me, Cheetah," Mabry said.

"Jimmy, you have the second element."

"Fine with me," Gander said. "Gaston, old hoss, no closer than three feet, got that?"

"It's night; I'll give you four," Greer said. He was a first class aerobatic pilot, and he was known for his ability to stay close.

"Let's mount up," Kimball said.

He walked down to ought-eight and did the walkaround with Virgil Thomas, who was the chief mechanic on the plane. Thomas was in his fifties, sprightly, and permed his gray hair into a curly mop. He was ex-Navy, with a lot of experience on Tomcats and Intruders.

"Tex told you about the air intakes?"

"He did, Virg."

"Sam Eddy bitches a lot."

Thomas opened a small hatch on the left side of the fuselage and worked the switches. The canopy rose with an hydraulic hiss, and the single-stemmed boarding ladder lowered from the fuselage, its two steps folding out. In an early design stage, the pilot design team had determined that they didn't want to have to mess with detachable ladders. The ladder was necessary since the Alpha Kat sat on landing gear that was stilt-like in its height. That allowed a wide variety of ordnance and accessory packages to be suspended from the hard points.

Ought-eight was outfitted with four AMRAAMs, two each on the outboard pylons. The missiles topped Mach 4 in speed and had a range of seventy miles. One inboard pylon carried a pair of AIM-9L Super Sidewinders, with a cruise speed of Mach 3 and a range of 11 miles. The left inboard pylon was mounted with a pod containing an M61A2 20-millimeter, rotating barrel gun and six hundred rounds of ammunition. On the centerline, one behind the other, were two simulated Mark 84 low-profile 500-pound bombs.

"You've got a full load, Kim," Thomas said. "Don't drop anything until you're ready."

"Got it, Virg."

Kimball gave Thomas his helmet, pushed in a spring-loaded handhold, got a grip, and climbed the ladder. He rotated his hips over the cockpit coaming, levered his legs inside, and stood on the seat. The seat pan was constructed of carbon-reinforced plastic, as were all major components of the aircraft, to reduce radar reflections. With this seat, modified to the Martin-Baker SJU-5/A ejector seat design, only the ejector rails used stainless steel.

Thomas came up the ladder with Kimball's helmet and parachute pack and helped him into it. The seat pan pack contained the survival gear, including a one-man raft. Thomas stayed long enough to help him strap in, don his helmet, and couple the communications, oxygen, and pressure suit lines, then slid back to the ground.

Kimball powered up the instrument panel and accessory systems, then ran diagnostic checks on each of the major systems, watching for green light-emitting diodes on the instrument panel. The Alpha Kat did have its own radar, but it was a low-power, fifteen-mile range set to be utilized in emergency situations. Since the odds were that the Alpha Kat would not be attacked by radar-guided missiles, there was no radar threat system. The AAR-38 infrared tailwarning system was mounted.

All of the radios and data link receivers came up and announced their availability with green LEDs. On the radio panel above the throttle handle, Kimball dialed the radios into the respective frequencies they would be using. The gyros came up to full speed. The Alpha Kat did not carry expensive navigational systems; it relied on data links to the Kappa Kat for navigation aids that were more exotic than the pilot's mind.

Kimball stuck his left hand outside the cockpit and rotated his wrist.

Thomas's crew powered up the start cart, and compressed air was forced into the turbojet intake. The RPM indicator (all readouts were digital) immediately showed the turbine blades beginning to turn. When he had 35 percent RPMs, Kimball initiated fuel flow and ignition.

The turbojet started to whine on its own.

He advanced the throttle slightly, tapping the key on the handle for Tac Two communications. "Bengal One. What have we got?"

"Two. Impatient," Mabry said.

"Three," Gander responded.

"And Four," Greer said.

Keying the button for Tac One, he said, "Uh, Phoenix Ground Control, this is Alpha Kat zero eight."

"Again, zero eight? You guys are hot on it lately."

"Got to make sure they work. How about permissions?"

"You're in good shape. There's a cargo transport due in about fifteen minutes, otherwise it's all going to be yours. Proceed to two-seven, zero eight, and go to air control."

Kimball released the brakes and pulled out of the line, turning right. The others fell in behind him and he left the air park, headed for the east end of the runways.

Changing to the tower frequency, Kimball checked in, "Phoenix Tower, Alpha Kat zero eight with a flight of four."

They were becoming accustomed to the increased traffic from Kimball Aero.

"Zero eight, Phoenix. You've got immediate clearance for two-seven-zero left. Barometric is three-zero-point-one-four."

Kimball checked to make sure that his altimeter setting agreed with the tower's.

"Wind is three knots southwest, maybe a thundershower in a few hours."

"That's wishful thinking, Phoenix."

"You're probably right, zero eight."

At the end of the taxiway, Kimball turned left, stopped short of the runway, and ran the engine up to full power for a few seconds. It responded immediately, its song vibrating in his ears and in the airframe.

He checked in both directions, lowered the canopy, released the brakes and moved onto the runway. Turning left, he braked until Mabry pulled up alongside him.

Mabry gave him a thumb's up.

On Tac Two, Kimball said, "Let's roll."

And he slammed the throttle to its forward stop.

Even with the full weight of the ordnance load, the Alpha Kat leaped forward. In seconds, the airspeed readout was showing sixty knots.

Mabry was right with him.

At 180 knots, the aircraft felt jittery, and he rotated by easing back on the hand controller.

The Alpha Kat utilized a fly-by-wire control system. The ergonomically-designed controller was located at the forward end of his right armrest and his hand gripped it snugly. Situated on the controller were buttons and keypads with different shapes and textures for controlling weapons release and other aircraft systems.

As soon as he had cleared the ground, Kimball verified the airspeed, then pulled in his flaps and landing gear. Putting the nose down slightly, he brought the speed up quickly.

"Five hundred," he said on Tac Two.

"Two at five hundred," Mabry said.

The two aircraft climbed steadily at a shallow five hundred feet per minute.

"Three and Four off," Gander reported.

By thirty minutes after midnight, they were cruising southwestward at 600 knots, in a loose four-finger echelon formation. The altimeter readout's blue numerals indicated 26,500 feet.

As they closed on the north end of the reservation, Soames came on the air from the Kappa Kat, which was doing lazy eights at 34,000 feet.

"Bengal One, Hawkeye."

"One."

"Squawk me once, so I can find you."

Kimball tapped in the IFF transponder, counted to five, and shut it down.

"This will be a breeze if you guys just listen close," Soames said. "Go right to two-one-five."

"One. Turning right."

Kimball eased the controller over and added rudder. The compass readout on the Head-Up Display slowly came around to 215. The HUD readouts, directly in front of him so he didn't have to glance down at the instrument panel, repeated the important information from the panel. The readouts were primarily in blue, though targeting information would appear in red.

Flying the Alpha Kat brought out polarized emotions in her pilots. On the one hand, it was back-to-the-basics flying, augmented by a few technological advances, like the HUD display. Without radar, navigation and advanced computer systems, they could be flying Stearman bipes or Spads. It was exhilarating, out on one's own on a clear, hot Arizona day, chasing coyotes and diving into arroyos.

Conversely, in an F-15, Kimball had had the ability to accept or reject the data provided by the computers and make his own decisions. In tactical situations with the Alpha Kat, he now had to rely on his air controller. It was difficult for hotshots like Gander and Greer and, he admitted, himself to relinquish that decision making.

Especially when it could mean a life.

"Bengal flight, put it on the deck," Soames told them. "Let's call it two thousand."

"Roger, Hawkeye, going to angels two."

Kimball eased back on the throttle and nudged the nose down with the hand controller. The airspeed began to increase, and he retarded the throttle some more. Supersonic flight wasn't programmed for this mission.

The stars were impressively clear tonight; bright, hard twinkles in the black sky. Moonset had occurred earlier, so the desert floor was almost invisible. To his right were the Sand Tank Mountains.

"What have we got for traffic, Hawkeye?" he asked.

"There's a couple choppers messing around over at Luke. What for, this time of night, I don't know. That's it."

Luke Air Force Range abutted the Papago Indian Reservation. It would have been nice to use their bombing and missile ranges, but Wilcox had vetoed the idea, not wanting to force the USAF any further after already requisitioning so much of their ordnance and gaining control of the two C-141s without identifying

KAT as the beneficial party. The request for Luke would have pinpointed Kimball Aero Tech and created a verbal firestorm in the halls of the Pentagon.

The readout wound down to 2000, and Kimball eased the power back in. Checking to his left, he saw Mabry a half-plane back. On the right was Jimmy Gander, and beyond him, Greer. If they hadn't been operating their low-wattage wingtip guidance lights, he wouldn't have known they were there.

"Bengals, take spacing and douse the lights," he ordered.

"Two."

"Three."

"Four."

The aircraft lights blinked out as the planes spread apart.

Tac Two sounded off. "Cheetah, we've got a UFO. I want two of your flight."

"Take whatever you want, Papa."

"Bengal Three and Four, jettison bomb load and climb to angels one-three, heading zero-nine-eight."

The intruder was off Kimball's rear quarter. He decided to let Gander take care of it and not worry about it.

Soames moved Gander and Greer to Tac Three, then said, "Bengal One, you've got a short peak coming up, but not short enough. Turn to one-nine-five."

"Roger, Papa. Going to one-nine-five."

"I'm going to need a guide, I guess," Warren Mabry said.

"Coming up, Two."

Kimball reached for the light panel and turned on his left wingtip guidelight. It was a red light that could be seen for perhaps a mile. The left or right guidelights were utilized by wingmen to keep track of the leader.

He would like to have listened to the dialogue between Soames and Gander, to get a feel for the attack of the aggressor aircraft, but knew that his job was to

101

concentrate on the ground attack.

"One, Hawkeye. You have a visual on ground lights?"

"Roger, Papa. At my ten o'clock."

They appeared to be a couple of farm yard lights, to be used as the Initial Point in his bomb run.

"That's the village of Ventana, Cheetah. When they hit your nine o'clock, that's your IP. Go to one-eight-zero. Target six miles. I'm feeding data now."

Kimball switched on his primary data receiver.

"Receiving, Hawkeye. How about you, Dingbat?"

"Two."

Mabry had always wanted a codename of "Othello," but somewhere along the line, got stuck with "Dingbat," and couldn't shake it.

The Alpha Kat computers accepted the data gathered by the Kappa Kat radars, compared it with on-board altitude, speed, and direction data, verified it, and displayed the results on the HUDs.

The center of Kimball's HUD showed him little spikes of light whenever the earth came closer than 500 feet, the altitude above ground for which he had set a tolerance.

"Bengal One, I'm painting the target now."

On the upper left of the HUD targeting screen, a red diamond appeared, the initial point to the target selected by Soames.

"Got it, Hawkeye."

"IP, One," Mabry reported.

"Roger that," Kimball said and started a turn to the left. When the HUD readout read 180, he stabilized.

The red diamond was now directly ahead.

"Bengals, Hawkeye. Bengal Three splashed himself a Fighting Falcon."

"Won't hear the end of that," Mabry said.

"Deploy IR," Kimball ordered.

"Two."

With his forefinger, Kimball found and depressed a

keypad on the control stick. That lowered a gimbal-mounted nightsight lens and infrared targeting lens from below the nose and simultaneously activated the interface with his helmet reader. He reached up and pulled the hinged infrared reader down over the Plexi-glas of his helmet visor. He could still read the instruments and the HUD, but he also had an irritating little yellow square in the center of his vision. It moved around whenever he moved his head. It also moved the gimballed lenses jutting from under the nose of the Alpha Kat.

"I want weapons, Hawkeye."

"Free fall weapons cleared," Hawkeye responded.

Kimball reached for the armaments panel with his right hand, the control stick always stayed in the position in which he left it; lifted the protective plastic cover, and snapped down the toggles for each of his two bombs.

On the bottom right of the HUD, two amber lights labeled "CL-1" and "CL-2" came on.

"I'm hot," Kimball reported.

"Two's hot."

The airspeed was four hundred knots, a bit high for the bomb drop, but they were experimenting a little.

The infrared lens picked up a heat source, and made it a red dot on the transparent screen of his infrared reader.

The landscape outside the canopy was utterly dark.

Kimball moved his head, sliding the yellow square over the red dot. With his forefinger, he pressed another keypad. From that point, the computer would track and stay locked on the red dot. He pressed the bomb release stud twice.

That only committed the drop. The weapons control computer would release the bombs at the optimal moment, considering altitude, speed, weight of the bomb, and the trajectory.

"Committed," he reported.

103

"Two, ditto."

A tall hill on the right penetrated the tolerance level of the computer and appeared on the HUD. He jinked slightly to the left.

"Watch it, One."

"Sorry, Dingbat."

One beep, then another, in his earphones signalled bombs away. The Alpha Kat surged upward a little as the weight dropped away.

"Bombs away," Mabry said.

Kimball eased the stick back and shoved the throttle in, climbing steeply away from the target.

There was no flash and no roar of thunder behind them. The two men tending the target would report the extent of their accuracy later.

"Felt good to me, Dingbat," Kimball said.

"Something missing though, Cheetah."

"What's that?"

"There wasn't anyone shooting at us. I kind of expect people to shoot at us."

"Not if we do it right."

"That one of Murphy's Laws, Cheetah?"

The compound rested on the brow of the hill, overlooking a deep, flat-floored valley. The view of the valley was not spectacular. There was a thin and meandering stream that eventually joined the Nam Hka. The stream was lined with deciduous trees, pines, and spruce. At two thousand meters of altitude, the jungle was not present.

At the head of the valley was a village composed of two dozen huts, shacks, and sheds. The village was blessed with electricity and a rude hospital, both gifts of the master.

In this part of the world, there was not much for the electricity to do. Each hut had a lightbulb, the hospital had a refrigerator, used by the entire village, and the chieftain's hut had a radio.

Midway up the valley, a hundred meters from the stream, running parallel to it, was an asphalt runway. It was nearly 4,000 meters long, and it was not particularly level. Along its length, it rose and fell by several meters. It was not crowned well, and in the rainy season, pumps had to be used to drain the water from the pools that appeared. Asphalt was as rare as electricity and bespoke great wealth.

A twin-rutted road that was not asphalted, and which became as slippery as snakes in the rainy season, wove its way from the runway, up the side of the hill, to the compound. There were six trucks that used the road frequently, in addition to occasional forays into the village. The trucks had been brought into the valley by large airplanes and had nowhere else to go but to the runway, to the village, and back to the compound.

It was a large compound, and as it had grown, had amazed the villagers who walked up the valley to personally view the construction. The perimeter was composed of thick walls six meters tall. From the outside, above the walls, could be seen red-tiled roofs which joined to the walls. At intervals along the walls, high up, were small openings that appeared suspiciously to be gun ports. No one in the village had ever seen a fortress.

One villager, who had paced off the perimeter during construction, had professed that the long sides were three hundred paces long, about three hundred meters, and the short sides were two hundred paces long.

Inside, before the massive central doors in the wall had been closed to them, the villagers had seen houses being erected against the outside walls. They were tall houses, narrow, with two floors. Some houses appeared to have been constructed for the trucks.

The trucks went back and forth to the runway, meeting airplanes bringing in the building materials and strange furnishings. Trees and shrubbery in heavy tubs were flown in. The machinery that made electricity was placed in its own house farther up the hill, and eventually the wires that carried the electricity were nailed high on the trees and brought down to the village.

There was a little ceremony in which the chieftain thanked the master of the compound for his largesse.

Bolts of fabric and exotic rugs were carried in on the airplanes. Utensils and china and clothing were reported by the young boys who spied on the airplanes.

And then, several years before, all of the people who had constructed the compound got on the airplanes and left.

But the airplanes continued to come and to go.

And the master was often in residence.

Brock Dixon took the call on his secure line.

"Marvin Nash, General."

"Where the hell are you?"

"Phoenix."

"Something wrong?"

"Kimball blew my cover."

"Shit! What happened?"

Nash reported the set-to with Kimball in the vacant hangar.

"He got the camera?"

"Yes sir, but it only had pictures of his own airplanes. He's already seen them."

"That's all?"

"Well, there's a few shots of some of his personnel."

Jesus Christ. All he needed was to have someone make a connection between Nash and the Air Force Intelligence agency. The papers would play it up for all it was worth: "AFI Spying on Civilian Manufacturers."

"Get the hell out of town, Nash."

"Yes sir. But you know something, General . . ."

"What, damn it?"

"That's a hell of an airplane, sir. I've been watching

106

it for two days, and—"

"Back to Washington, Nash. Report to me."

Kimball landed his Alpha Kat at the Buckley Air National Guard Base east of Denver at three o'clock in the afternoon. He fell in behind a blue Chevy pickup with a "Follow Me" sign on the back, and taxied to an area where a dozen elegant F-4 Phantoms were parked. He had always liked the Phantom, a stalwart of the Vietnam era.

An airman waved him into line, then gave him a cutthroat signal. Kimball shut down the turbofan, then the rest of his systems. Raising the canopy and lowering the ladder, he shrugged out of his harness and parachute, then unstrapped his helmet and placed it on top of the instrument panel.

He stood up in the cockpit and stretched. The flight from Phoenix had taken less than an hour. He had gone supersonic for about half of it.

While a couple of ground crewmen chocked the wheels, he slipped his legs over the coaming, found the spring-loaded toehold doors for his boots, and worked his way down to the ladder, then to the ground.

A beige Plymouth sedan crossed the tarmac and pulled up beside him. The back door opened, and he looked in to see Wilcox.

"Jesus Christ, Kimball! You weren't supposed to bring the goddamned airplane."

A crowd was already forming. Puzzled airmen and weekend fighter pilots emerged from hangars and airplanes and gathered to inspect the strange-looking Alpha Kat.

"It'd have been out of character for me not to bring it," Kimball said. "I advertise, remember? And would I give up a chance to park the Alpha on a military base?"

"Get in."

Kimball got in and sat next to Wilcox.

The driver kept his eyes trained forward. He was dressed in a dark suit, but he wasn't a chauffeur by career choice, Kimball guessed.

"We going to get us a drink or dinner?" he asked.

"I was going to, yeah, but now I want you back in that plane and off this base."

Wilcox handed him a black attaché case.

Kimball rubbed his thumb over the leather. "Nice case."

"Keep it. The data we have on Lon Pot's operations is in one folder. All of your clearances and permits are in there. Also duplicate sets of passports and visas."

"Duplicate?"

"For all of your pilots. If somebody goes down somewhere sensitive, we want him carrying bogus ID."

"That's a little silly, isn't it, Wilcox? All they'd have to do is round up a few pieces of airplane, and they could figure it out."

"Tomorrow morning, a Federal Express truck will deliver some packages."

"Christmas, already?"

"They're self-destruct devices. I want one mounted in every damned plane you've got."

"Ever since I said yes to this little enterprise, you've gotten pretty damned bossy, Wilcox."

"You going to do what I say."

"Do I have a choice?"

"Not in this particular case."

"Then I guess we'll sabotage the airplanes."

He was going to do it, anyway. Kimball didn't want any of his personal high-tech secrets falling into the wrong hands. But if he could irritate the man from the CIA, he didn't mind doing that, either.

Despite what he had told Emilio Lujan, Derek Crider did not return immediately to Washington. If he could avoid the truth, he always did. It kept people from knowing too much about him or about what he was doing.

He flew to Puerto Rico and checked into the Condado Plaza Hotel in San Juan.

After an excellent and leisurely dinner of lobster tails, Crider took a taxi to Old San Juan, then got out and strolled along Avenida Ponce de Leon. The tourists swirled around him, reacting negatively and positively to the chants and promises of the hawkers outside storefronts. Trinkets and T-shirts, scarves and baseball caps were offered at supposedly cutthroat prices. A little something to prove to the neighbors that Thelma and Walter had actually made it to the island.

It was a sultry night, the heat not dissipated by any breeze from offshore. Crider ambled along the sidewalk, letting others dodge him since he was bigger. Everyone was happy. No one seemed to notice the cold gray eyes that swept the street, looking for inconsistencies in the crowd.

He saw no problems for himself, and he turned down a side street to the Avenida Fernandez Juncos and slipped into a small bar. It was smoky and loud. A jukebox thumped hot reggae. The long bar was crowded, and all of the tables were occupied. He found the one he wanted far back, just outside the corridor to the reeking bathrooms.

He walked up to it and looked down at the four men sitting around it, drinking from long-necked bottles of *Corona.*

"Hey, Crider. Take a load off."

The man named Wheeler slid his chair sideways and grabbed a fifth chair from the adjacent table.

Crider sat down and nodded at the others. He had met them and fought with them at various times in his life.

Wheeler, the only name he ever gave, was an ex-Navy SEAL. The right side of his face was scarred from a

109

splash of napalm.

Del Gart had been in the Fifth Special Forces at the same time as Crider. He was as hard and tough now as he had been then, though now his skin was tanned the color of deer meat and his fair hair was bleached to white. His specialties were munitions and communications.

Corey O'Brian started out with the Irish Republican Army and, when the manhunt for him became too intense, volunteered elsewhere. Crider had met him in Angola. He was almost as good as Gart with bombs. Almost, since he was missing three fingers on his left hand.

Alan Adage was a hell of a sniper, a trade taught him in the Marines' First Recon. His dark blue eyes were as cold as an Arctic night, and his nerve was smooth and steady. He wore a full beard which matched the brick red of his hair.

"Everybody must be hungry," Crider said, "or you wouldn't be here."

"Always use a spot o' cash," O'Brian told him.

"Anybody to wonder where you went?"

They all shook their heads. They lived in places like Guatemala, El Salvador, and Honduras, and their neighbors were probably glad to see them leave.

"You said the money'd be good," Wheeler said. "How good?"

"Hundred grand apiece. You're in for the duration, but that's maybe a month, five weeks. If it goes longer, I'll boost the money."

"Who's the contractor?" Adage asked.

"No need to know," Crider said. Hell, he didn't even know, but he had some good ideas. He would never pursue them, of course, because people in his profession did not do that. Not if they wanted future work.

Wheeler asked, "This gonna to be wet work?"

Crider canted his head sideways and raised his hands palms up. "Don't know about that, yet. Could get that way, but preferably not. If it gets to hostile fire, you get a bonus of twenty thou."

"I'm in," Adage said.

"Why not?" O'Brian agreed.

Wheeler nodded his head.

Gart asked, "We get to play with HE?"

Crider said, "High Explosive figures prominently in this job."

"Yeah, I'll go along," Gart said. "What's the action? Political?"

"There's probably some politicking involved, but nothing that concerns us. We just guarantee that some airplanes don't fly."

"Piece of cake," Wheeler said.

TAKEOFF

Eight

Shortly before four o'clock in the morning, Jimmy Gander turned his F-150 Ford pickup into the parking lot. From the height afforded by the oversized wheels and tires, he could see across the lot to three rows of cars idling in front of the hangar. The violet sodium lamps of the lot cast an eerie glow over everything.

He pulled up in the third row behind Luke Frale's Buick Regal, and the pickup's headlights shone through the rear window, illuminating Luke saying goodbye to his wife and three kids.

Shifting to neutral, Gander set the parking brake.

"I thought I was long past being an Air Force wife," Mollie said.

"Hey, baby, it's only for a couple of weeks. We hop into one place, hop out, and head for another place. It'll be over in no time."

Gander shifted around to face her, leaned forward, held her cheeks in both of his hands, and gave her a kiss on the lips.

"You be careful, James Gander."

"Yes, ma'am."

"I mean it. No risk-taking."

"You know me, Mollie."

"You're damned right I do. That's why you've got to promise me."

"No risks," he said.

"Cross your heart?"

"And yours," he said and did.

He kissed her again, then opened the door and slid to the ground. He fished his duffle bag out of the pickup bed as Mollie closed the door and rolled down the window.

"Tell Timmy goodbye for me."

"We could have wakened him."

"He needs his rest."

"And I need you," she said. "Remember your promise."

"Yes ma'am."

She leaned through the window to kiss him again, then released the brake, shifted into first, and rolled away. The dual exhaust gurgled merrily behind her, and Gander watched after her until the truck turned out of the lot.

Heading for the door, he said hello to wives and kids he knew and greeted the sleepy-eyed men who would be going with them. The atmosphere had a carnival edge to it, and once inside the hangar, away from their families, the male voices picked up tempo and volume. They were off on a happy crusade, a long-promised quest to sell the airplanes and realize some of the gold.

It was a vacation, long overdue.

His cowboy boots clacked on the linoleum as he went down the hall and into the hangar proper. A crowd was gathering near the hangar door, and the chatter was lively and vibrant.

Sam Eddy McEntire stood near the Judas door in the sliding hangar door, and he called out, "All right, you guys! Nobody goes through that door until I've checked your passports and luggage. Ain't no snakes, booze, Gila monsters, or *Playboys* going with us, so get rid of them now. We're not taking this trip to offend our hosts."

"Ah, hell!" somebody called back to him.

"Shed the contraband and line it on up, boys! Let's get this show on the airways. Command pilots, check in with A.J. first thing."

Since he was a command pilot for the first leg, Gander sidled through the crowd to where Kimball and Soames stood together.

"Mornin'," he said.

Kimball grinned at him. "Come on, Gandy, smile!"

"It's too damned early in the morning. But I'm happy, Kim, believe me."

"Good deal."

Soames handed him a thick attaché case. "There's your paperwork, Jimmy. It's so pristine, it squeaks."

"Damned better squeak," Gander said.

"Main thing," Soames said, "don't get nervous when the Customs boys are going through your stuff."

"I got bogus passports stowed all over the plane, and I got fifteen tons of illegal missiles, A.J. Why should I get nervous?"

"You're a good actor," Kimball said, "that's why you drew the assignment."

"Never acted in my life."

"You're a natural," Soames said.

"Break a leg," Kimball added.

Shaking his head, Gander moved over to get in line for McEntire.

When he reached him, McEntire said, "What's in the bag, Gandy?"

"Shorts and socks."

"Good enough. Passport?"

Gander handed it over, and McEntire leafed through it, then gave it back.

"You're all set."

"You want to trade places, Sam Eddy?"

"I know too much. Luck be with you, Gandy Dancer."

Gander stepped through the Judas door and crossed the tarmac to the transport. He met Walt Hammond, who was serving as crew chief on the C-141, and they did their walk-around together. They poked their heads into wheel wells and access doors, looked for fluid leakage, and checked for free movement of surfaces that were supposed to be free-moving.

People were clustered around both Starlifters when he climbed through the crew hatch and shoved his duffle into one of the lockers in the crew compartment.

He opened the door into the cargo bay, turned on the overhead lights, and walked through the seventy-foot long space.

The loadmasters, sternly governed by Tex Brabham, had carefully placed the cargo, spreading the weight. Most of the ordnance was tied down near the front end, the specially marked boxes and crates at the bottom of the stacks. There were 30,000 pounds of live missiles, bombs, and cannon rounds under there somewhere, and a like amount was aboard the other C-141. Thirty tons of lethal weaponry on both transports. Just enough to allow them seven sorties, if that many were required. Kimball and McEntire seemed to think they could accomplish the mission with three raids. On top of that in each plane was another twenty tons of demonstration ordnance. The rest of the bay was filled with two startcarts, a tow tractor, missile dollies, big tool chests on casters, crates and cardboard boxes of replacement parts, jerry cans of lubricating oil, water cans, and boxes of Meals Ready to Eat (MREs) in case anyone got hungry along the way.

His plane carried a small portable crane, its boom folded back over its squat body.

There was slightly over forty tons of materiel, near the cargo weight limit for the transport.

The other Starlifter, commanded by Mel Vrdlicka, was provisioned the same way except for the addition of a spare KM-121 turbofan engine on its own dolly. It was the only complete spare engine they had.

As he headed back toward the front, Howard Cadwell stepped through the hatch.

"How's she look, Jimmy?"

"All tied down, Cardsharp."

"How come you don't look proud?"

"If I wanted a bunch of passengers on my airplane, I'd be flying for United. I like a cockpit with just me in it."

"Ditto."

They went back to the crew compartment, and Cadwell climbed the short ladder to the flight deck to begin the checklist. From his attaché case, Gander took his passenger manifest and checked off everyone that was supposed to be with him. Counting Cadwell and himself, there were ten.

The count of noses came out right, and Gander said, "Okay, Walt, button her up."

Hammond secured the hatch, and Gander climbed to the flight deck. George Wagers, known as the "Gambler," followed him up. Wagers was acting as navigator/flight engineer for the cross-country trip.

Sidling into the lefthand seat, Gander took off his cowboy hat, hung it on a bulkhead hook, and donned his headset. He rested his feet on the rudder pedals. Checking his watch against the chronometer on the instrument panel, he said, "Six minutes after four, gentlemen. We're already late."

"We're late, we're late! For a very important date," Cadwell said.

"Ah, shit, Howard. Don't go quoting literature all the way to Africa."

"You know Alice?"

"She's the only one I know."

"The Alice I like," said Wagers, "is from Massachusetts. She used to run a restaurant."

"Goddamn it. This is going to be one damned long trip," Gander said. "Light 'em up."

He wished Kimball had assigned him to an Alpha Kat, where he could be by himself.

Since the view all around the compound he called

119

Fragrant Flower was so dismal, Lon Pot had provided his own view. The window wall of the main house looked out upon a garden fabricated by his architects and landscape designers. It filled the entire courtyard of the compound.

Orange trees, Russian olives, pine, and Colorado Blue Spruce had been imported in near full-grown sizes and planted randomly. Gravelled walks meandered through the forest, skirting elevated ponds that spouted miniature waterfalls. Rocky outcroppings had been transposed from the nearby mountains, and their crevices were filled with gold, red, and yellow blossoms.

The garden seemed to flow inside the house, which is what it was supposed to do.

The two-story-high ceiling of the living room and the walls were finished in matte white, and one wall was spanned from one end to the other by a black marble mantel. Centered beneath the mantel was a large fireplace, flanked by sunken bookcases. All of the books were bound in black leather, and their titles were stamped in gold. There were over three thousand books written in English, and although Lon Pot's reading ability in English was not yet rapid, and he stumbled over many of the longer words, he intended to read them all. He had already read Thackeray, Machiavelli, some of Emerson, one volume of Winston Churchill's work, and a Harold Robbins's book called *The Adventurers*.

He particularly liked Machiavelli.

His living room had been copied from a picture he saw in a magazine in Hong Kong, though many of the touches were his alone. The carpeting was deep and plush and ultra white. The tables and sideboards were of hammered brass and had come from Saudi Arabia. All of the randomly spotted chairs and sofas were upholstered in bright red. The lamps were of crystal, and their shades were covered in pure white silk. Over the fireplace was an oversized copy of a Picasso print.

The room reflected the soul and the essence of Lon

Pot, Lon Pot thought. It was progressive, with clean lines, and bright spots of creativity.

There were six bedrooms, with at least four of them occupied at all times by visiting young beauties of Burmese or Thai ancestry.

For guests, there were four guest houses in the compound. Each of his chief deputies were also provided a house.

This compound of houses was a refuge for him and his lieutenants.

It was also an island of solitude on the high plateau, but solitude was no longer what he craved. He had built the compound years before at a time when he might have been considered an outlaw, yet now, in most of the region, he was the law. His words alone directed the energies of thousands of people.

Lon Pot had already achieved his first objective. He was a man of immense wealth, and the accumulation no longer had the same importance it had once had. He had come to realize that he was more than a man, and as such, he had to give more of himself to his people. His existence, his very core, was meant to serve a higher cause.

He had determined that he would help his people, and he would help them in the most efficient way he could. He had read *The Prince,* after all.

He turned from his contemplation of the garden and faced the four men seated on two of the red sofas. They were his most trusted advisors and subordinates: Dao Van Luong, Micah Chao, Vol Soon, and Henry Loh.

"I feel that soon I must live in a city," he said.

The four men nodded their agreement.

"Then let us make it so."

All four men rose from the sofas and left the room to make it so.

Which was the way Lon Pot preferred to accomplish his objectives.

* * *

The Kappa Kat, piloted by A.J. Soames, and carrying mechanics Tex Brabham and Elliot Stott along with Conrad Billingsly as air controller, had taken off from Sky Harbor International fifteen minutes before.

The six Alpha Kats were parked in one row, surrounded by their pilots and the ground crewmen who weren't going along and were therefore understandably sullen. Kimball stood with Sam Eddy McEntire and Susan McEntire next to zero-eight.

"You're the acting president," Kimball told her.

"Hell, hon, you're the whole damned acting corporation," McEntire added.

"Do I get an acting salary?" she asked.

"You can have mine," Sam Eddy told her.

"You've already borrowed against yours into the next century, she said, then leaned toward him and kissed him on the cheek. "Be very careful, Sam Eddy."

"Just for you," McEntire said, gave her a thumb's up, and headed for Alpha Kat one-five.

Kimball had never been very nosy about relationships, and the ebb and flow of tensions between the McEntires could easily confuse him.

"Watch him, Kim," Susan said.

"What?"

"Watch him closely. For me."

"Sam Eddy can take care of himself pretty well, Susie."

"Please."

"I'll watch him."

"Thank you."

"May I ask—"

"No," she said. Emphatically.

Abruptly, she rose on her toes and kissed him on the mouth. There was a lot of heat behind it, and she held the kiss for some time.

Kimball gripped her upper arms to stabilize himself

122

physically and mentally.

She pulled away.

"Most important, you take care of yourself, Kim."

She spun away, headed for the hangar, but not before he saw the tears spilling down her cheeks.

Jesus. There's not enough time in a lifetime to understand women.

Kimball swung around to his plane and went up the ladder. Eight minutes later, he was buckled in, hooked up, and turning the turbofan.

Ground control gave him permission to use Runway 9-R, and he led the other five eager fighters into position just off the runway.

"Phoenix, Alpha Kat zero-eight with a flight of six."

"Got you, zero-eight. Let me get a UPS freighter off, then it's all yours."

"Appreciate that, Phoenix."

"When you get airborne, zero-eight, I'd like a squawk from all of you. All modes and codes."

"Roger, Phoenix."

The squawk-ident—or for the military, the Identification Friend or Foe (IFF)—transponders aboard aircraft identified their blips on the screens of ground radars. Depending on the modes set on the transponder, various data, such as altitude, were also displayed. Since they were stealth aircraft, the KAT aircraft mounted modified transponders that also sent a signal that created a radar blip in the first place. The FAA was conscientious about wanting to know what was in the air, especially when it was civilian.

Sixteen minutes after takeoff, they rendezvoused with the Kappa Kat.

In the clear skies over the Arizona desert, with day fully broken at their altitude, Kimball saw the controller craft from several miles away.

He used Tac Two. "Hawkeye, Bengal One."

"You took your sweet time, Cheetah. I want the lead. Form on me in echelon," Billingsly said.

"You got it, Papa. Bengals, let's put the odds on the left."

Kimball drifted upward until he was slightly above the Kappa Kat and flying behind and to the left of its left wing. Bengals Three and Five formed up on him. The three Alpha Kats with even codenames took up stations off the Kappa Kat's right wing.

Below, the shadows of the mountains were getting shorter, but they were too high to distinguish the bright colors of wildflowers and cacti.

"Bengals," Billingsly said, "we're going to stay at angels two-zero and heading zero-eight-seven. But we're going to goose it to Mach one-point-two. Everybody stay with me."

Kimball eased his throttle forward as the Kappa Kat accelerated. He easily maintained his position until the HUD readout, switching from a reading of knots when they crossed through the sonic barrier, displayed 1.2.

He looked over the formation, and he couldn't help but feel an elevated sense of pride in its appearance. The craft appeared lethal and agile, and he was responsible for that, for the initial design. Others had contributed in many ways: electronics, weapons systems, and engines, but the Alpha Kat was his in her beautiful heart and soul.

The dark bronze tinting of the canopies prevented him from distinguishing the identities of specific pilots, but he knew them all, and he was proud of them, too. They were the kind of men he could trust.

"Okay, Bengals, I'm giving you a data feed. Just in case you missed your naps."

"That's what I've been waiting for, Papa," McEntire said.

"Except for Irish. He needs the exercise," Billingsly responded.

Sam Eddy had picked up the nickname of "Irish Eyes," not for his surname and his good-humored handsomeness, but also for his reputation with the ladies. In his Air Force days, there had been many waiting for him at every base.

The autopilots aboard the Alpha Kats were rather rudimentary when used stand-alone. They maintained the course, speed, and altitude input by the pilot. When connected to the Kappa Kat by data-link, they were as sophisticated as anything in the skies. The AWACS craft's navigation system interfaced with at least three or four of the satellites in the Global Positioning System, providing it with navigational accuracy that was within a few feet of geographical position and a few knots of speed. Coupled with input from the Kappa Kat's radars, the data fed to the fighters provided them with navigational information that was just as accurate.

Kimball activated his primary data-link receiver, the frequencies determined at the pre-flight briefing and set during the cockpit check. He cut in the autopilot and felt the control stick tremble as the computer took over. If he turned on his data-link feedback transmitter, the Kappa Kat could also fly his plane for him. It was considered a backup system. If a pilot became disabled—something none of the pilots talked about—there was a possibility that the Kappa Kat air controller could get him back on the ground in one or two pieces by remotely operating the autopilot.

In the center of the instrument panel was an eight-inch cathode ray tube, and Kimball switched it on, then pressed the keypad for navigational display. Immediately, the screen showed him the seven blips in the formation, all in blue. His blip was in the center of the screen and blinking, and at the bottom of the screen, blue lettering displayed his geographical coordinates. In a tense combat situation, Billingsly's computer would paint the opposing aircraft red, to help track friend and foe.

"In case any of you are lost," the AC said, "I'm going to give you a map overlay."

The Kappa Kat's computer disk reader would accept

mapping information stored on small hard disks, each disk containing data for various parts of the world. That kind of information was good, and often essential, for flying in unknown regions or flying close to the terrain during invasions.

Using data relayed from the Kappa Kat, the screen showed the overlay of map grid lines, each five miles apart. The entire screen displayed the current setting of the Kappa Kat's ninety-mile scan. Several of the major highways were shown, to aid in orientation. At the top right of the screen, the city of Globe was shown. Globe was east of Phoenix, but on the screen appeared to be north. That was because the top of the screen was always the direction of travel, 087 degrees magnetic currently.

Kimball loosened his harness a bit, took his feet off the rudder pedals, and relaxed. He squirmed a bit to settle into the survival and parachute packs of his seat, then reached between the seat and the fuselage wall and found his leather portfolio. The leather wasn't as good as that of the attaché case Wilcox had given him, and was scratched and stained from fifteen years of use.

Opening it on his lap, he studied the itinerary that had been finalized only two days before:

  July 16: N'Djamena, Chad
  July 18: Riyadh, Saudi Arabia
  July 21: Islamabad, Pakistan
  July 23: New Delhi, India
  July 26: Dacca, Bangladesh
  July 28: Rangoon, Burma
  July 31: Bangkok, Thailand
  August 3: Manila, Philippines

Andrea Deacon had had to do some rescheduling when Kimball had finally firmed up the last demonstration dates, for Riyadh and Dacca, but it was all in place now.

126

In some cases, Susan McEntire had had to secure separate lines of credit from local banks to cover their fuel and other expenses, but there hadn't been many obstacles. He and Susan had always been compelled to pay enough on the Kimball Aero billings by the time they were due in order to maintain an excellent credit rating.

Below the itinerary sheet were slim file folders containing information about each site's landing and parking conditions, the hotel and meal accommodations, and other practical matters. Each of the aircraft command pilots had aeronautical charts and local regulations for each stop along the way.

Also in each of the folders in Kimball's portfolio were profiles and background information on influential members of the nation's defense ministries and military. They had been compiled by Soames and McEntire, often with information supplied by Ben Wilcox. Wilcox had been very helpful in a number of areas, coming up with arcane information about the bribability and sexuality of many important military and civilian leaders. Kimball had been cautioned to destroy the profiles before landing at each destination.

There were also short summaries of the economic, military, and political climates of each nation.

Kimball pulled the file labeled for Chad and began reading.

The French have long supported administrative and military objectives in Chad, particularly in regard to occasional incursions from Libya. It can be expected that French companies such as Dassault-Breguet will resist the potential loss of sales revenues, and that they will be supported by French sympathizers in the administration.

However, a cadre of new administration and military people is beginning to emerge, and. . . .

127

At 10:15 A.M., they were on the ground in Atlanta after a three-and-a-half hour flight from Phoenix.

The tanker trucks were nearly finished with the refueling of booth Starlifters.

Gander and Vrdlicka stood near the nose of Gander's aircraft, out of the mild breeze wafting the stench of JP-4 across the tarmac. The humidity was like a soft, sopping washrag, oozing from the cracks in the concrete. Heat waves flickered over the hot metal of the wings. The sweatband of his Stetson was already permeated.

"Just another measly seventy-five hundred miles to go," Vrdlicka said.

"It's a piece of cake, Mel. A piece of boring damned chocolate cake."

Loaded the way they were, the C141s had a range of 4,500 miles, and straight lines being what they were when the curvature of the earth interfered, they were headed next for England for refueling before taking on the last leg to N'Djamena, Chad. Spain had refused them a refueling stopover.

"You know what Hamilton and Carl Dent are doing in the back of my buggy?" Vrdlicka asked.

"What?"

"They put a sheet of plywood on some crates, and they're running a ping pong tournament."

"No lie? Who's winning?"

"I don't think anyone is. The ball does funny things when the plane changes attitude."

Back by the hatchway, Gander's hitchhikers were standing around stretching their legs. As he looked at them, one of the Customs agents stuck his head out of the hatch.

"Mr. Gander?"

"Yo."

"You want to come here a minute?"

Trailed by Vrdlicka, Gander walked back and climbed through the hatch.

"Do you have a key for this locker, Mr. Gander?" the officer asked, pointing to one of the tall and narrow hanging lockers for crew use.

Uh oh.

"Sure."

He shoved his hat back on his head, dug his keyring out of his Levis, and found the one for the Masterlock padlock. The lock popped open readily, and he swung the door back.

Four M-16 assault rifles leaned into one corner of the locker, and two Browning 9-mm. automatics in holsters were stashed on the top shelf. Boxes of ammunition and a dozen loaded magazines were stacked at the bottom.

"What's this?" the Customs officer asked.

"M-16s and automatic pistols."

"I can see that. What for?"

"We've got a hundred million dollars' worth of airplanes that are going to be parked in some exotic locations," Gander said. "We provide our own security."

"Uh huh, yeah," the agent said. "You have a clearance for this, of course?"

"Should be in the bunch of paper I gave you."

"I don't have anything like that." He held up his clipboard.

Gander glanced at Vrdlicka standing in the hatchway. Vrdlicka spun away toward his own plane. Maybe he had the damned release.

"Look, Officer, we've got a schedule to follow, and we need to get in the air. The flight plan's already filed."

"Then you'd better suspend the flight plan," the man told him.

Gander shook his head in disgust. Damned paper was going to be the downfall of humanity.

Ben Wilcox had a copy of Clive Cussler's *Sahara*

with him as cover, but he had found himself getting caught up in the story a couple of times, forgetting to keep an alert eye on the activities taking place at the general aviation section of the airport.

He had spent much of his morning on the observation deck level of Hartfield-Atlanta International Airport. Two gooey donuts he didn't need had already been consumed, and he was on his third cup of styrofoam-encased coffee.

The two C-141's, distinctive with their high-set stabilizers, hadn't moved since landing. They were a distance away, and the people moving around them looked like oversized ants. The airport's tanker trucks had departed some time before, and the aircraft engines still hadn't been started.

Some kind of problem.

He didn't need problems.

He glanced back at his book. Dirk Pitt was getting roped into something he. . . .

"Mr. Ben Wilcox, please go to a white paging telephone."

The soft-spoken monotone almost didn't register until the second repetition. Wilcox got up and looked for a white telephone, carrying his book and coffee with him.

The voice on the other end of the phone told him to call a Washington number.

He found a real telephone on which to dial it.

"Happy Hour."

"This is Montrose," he said, providing the code name.

"Donegal reported in."

"And?"

"Phase One is under way."

"Damn." Much earlier than expected. "Did Donegal say it was going the way we'd discussed?"

"Donegal did not elaborate," the disembodied voice told him.

Wilcox hung up and went back to his seat.

He sipped his coffee and watched the inaction around the transport airplanes. The itinerary that Kimball had faxed him would barely make the deadline that Wilcox had imposed. Now, that deadline may have been advanced.

He couldn't take many delays.

Especially if Lon Pot had jumped the gun on his starting date.

Just thinking about that made him more antsy. He wished he had talked to Donegal himself.

He looked across the field at the dormant transports and almost decided to interfere.

But he wouldn't.

If Kimball and his people couldn't pull themselves out of the crap, the Agency wasn't going to do it for them. Not from here on in. If or when Kimball got in trouble, the Agency would be looking the other way.

That was the only way it could be.

Nine

Atlanta appeared on the horizon just before eleven, eastern standard time. Kimball had already advanced the secondary chronometer on the instrument panel, as well as his watch. The primary chronometer was always set to Zulu, Greenwich mean, time, so that the computers didn't become confused.

At Mach 1.2, their flight time from Phoenix was just over two hours.

There was a haze stretched over the verdant countryside that threatened to thicken into an opaque cloud cover by later in the afternoon. The local meteorologists concurred with that prediction, but Kimball intended to be a long way from Georgia before it happened.

"Bengals, Hawkeye. Everybody awake?" Billingsly asked. "I'm taking my data feed back."

Each of the pilots responded with his number, and Kimball deactivated the autopilot.

The fighters broke away from the Kappa Kat and formed on Kimball.

He contacted Atlanta Air Control on Tac One, and they were put in the stack for landing. Traffic was heavy.

It was 11:20 A.M. when he and McEntire landed as a pair and taxied off the runway.

"The big birds are still here, Cheetah," McEntire said.

"Could we have expected more, Irish?"

"I guess not, buddy."

Kimball got on the radio and requested permission to

park near the Starlifters for refueling, and the request was promptly granted.

He had the turbofan shut down, the brakes locked, the ejection seat safed, the canopy open, and was mostly out of his gear by the time Gander, Vrdlicka, and three uniformed officials reached the plane. The Customs agents took their time looking the Alpha Kat over.

Kimball got his portfolio from its crevice next to the seat and made his way to the ground. The sweat broke out on his forehead right away.

"Damn, we're glad to see you," Vrdlicka said.

"You got a problem, Mel?" he asked.

"Are you Mr. Kimball?" one of the agents asked. He seemed to be in charge, and he took an inordinate amount of interest in the bluish-brown blemish on Kimball's forehead. The swelling had disappeared.

"Got me."

"You have weapons on those planes that are not cleared for departure."

"Oh, shit! You don't have the releases, Jimmy?"

"Hell, no."

"Well, let me see what I've got here." Kimball took his time opening his leather envelope and leafing through his file folders.

McEntire came around the nose of zero-eight and joined them. "Good morning, gents."

"Sam Eddy, have you seen the releases for the security weapons?" Kimball asked.

"Not me. I don't believe in red tape."

The Customs agent gave him a sour look.

"Here we go," Kimball said, withdrawing the two sheets of paper. They had enough Transportation, State, Commerce, Treasury, and Bureau of Alcohol, Tobacco, and Firearms counter-signatures on them to start their own government.

The officer looked them over.

"Every serial number will agree with what's listed there," Kimball assured them.

The other two agents peered over the first one's shoulder and gave him nods. He raised his clipboard, signed the two top papers, and passed them to Gander and Vrdlicka.

"I guess that takes care of it, Mr. Kimball."

"Well, I appreciate it. Now, we've got seven more airplanes for you to take a look at."

"Yes sir, we'll do that."

The three of them wandered off for a closer look at the Alpha Kat.

Two more Alpha Kats rolled in from the taxiway and parked in line.

Gander moved closer to Kimball and McEntire.

"Jesus, I was worried as hell. A.J. said we had all the documentation we needed."

"He did say that," Kimball agreed. "Except we pulled these on purpose."

"What! And put me through all this shit!"

"It seemed like a good idea at the time," Kimball said. He and Sam Eddy had discussed the tactic in detail.

"It wasn't a good goddamned idea, not at all," Gander countered.

"Sure it was," McEntire said. "You give a guy a little problem to worry about, you think he's going to worry about a larger problem?"

Vrdlicka laughed and slapped Gander on the shoulder. "Hell, yes! I'd rather worry about twenty pounds than fifteen tons, any day."

Gander gave him the finger.

Derek Crider was stretched out on the bed in his hotel room when the phone rang.

He rolled over and picked the receiver from the bedside stand.

"Yeah."

"They filed a flight plan out of Atlanta for the capital of Chad."

134

"Chad?" he asked.

But the caller had already hung up.

Crider sat up, made five calls to other rooms in the hotel, then got up and packed his small valise. By the time he got down to the lobby, the others were already in line at the cashier's counter, checking out.

The six of them took two taxis out to Isla Verde Airport where they went through the immigration checks without one question being raised about the six passports Crider had supplied. He knew very competent people in the passport business.

While Lujan went to file his flight plan, Crider led the others out to the airplane, a Gates Learjet 25B that normally carried ten passengers. This one was modified with two additional fuel tanks in place of four seats in the rear of the passenger cabin.

One could assume that it had seen service between South and North America. Crider was confident that Lujan had vacuumed, dusted, washed, and rinsed the plane inside and out. There would be no traces of prior cargoes to trip them up.

Wheeler opened the swing-down cabin door, and they climbed inside, stowed luggage, and selected seats. All of them were big men, and the space disappeared quickly.

Del Gart opened a small case and pulled out a bottle of Jim Beam. He held it up toward Crider.

"I don't drink on an operation, Crider, but we aren't starting anything today, are we?"

"Go ahead," Crider said.

Gart started filling paper cups.

Lujan arrived a few minutes later, his brown eyes excited by the prospect of adventure and money, and clambered up the steps. He turned to pull the doors closed behind him.

"What's the route, Emilio?" Crider asked.

"We're goin' to the Azores, man."

"Can we make it on fuel?"

135

"If the wind's right."

Henry Loh was a multi-millionaire. His accounts in Hong Kong, Singapore, and Bern kept accumulating higher totals, but he never worried too much about it. He had never had any trouble making money, but he preferred having it in his accounts to flaunting it.

His wardrobe contained nothing worthy of ceremonial or formal occasions. There were two pairs of blue slacks and a couple of white, short-sleeved cotton shirts. A dozen sets of khaki pants and shirts, along with a couple of safari jackets rounded out his closets at the Fragrant Flower compound and at the small flat he kept in Bangkok.

Retirement to an exotic, peaceful island did not enchant him, whether or not he could afford it. Loh was addicted to activity, preferably activity involving aircraft, and Lon Pot had offered him the most attractive deal in his world.

As one of Lon Pot's four chief lieutenants, Henry Loh received a salary equivalent to one million U.S. dollars a year, paid to him in automatic dollar, *franc, baht, kyat,* and *riel* deposits to his accounts. He generally carried with him ten thousand dollars because he never knew when a bribe might be required.

As much as he disdained money, Henry Loh was always ready to accept it when it was offered. It was primarily a way of keeping score, but it did not substitute for his other needs.

Better, to his way of thinking, he was chief of Lon Pot's air arm. Where else in the world could a poor boy from Taiwan become the general of his own air force?

The air force was spread all over the State of Shan, with two additional bases, Muang and Chiang, hidden in the geography of northern Laos and northern Thailand. The core of the fleet, naturally, was composed of aged transport craft, operating under cover of a half-dozen airline names. The transports could be found anywhere from Rangoon to Bangkok to Mandalay to several dirt strips hacked out of the jungle and the hillsides.

Slowly, however, with careful orchestration of Lon Pot's ego, and working through foreign intermediaries, Henry Loh had amassed two MiG-23s, two MiG-27s, four Maruts, and five French Mirage 2000s. His helicopter squadron consisted of an Aerospatiale Gazelle dedicated to the transport of Lon Pot, several Super Frelons, and five Augusta-Bell AB 212s, a version of the famous Huey produced under license in Italy.

At nine o'clock at night, Air Force Chief Henry Loh landed his AB 212 in a self-raised dust storm twenty meters from the village administrator's house in Mawkmai. Loh always took the controls when he was aboard any aircraft, and the helicopter's regular pilot had assumed copilot duties.

As the rotors wound down, a flight of two MiGs passed overhead and began to circle the village at less than one thousand meters. They were there for emphasis, though they were unlikely to be needed.

Eight men scrambled from the helicopter's cabin. Six of them were uniformed in camouflaged fatigues, with no badges of rank, but with the authority of new model Kalashnikov AK-74 assault rifles.

Two of the men were assistants to the new village administrator, who was also a passenger.

The last man was Police Chief Micah Chao. He was a small and tidy man, with oiled blue-black hair, and eyes the color of flint. Like his squad of men, he was dressed in fatigues, but he wore a Sam Browne belt . . . a reincarnation of colonial British oppressors Loh frequently thought . . . with a holstered Colt .45 automatic that was nearly as large as Chao. Loh thought that if Chao ever fired the weapon, he would find himself rocketed into China.

Loh also thought that Lon Pot's organization reflected the leader's mind. A police chief, an air force chief, an army chief, and a finance chief were close to the head of the new government. Posts in domestic and foreign affairs and policy would be designated later, if they became necessary, and would report to one of Pot's deputies.

He did not care, one way or the other, as long as he headed the air force.

Sliding out of his seat, Loh joined Chao as they walked toward the house. The noise of their arrival had alerted the occupants, and lights were coming on.

"This man may be more difficult," Chao told him.

Loh shrugged. A few had resisted, but most had not. Throughout the Shan state, helicopter teams had visited the key villages, urged the old administration to step aside, and installed new administrators. It was a warlord society, the custom of generations, and warlords changed.

The least difficult had been in Taunggyi, the capital city of Shan. Lon Pot already owned most of the government officials there, and they had readily signed new oaths.

The transition of power was taking place smoothly and with less bloodletting than Loh had anticipated.

By the end of the week, Shan State would be Lon Pot's. Within a month, the master anticipated having control of Kachin State in the north and Kayah State, which lay just southwest of this village.

The governments of Burma had been in chaos for years, and neither Lon Pot nor his deputies expected heavy resistance to subtle and unadvertised transfers of loyalty. As the tide of change rolled south, toward Rangoon and the national government, key members of the incumbent armed forces and police would either be converted or terminated.

Loh followed Micah Chao to the door, which opened immediately.

The administrator stood in the doorway and bowed

his head in recognition.

Police Chief Micah Chao, whose new title was unknown to the administrator, but whose relationship to Lon Pot was, said, "You have been demoted. You must now collect your belongings and move."

The man's eyes widened. They shifted to peer into the darkness beyond Chao's shoulder and weigh the threat of the armed men. The jet fighters circled, their throttled-back engines still an ominous thunder.

"I have not been advised of this change."

"You are being advised now."

"I should contact the capital."

"Which will tell you the same thing," Chao said. "You will leave immediately."

"But my family! It will take time. . . ."

Chao unsnapped the flap of his holster.

Loh was not certain whether the policeman would be able to lift the Colt from the holster. He stayed behind Chao, an observer of one of life's lesser events.

"I insist upon seeing your credentials and a written order," the administrator said.

Unfortunately.

The Colt came out of the holster with ease.

Exploded loudly in the night.

And Chao was not rocketed into China.

On the last leg, A.J. Soames moved to air controller in the Kappa Kat's backseat, and Fred Nackerman, a hazel-eyed, redheaded youngster of twenty-eight years, took over the controls. Nackerman was a New Jersey native, and he had never gotten it out of his speech.

Kimball had set up a rotation schedule for all of the pilots, and not one of them was in the same seat in which he had left Phoenix.

The stopover at Greenham Common Air Base in England had been uneventful, primarily since there was no concern for the import or export of cargo aboard the C-141s. Whatever it was, it was going straight through.

139

They had refueled the planes and fed the personnel and taken off.

Eleven-and-a-half hours out of Atlanta, at four-thirty in the morning in North Africa, the flight of KAT aircraft was approaching their destination. They had been allowed to overfly France, as long as they stayed above 30,000 feet, but they had had to circumnavigate Libya, flying across Tunisia, Algeria, and a large segment of Nigeria.

Soames estimated that the Starlifters were now about twelve hundred miles behind them. The squadron had passed them just south of Paris.

Tex Brabham was still in the copilot's seat, having overruled Kimball's rotation plan because, he said, he didn't often get such a chance to fly the beast. Nackerman had let him take the controls for a couple hours.

Kimball was in the seat next to Soames, sound asleep.

The stars were crisp and clean in a moonless sky. Soames hadn't been to Africa in so long that he had forgotten that clarity. They were at 20,000 feet above ground level (AGL), and not much of the terrain was visible in the darkness, but it wouldn't have been very scenic if he could have seen it. He remembered that.

Jay Halek was Bengal One, and Soames called him on Tac Two.

"Barnfire?"

"I'm awake, Papa."

"ETA in twenty."

"I see the lights," Halek said.

In the far distance, there was a slightly warm glow on the horizon.

"Your eyes are better than mine," Soames said.

"Nah, Papa, just my anticipation."

"All right, Bengals, let's go to work. I'm cancelling data feeds and you're coming off autopilot. Let's begin our descent. Take it slow to angels ten," Soames said, and on the intercom, added, "You want to lead the way, Flapjack?"

Nackerman was fond of big breakfasts, and often ate them for dinner.

"Roger, Papa."

The steady drone of the turbofans changed pitch, and the Kappa Kat began to settle.

Soames checked the running lights of the fighters off both wings and found them matching the descent.

When he saw starshine reflecting from the surface of the huge Lake Chad, Soames checked his chart under the red map light and dialed in a new frequency on the Tac One channel.

"N'Djamena Air Control, this is Kimball Aero Tech two-two."

"Two-two, N'Djamena." The voice was in the upper ranges, with a pronounced British accent. "We indicate a flight of seven aircraft."

"Affirmative. I have a flight of seven."

"You are ahead of schedule, two-two."

"I had nice tail winds. I'm requesting permission for landing."

"Permission to land is granted. There is no other traffic in the area. Visibility unlimited, winds northwest at five knots, gusting to twelve knots."

Soames went back to Tac Two and broke off the Alpha Kats, setting them up in landing pairs and spacing them ahead of the Kappa Kat.

At 8,000 feet, he released his oxygen mask and let it hang from the side of his helmet.

The capital of Chad had about 200,000 residents, and the city was sprawled widely around the confluence of the Logone and Shari rivers, which fed Lake Chad. That early in the morning, the lighting appeared dim and the city sleepy as they circled it to the north. The runway lights were bright and welcoming.

The lead pilot in each pair of fighters checked in with the tower, then landed smoothly.

Nackerman brought the Kappa Kat in last, and it

141

wasn't until the main gear touched down that Kimball stirred.

He sat up, rolling his head to stretch his neck muscles, and looked out the canopy. Unsnapping his oxygen mask, he licked his lips. The oxygen mixture tended to dry out the mouth.

On the intercom, he said, "Damn, A.J., I didn't think I'd sleep that long."

"It's good for you, boy. There wasn't anything to see anyway."

"The Starlifters?"

"It'll be a couple hours before they get in."

"Any glitches?"

From the front seat, Brabham asked, "With my birds, Kim? You crazy?"

"It was just a loose thought, Tex."

"As soon as my equipment gets here, we'll tear into 'em and see how they fared," Brabham said. "I don't think we'll find much of anything wrong, though."

A white Toyota pickup was leading the string of fighters down a taxiway, and Nackerman fell in behind them. On the far side of the airport was the commercial terminal. On this side, they passed several large hangars and parked military aircraft, primarily of French manufacture. Soames saw a couple Hueys and several varieties of Cessna and Beechcraft light-twins that had apparently been converted to military use.

"I'm going to uncork us, Flapjack."

"Go ahead."

Soames found the canopy control and raised the rear canopy. Desert air, surprisingly cool, rushed in. It felt dry, but after his years in the Southwest, not uncomfortably so.

A couple of Chadians, Soames didn't know whether or not they were military, directed them into parking places.

"Damn," Brabham said. "They're only giving us two helpers? I'm the only mechanic here."

"But the best one," Soames reminded him.

"Goes without saying," Brabham said.

After Nackerman shut down, the four of them unstrapped and took turns descending to the ground.

Brabham rubbed the toe of his polished and worn cowboy boot over the surface of the asphalt. There was a heavy coating of sand on it.

"First thing, I've got to get the intakes and exhaust covered. Close the canopies. Otherwise, we'll be taking this desert along with us."

The protective covers were aboard the transports, Soames knew.

"You want my flight suit for that, Tex?" he asked.

"Naw. These guys're bound to have some canvas around somewhere."

Brabham walked off to meet the Chadians.

Soames stretched his arms out and took a deep breath.

"I may be getting too old for this, Kim."

"Can't see it, A.J. You like hot airplanes and strange new air fields too much."

"I like showers, too."

Nackerman, Kimball, and Soames started walking back toward the hangars they had passed.

"You'd think somebody would have sent a car or a bus," Nackerman said.

Soames told him, "You can bet there was a Frenchman in charge of ground transportation."

At six o'clock in the morning, which was not an unusual time for him to be up and around, Major General Brock Dixon stopped on his way to work at his nearby 7-Eleven. He went inside and bought a large, hot, and black coffee.

He carried it and a morning *Post* outside, skipped getting into his Buick, and went to the end of the building to lean against the brick exterior. He sipped from the cup and leafed through the first section.

143

All around him, Alexandria was coming awake. The traffic on the streets was picking up.

At 6:06 A.M., the phone rang, and he reached into the bubble and picked it up.

"Six-oh-six," he said, checking his watch. It was six minutes after eleven in Chad.

"Cable car," Crider told him.

"Status?"

"All the players are here."

"And the condition?"

"I think they all look good."

"That's too bad," Dixon said. "There should be an accident."

"Fatal?"

"Of course not. But embarrassing would be all right."

"One embarrassing event coming up," Crider said and hung up.

Kimball was tired, but not sleepy, and he spent the morning in his hotel having breakfast and getting cleaned up. The hotel was bare bones, but presentable, and the menu had a Continental flair to it.

His room had a telephone and a radio, but no television. The radio lacked a tuning knob, and the station it was locked into broadcast staccato Arabic.

He was rereading his fact sheet in preparation for the afternoon meeting with the defense ministry officials when the phone rang.

He picked it up. The connection was weak, and he found he had to double his volume.

"Kimball."

"H'lo." Almost unheard.

"Kimball," he said louder.

"It's Susan."

"Hi, boss lady. What's up?"

"Everything is fine here, Kim. I wanted to make sure you'd arrived all right."

"Now, mother . . ."

144

"Don't give me that. I'm not asking for much, and some of the wives have been calling."

"All personnel are healthy and present. We went through Atlanta just as planned. Equipment-wise, we had one hydraulic leak, and that was on a Starlifter. Okay?"

"Okay," she said. He had to strain to hear her.

"How's Sam Eddy?"

She could have called McEntire directly, but Kimball didn't mention it.

"He's fine."

"Good. Call me tomorrow, after the demonstration."

He sighed, remembering his collegiate days, when his mother had insisted on a call a week since he wasn't writing letters. His parents were both dead now, and every once in a while, he regretted some of those missed phone calls.

Kimball left the hotel at noon, still feeling some of the effects of jet lag, and shared a cab with McEntire out to the airport.

"Susie called."

"Oh. Any particular reason?"

"Wanted to know if we made it."

"We did," McEntire grinned.

"Wanted to know how you were."

"And you told her?"

"Fine."

"You're a terrific observer, Kim."

McEntire obviously wasn't going to get into personal discussions, and Kimball wasn't going to probe any deeper. They talked tactics for the rest of the trip to the airport.

Their space at the north end of the air field had been cordoned off with standards and yellow tape. Two men with slung, and unloaded, M-16s walked the perimeter. The two Starlifters were parked side by side, with their tails pointed toward the row of KAT aircraft. The ramps were down, and people hustled in-and-out

145

of the cargo bays, which were being used as portable workshops.

By the time Kimball and McEntire crawled under the yellow tape, Carl Dent was supervising the uncrating of the first practice missiles. A stack of wood was growing next to the ramp as the crates were pried open with crowbars, and the small portable crane was used to lift the missiles from their wooden cradles and move them to dollies.

A few Chadian pilots were being escorted for sneak previews of the fighters by KAT pilots.

They found Soames in the middle of the confusion, directing it with clipboard in hand. "About time the executives showed up," he said.

"Where are we at, A.J.?"

He checked his clipboard.

"I've got Conrad and the demo pilots at the hotel, sleeping. Ito and Jimmy joined some of our hosts and flew out to the target site by helicopter. They're going to show them how to best set up their radar and defensive network."

"Not that it'll do them any good," McEntire said.

"Of course not. Howard Cadwell and George Wagers are briefing the Chad pilots who will act as the defenders in tonight's exercise."

"It's not often that the aggressors come in and brief the defenders before an attack," Kimball said.

"They need all the help they can get," Soames said. "There seems to be quite a few French advisors tagging along."

"I'm not going to worry about that," Kimball said. "In fact, it'd be nice if we could impress them, too."

"I'm resting the guys every twenty minutes," Soames said. "It's a hundred and four degrees on the asphalt, and I sent Keeper into town earlier to buy a few hundred pounds of ice. There's iced tea and water in the first Starlifter if you want it."

"I want," McEntire said.

They climbed the ramp into the plane and got tall paper cups of tea from five-gallon, insulated vats. The shade of the interior was deceptive; the temperature wasn't three or four degrees less than on the tarmac.

Carrying their iced drinks, Kimball and McEntire ran down Brabham and the three of them toured the airplanes. Brabham assured them that every system hummed.

Carl Dent stopped Kimball and asked for permission to start loading missiles.

Kimball gave it.

Despite the oppressive heat and the heavy work, everyone was in good spirits. Kimball didn't hear one argument. If someone needed help, someone else jumped to his aid, mechanic or pilot.

At 2:30 P.M., the Kappa Kat and two Alpha Kats took off for the afternoon demonstration. The short daylight exercise was necessary so that observers on the ground could see that the Alpha Kats actually engaged and destroyed an aerial target under the direction and control of the Kappa Kat. The target was one of a dozen weather balloons they had brought along.

The aircraft were back on the ground by 3:30 P.M., Brabham and his technicians swarming over them, sweating profusely in the heat.

At 4:30 P.M., Kimball, McEntire, and Soames gathered their easels and other paraphernalia and carried it the half-mile to the small building near the large hangars that housed the air defense headquarters.

The briefing was scheduled for five o'clock, and they spent the waiting time meeting the officials who were there to attend it. Almost all of them spoke English, and for those who didn't, there were interpreters available.

The defense minister was there, along with a gaggle of assistants. Most of the officers present carried hats with lots of braid on the visors. There were three French advisors meandering around the conference room.

McEntire, who was KAT's vice president for public relations, was in fine form. He melted into the crowd, shaking hands and slapping backs and promising grand receptions in the United States, should anyone ever get over there.

Kimball often envied Sam Eddy his ease with people.

He and Soames tended to get locked into serious discussions with people who didn't understand the first thing about the technologies involved. There was a great deal of hand movement and sign language involved in the dialogue.

At five o'clock, the defense minister achieved silence by raising his arms. The man was almost seven feet tall, and raising his arms almost raised the ceiling.

Kimball moved to the head of the room to start his presentation. McEntire stood next to the easel, ready to flip the charts in coordination with Kimball's prepared speech. A.J. Soames stood by on the other side of him, holding a thick binder, ready to come up with factual responses to any detailed questions.

Kimball cleared his throat and said, "Gentlemen, thank you for inviting us to your country. You've been very kind hosts."

The defense minister smiled.

At Kimball's signal, McEntire flipped up the chart cover, revealing a large, detailed rendering of the Alpha Kat, bristling with firepower, and adorned with the blue, yellow, and red flag of Chad on her canted rudder.

"Please take a close look at the Alpha Kat, gentlemen. As soon as night falls, she will disappear, and try as you might, you will be unable to find her."

FLIGHT

Ten

"We could always abort the mission," Ted Simonson said.

Wilcox had to watch the eyes of the Deputy Director of Operations closely to be certain he was sincere.

"I . . . well, we have got three million invested," Wilcox said. "Not to mention the favors we called in with other agencies in order to secure all the permits."

He got up from the easy chair in Simonson's office and crossed to stand at the window. It was a nice view, better than his own, which had part of a parking lot in it. The one o'clock sun was hot in a clear sky, bringing out a wide range of color. The green forest that encircled the CIA headquarters had a tinge of yellow to it. It would not hurt to have some rain.

"You really worried about the money, Ben? It's cheap at ten times the price. We spent thirty mil trying to change leadership in Iraq."

"No, the bucks don't bother me. I'm worried about the consequences. If the timing is off by a day or two, Kimball's shit outta luck."

"Can we push him ahead?"

"I don't think so. His schedule is locked in, Ted. Changing it means raising questions in too many governments."

"They're going to be suspicious anyway."

"After it's over, and if it goes as planned, they're going to be suspicious," Wilcox said. "With precision and a hell of a lot of luck, that's all they'll ever be, suspicious. There won't be any evidence."

Wilcox moved back to the desk and leaned over Simonson's shoulder to study the map spread over the blotter. It was a coarse scale depiction of Southeast Asia, and it had come off the laser printer in color. The colors did not follow national boundaries. A yellow stain inundated the Shan State of Burma, but also slopped over into Kayah State and Kachin State, as well as into northern Laos and a piece of Thailand. There were a few dots of yellow beginning to bleed into the blue that was Kampuchea. On the northwestern coast of Burma, around the cities of Sittwe and Myebon, the yellow had also taken over.

The yellow represented local governments and influences that had moved to the Lon Pot camp.

"I knew Lon Pot could move fast," Simonson said, "but I didn't think it was going to be this easy for him."

"Two reasons, I think. Those are the areas where he's bought his loyalties. There was little resistance to change, according to the numbers we've gotten so far. Only sixteen dead."

"And the second reason?"

"The Burmese military is tunnel-visioned right now. The government's in disarray, and they're mainly worried about the *banditos* in the hills who are yelling about human rights and democratic reform. They're not paying attention to the Lon Pot faction because he's spent twenty years being nonpolitical. His influence has been economic, and Rangoon thinks that's all right."

"I can buy that," Simonson said. "Plus, Pot's cadre of advisors and henchmen is multinational. From one point of view, that might seem less threatening. On the other hand, it gives him *entrée* into at least four countries. I don't think he'll tackle China."

"Pot is simply moving into a political vacuum. The

same thing is going to happen in Laos and Kampuchea. Two bits Kampuchea goes next," Wilcox offered.

"No bet."

"There will be resistance from the dissidents and revolutionaries with other visions in their heads when Pot hits Sagaing State and maybe parts of Kachin, but Pot's too well organized. He may just bypass them and starve them out. Arakan State, along the coast, is mostly his for the asking."

"But the peninsula? Pegu?"

"I think, Ted, that he's got a lot of the key bureaucrats in his wallet pocket. They'll roll over, and they'll bring the military and police with them. It won't be as tough as we think it could, or should, be."

"You're going to have an intelligence estimate for the White House in the morning?"

"Yes."

"Best guess?"

"Right now," Wilcox said, "we're going to project that Burma falls to Lon Pot in ten days. Call it July twenty-sixth, and give it a day or two tolerance. That date is fifteen days ahead of our last projection."

"Damn."

"On down the road, we think he'll wrap up Kampuchea by the end of the year, and Laos shortly after that. Then he's got Thailand encircled. Three years, maybe."

"In three years, he controls . . . what?"

"Eighty-six million people. Six hundred thousand square miles, about half the size of India. In ten years, with either outright invasion, or by treaty, he could encompass Malaya and Vietnam."

"Drug money," Simonson said, "turned into a mini-superpower. One that will be just as ruthless and just as unpredictable as Saddam's."

"Money talks. Fear talks. Lon Pot has twenty billion personal dollars that we can track. With what we can't trace, we can figure at least a fifty billion dollar total, and that much moola leverages maybe another two hundred billion. When he gets control of Burma, he'll better than quadruple his fiscal control.

"For the people who disagree with him, he's got a little squad of zombies, headed by Micah Chao, who specializes in erasing disagreement."

"Plus his army," Simonson added.

"It's not large, but it doesn't have to be. He'll subvert existing military organizations. They tend to report to the people footing the payroll."

Simonson went back to the timetable. "So, if Kimball doesn't get there in time, rather than taking a poke at the big, bad druggie, he's attacking a sovereign nation."

Simonson's comment was not a question.

"The U.N. probably wouldn't take kindly to that. Unapproved aggression is frowned upon," Wilcox said.

"Kimball's not stupid," the DDO said. "He's going to read a paper, now and then. He'll know if Burma falls to Lon Pot. Will he cancel on his own?"

Wilcox turned and sat on the edge of the desk.

Simonson pushed his castered chair away from the desk and put his feet up on the map, waiting.

"Maybe not."

"Jesus, Ben, I hate all these 'maybes.' "

"Kimball had a baby brother, ten years younger. Good kid, straight-As through high school, played football. Got to graduate school and got into heroin."

"Deep into it?"

"Yeah. He was home for summer vacation, driving his parents somewhere, flying high, and took them into the back end of a semi-truck stalled on the highway."

"Shit! No survivors?"

"None," Wilcox said.

"That's why you knew he'd go along with you, isn't

it? More than the precarious financial position of Kimball Aero?"

"I thought that might be the kicker, yes."

Simonson's chin dropped to his chest as he pondered the alternatives.

"You want to try getting a shooter close to Pot?" Wilcox asked.

"It's not going to happen, Ben. He's too well insulated by either space or bodyguards. That's why I went along with your massive firepower scenario."

"How do you think the White House is going to react to the new timeline?"

"Not well, I assure you."

"Any guesses?" Wilcox asked.

"If Kimball can make a move before Pot hits Rangoon, we'll get a green light."

"And if he can't?"

"I'm not going to guess at that," Simonson said.

"Even if we get a red light, I don't know if I can stop Kimball. He bought into the drug concept, and he may not put the brakes on just because Pot owns a country."

"The Agency's at arm's length?"

"Much farther than that," Wilcox said.

"Then we probably don't want to stop him, White House approval or not. He's expendable."

"He's got thirty damned good people with him, Ted."

"Thirty people versus eighty million? Thirty people versus what Lon Pot's operation is doing to America? Do you know how far his tentacles reach, Ben?"

"We think he owns a shopping center in Atlanta. There's probably others. He's got that twenty billion doubling every three or four years."

"Kimball's expendable," Simonson repeated.

Wilcox had known that from the beginning. It was part of the profession. Sometimes, though, it was difficult to admit it to himself.

Dao Van Luong had once told Lon Pot that his father was Vietnamese and that his mother had been Laotian. He had only known them for fourteen years, the age at which he had been conscripted into the North Vietnamese Army, (NVA). They had been killed in one of the American B-52 raids of the Linebacker operation.

It was not out of compassion for the fate of his parents that Dao had received an education. Rather, some officer had noted his penchant for arithmetic and made him a clerk in an NVA accounting office. He had moved successively to battalion, then regimental levels. After the war had been won, he had been encouraged to pursue an accounting degree while working for the national bank.

And several years after obtaining his degree, he had created some phantom accounts, transferred a large amount of the government's *dong* to Shanghai, then converted it to American dollars and shipped it to New Delhi where he met up with it.

Vietnam was still trying to get it back, or to extract its equivalent in blood, and twice in earlier years had almost managed to do so. After the second attempt on his life, Dao had arranged a meeting with Lon Pot and offered his creative financial services in exchange for protection.

The arrangement had been beneficial for both of them, Lon Pot thought. The man had orchestrated the investment of Pot's excess cash, which was considerable, and much of it was now considered legitimate by any government's definition. The rate of return was immense, considering that little or no taxes were ever paid on the income.

He was certain that the small, dark-haired man sitting opposite him on the couch had made parallel investments of his own and had also benefited. He was also certain that Dao had never mismanaged one *baht* of Lon Pot's money. Dao had already learned of the ferocious revenge sought by the Vietnamese government, and he knew that Lon Pot's vengeance, unlike a mere government's, could not be blocked.

They understood each other.

Dao had spent an hour reporting, as he did each month, on the current state of Lon Pot's financial affairs. Lon Pot found the reports boring in the extreme, but he always listened in rapt attention and asked what he thought were pertinent questions. He did not understand much of what went on: shell companies, foreign exchange rates, blind corporations. But, he thought it important that he display some degree of knowledge.

"And the Pegasus Fund?" he asked.

Dao searched the papers littering his lap, found one, and said, "Twenty-two million dollars."

"It is all in dollars?"

"Yes. The recipients prefer dollars."

The fund was tapped for bribes and for greasing the wheels of various bureaucracies. Lon Pot thought he would eliminate a lot of bureaucratic functions in the future. If they could be bribed by him, they could be bribed by anyone.

"And the change?"

"It is down almost three million from last month," Dao Van Luong said. "We have paid out much in the last week."

And well worth the price, Pot thought. Most of the northern coastal villages had quietly reported their change in allegiance. Within a week, he told himself, the Rangoon government was going to wake up and have no government to manage.

"And speaking of the Pegasus Fund, Henry Loh wants me to give him a million dollars in cash tomorrow," Dao said.

"Let him have it, then. He is going to the capital to meet with old friends. It will be used to our advantage, I am certain."

"Of course, Prince."

Lon Pot liked the sound of that. When he had passed out the "Chief" titles to his key advisors, he had told them that, from now on, he would assume his rightful position as a prince of the realm. The only prince of the realm.

He had liked it in Machiavelli, and he liked it in himself. There was a pure sense of tradition and custom and power in the title, unlike that of president or chancellor or prime minister, any of which could be transitory and fleeting.

"Henry Loh also wants to buy four more airplanes. Attack aircraft from the French."

Pot pondered the request. In a week, Loh would have the entire Burmese air force at his disposal.

If the air force did not put up a strong resistance. Was Loh concerned about that?

"He had a rationale?" Pot asked.

Dao smiled his little grim smile. "It is to be a reserve unit for your personal air guard, or so I was told."

"Nothing beyond that?"

"There may be a squadron or two of the national air force that might not capitulate readily. That is my own interpretation of possibilities, Prince."

"We should have prepared long before this."

"Perhaps the information was not known to Loh until recently?"

Lon Pot pursed his lips. "Perhaps. Very well, let him obtain bids from his sources, then we will discuss it."

Dao Van Luong nodded.

He waited.

Dao waited also.

"Is there anything more?" Pot asked.

"There is your wife."

Lon Pot had many wives, some as transitory as the titles of leaders, but this one was legal.

"She has a complaint?"

"She would like to have larger living quarters. And she insists upon an increase in her allowance."

He could tell that Dao did not relish bringing up these matters any more than Lon Pot relished hashing over her insistent and unreasonable demands. In the infrequent times when he met with her, she was as complaisant as ever. When she found pen and paper, she created elaborate and expensive plans for herself. She felt as if she must present to the world the facade of a queen, simply because Lon Pot had some resources.

"No to both demands," he said.

Dao Van Luong nodded.

Derek Crider drove the rented Renault. It was fifteen years old, and the wind whistled past holes rusted through the floorboard.

He bitched at the inane traffic from time to time, but they had left the hotel early enough to find their spot. The sun would not go down for another hour. They passed one policeman on their way to the airport.

"No security to speak of," Alan Adage said.

"I didn't think there would be. Kimball's not a visiting dignitary."

He glanced over at Adage, who opened the attaché case. Nestled in foam was a broken down Husqvarna Monte Carlo de Luxe. There was a Weaver scope, a hand-machined silencer, and five hand-loaded 7.62 millimeter rounds in the case also. There had been eight cartridges, but Adage had used three to fire in the weapon earlier, out in the desert.

The attaché case had been waiting for them when they arrived at the hotel. All it had cost Crider was a phone call from the Azores and five thousand American dollars. He had lots of friends and acquaintances, and friends of friends, all over the world who liked money.

Adage lifted the receiver from the case and began fitting the stock. His fingers moved over the blued metal surfaces with a loving touch. Adage's old man had taught him the finer points of hunting in the Kentucky hills, and the Marine Corps had refined his trade for him. The man loved a well-designed weapon more than he would any woman.

He had a blue stocking cap pulled down over his telltale bushy red hair, but not much was going to disguise his flaming red beard. They both wore dark blue windbreakers and black denim jeans.

Crider bypassed the entrance to the passenger terminal, jamming the gear shift into third, and lurching onto a service road headed north. The transmission required jamming, and the clutch was on the ragged end of its useful life.

The engine screamed through a ventilated muffler until he could get enough speed to shift to fourth.

"Didn't have a better car, did they?" Adage asked.

"Nothing that didn't stand out like a sore thumb."

Crider had scouted the area earlier. He passed several freight and industrial transfer companies housed in small buildings. They were already darkened, their inhabitants gone for the day.

Adage screwed the silencer into place.

Crider turned into a small gravelled lot, keeping an eye on the rearview mirror. There was no traffic behind him.

He downshifted twice, bouncing through the lot.

Adage fitted the Weaver scope to its mountings and

160

tightened the thumb screws.

At the edge of the lot, Crider whipped a hard left, slammed on the brakes, and ground the gearshift into reverse. He backed over a set of dried-mud ruts and into the narrow space between two buildings. They were both constructed of corrugated steel that shimmered with rust.

With his arm over the back of the seat, peering through the dirty rear window into the shadowed alley, he gripped the wheel with his left hand and raced in reverse toward the chainlink fence that guarded the airport proper.

Easing on the brakes, he slid to a stop a few feet before hitting the fence. He left the engine idling and they both got out.

Adage glanced up to check his sunlight, then looked across the runways to where Kimball's aircraft were parked.

"That's them?" Adage asked.

"That's them."

"No sweat. About six hundred yards. Where do you want it?"

Crider squinted to clarify his image of the six Alpha Kats lined up with their noses toward the runway. Behind them were the two giant transports and the Kappa Kat.

He had been thinking about it.

"They're due to take off just before dusk. Before that, the ground crews have got to pull off the protective covers on the intakes. As soon as they do, you put a slug right up the intake."

"Why wait for the covers? We do it now, and take off."

Crider tried to be patient. "Because a bullet hole in an intake cover gives us away. We want it to look like engine failure."

"They're center-line mounted, Crider? The engines?"

161

"Right."

Adage moved toward the building on the right, got right next to it, back by the fence, and squatted down.

"Yeah, maybe," he said. "I might just have enough angle, if I put the round to the right side of the left intake. Can't guarantee much, though, since I don't know what kind of interior curve the intake has."

"Do what you can, Adage."

"Oh, I will."

The sniper stood up and went back to the car to get his rifle.

Crider turned the engine off, crossing his fingers in the hope that it would start again.

The shadows were long, and between the buildings, they were in semidarkness.

Adage went back to the fence and stretched out on the ground, lifted the Husqvarna to his shoulder, and peered through the scope. He wet his finger with his tongue and tested the wind. There was none that Crider could feel.

Adage adjusted his windage and elevation knobs and then lowered the rifle gently to the ground.

Crider sat down on the driver's seat with the door open, his feet planted in the dusty earth.

They waited.

The shadows got longer. The sky dimmed toward gray. It did not get cooler. The sweat beads formed on his forehead and slithered down his cheeks.

Adage retrieved an already sodden handkerchief and used it frequently.

Twenty minutes went by before Crider saw mechanics begin to move around the airplanes with some purpose.

"I could take out five of them," Adage said.

"Just one. We don't want questions about unexplained coincidences."

The intake covers started coming off.

"Any one in particular you'd like?" Adage asked.

"Take the fourth in line."

"Good. The angle should be right."

The ex-Marine pulled the Monte Carlo sporting rifle tight against his shoulder, aimed more quickly than Crider expected, and squeezed the trigger.

Phut!

Adage stood up, already disassembling the weapon. "You got it?"

"Of course. Let's go get something to eat."

The Aerospatiale Super Frelon, capable of handling thirty combat-loaded troops, but equipped as a military VIP transport, lifted off shortly after dark. Its massive rotors kicked up a dust storm that should have obliterated N'Djamena.

Kimball sat in one of the over-cushioned flight seats next to Sam Eddy. Soames had gone back to manage the flight operations, and Kimball felt like he was sidelined. He should be flying, or at least directing the mission, but here he was playing salesman.

One look at McEntire in the dim reddish cabin lighting told him that Sam Eddy had the same thing on his mind.

The Chad air force and defense ministry people were in good humor after a heavy dinner that Kimball had picked his way through. They lounged in their seats and tried to chat above the roar of the engines. It was a lark for them, and Kimball couldn't help thinking about the lack of thought that had gone into putting all of the heavy brass and high defense people into the same vulnerable transport helicopter.

One missile.

Exit the command structure.

No problem at all for the Alpha Kat.

He flipped open his notepad and looked at the roster he had set up for the demonstration:

BENGAL ONE: Mel Vrdlicka
BENGAL TWO: Alex Hamilton
BENGAL THREE: Jay Halek
BENGAL FOUR: Howard Cadwell
BENGAL FIVE: Warren Mabry
BENGAL SIX: Tom Keeper
HAWKEYE ONE: Sam Miller
HAWKEYE TWO: Fred Nackerman
HAWKEYE THREE: Conrad Billingsly
HAWKEYE FOUR: Phillipe Contrarez
ZOOKEEPER: A.J. Soames

He studied the list, fingering the walkie-talkie resting in his lap. His codename was Lion, but he would only be able to talk to Soames since the portable radio couldn't manage the scrambled channels. If something drastic. . . .

McEntire slapped him on the shoulder and leaned over to practically shout in his ear, "Quit fretting about it, Kim. The right decisions have already been made."

He shook his head, unable to stop worrying.

There was a lot riding on this program.

McEntire grinned at him. "Dumb shit. If I'd known you were going to turn all sour on me, I'd never have married you."

Sixty miles later, according to the map they had been given, the helicopter set down, deplaned its passengers, then raced away into the night.

Despite a couple of generators chugging away to provide electricity and a couple of trucks that were idling a hundred yards to the east, it seemed magnificently quiet in the middle of the desert.

The night would have been utterly black but for the thousands of stars that ranged over and around them like a bowl. They stretched from one horizon to the other. The whisper of a mild wind touched his cheeks, cooling them. What he could see of the landscape was rugged and barren. There wasn't all that much sand, and the ground was hard, cracked and creviced from intense heat.

Two large canopies had been erected, lit on the inside with red bulbs, and straight-backed chairs were arranged in rows facing north. Several folding tables had been set up, and radios rested on them. The radio operators spoke in clipped, guttural Arabic and passed hand-written messages to several junior officers.

General Haraz, the air force chief of staff, waved toward several chairs, and Kimball and McEntire sat down with him near one of his radios.

Kimball raised his portable unit to check the operation. "Zookeeper, Lion."

"Five by five, Lion," Soames came back.

"Status?"

"Ah . . . we're ready to pounce."

Kimball looked to the general, and he nodded.

"Launch them, Zookeeper. Let me know if you have a problem."

"Roger that, Lion. Launching in ten."

Haraz spoke quickly to a colonel in Arabic, who passed the word to his radio operator. Kimball figured that the ten Mirage defenders had been ordered into the air.

In his cultured and stiff English, the general said, "Let me orient you, Mr. Kimball and Mr. McEntire. The map is never quite the same as the reality, is it? Out there," he pointed with a stiff right forefinger, "directly ahead of us by two thousand meters is the target, the old truck. It is radiating a signal on UHF

165

radio."

The finger moved in a large circle. "We have emplaced four mobile surface-to-air missile units around the target. Their crews are very reliable."

"I'm sure they are, General. As are your pilots, but I'm afraid they won't see anything to shoot at."

The general smiled. "We shall see."

Sam Eddy got up and went to look at a repeater monitor that was relaying the radar picture from one of the SAM sites. When he came back he said, "The Bengals are moving north at about Mach One, Kim. Give 'em another five minutes."

He went back to the radar screen.

Kimball checked his watch, and when the time elapsed, called Soames on the portable.

"Zookeeper, kill the IFF."

Twenty seconds later, from next to the radar repeater, McEntire said, "We just went incognito."

A large group of field grade officers had begun to gather around the radar screen. Kimball couldn't interpret the rapid chatter, but the various tones ranged from skeptical to incredulous.

The colonel supervising the radio operators reported to General Haraz, again in Arabic.

"Our fighters are closing in," he said to Kimball. "They have targeted your command plane."

Kimball heard the moan of one flight of Mirages passing high overhead.

The dialogue on the radios started to get excited. Messages flew back and forth.

Kimball was getting anxious.

"You mind if we take a look at the radar, General?"

"Not at all."

Haraz came out of his chair as if he'd been waiting for the excuse, determined to have Kimball make the request.

The crowd made way for them and they stood near the set and watched.

The sweep left eleven blips behind as it rotated. Ten blips in two flights were closing on a single target, some thirty miles to the northeast.

"General Haraz," McEntire said, "your defenders are concentrating on the AWACS. You don't want them to forget there are six more aggressors out there."

"Whose side are you on?" Kimball asked him.

The general smiled, spoke to the colonel, and some message went out to the fighter pilots.

Almost immediately, the blips on the screen began to separate.

"They're setting up a search pattern," McEntire observed.

Then the target blip disappeared as Connie Billingsly stopped radiating emissions.

The Mirages circled, climbed, dove. The screen looked like a random kaleidoscope.

It remained empty of all but scrambling Mirages for nearly four minutes.

Abruptly, without warning, a heavy thump sounded out in the desert ahead of them.

Everyone whirled toward it.

Another thump.

"Bet that truck's got a dented hood," McEntire said. "Those five hundred pound dummies don't make a lot of noise, but they make a big dent."

Thump.

Thump, thump.

And then, like bats from a darkened cave, the Alpha Kats shot overhead in trail, one after the other, at less than three hundred feet. They were throttled back, almost silent, and they were just shadows against the stars as they went by.

Almost everyone under the canopy scrambled outside to get a better look, Haraz included.

But they were gone.

All five of them.

Five thumps, five shadows.

Kimball swore under his breath and raised the portable radio to call Soames, but McEntire grabbed his arm.

"Let it be for now, Kim."

Eleven

Hanging around at the demonstration site rasped heavily on Kimball's nerves, even after Soames radioed the message that the aircraft had been recovered and that the Alpha Kat pilots were claiming four Mirage kills. Out of earshot of their hosts, Sam Eddy kept telling him that, if some tragedy had occurred, Soames would have called it in.

Kimball wasn't so sure. The frequency used by the portable radio wasn't secure, and A.J. might not have wanted to broadcast an accident to the world.

His mind kept replaying five shadows when there should have been six.

Kimball's fingers worried at the transmit stud on the radio, but he managed to restrain himself as they loaded aboard the trucks and drove out to the target.

Two of the dummy bombs had missed the target by fifteen or twenty yards, but three of the five-hundred-pounders had nearly obliterated the sheet metal of the junked bus.

The two Americans followed General Haraz around to the SAM units and listened to the interrogations of the crews without understanding a word. It was clear to Kimball, however, that none of the SAM radars had ever detected an intruder.

The Mirage pilots reporting in by radio insisted that none of them had been shot down, but none of them would claim a kill of an Alpha Kat. For any one of them to do so, they would have had to identify the symbol emplaced on each of the Alpha Kats with white tape: cross, diamond, circle, square, rectangle, or octagon.

After an hour of collecting information, General Haraz said, "I think we have most of what we need, Mr. Kimball. We shall go back now, and then debrief in the morning."

"That'll be fine with us, General. We're looking forward to it."

The helicopter ride back to N'Djamena took forever, and the Aerospatiale landed next to the headquarters building at eleven o'clock.

As soon as they deplaned and performed their glad-handing with the dignitaries, Kimball and McEntire began the long walk back to their ramp. Except for a few floodlights near the hangars, it was dark, and neither of them had anything to say to the other. Kimball figured Sam Eddy was just as worried as he was.

Closing on the aircraft park, Kimball counted the silhouettes in the front row. There were only five.

The Kappa Kat was lined up next to the Starlifters, and there seemed to be a lot of light emitting from the space between the C-141s, but his view was blocked.

McEntire stopped to squat down.

"We've got six," he said. The relief in his voice was evident.

Kimball bent over and looked. Sighting beneath the Kappa Kat and the first Starlifter, he saw the tires and oleo struts of the sixth fighter.

They both stood up and started to trot.

Light spilled from the cargo bays of both transports, illuminating the lowered ramps. Quite a few men seemed to be moving around the planes.

As he rounded the Kappa Kat, Kimball saw that the sixth Alpha Kat was parked between the two C-141s, enclosed by canvas windscreens stretched on ten-foot-

170

tall aluminum frames. Seven floodlights were mounted on top of the frames, lighting the enclosed space.

He slowed to a walk and slipped through a gap into the makeshift work area.

The entire aft fuselage skin had been removed from the Alpha Kat, and at the moment he entered, the massive turbofan engine was being lifted from its mounts by the portable crane. The crane's engine groaned with the load; it hadn't been designed for lifting that amount of weight. Four men stood on the back end of the crane's squat body, attempting to keep it from tipping over. It had four small tires, and the two front tires appeared to be almost squashed flat.

Everyone had turned out to help. Technicians and pilots both were manning tools and diagnostic equipment. Three men stood on top of the wing, guiding the engine as it rose from its bed.

Tex Brabham was standing next to the crane, helping the operator, Elliot Stott, with a long series of colorful and innovative invectives.

A.J. Soames spotted him, slapped Tom Keeper on the arm, and led him over to Kimball and McEntire. Keeper was limping a little. He had an arthritic knee, which was why the Navy medicos had suggested another line of work for him.

"What the hell, A.J.?"

Keeper responded. "She cranked up just fine, Kim. But when I ran it up to full power, I got a hell of a vibration, so I shut it down right away."

The ex-Navy aviator was also an aeronautics engineer, and he had completed a duty tour at the Patuxent Naval Air Test Center. His "hell of a vibration" was magnified by his sensitivity to potential design or operational problems.

"I only sent five on the mission," Soames said. "And I didn't want to broadcast the fact that we had a malfunction."

"I think it's okay," Sam Eddy said. "We never told them how many we were sending. If they couldn't see them, they couldn't count them."

Kimball was both relieved and concerned. He didn't want to hide problems if it meant the safety of a pilot. If a fighter had gone down on the mission, he wanted rescue units dispatched as soon as possible.

Soames read his mind. "If somebody'd plowed ground, Kim, you'd have heard my yell without the radio."

"All right, good. I should know that. What's with the engine?"

"The end of one turbine blade snapped off," Soames said. "There wasn't a hell of a lot of vibration, but I'm damned glad Tom caught it. In the air, at Mach One, the whole unit might have started coming apart."

"Shit!" McEntire said. "It can't happen."

He headed for Tex Brabham.

The turbine fan assembly was McEntire's design. Kimball knew how he felt.

"What do you think, A.J.?" he asked.

"I've been hassling with the alternatives, Kim. If it's a design flaw, we don't have a choice but to ground the airplanes. Right in the middle of the demo tour, that'll kill us."

"It won't be a design problem," Kimball said with conviction. "How about a casting flaw?"

"Yeah, that's my best scenario. We've got nine engines with us, counting the spare. There's always that slim chance that one of the nine got a bad set of blades."

"Jesus! We checked and double-checked everything," Kimball said.

One of the canvas panels was lifted and shunted aside, and eight men shoved the dolly with the spare engine inside the enclosure.

"We put the windscreens up to protect us from prying

eyes more than anything," Soames said. "As far as anyone out in that desert knows, we're running routine maintenance."

The engine at the end of the crane's cables came free of the airframe mounts, the airplane rose on its oleo struts, and the crane backed the turbofan away from between the rudders. Brabham barked orders. Mechanics scrambled to place four-by-fours on the ground to receive the engine as the crane's boom swung to the side.

"Tex is going to disassemble it as soon as we can get it aboard the Starlifter," Keeper said. "Warren's in there now, setting up the portable X-ray unit."

"Do we even want to install the new engine?" Kimball asked. "At least, until we know?"

"Tex thinks so," Soames said, "for two reasons. He needs the dolly for the bad engine, and he's like you. He doesn't think it's a design flaw."

It took nearly an hour to get the new engine settled correctly into the mounts and bolted in place. While a dozen men swarmed over the plane, connecting wire bundles, fuel lines, and control systems, Kimball and McEntire helped Brabham raise the damaged engine from the timbers with the crane and get it on the dolly. It took sixteen of them to shove it far enough onto the ramp of the transport so that the ramp could be raised and the engine slid into the cargo bay.

It was nearly four in the morning before Brabham had the turbine wheel out of the engine casing and X-ray photos of the offending blade printed.

Kimball, McEntire and two mechanics stood around a worktable while Brabham went over the photo with a magnifying glass. All of them knew better than to interfere with the expert when he was at work.

He finally stood up straight and stretched his back. He shoved his cowboy hat back on his head.

"Not our fault," he said.

McEntire grabbed the magnifying glass and bent over the photograph.

"No flaw marks at all in the casting," Brabham went on. "Take a close look at the break, Sam Eddy, near the right-side outer edge of the blade. There's a chip there, kind of rounded. Then, too, the break is too jagged. A flaw would likely have broken along cleaner lines."

McEntire handed the magnifying glass to Kimball, and he took his own look.

"Couldn't have picked up a rock," McEntire said.

"A rock wouldn't have had the velocity," Kimball agreed. "The fragment wasn't in the engine?"

"Naw, it'd have gone right out the back, the minute the turbine started to turn. The magnets—which attracted metal shavings and dust to provide evidence of bearing wear—didn't have much on them, and certainly wouldn't have caught a rock. We're not going to find it in the dark."

"When it started to turn . . . you're right, Tex!" Kimball said.

McEntire whipped the magnifying glass out of Kimball's hand and bent over the photo again.

"Son of a bitch!" he said.

"If that engine had been turning," Brabham said, "three or four blades would show some damage. That blade there got hit when it was stationary."

No one wanted to say anything for a while. Kimball crossed to a canvas seat and sat down. One of the mechanics, Mark Westergood, turned the tap on an iced water vat and filled a paper cup.

"Bullet?" McEntire finally asked.

"Heavy slug, I'd say," Brabham said.

"That's sabotage," Kimball told them. "That's damned scary."

The cargo bay lights suddenly seemed too bright. Kimball looked out the back of the plane, but saw only

174

the line of Alpha Kats and the lights of the passenger terminal on the far side of the lighted runways.

McEntire turned around and leaned against the worktable.

"Okay, boss man, where do we go from here?"

"Tex?" Kimball asked.

"We've got a couple spare turbine wheels with us. Mark and Darrell, here, are going to get one of them and rebuild this engine so we've got a spare. They're also going to make damned sure that slug didn't cause any damage to the casing. Me, I'm going outside and keep a close watch on the heavy-handed people out there while they put two-seven back together right. I want the fuselage back in place before daylight so the Chadians don't know we've done a full engine swap. Then, we'll need a couple, three hours to run it in. I don't know what you guys are going to do."

Kimball rubbed his fingers over the whiskers on his jaw. "Sam Eddy and I have a debriefing at nine. We'll go back to the hotel and get cleaned up."

"And get a couple hours sleep," McEntire said. "Our audience will expect cheery."

"And ship about thirty breakfasts out to us," Brabham said. "I'm not eating MREs."

"And call Mr. Washington," Sam Eddy said. "Right?"

"Right," Kimball told him.

Jimmy Gander kept thinking of the word, "broast."

He didn't know what it meant, though he thought he recalled seeing "broasted chicken" on a menu once.

He thought he was being broasted.

Slowly, to retain the flavor.

The heat rose off the tarmac in waves that made him think his vision had gone bad. Carl Dent had measured the temperature in the Kappa Kat's cockpit at noon and had reported a dysfunctional thermometer or an actual reading of 145 degrees Fahrenheit.

A passenger airliner had taken off forty minutes before, but that was the only activity he had seen. No one was moving around on the ramp or in the planes.

Gander was sprawled on top of a couple of parachutes, leaning back against a missile crate. Tex Brabham was next to him, his hat tilted over his eyes, sound asleep. He snored like an underpowered McCullough chain saw attacking a giant redwood. Gander and Brabham stuck together since they were the only two who wore, and respected, Stetson hats.

The temperature inside the cargo bay of the transport was well over 110, and movement from one point to another was akin to heavy exercise. About half of the crew were curled into one corner or another, trying to sleep, but only Brabham seemed to be having any success. Added to the aromas of Cosmoline and lubricants was the body odor of the great unwashed.

Jay Halek was on his fourth unlit cigar of the day, rolling it back and forth in his teeth. Mel Vrdlicka had a water-soaked rag draped over his eyes. Conrad Billingsly had suggested a game of bridge and had been speared with pears and Mandarin oranges left over from breakfast.

Outside, the Alpha Kats were ready to go. They were "clean," the dummy missiles not used the night before removed and repacked. Chunks of white canvas were draped from the opened canopies in the attempt to keep the cockpits cool. Or at least cooler. Two-seven had been ground-tested for several hours in the early morning, and Brabham had declared it one hundred percent operational.

Gander heard a car pull up next to the plane, but he didn't have the ambition to get up and go see who it was. No one else did, either. If it was a terrorist, they were all going to be blown to hell.

A car door slammed, the engine revved up, and then

died away as it drove off. A minute later, Soames climbed the ramp into the bay.

"I want to know," Soames said soberly, "who it was that forgot to bring the fans."

"Who needs fans?" Speedy Contrarez asked. "I was dreaming of this very tall bottle of *Carta Blanca*. It's so cold that the beads of moisture on the outside have turned to ice. You pick it up and—"

"Jesus Christ! Shut him up, Papa," Alex Hamilton said.

"You're dreaming of donuts, right, Alex?"

"No, but it's a good thought."

"Kim and Sam Eddy aren't back yet?" Soames asked.

"Not yet," Gander said, trying to sit up without disturbing Brabham.

He got off the parachutes and went to get himself a cup of iced tea, When Soames raised a finger, he filled two from the vat and carried one over to where Soames had collapsed on a canvas seat.

"You get us checked out of the hotel, A.J.?"

"Yeah. Probably maxed out the company Visa card. I didn't check the rooms, so if anyone left anything behind, he can come back and get it on his own."

Gander took a small sip of his tea and held the cool liquid in his mouth for a minute. He felt like he was dehydrating rapidly.

"How come this seems so much like the USAF?" Hamilton asked.

"Hurry up and wait. Get in line. Wait."

"We wanted you to feel at home, *compadre,*" Contrarez told him.

Gander was about to sit down next to Soames when he heard more car doors slamming. Kimball and McEntire walked up the ramp, and Sam Eddy headed straight for the water can.

Soames asked, "Well, Kim?"

"Seemed to go all right, A.J. They kept us for about

177

three more hours than we'd figured on. Lots of questions, and lots of them were good ones. I think we handled it."

"They're interested?"

"Interested!" McEntire said. "They were drooling. Or maybe it was just the heat."

"We ran our tapes, and we listened to a few of the audio tapes from the Mirages," Kimball said. "Not that we understood the language, mind you. But I think we reached consensus on the fact that no Alpha Kat was spotted. We agreed that at least two Mirages would have been our trophies."

"They had some gun camera video," McEntire said. "But there was never a target on the film."

"They ever get close to the Kappa Kat?" Soames asked.

"They swear they did, but they don't have video, audio, or a visual sighting of the taped double cross symbol to prove it."

"So they're going to buy five squadrons?" Gander asked.

"Who knows?" Kimball said. "They've all got our brochures and two sets of specifications. They've got the demonstration data, and they've set up an analysis committee. The committee will study the options for a couple of months, then make a recommendation to some bureau in the ministry."

"Yeah, but did you get any personal feedback?" Gander said.

Sam Eddy responded to the question. "General Haraz, who I think swings a lot of weight, tried to appear neutral. On one side of it, he's being loyal to his pilots, and maybe to the two French guys who sat through the whole show. On the other side of it, I got the feeling he was impressed. He mashed my hand when we finally said goodbye."

"Can we go now?" Soames asked.

"It's not going to be any cooler in Riyadh, A.J.," Kimball said.

"Not for you, maybe. I'm thinking about my hotel and my bed. Us old guys get wrinkled pretty bad if we don't get our sleep."

"Well, hell," McEntire said, "if you're going to get cranky, we might as well saddle up."

"I'll take two-seven," Gander said, "and shake her out."

"She's mine," Sam Eddy claimed.

"Flip you for it."

"Not before I flip you."

Kimball reached in his pocket, found a quarter and tossed it. "Call it, Jimmy."

"Heads."

The coin landed on the deck heads up.

Gander tapped his boot toe against Walt Hammond's left foot.

"Come on, Walt. Find me a start cart, so I can get the air conditioner going."

Hammond grunted an obscene suggestion about the start cart, but rolled over and got to his feet. The other mechanics, also complaining, began to stir.

Everybody, including himself, Gander thought, would bitch and moan about the routine duties, but when it came to staying up all night to change an engine, they all got their hands dirty and the complaints were left outside.

He walked forward to the crew compartment, found his duffle bag, and changed out of his boots. Stripping to his shorts, he donned his Nomex flight suit and then pulled on the pressure suit.

When he emerged into the sun wearing his Stetson and carrying his helmet, the men from the other transport were also slithering down the ramp, headed for their airplanes.

He clambered up the ladder of two-seven, pulled the

179

canvas from the canopy, and slid inside. He found a place behind the seat for his hat, and Hammond helped him buckle into the chute and seat harness.

It was sweltering in the cockpit. The perspiration from Hammond's forehead dripped on him.

"Go easy with her, Jimmy, until you're sure she checks out a hundred percent on all systems."

"Got it, Walt."

They took longer than usual with the checklist, making absolutely sure all of the switches were in the right position and all of the readouts were in the green.

They had to wait for a start cart, and when they finally turned the engine, it came to life immediately.

Gander gave Hammond a thumb's up, and the ex-master sergeant pulled the chocks.

McEntire was in zero-eight and signalled with his hand for Gander to pull up alongside him.

He released the brakes and the Alpha Kat rolled ahead. McEntire pulled out of line, turned onto the taxiway, and Gander fell in off his right wing.

Ten minutes later, they were climbing through eight thousand feet, and cool air was blasting from the vents of the air conditioning system.

Things were looking up again.

Brock Dixon took the next call at a public phone in an Arlington Heights shopping center. Crider had a whole list of telephone numbers and calling times, and none of them were repeated.

"Negative," Crider said.

"What do you mean, negative."

"We tried to decommission a jet engine, but they caught it and changed it out. They took off for Riyadh about an hour ago."

"Shit."

"Couldn't be helped. Not if you want us to be subtle."

"I want you to be subtle."

"Soon as we get our flight plan filed, we're taking off."

"Good. Make sure something embarrassing happens, and damned soon."

"Subtle, huh?"

Dixon thought about it. "Maybe less subtle, as long as it appears to be a KAT problem."

"That makes it a little easier," Crider said and hung up.

It was cooler in Saudi Arabia, but that was because the sun had gone down.

It also helped to be inside the Hilton, sitting in an easy chair, sucking on a Coke. Soames thought longingly about Chivas Regal poured over four ice cubes.

His roommate Conrad Billingsly said, "I'm going down the hall and get another Coke. How about you?" Susan and Andrea had doubled everyone up to save on expenses.

"You suppose the bellboy could find us something more suited to our taste, Connie?"

"I doubt it, unless you're talking females."

"I'll have another Coke."

Billingsly walked out, leaving the door open a crack, and the phone rang.

Soames got up and crossed the room to pick it up.

"Soames."

"A.J., it's Susan."

"Hi, Susie."

"I tried Kim's room, but no one answered."

"They're still downstairs, working on dinner. They've got a couple Saudi air force officers with them, one of whom is a prince, I think."

"Tell me about Chad."

Soames related the details of the demonstration, and

181

being naturally circumspect, neglected to mention the sabotage of two-seven.

"Sam Eddy felt good about it? About the reaction to the demo?"

"Said he did."

"And Kim?"

"You know Kim. He's not very speculative."

She took too much time framing her next question, he thought, and made it too general. "How are they doing?"

"About the same as the rest of us," he said.

"You know what I mean, A.J. They're both under a lot of pressure."

"About the same as the rest of us," he repeated.

"A.J."

"Look, Susie, ask your question."

"Sam Eddy didn't look at all well when he left. I thought he might be coming down with something."

Soames thought about it. McEntire never seemed to change, at least in any way that Soames had noticed.

"He's lost a couple pounds, maybe. Hell, I've lost five pounds in this heat, but I needed to lose it. What are you worried about, Susie?"

"I'm as involved in the company as anyone," she said. "Can't I worry?"

"Feel free," he told her, and then they spent ten minutes on the details of what was going on in Phoenix. She had upped the working hours of several people. Some avionics systems had been back ordered on them. DJ Alloys wanted more money on account before they would ship the next order.

"Send them a check," Soames said. "I'll clear it with Kim."

Billingsly had returned with their Cokes by the time he hung up.

"All's well along the Salt River?" he asked in his deep voice.

"The normal logistics screw-ups, Connie. Abnormal concerns from Susie."

Billingsly kicked his shoes off and stretched out on his bed. "In what way?"

"We both know she's a bit of a mother to all of us—"

"Some of us would prefer a slightly different relationship, I think."

"My wife has mentioned that possibility and nixed it in my case," Soames said. "However, she seems particularly worried about Sam Eddy and Kim."

"You think she knows something important the rest of us don't know?"

"I don't know what to think. She and Sam Eddy were divorced—almost two years ago. Lately though, she's been watching him like a hawk."

"Maybe she wasn't in favor of their divorce?" Billingsly said.

"What? I thought it was amicable."

"Sam Eddy initiated it."

"The hell he did. I didn't know that. With Sam Eddy, it's usually the other way around."

"Yeah. He's an unreformed womanizer, and he always gets caught. This time, though, he dumped her."

"Shit," Soames said. "Tells you what kind of observer of human nature I am. I thought she'd been making eyes at Kim for the last few months."

"Well, that's true, too," Billingsly said.

"Damn it, don't confuse me, Connie. I thought Susan was the confused one."

Billingsly sipped from his can and said, "Nothing confusing about it, A.J. She's in love with both of them. At least, that's the way I see it from my limited perspective."

Soames tried to recall various interactions in the last year. "Yeah, I could maybe buy that. And Kim hasn't figured it out."

"I don't think so. Or maybe he missed seeing *Paint Your Wagon*."

"You think Sam Eddy knows?" Soames asked.

"He knows."

"And that's why he divorced her?"

"I don't think so," Billingsly said, but he wouldn't elaborate.

Henry Loh and Jean Franc landed their Cessna A-37 Dragonfly in Rangoon in mid-afternoon.

The Dragonfly was a two-seater fitted out as an unarmed jet trainer, and Loh liked to fly it when he was going into populated airports. Rangoon Air Control might have rebelled if he had requested permission to land a Mirage 2000 that did not belong to an established air force.

That would soon change.

He did not know whether the change would be for the better or for the worse, nor did he care. Henry Loh simply looked forward to the change, to some kind of action.

After parking the Cessna in the commercial section, he and Franc shut down the systems and opened the canopy. The air was humid and fetid with the aroma of the Irrawaddy River. Standing on the wings outside the canopy, the two of them quickly changed clothes, swapping flight coveralls for short-sleeved khaki shirts and shorts. The garb was almost, but not quite, military uniforms.

Loh had never been enamored of uniforms, but he suspected that Lon Pot would soon expect his army and air force personnel to become more ceremonial.

Franc disappeared to pursue one delight or another, and after closing out the flight plan, Loh found a taxi and ordered the driver to take him to the Americanized bar called the Wild West.

The journey was more death-defying than combat flight. Drivers in Rangoon, as in most of Southeast Asia's large cities, observed traffic laws as misguided suggestions. Pedestrians and bicyclists were less fellow travellers than targets of opportunity.

While the streets were crowded and the storekeepers stood on the sidewalks hawking the sapphires, Sony stereos, eyeglasses, and tailored suits of their inventories, Loh thought that there were probably few buyers. The worldwide recession had cut heavily into tourism, and very few of the potential customers were Westerners. When they were, they appeared more likely to have pockets lined with hashish than with American Express cards. Then, too, the civil war had deterred many from visiting the sights of Burma.

Loh knew that the proportion of poverty-stricken peasants was on the rise, along with inflation. The time was ripe for change, and he felt he had chosen the side that would emerge in control.

The Wild West Saloon was set back from the sidewalk, its entranceway festooned with an unlikely mix of pepper trees, imported yucca plants, and a papier-mâché Saguaro cactus that had large holes punched in it.

He paid off the driver with a few more *kyat* than necessary, walked up the flagstone path to the door, and pushed open both swinging doors.

The interior was fogged with cigarette smoke, making the full-width bar at the back vaguely more distant. A high-wattage amplifier boomed American country music through ceiling speakers. Some male singer he had never heard before sang about lost love, a typical theme.

The bar was crowded to overflow with Burmese cowboys, Thai and Burmese whores, ex-patriot Americans and Brits. The mob at the bar was three-deep, and the thirty-five or forty tables were all taken. More people stood around or sidled through the throng on seemingly important errands. He saw at least a dozen blond and blue-eyed giants dressed in the ancient fatigues of Vietnam veterans or deserters. Having made their decisions twenty years before, they had no other place to go now.

There was sawdust on the floor and the smell of tobacco and marijuana and spilled beer hung in the air. Wagon wheels with lantern globes over forty-watt bulbs were suspended from the ceiling. The bar was twenty meters long, and the back wall was liberally decorated with oil paintings, prints, and photographs of nude women, all Westerners, and all large-breasted.

Loh stood just inside the entrance for several minutes, allowing his eyes to adjust to the dim interior. When he could see clearly, he scanned the tables and found his quarry.

There were four of them. They were dressed in slacks and white shirts, but their normal attire would be that of the Burmese Air Force. They were sipping cautiously from bottles of Budweiser beer and surreptitiously watching the entrance.

He forced his way through the milling crowd, declining three less than suggestive offers from girls who were probably less than fifteen years old.

Colonel Kun Mauk nodded at the chair they had saved for him, and Henry Loh sat down in it. He waved off the girl serving the table.

No one offered a greeting. They had known each other for many years, and they knew why he was here.

Mauk said, "Well?"

"You will be promoted one grade immediately, and your salaries will advance by half-again what they are now."

They all looked at each other, then back to Loh.

"And there is a bonus."

He reached inside his shirt and withdrew four envelopes, somewhat dampened by contact with his skin.

186

He glanced around the room, then divided the envelopes and slid them across the table to each man.

Each slit his envelope and peered within. Loh watched them closely.

At the sight of the American dollars, no one smiled, but the lines around their eyes eased considerably.

Mauk asked, "When?"

"Very, very soon. I will notify you."

Mauk looked to the others and received curt bobs of the heads in reply.

"We are committed," Mauk said.

"You have chosen the correct path," Loh said.

"If it is not, we will make it so."

The statement was one that Lon Pot would enjoy, Loh thought.

He also thought that his air force had just expanded by sixteen fighter aircraft.

Twelve

The Saudis were much better organized, and their military had a great deal more discipline than the Chadians. The military section of the airport, where the Kimball Aero aircraft had been parked, was under constant surveillance by army units patrolling on foot and in jeeps.

It was a large complex, with long rows of first-class aircraft. Crider recognized Northrop F-5E Tiger IIs, McDonnell Douglas F-15 Eagles, Lockheed C-130 Hercules, and some British Aerospace Strikemasters. The activity level was high, with flights of aircraft constantly on the move, taxiing, taking off, landing.

The Learjet's twin engines were toned down to a muted roar as Lujan taxied slowly toward the spot where he'd been told to park.

Crider, Gart, and O'Brian were settled low in their seats so they could get decent views of the ramp where the Alpha Kats were parked. Wheeler and Adage were on their knees in the aisle, peering over their shoulders.

"Security's damned tight," Del Gart said.

"And it's a big fucking base," Alan Adage added.

His beard could use a shampoo, Crider thought.

"One of the largest airports in the world," Crider told him. "The Saudis have to spend their bucks somewhere."

"They could have spent it somewhere other than in the middle of the damned country," Wheeler said.

"Christ! I haven't seen so much nothing in my life."

Saudi Arabia was one fourth the size of the United States in land area, but not much of the land area was hospitable. Twentieth Century warplanes broke the sonic barrier directly over nomadic tribes whose routines and way of life had not advanced much past what they were at the time of Jesus Christ. Or of Mohammed, Crider reminded himself.

The KAT planes slid out of view as Emilio Lujan turned the Lear into a parking place.

"Any ideas?" Crider asked.

"We can get *plastique?*" O'Brian asked.

"Yeah, I've got some contacts around the Gulf. Shouldn't be too difficult."

Gart turned around in his seat to look back at Corey O'Brian. The two munitions experts stared at each other for a few minutes.

"Fuel tank?" Gart asked.

"That would be the best and quickest by far, I think," O'Brian said.

"No," Crider told them. "Any goddamned plane can have a fuel tank explode. This has to be a problem peculiar to Kimball's airplane."

"We tried the engine," Adage said.

"Control, then," Gart said.

"They're fly-by-wire," Crider said.

"What we want," O'Brian said, "is just the teeniest little charge placed against the electronics box, wherever it is. At speed, the pilot won't even hear it before he loses control. He may then broadcast his sudden new problem over the air, so everyone knows."

"We don't want it discovered during the post-crash investigation, Corey," Crider insisted.

"We'll give it a couple minutes delay, then the fuel tank goes," Gart said. "That should obliterate any evidence."

"Or fatalities, Del," Crider reminded him. "We're supposed to avoid fatalities."

"Give it five minutes, then," the Irishman said. "The pilot can eject, and the plane blows up on crashing. For certain."

"I like it," Crider said.

"One problem," Wheeler said.

"What's that?"

"If the guy's at ten thousand feet, he's got time to eject. If he's showing off, flying fifty feet off the sand, that son of a bitch is going to dig a hole immediately."

"Well," Crider said, "we'll have done the best we can do, under the circumstances."

Lujan shut down the jets, then came back from the cockpit and opened the hatch.

O'Brian said, "Well, and now that's settled, let's find a hotel, hey?"

Ben Wilcox was acutely aware of the calendar on his desk. Three hours before, at exactly midnight, he had flipped the page. July 19.

Simonson's assets in Burma and Thailand were now saying July 27 looked like a good bet.

Worse, his own source confirmed it.

The White House was saying that, if civil war erupted in Burma, the CIA was to stay out of it. The President would go to the UN and raise hell, but U.S. covert actions were to be suspended.

It was dark outside, and though there were a few hundred people still working in the building, he felt quite alone on his floor.

The digital clock that was part of his elaborate telephone set read 3:06.

It was six minutes after ten in Riyadh.

Where in hell are you, Kimball?

He got up from his desk chair and paced around the room. He started to fill his mug from the automatic drip pot on the sideboard, then put it down. Caffeine was beginning to become his life.

The stubble on his face rasped loudly in his ears when he ran his hand over his cheeks.

The telephone rang.

He whipped around and went back to the desk, snatching the phone from its cradle.

"Wilcox."

"You called?" Kimball asked.

"Damned near two hours ago."

"My business is selling airplanes. The customer comes first."

"Let's not forget, Kimball, that I'm your first damned customer."

"What do you want?"

"How secure is your line?"

"As secure as Sheraton makes it. First things first. What did you find out about my ... engine problems?"

Wilcox sighed. At least, Kimball was being circumspect on the phone.

"I haven't found out anything yet. I've got a couple people taking a look at it."

"I want to know what's going on, and damned soon. If my people are in greater danger than I expect them to be, I want to know why and how."

"We're doing what we can, Kimball."

"Do more."

"Damn it, we're doing everything we possibly can," Wilcox said, but had to go on. "You've got to be in Rangoon on the twenty-sixth."

"No way. We get into Dacca that day."

"Hell, no one in Bangladesh can afford to buy your aircraft."

"They want to look at them, and I'm going to let them look, Wilcox. Hell, for all you know, they've got a secret treasury stashed away."

191

"I don't . . ."

"Besides," Kimball continued, "if I try to change the schedule for Burma and the rest down the line, somebody's going to get suspicious."

Wilcox damned the lack of a secure line, but asked, "Can you make your first . . . priority flights out of Dacca?"

Kimball only thought it over for thirty seconds. "That can be done, but why? What's the sudden rush?"

"New developments."

"What new developments?"

"I can't talk about them on the phone."

"Then you'd better get your ass over here and tell me in person. I'm not deviating from the original schedule unless I've got a damned good reason."

Kimball hung up.

Shit!

He didn't want to go to Saudi Arabia.

A.J. Soames sat with Kimball, McEntire, and Hamilton at a linen-covered table in the hotel's dining room. After the morning spent in the heat blistering the concrete at Riyadh International, the air conditioning was one step away from paradise.

The waiter took away the scoured hamburger plates and delivered the bowls of ice cream with a flourish that was beyond necessity.

Soames said, "Hell, Kim, I don't know how great a salesman I am."

"You and Alex will do fine, A.J. The prince is easy to get along with, and about all you have to do is flip through the charts."

"And stand around during the demonstration," Sam Eddy added. "The questions aren't all that hard to answer. Just remember to keep a straight face when their planes go so far off the target. Smirking is off-limits."

"I smirk easily," Hamilton said, scooping into his vanilla ice cream. "I'd better stay in the airplane."

"Who's going to stand in as Zookeeper?" Soames asked.

"We'll put Vrdlicka on it," Kimball said.

"Are we fouling up the planned rotation just because you and Sam Eddy want to fly?" Soames asked.

He wasn't above adjusting to emergencies or revised circumstances, but if there was an emergency, he wanted to know about it.

McEntire answered, "We want to be closer to the operations because of the event in Chad."

Hamilton asked, "Are you sure you're going to eat your ice cream, Kim?"

"No, you can have it."

"Ah shit," Soames said. "I guess we move to public relations."

"You speaking for me?" Hamilton asked.

"Damned right."

"You'll probably be better at it than we are," McEntire told them. "In fact, I'm sure you will be."

"If we sell some airplanes, do we get a commission?" Hamilton asked.

"We're all on commission," Soames said, thinking of his stock.

"Okay, good," Kimball said. "How are we doing? What's the status?"

"The birds are all pre-flighted," Soames said. "Most everyone is on a sleep- or recreation-break right now."

"You mean there's recreation somewhere around here?" Sam Eddy asked.

"If you look for it," Soames said. "The Saudis have the base well-secured, but I've got Perry Vance and Dave Metger standing afternoon guard on the aircraft. We won't load weapons until just before the demonstration."

"We want an intense inspection of all aircraft before

193

takeoff," Kimball said.

"I've got it on my chart."

"And then, at three o'clock, during our afternoon exercise, the prince is taking a little joy ride."

"Oh, damn!"

"I couldn't very well refuse him," Kimball said. "He's an active air force pilot, he's rated in F-15s and F-16s, and he's loaded up with flying time in both. Plus, he's got combat experience in the Gulf war."

"I don't think he'll break the airplane," McEntire said, "and if he does, he can afford to pay for it."

"You'll go with him, Kim?" Soames asked.

"Sam Eddy's going to fly his wing."

"Don't shoot him down or do anything silly, Sam Eddy," Soames said.

"I know a golden goose when I see one, A.J."

Derek Crider's credentials and business cards, describing him as an assistant vice president and a field engineer for Rockwell International, worked very well.

Twice.

Along with Del Gart, who carried a similar set of forged documents, he whisked through a chainlink gate manned by a Saudi military policeman. Corey O'Brian had stayed behind because they thought his maimed hand, with its missing three fingers, might have drawn too much attention.

They were dressed almost alike in sturdy work shoes and khaki cotton pants. Gart wore a pastel blue shirt with a half-dozen pens and pencils in a pocket protector. Crider thought it might have been over-kill. He himself wore a white shirt and an open tan safari jacket that whipped in the light breeze. He had an expensive Hewlett-Packard calculator clipped to his belt.

Gart wore a beat-up straw hat, an essential ingredient of his uniform.

The two of them approached a short slim man sitting on the lowered ramp of a C-141. The guy lolled there, a black Los Angeles Raiders baseball cap pulled low over his eyebrows, and watched them approach. He had an M-16 with a clip in place leaning against the ramp beside him. A trickle of sweat ran down the side of his face, and he wiped it away.

Pulling out his wallet and offering the credentials, Crider said, "Good afternoon."

"Afternoon," the man said, pushing himself to his feet. "What can I do for you guys?"

"We're with Rockwell, been working on a Saudi air control project for the past eighteen months."

"Chip Block," Gart said, offering his hand. "It's a nickname, for the obvious reason."

"Dave Metger," the guy said and shook Gart's hand, then Crider's.

"Bill Torrington, Atlanta," he identified himself with a drawl he had spent half of his life trying to lose.

"You working on the base?"

"Yeah, back theah at the main towah." Crider flipped a thumb over his shoulder.

"And you've been here a year and a half?"

"Hard to believe, isn't it?" Gart said. "Another six months, and I'll go nuts."

"What it was," Crider said, "we all saw fellow Americans with their own planes, ya know, and we thought we'd walk over and see if ya'll didn't have somethin' ta wet a whistle with."

Metger grinned. "Yeah, I'll bet you've been here a long time."

"Long damned time."

"But I can't help you out. Unless you want a cup of iced tea."

Gart made a long face. "Well, we didn't hold out much hope. Thanks, anyway."

Crider turned to look at the row of Alpha Kats.

"Nice lookin' planes."

"Thanks. We're kind of proud of them."

"Ah worked the B-1 bombah program till Jimmy Carter dumped all over us."

"The hell you did? That was a nice airplane."

"SOB was a fellow Georgian, too. But that's how come I ended up playin' with ground computers."

"You mind if we take a look?" Gart asked.

"Oh, hell no! Come on, I'll take you around."

Metger loosened the sling on his assault rifle and draped it over his shoulder, then led them across the tarmac to the Alpha Kats.

He was a right proud airplane salesman. Opened access panels and showed them the kinds of things engineers would be interested in. Helped Crider up a ladder to peer into the cockpit. Ignored Gart as he wandered around to the other side of the aircraft.

Metger showed them the other planes and the Kappa Kat, explaining the tactics briefly.

They spent twenty minutes on the tour, then Gart said, "Damn, Bill! We'd better get back before the royal family crawls all over us."

Crider lifted his wrist and looked at his watch. "No shit. Hey, Dave, we all 'preciate the tour."

"No sweat. Come back and meet some of the others when they're here. We're going to be hanging around for a couple days."

"We all will just do that," Gart said and offered his hand again.

Walking back toward the chainlink fence, Crider said, "That asshole's not mean enough, or suspicious enough, to be in the aerospace business."

"You're telling me?"

"Any trouble?"

"None at all," Gart said, taking his straw hat off and wiping his forehead with his forearm.

Crider saw that the small explosive charges that had

been hidden in the hat were gone.

"Where in hell'd you get that accent?" Gart asked.

"My childhood's comin' back to me."

Kimball wasn't particularly worried about the prince. The man was qualified in the Falcon, so he was accustomed to the fly-by-wire controls.

Still, he was on edge until he saw both Alpha Kats on the final approach. When they touched down, one behind the other, the prince's landing even smoother than Sam Eddy's, and slowed to a crawl, he let his breath out.

"See?" Gander said. "Nothing to worry about."

"Me, worried?"

"You're getting to be a regular old fuddy duddy. Chill out, Kim."

After the turbojets were shut down, he and Gander crossed the ramp to the planes. Tex Brabham was the first up the ladder to help the prince out of his harness and connections.

Four mean-looking and heavily armed Saudis in desert camouflage also moved in close to the plane. They hadn't been introduced, and Kimball assumed they were in the bodyguard business.

The prince, who was both earnest and agile, scrambled down the ladder behind Brabham.

"Delightful!"

"I'm glad you enjoyed it," Kimball said. And he was glad. There was nothing like hands-on experience to promote love for the airplane.

"It is a joy to fly."

"We warned you," McEntire said, coming around the nose of the next plane in line. He was holding his hands up, palms out, in deference to the bodyguards.

"I am, naturally, both concerned and intrigued about the capability in tandem with the Kappa Kat."

"You'll see that tonight," Kimball said.

"But I wonder . . ."

Uh oh, Kimball thought.

". . . if we might not change the demonstration somewhat?"

"In what way?" Kimball asked.

"I am certain that you have carefully choreographed your program, in the interest of safety as well as of showing off the talents of the craft. However, our interest lies primarily in defense, rather than the attack mission."

"You'd like to see us fly defense?"

"Exactly!"

Kimball looked at McEntire.

"That's my preference, actually," Sam Eddy said.

"Fine with us," Kimball echoed.

"Wonderful. I will have my two squadrons attack the target, and you will protect it."

Kimball's watch read 4:30 P.M. "I'll get my people together, and we'll brief them for the change."

"You have the maps, Kim?" the prince asked.

"We've got everything we need, thanks."

"And then we'll see you for dinner."

"What we'd like to do is have A.J. Soames and Alex Hamilton brief you and your officers over dinner. Sam Eddy and I are leading the flight, so we'll have some of our own preparations to make here."

"I like a man who demonstrates his own convictions," the prince said. "I will lead the attackers."

Kimball grinned at him. "I'll see you before you see me."

The prince smiled back. "Perhaps."

As soon as the prince and his party departed, the KAT crews went into action. A refueling truck was ordered up for the two Alpha Kats just returned. The ordnance teams began wheeling the dollies beneath the fighters and loading air-to-air missiles. Carl Dent dutifully checked each missile to be certain it was a dummy.

Kimball specified only four missiles per Alpha Kat. They wouldn't actually be fired, but their heat-seeking or radar-tracking heads would be utilized to designate contacts. Additionally, the lighter ordnance load increased the stealth of the planes. The missiles were not constructed with stealth technology, and at close ranges, would provide a radar return. The absence of iron bombs on the centerline hardpoints also improved the fighters' performances and lowered their radar cross sections.

One of the techs, Paul Diamond, took one of the jeeps provided by the Saudis and went to find a restaurant that would box some dinners for them.

Kimball and the day's demo team (McEntire, Gander, Mabry, Halek, and Cadwell) met with Billingsly and Vrdlicka around a stack of missile crates in the Starlifter.

Billingsly was Hawkeye Three and Vrdlicka would handle the headquarters chores as Zookeeper.

Sam Miller, Ito Makura, and Phillipe Contrarez, the rest of the Hawkeye crew, listened in from their places on the drop-down canvas seats along the fuselage.

They spent the next three hours revising their plan of operations, chewing slowly through cold chicken when Diamond got back with it. Everyone argued freely about the methodology, and it began to refine itself around 7:30 P.M.

The target, a tin shanty that had been moved into the desert by cargo helicopter, was two hundred miles to the south.

"Seems to me," Gander said, "that the Saudis will figure us to all be at altitude."

"They'll also come in low, trying to avoid the radar coverage," McEntire added.

"You want us to stay low, then? Use pop-up tactics

like the MiG-23s did in 'Nam?"

"The prince is familiar with American tactics," Billingsly said. "So let's not be absolutely traditional."

"How about CAP?" Sam Eddy asked.

"They're coming in with eight Eagles," Kimball said. "If Connie would give up his CAP, we could have six planes available when they're only expecting four."

"I can live without the CAP," Billingsly said, "if you can live with the fact that I might have to go off the air more frequently."

"What the hell? Let's try it," McEntire said.

Tex Brabham walked up the ramp and asked, "Got to interrupt. Who gets what?"

McEntire wrote quickly on slips of paper, and they drew N-numbers out of Gander's Stetson.

Kimball opened his slip and saw: one-five.

Brabham memorized the roster and went back to do the final checks.

"Hey, Tex," Kimball called after him.

"Yeah, Kim."

"Look real close, huh? Flashlights everywhere."

Brabham gave him a dirty look. "Yo, boss."

The flight crews split up and headed for the crew compartments of whichever C-141 held their flight gear. Kimball dampened a towel with ice water and carried it into the compartment with him. He stripped and used the towel to give himself a sponge bath before donning his flight suit and G-suit. He carried his survival equipment, helmet, and oxygen mask out to one-five.

Brabham was waiting for him, and they did another walkaround together.

"She looks clean, Kim. But I'm worried."

"About what, Tex?"

"These honeys are so complicated, it's easy to hide something when somebody wants to hide something."

"Engines check out?"

"We put floodlight through them and turned them on

200

the starters. They're okay."

"We'll be all right," Kimball assured him and climbed into the cockpit.

The Kappa Kat took off while the fighters were being started. All six fired without complaint, and all six stayed in place and ran their engines up to one hundred percent, then idled back.

"Anybody?" Kimball asked on Tac Two.

"Two's good."

"Three."

"Four."

"Five, yo."

"And Six," McEntire said. He had elected to ride wing on Five, flown by Jay Halek.

Kimball called ground control, then the tower, and got them airborne ten minutes later. Two minutes after that, air control allowed them to kill their IFF transponders.

"Kimball Aero one-five, Riyadh."

"Go Riyadh."

"That's scary, one-five. You should not just disappear like that."

"It's supposed to be scary," Kimball told him, then went to Tac Two. "Hawkeye, Bengals are up."

"Let's hope so," Billingsly came back. "Five and Six, go to Hawkeye Four on Tac Three. One through Four, let's keep hot mikes. I want to hear you breathing."

Kimball reached for the communications panel and flipped the toggle that kept his microphone on transmit. The receiver for his Tac Two channel, carrying Hawkeye's voice, was on a different frequency.

"One and Two, take up a heading of one-three-five. I'm aiming you toward the coast. Three and Four, go to one-seven-five. Let's keep 'em two hundred feet off the deck, airspeed four-five-zero knots."

"One. Roger one-three-five, two hundred feet, and four-five-zero," Kimball answered for himself and his

201

wingman, Cadwell.

"Two. One-seven-five, two hundred feet, and four-five-zero."

The terrain rolled easily ahead of them, vaguely visible through the windscreen, but clearly shown on the night vision camera's image displayed on the instrument panel CRT. The desert was green in the image, and Kimball couldn't find one distinctive piece of geography that he would call a landmark. The big turbofan purred with a lion's pleasure behind him.

Sixteen minutes later, Billingsly called, "Bengal One, go to one-eight-zero now."

"Going one-eight-zero."

Kimball eased the stick to the right and pressed lightly on the rudder pedal.

Nothing happened.

He jiggled the stick.

Nothing.

Glancing down to his right side, he saw the red light right away.

"You turning or not?" Cadwell asked him.

"I'm showing malfunction on the control computer," Kimball said.

His throat had tightened up on him almost immediately.

Instant sweat coated his palms under the flight gloves.

The plane stayed level, but the desert scene on the screen suddenly appeared way too close. Low-level flight was normally accomplished in unexpected turbulence. The day's heat bleeding off the desert was fairly steady now because of the flat terrain, but could change at any moment.

"Cheetah, list for me."

"No rudder, ailerons, or elevators, Frog."

"Leave the throttle alone."

"Wouldn't touch it for the world," Kimball said,

switching on his running lights so Cadwell could see him.

"We're way too damned low," Cadwell said.

"Okay," Billingsly said. "Let's get you some altitude. See if you can trim in some elevator and give it a bit of power."

Kimball gingerly touched the throttle and eased it forward. He was afraid that the turbulence of their low flight was going to destabilize the plane once he changed the setting.

Tapping the rocker switch on the throttle handle, he fed in some up-trim on the elevator.

"That's it, good," Cadwell said.

He glanced at the HUD. The rate-of-climb readout was positive.

"I'm showing fifty feet per minute, Frog," he said.

"Good, that's enough. We'll just work you up to altitude slowly."

It sounded good to Kimball.

Until the back end of the Alpha Kat erupted in a yellow-red flash of light that erased his night vision.

Thirteen

Because the mikes were hot, Jimmy Gander, Bengal Three, heard one explosion and what might have been part of a second explosion before Kimball's transmitter whistled loudly in his ears and then went dead.

"Jesus Christ! The son of a bitching plane blew up!" Cadwell yelled.

"Chute?" Billingsly asked.

"Goddamn!"

"Did you see a parachute, Two?" Billingsly asked, his voice as calm as water confined to a lagoon.

"Hell no! I went by too fast. Took some debris hits. I'm turning back now."

"Hawkeye, Three," Gander said. "Vector me in."

"Go to zero-nine-eight, Three."

Gander eased the controller over, added rudder, and took up the new heading. He flashed his wingtip guide-lights twice so Warren Mabry could stay with him, then slammed the throttle forward.

The Gs shoved him back in the seat, and the HUD readout quickly rose through the numbers, switched to Mach, and climbed again to Mach 1.5.

Seconds later, he saw the glow on the horizon.

"Got visual, Frog."

Speedy Gonzales must have notified Bengals Five and Six because McEntire came in on Tac Two. "What the hell's happening?"

"Two here. I've got an orbit. The plane's destroyed,

scattered all over the damned desert. Fuselage is still on fire."

"Beeper, Two?" Billingsly asked.

"No beeper. No chute."

"Bastard!" McEntire yelped. "Vector me, Frog."

"Hold on, troops," Billingsly said. "I've got hostiles. Charlie, Delta, and Echo coming hard from the east. Fox and George high to the south."

"Screw 'em," McEntire said.

Gander searched the skies ahead for Cadwell, but couldn't see him.

"Two, give me some lights."

He switched on his own and was aware that Mabry had illuminated alongside him.

The fire was dying as he approached, retarding his throttle and getting back down through the sonic barrier.

He spotted Cadwell's lights low to the south of the burning fighter.

Slowing until the HUD readout displayed 300 knots, Gander dialed his Tac Four transceiver to the Guard channel, 243.0, where it was supposed to be anyway. Someone—himself—had missed it in the pre-flight checklist.

"How about you, Cheetah? Talk to me."

Nothing.

"Come on, Cheetah, quit horsing around. Tell the Gandy Dancer all about it."

"Got me, Gandy."

Kimball's voice sounded weak, or maybe it was the survival radio. He eased into a wide turn.

"Can you give me a flash?"

A flashlight beam erupted from the dark desert floor, nearly a mile north of the wreckage. Gander rolled out of his turn and headed for it.

Everyone tried to speak on the Guard channel at once.

"Shut up!" Gander yelled. "Give me a rundown, Cheetah. How you feeling?"

"Like I've been kicked in the ass."

"How about something more objective?"

"No broken bones that I can detect. I'm not bleeding anywhere obvious. The flying suit's a loss. Nearly burnt through in spots. The damned chute was barely open when I hit the sand. Knocked the wind out of me."

"Hostiles Charlie, Delta, and Echo are seventy miles out, turning for the wreckage," Billingsly said. "They've spotted it."

"Go get 'em," Kimball said.

"I'll orbit you," Cadwell said.

"Get the hell out of here, now! Frog, send me a chopper when it's over."

Gander wagged his wings when he flew over the flashlight beam, then cut his running lights and switched back to the Tac Two radio.

Billingsly was reporting to Vrdlicka, who wouldn't have heard the Guard channel conversations because of the line-of-sight interference.

"Zookeeper, that Saudi SAR chopper still standing by?"

"Roger, Hawkeye. Sitrep, please."

"He's fine, but scratch one Alpha."

"Call them all back, Frog."

"Cheetah won't go for it."

"Neither will Irish Eyes," McEntire cut in.

"It's the safest course," Vrdlicka said.

Gander broke in, "I'm still waiting for a vector, Frog. Fuck the recall."

Billingsly barely paused before reading off a set of coordinates. "Send the chopper two minutes after the exercise is completed, Zookeeper."

Vrdlicka obviously didn't like it, but read back the coordinates and said, "Roger the chopper."

McEntire came in, "Give me Fox and George, Hawk-eye."

"Two, join on Three and Four. Three, go to zero-eight-seven. I'll tell you when to pop up. Five, reverse course and pick up zero-zero-nine. . . ."

Kimball sat in the sand, still trying to catch his breath. He shut off the flashlight and laid it next to the radio beside his leg.

Once again, he ran his hands over his whole body, and once again was amazed that they didn't run into protruding bones or organs. The backs of his G-suit and his flying suit were scorched. He tugged at the fingers of his gloves and slipped them off.

He realized that he still had his helmet on and unsnapped the straps, then lifted it off. The air caressing his face felt better, though it was still hot.

Some of the hair on the back of his neck felt like it was singed.

He rolled onto his stomach, got his knees under him, and pushed himself to a kneeling position.

Felt a little dizzy.

Waited.

The dizziness passed and he stood up. The sand shifting under his feet felt like heavy seawater, and he spread his legs to keep his balance.

Another short flash of dizziness.

With trembling hands, he unbuckled the parachute harness and dropped it to the earth.

He waited three full minutes before squatting to pick up the radio, flashlight, and helmet.

He barely remembered the last minutes in the Alpha Kat. It was a safety quirk of the mind, he thought, which didn't want to remember.

Because he had no control of the aircraft and expected to go wing-over at any minute from turbulence, he had had his right hand lightly gripping the ejection handle between his legs. The second he heard the dull thump of the explosion, felt the heat, and was blinded by the light, he had ejected. He thought he went out at about a thousand feet AGL, tumbling over backwards. The Martin-Baker seat parted from him as advertised, and the drogue chute streamed out of his pack, tugging the main canopy behind it.

He remembered looking upward for the canopy deployment, seeing the white nylon blossom, felt the tug, and boom . . . ! He slammed into the earth.

The air whooshed out of his lungs.

Followed immediately by the muted concussion of the fighter crashing into the earth south of him.

He had a headache.

His back hurt. He felt as if he were two inches shorter, his vertebrae squashed together by the ejection.

He was going to write a long letter of appreciation to the people at Martin-Baker.

He was thirsty as hell, but he had lost his water bottle in the ejection.

Walking carefully in the oozy sand, he started out toward the wreckage. The dunes weren't high, but they felt as if they were as he struggled with the shallow inclines.

He was damned certain it was sabotage, this time. He had too much faith in the airplane. If he had been in some maneuver when the fly-by-wire went out, rather than in trimmed-out level flight, he wouldn't be walking in the sand now.

And he tried not to wonder if one of the other planes had also been compromised. He should have sent them all back to the airfield.

But then, he reasoned, two similar crashes would have been too coincidental.

He felt better.

Mentally.

His back still hurt, and his head was throbbing.

A.J. Soames appreciated the thoughtfulness of the prince. Before taking off with his two flights of F-15 Eagles, the prince had ordered everyone who could manage it to use English on the radio, in deference to the guests.

He and Alex Hamilton sat in comfortable chairs, along with a dozen dignitaries, in the underground combat center. It was well outfitted with computers and radar repeater screens lined up along two walls. A huge map of the Middle East was projected onto a wall screen. Symbols moving across the southern portion of the map were identified as the aggressor Eagles. Commercial and other flights had been routed to the north, to stay clear of the exercise.

The aggressors had split into three groups of two aircraft and taken three different headings, circling the target wide, and then beginning to move in on it in a pincer movement. They were all above twenty thousand feet, and two of them had already identified the Kappa Kat by its radar emissions.

He leaned over to his right and said, "What do you think, Alex?"

"I think they're in for a surprise."

The pilots' dialogue was broadcast over ceiling speakers, and some of it was confusing when it overlapped or reverted to Arabic.

"Blue Dart One, Sapphire One. I have visual on a fire."

The Sapphire flight was headed for the target from off the Persian Gulf.

In response to a question, Sapphire One said, "On the ground."

"In the target area?"

"Negative."

"Investigate, Sapphire. Dart One out."

Soames felt himself holding his breath.

"Now, I know why we're here, and Kim's flying," Hamilton said. "He couldn't take the suspense."

"I can't take it either. We may have to renegotiate," Soames said.

Two more Eagles, Red Fox flight, began to converge on the target from the west. One of them split off and headed for the Kappa Kat.

Which promptly disappeared from the screen.

"Hey," one of the Saudi pilots called, "I have got a J-band threat. Missile locked on me."

"I will check your . . . what! Threat receiver. Missile lock on."

It was all over in twelve minutes. Not one of the F-15s got close to the target or to Hawkeye.

As soon as he was shot down, the prince, Blue Dart One, began to chuckle.

"The fire was a ruse, I think," he said over the radio.

"If it was, Kim didn't bother to tell me about it," Soames said to Hamilton.

"It was a damned good idea, though," Hamilton said.

Four choppers came.

They were directed to his position by Billingsly who had moved the Kappa Kat to an orbit position some three thousand feet above him.

The fire had gone out, but the wreckage was still hot, and Kimball had not been able to get close enough to inspect it thoroughly.

He was pretty certain that the explosion and fire had completely destroyed any of the electronics and computer software that Kimball Aero had patented or would like to have protected. If the detonation of the fuel cell hadn't done the job, the small self-destruct charges provided by Wilcox would have.

Tex Brabham was the first one out of the first chopper, some three feet before it would have officially landed. He ran clumsily in the sand toward Kimball's flashlight.

Sliding to a stop in front of where Kimball sat, he said, "Kim?"

"I'm all right, Tex. There's a couple bruises and a hell of a headache."

Brabham went to his knees and dug into a canvas bag. He came up with three aspirin and a thermos of ice water. "Take these."

Kimball followed orders. The cool water tasted damned good. He swirled it around in his mouth.

"Goddamn, boss. I should have caught it."

"Not necessarily, Tex, but yeah, I think it's sabotage, too. But I can't figure out how they got to the planes."

"Rockwell International."

"What!"

"I doubt they really worked for Rockwell, but they had papers that said they did." Brabham told him what he had learned from Dave Metger

"Dave's pretty shot," he added.

"I'll talk to him," Kimball said.

Floodlights began to wink on. KAT personnel came by to check on him, then began to search for the scattered debris. Saudi air force investigators were directing everyone, shooting video and still camera shots.

Vrdlicka showed up, shaking his head.

"How'd it go, Mel?" he asked.

"We downed all of them. They downed you."

"I don't think we're talking about the same enemy."

"Come on, Kim, there's a chopper headed back now," Vrdlicka said

"I'm going to stick around here for a little while longer," Kimball said.

"Bullshit," Brabham said. "I'll be here, and you're

getting on the bird. The easy way or the hard way."

Kimball chose the easy way and got up to walk over to the helicopter, a twin-rotored Boeing Chinook.

Slightly over an hour later, with his headache only mildly diminished, he slid out the helicopter's wide doorway onto warm concrete.

Sam Eddy McEntire, A.J. Soames, and the prince were waiting for him.

He told them the story. It seemed as if he had repeated it a dozen times.

In his mind, he probably had.

"No control at all?" McEntire asked. "That system's redundant. You don't lose both of them at once."

"I don't think the guy who set it up knew that," Kimball said. "There's no way it was going to look like an accident or system failure, but he thought it would."

"We have the descriptions of the men," the prince said. "Unless they have already left the country, they won't be leaving soon."

Soames went back to their ramp area to coordinate the investigation, and over Kimball's objection, Sam Eddy loaded him in a jeep and took him back to the hotel.

The prince had a doctor waiting in the room for him, and Kimball submitted to a thorough examination before stumbling into the shower.

When he came out with a towel wrapped around his waist, feeling a smidgen better, McEntire handed him a glass.

"What's that?"

"Johnnie Walker Black cough syrup."

"In Riyadh?"

"Understanding doc. Drink up."

The liquor burned nicely going down. "What'd the doc tell you?"

"You're mostly in one piece. Slight concussion. You'll live, whether you want to or not."

212

"Good deal."

Kimball crossed the room to his own bed and sat on the edge of it.

The phone rang.

He looked at his watch. 12:15 A.M. in the morning. 3:15 A.M. in Phoenix.

The phone rang again.

"You want to take that, Sam Eddy? It'll be Susan."

McEntire splashed more scotch in their glasses.

The phone rang again.

Finally, he picked it up. "Grand Central Zoo."

He listened for a minute, then told Kimball, "She wants to know how our day went."

"Tell her about yours. Tell her mine was a bust."

Kimball lay back and closed his eyes to rest them, but they didn't want to open again.

Fourteen

Bangkok was teeming with life. Too much life. It flowed through the jammed streets on tireless, sandaled feet and in shrilly honking, smoke-emitting trucks, automobiles, and weaving motorscooters, and it sailed along the edges of the Chao Phraya River and the canals, the *klongs,* in thousands of well-maintained or decrepit longtail boats called *hang yao,* propelled by ratty motors driving propellers mounted on long driveshafts.

The silver and gold spires of the city were slowly becoming hidden by the glass-faced highrises imported from Western architects. This holiest of cities was being subverted by the devils of America and Europe. Still, Buddha reigned, and foreigners who wished to reside in the city paid at least superficial homage to the prevailing attitude of serenity. A Thai did not increase the volume of his voice, debate meaningless issues, nor demonstrate anger.

In a city that appeared so wealthy, where gold leaf was left at the feet of the Buddha in innumerable temples, there was still an underlying patina of vast poverty.

It seemed to Lon Pot that almost every citizen of the Thai capital either had his hand out, pleading for alms, or had his hand out, offering breadfruits, orchids, and cheap watches in exchange for pitifully few

214

baht. The gem dealers were scarcely more subtle.

Lon Pot's white Lincoln passed over the main canal, Phadung Klong, coming close to mashing a pedicab. His driver was more concerned with his destination than with those who might possibly get in the way of it.

The Lincoln dwarfed most of the automobiles on the street and signified that a great personage sat behind its darkly tinted windows.

The personage, Lon Pot, was accompanied by two bodyguards in addition to the driver. He was dressed in a white silk suit, silver-blue shirt, and spotless white tie. When he came to Bangkok, he liked to dress for the occasion.

They passed the small temples that proliferated through the city, bedecked with purple orchids, yellow roses, and white jasmine. Monks in saffron robes moved along the sidewalks, appearing and disappearing in the crowds. The city of six million international souls had grown too fast.

Pot ordered the car stopped at a grocer's stand, and Dhat, one of his guards, got out and bought mangoes and durian, a spiky fruit that he loved.

Just before reaching Yawaraj Road, the driver turned left into a narrow alley containing several houses and apartment buildings. He drove slowly until reaching the front of a narrow, newer building, then stopped at the curb.

Dhat got out of the car and explored the street with his eyes. He walked to the nearest structures and examined the doorways, then walked back and opened the rear door of the Lincoln.

"All clear?" Pot asked.

"*Chai,* Prince."

Pot got out of the car and was nearly run over by a bicycle that appeared from nowhere. He jumped back against the car as Dhat backhanded the boy on the bicycle.

The boy and the bicycle landed four feet away.

After examining the boy, no more than nine years old, for hostile intent, Dhat helped him up.

"I apologize," the bodyguard told the boy. "It was a mistake."

"Mai pen rai," the youngster said, pushing his bicycle away.

Never mind. It was the philosophical bent of the Thai people.

Pot crossed the sidewalk, and unlocked the front door with his own key. He pushed open the steel door, which had a wrought iron grille over its window, and stepped into a small foyer. There were two apartments in the building, the main floor quarters dedicated to Pot's employees who happened to be in the city on one errand or another. The upstairs apartment was his own.

A flight of steps with a black wrought iron railing climbed along one wall, and he immediately took them. On the landing at the top of the stairs, he was faced with another locked steel door which yielded to his key.

He shoved it open with a bang.

"Aie!" a small boy yelped, then gushed, "Father!"

He rose to his feet from the carpet of the living room, where he had been reading a book, and bowed to his father. At ten years of age, he had his father's lanky, black hair, and nothing else. He wore round, thick spectacles, and his chin receded as if he had no jaw at all. His stature was tiny, his shoulders thin and slumped. All in all, he was not very regal, and he was a disappointment to the Prince.

"Where is your mother?"

"I will get her."

He raced from the room.

Dhat stepped inside and looked around. It was a

large room, the far windows overlooking a large balcony decorated with white-painted wrought iron furniture and potted orange trees. The railings were draped with bougainvillea. Beyond the balcony was a view of Yawaraj Road and beyond that, the river and Chinese Town.

Satisfied that only the proper persons were in residence, Dhat withdrew and closed the door behind him.

Besides the large living room, the apartment contained a small kitchen, a dining room, a very nice Western bathroom, and two bedrooms. It should not have been difficult for the boy to locate his mother.

Pot walked across the deep-pile carpet to the sideboard and used another key to unlock it. He withdrew a bottle of Glenlivet scotch, checked the mark on the bottle to be certain it had not been tampered with, and poured several centimeters in a lead crystal glass. Lon Pot had acquired the taste for Scotch whisky from an American CIA agent with whom he did business during the crisis in Vietnam. He put the bottle back and relocked the cabinet.

"Master."

She said it in such an even-toned, noninflected way that it was difficult to interpret her as either softly yielding or brazenly insubordinate.

Lon Pot turned to face his wife, who stood in the entrance to the hallway. She was tiny, less than one-and-a-half meters tall, and obviously the source of his son's stature. She was also an exquisite miniature, with finely formed features, flowing hair so shiny it appeared to be silk, and delicate, almond-shaped brown eyes. She wore the traditional *ao dai* of her Vietnamese culture, this one a pale-cream with an intricate embroidery of rose petals outlined in gold.

He had bought her when she was fourteen, and she was now twenty-five.

"Hello, Mai."

"It is a pleasure to see you after so much time," she said. "Will you be here long?"

Again, the even tone of her voice displayed no pleasure, nor any reticence. Her vocal presence was always less demanding than the words she placed in her letters.

"Perhaps a week. It depends on events."

"We can look for a new apartment?" There was the first hint of a light in her eyes.

"Perhaps," he said, though he had no intention of doing so. A week from now, who knew where he might wish to live? It could be here, it could be in Rangoon.

Her flower-red lips parted in the trace of a smile.

"We will go to our room," he said.

She pivoted gracefully toward the hall and led the way.

The lady in the pink sweatband and stuffed blue sweatsuit yakked on and on. Dixon figured she was not talking to her lover, so it had to be her mother.

He sat on the blond wood bench in the middle of the mall and watched the people sauntering up and down the shiny, rose-tinted tile. They were dressed in ultra casual, and not many were carrying shopping bags. They weren't buying; they were cruising the neighborhood.

Brock Dixon felt out of place in his thousand-dollar charcoal suit.

Every few seconds, he glanced back at the woman gripping his telephone. Beside him, a huge, plastic philodendron in a redwood planter was coated with dust.

Two boys and four girls dressed in black leather and multi-hued tattoos stopped to peer in the window

218

of a formal wear shop. With the haircuts that made them nearly indistinguishable as to gender, he could not imagine them in tuxedos and gowns. Maybe they were going to have their own prom.

He checked his watch. Eight minutes late.

Get off the damned phone, lady.

A mall security guard moseyed along, staying close to the black leather.

Finally, she hung up and jogged away from the public phone, most of her moving in up-and-down directions.

Dixon stood and crossed to the telephones. There were three of them, side by side, but she had taken his.

He had almost reached it when it started to ring.

The security guard cast a questioning look in his direction, and Dixon chose to ignore it.

He grabbed the receiver.

"Yeah?"

"We're in New Delhi," Crider said.

"You think that's where they're going next?" Dixon wished he knew Kimball's schedule. He could have discovered just what it was with a few phone calls, but he did not want anyone remembering who made those few phone calls.

"Who knows? But we got out of Riyadh just as soon as the package was placed. Anything in the papers there?"

"The *Post* gave it almost two inches on page fifteen," Dixon complained. "All it said was that a plane crashed on a Saudi training mission and that there were no casualties. No mention of the manufacturer."

"Same thing in the international edition of the *New York Times,*" Crider said. "The Saudis are protecting Kimball's reputation for some reason."

"I can figure out the reason easy enough."

"What?"

"They know it wasn't an accident or design flaw. You screwed it up."

"You want to do it?"

"How did you set it up?" Dixon asked.

Crider told him about the small dab of plastic explosive in the electronics compartment.

Dixon shook his head.

The kids in leather had moved on, and so had the security guard.

"That was stupid, Crider. Those planes have two, maybe three systems. Even if the black boxes are side by side, and they must be if you succeeded, they have armor protection from the exterior. Two or three systems aren't going to fail at the same time, not for electronic reasons. They'll examine the armor and know the explosion came from inside the plane."

"You wanted aircraft engineers, you should have hired aircraft engineers. We can quit now and go home," Crider told him.

"No, damn it! You've got your money. Earn it!"

"Find me an itinerary," Crider ordered, which Dixon did not like. "Working off the cuff, on the spur of the moment, isn't going to do it. We need some planning time."

"That's too damned risky."

"Let's compare your risk to mine."

"I'll see what I can do," Dixon said and slammed the phone down.

Digging some quarters from his pocket, he picked up the receiver and dialed a number.

"Weapons Procurement, this is Linda."

"Is General Ailesworth in, Linda? This is Brock Dixon."

"Just a minute, sir."

When Ailesworth came on the line, the first thing he said was, "Pretty disappointing, Brock."

220

"You read the paper?"

"I read it every morning. Our friends aren't getting their money's worth."

"This last one was a good idea. It just didn't come off well."

"Banner headlines would be better. Lots of discredit falling where it belongs."

"You'll get them. Just hang on."

"It's a funny thing about time, Brock. When it runs out, it's gone. If the man from the desert makes one good sale, then he's a contender, and the committees on the Hill will take a good look at what he has to offer. We'll have civilians dictating hardware purchases to the services. Given the penny-pinching attitudes, I think there may well be a shake-up in traditions that have lasted decades. Where were you planning to work after you retired, Brock?"

Dixon had always thought that, after he earned his third star, he might snoop around for one of the major aerospace contractors. They always had a need for decent intelligence-gathering.

"Same place as you, Jack."

"They might not be there," Ailesworth said.

Which was overstating the case, Dixon thought. The industries would still be around, but they would be downsizing and scrambling and not hiring retired generals at inflated salaries. Unless, of course, they knew by word of mouth or some other way that Brock Dixon had helped them out when they needed it most.

"We're working on it," he said.

"Work fast. Time is money, as they say."

Islamabad was not Ben Wilcox's idea of an exotic paradise, not even close to it.

Kimball's recital about his downed Alpha Kat was

221

also not a story he wanted to hear.

Wilcox, Kimball, and McEntire were in Wilcox's hotel room. It was a small room, and they sat in straight chairs around the double-sized bed. McEntire had his big feet up on Wilcox's pillow.

"You said you were working on it," Kimball said. "What have you found out?"

"To date, not a damned thing." Mostly, that was because he had not been actively investigating who might be sabotaging Kimball's aircraft. There was no way in hell that he was going to get the Agency crosswise with the law concerning domestic activity.

"Shit."

"That's right, Kimball. I have my suspicions, of course, but there's not a rumor, not a whisper, out about any group that's targeting you."

"We all know who wants us to fail," Kimball said, with some earned bitterness.

"We all *think* we know," Wilcox said. "I'm looking around . . . I've got my people looking, but you've got to remember that we're not dealing with nerds. I don't think I'll ever be able to make a connection between the attempts on your aircraft and anyone who matters."

"I think you're probably right," McEntire agreed. "The CIA couldn't find its ass with ten assistant directors and a flashlight. We'll do it ourselves."

Wilcox gave him a dirty look, but decided not to get in a pissing match with him. Not just now, anyway.

"What do the Saudis say?" he asked.

"They're still investigating the remains from the crash scene, but offhand, they seem to agree with us. That bird was sabotaged," Kimball said.

"Any salvage at all in it?"

"No," Kimball said. "There was a secondary explosion, either fuel or another bomb. Then, the little packages we got from you went off and evaporated most of what was left."

"And you?"

"I'm okay. The back's a little stiff, but the headache's gone."

"We're out an airplane," McEntire said.

"You knew there was going to be a risk."

"Not from in back of us, we didn't. We're still a couple thousand miles from the danger zone."

"You're insured," Wilcox said, knowing they were not.

"On experimental fighter aircraft? How dense are you, Wilcox?"

"If I dig deep, I can maybe come up with another million," Wilcox told him.

"That's about two million short," McEntire said. "Transfer it to our accounts this week," Kimball told him.

On this quiet, hot night in Pakistan, there was a difference in the personalities. In Colorado, Kimball had been the reticent one and McEntire had been more than a little flippant. Here, the flippancy had disappeared. McEntire was being tough. There was a heavy current of anger running through the man, and Wilcox guessed it was probably the result of the near-miss with his best friend. McEntire was not likely to be very demonstrative with male friends though the feelings would run deep. That was contrary to his behavior with his female friends.

Kimball was very reserved, though not as negative as he had been in Colorado. He hadn't mentioned dropping the mission, so Wilcox figured he was still locked in on that.

"You've got to skip New Delhi," Wilcox said.

"Fuck that," McEntire said.

"I second Sam Eddy. Motion passes," Kimball said. "We're not going to blow even one of our chances to

223

show the airplanes. It might not ever come around again."

Wilcox weighed his alternatives, but the options were fast depleting. Simonson would not be happy with his divulging the information, but time was now crucial.

"There's a new factor," he said.

Kimball grimaced. "There always is."

"Tell us about the new factor," McEntire urged. "Then we'll cancel everything and go home."

"Our sources tell us there's a deadline."

"What sources?" McEntire asked.

"What deadline?" Kimball asked.

Wilcox shifted his gaze to McEntire. "There's no way in hell I'm going to give you a name. But the source is damned highly placed."

"Deadline?" Kimball asked again.

"July twenty-seventh."

"For what?"

"That's the tricky part of it," Wilcox said. "Lon Pot is staged for a coup. He's planning to take over the Burmese government."

"Shit!" McEntire said. "The druggie becomes a dictator? Never happen."

"Look at Colombia. Who's really running the important things?" Wilcox asked.

Kimball got up and paced in small circles near the end of the bed. Both Wilcox and McEntire watched him.

Kimball stopped suddenly and turned toward him. "You knew this from day one, right?"

Wilcox only considered lying for ten seconds. "Yeah, we did. Not that the drug angle doesn't weigh heavily, Kimball, it does. The major concern, though, is that Lon Pot could buy himself one government, then another."

"He's bought this one?"

"A lot of palms have been greased. We expect very little resistance to the takeover. And once he's got himself a country, he legitimizes his operations. That makes it tougher to combat, without obtaining UN sanctions. And those sanctions might be watered down."

Wilcox forced himself to slow down. He did not want to oversell.

"And more countries after that?" McEntire asked. "Is that what you're saying?"

"He's got his fingers in some Cambodian and Laotian pockets, too. The intelligence estimate . . . top secret, by the way, and not something I should be giving you . . . says he'll run into very little opposition."

"You believe the intelligence estimate?" Kimball asked.

"I wrote it."

"Damn it. Is this your scenario alone? How high does it go?"

"High enough."

"I want to know."

"That won't happen, Kimball. You got the money, didn't you? That tell you anything?"

"Have you been working this from a single source?" Kimball asked.

"Hell, no! I have five, one of whom is in a sensitive position." Simonson had four, and Wilcox had one.

"This highly placed spook," McEntire said, "he's naturally reliable."

"Naturally."

"For money, or for ideology?"

Wilcox thought about hedging on that one, but did not. "Money."

"That makes me feel better," McEntire said.

"The spook confirms your domino theory of coun-

225

tries tumbling to Lon Pot, one after another?" Kimball said.

"Lon Pot has started calling himself the Prince of Southeast Asia."

"Christ! How come the world has so many self-ordained saviors?"

"We see him becoming another Idi Amin, another Saddam Hussein."

Kimball abruptly plopped into his chair. "I wish we had something to drink."

"The twenty-seventh," Wilcox repeated.

"We're in Dacca then," Kimball told him.

"After the twenty-seventh, you'd be taking on a country, rather than a druglord."

McEntire dropped his feet to the floor with a thud. "He's still the same asshole."

"If things go the way they're supposed to go," Kimball said, "nobody sees us anyway. Who cares if we go up against Lon Pot or the next Burma?"

"The odds change," Wilcox said. "Lon Pot has already bought himself four Burmese squadrons for sure. There might be more. After the twenty-seventh, they're fighting for him."

"And what about before the twenty-seventh? If they're already bought?"

"They'll be confused. The squadron commanders won't want to commit themselves until they know which way the wind is finally going to blow."

Kimball leaned forward and placed his elbows on his knees. His eyes seemed particularly blue and particularly penetrating as they stared into Wilcox's.

"Bottom line, Wilcox. If we don't initiate sorties before the deadline, what?"

Wilcox hated the requirement of uttering the party line. "We call it off."

"Well, shit," McEntire said. "We're home free, then. We made us a few bucks, got the demo tour, and go

226

home without risking the guys. Good-fucking-deal."

Wilcox thought he read sarcasm in McEntire's statement, but he was not certain.

Kimball still had an eye-lock on him. "But you don't agree with the big boys?"

"Hell, no. I don't want to see Lon Pot convert Southeast Asia into his own playground. We'd see official sanction of his poppy-growing."

Kimball swung around to look at his partner. "Sam Eddy?"

"You and I need to talk by our lonesomes."

"Take a walk," Kimball said.

"Hey, it's my room," Wilcox protested.

"Go down to the lounge."

"They only serve tea."

"Drink tea."

Wilcox got up, grabbed his suit jacket, and headed for the door.

Kimball called after him, "Keep in mind, Wilcox, that we can't trust you anymore. You keep fucking with the story."

"You didn't trust me before."

"Maybe, maybe not."

Henry Loh met with his commanders.

Jake Switzer, a wizened and weatherbeaten ex-American whose F-4 Phantom had been shot from under him over Vietnam, and who had decided to walk away from his parachute landing rather than go back to the Marines at Da Nang, led the First Squadron. The unit, composed of four HAL Maruts and one Mirage 2000, was housed at Shan Base near Mong Tung. The well-camouflaged and equipped airfield also maintained several helicopters and seven transport aircraft.

The Second Squadron, composed of three MiG-23s

and four elderly MiG-19s, was hidden away at Muang Base on the Nam Tha River in Laos and was commanded by Pyotr Burov. A seasoned veteran of the Soviet conflict in Afghanistan, Burov had been a colonel in the Red Air Force at the time of the coup. It had occurred to him shortly after the coup's failure that his safety, his future, and his financial success might be better assured elsewhere.

The Chinese, Kao Chung, headed the Third Squadron of the Prince's Dragon Wing, the only wing currently. Chung had done most of his flying for the Chinese air force in the Fantan, a redesign of the MiG-19 which the West called the F-6bis. Now, he commanded a force of five Mirage 2000s, three Super Frelon helicopters, and six multi-engined, well-abused transports. Sited in northern Thailand, his squadron occupied what was known as Chiang Base.

There was another squadron, called the support squadron, composed primarily of tankers and transport craft for supplying the hidden bases, and Loh oversaw its operation.

The hierarchy of command in the Dragon Wing was meeting in Loh's headquarters at Shan Base. His headquarters was a Quonset hut concealed in the trees alongside the single runway and the interior was baked with the heat of day.

"At seven o'clock in the morning of the twenty-seventh," Loh briefed them, "Colonel Mauk will make an announcement on Rangoon radio. This will coincide with proclamations made by several army and police leaders. Mauk will say that the alteration in direction is positive and that his units will not interfere with a change in leadership."

"They will stay on the ground?" Chung asked.

"No. He will launch all aircraft before making his speech, and he will urge his fellow senior commanders to join him. He will also inform them that their units are grounded. Any aircraft taking off will be shot down."

Since Mauk commanded most of the Union of Burma Air Force strike aircraft, comprised primarily of Lockheed AT-33As and propeller-driven SIAI-Marchetti SF.260MBs, it seemed unlikely to Loh that any commander would oppose him.

"We will want show of force," Loh said. "The First Squadron will make its presence known in the north and the Chin State. The Second will fly high-visibility missions through southern Shan and along the coast. The Third will stay close to the southern coast and Rangoon, but not intrude unless I learn from Mauk that it is necessary. Within hours, by nine o'clock, I should think, I will notify you of airfields which have capitulated, and where you may land for refueling."

Pyotr Burov seemed less optimistic than the others. "What if this passive transfer of power does not occur? Mauk could betray us. Some of the helicopter commands may join with the army in opposition."

Loh grinned at the Russian. "If it occurs, it will make our day more interesting. Micah Chao will be in Rangoon, directing our efforts there, and he will keep me informed. I will instruct you and your flight elements if assistance is necessary at any point."

"And on the twenty-eighth?" Switzer asked.

"In the morning, I will fly to Bangkok and bring the Prince back. In the afternoon, we will proceed with the reorganization as we have discussed it. Jake Switzer will assume command of Dragon Wing, with the First Squadron and two T-33 squadrons of the UBAF. Pyotr Burov will have the new Lotus Wing, including the Second Squadron and the SF 260s."

Burov did not appear enthused about adding ten dual role strike/training craft to his new wing.

"And Kao will assemble the Moon Wing with his Third Squadron and the helicopter companies."

"What of Mauk?" Chung asked. "You have promised him a command, have you not?"

"Of course," Henry Loh replied, "but his usefulness will have come to an end."

It was after 11:00 P.M. when the Kappa Kat finally landed. Jimmy Gander was Hawkeye One, and it wasn't until Gander shut down the twin turbofans that Kimball felt the tension go out of his shoulders.

He crossed the ramp in the darkness and stood next to the command craft as the canopies raised. Walt Hammond and Wes Overly chocked the wheels and set the tie-down lines.

Soames climbed out of the lead controller's seat first, hefted a leg over the coaming, and came slowly down the ladder rungs.

"Smooth as silk, Kim."

"Hell, A.J., I'm beginning to worry if something doesn't go wrong."

They waited for Gander, Wagers, and Contrarez to descend from the cockpit, then they all headed for the lighted cargo bay of the C-141. It had become their mobile briefing room, as well as warehouse and workshop.

Kimball spun around to check the perimeter and counted all four guards. He had doubled the guard contingent. No one was allowed to look at the aircraft without an escort.

Inside the transport, Tex Brabham was passing Cokes around, and Sam Eddy was finishing a joke which must have been good. It drew a few heartfelt guffaws.

Kimball walked to the front end of the bay and scrambled on top of a missile crate. He turned to look at the faces aimed at him and raised two thumbs.

"Good show, guys. Not one hitch. Alex, how did your end go?"

Hamilton was dressed in a lightweight blue suit, but he had pulled his tie off. "Sam Eddy made a credible presentation. I outshined him, naturally."

"Naturally," McEntire said.

"There was one general," Hamilton said, "by name of Abassi, who kept giving Sam Eddy this come-on look. I think he's in love."

"What he is," McEntire said, "is needy. He's looking for a little cash in hand to help him make up his mind."

"We going to do that?" Soames asked. "Grease palms?"

"I'm not much in favor of it," Kimball said, "but you all know this part of the world. If a little *baksheesh* is expected, when and if the negotiations get further along, I suppose we'll have to oblige."

"We could give round-trips to Hawaii, instead," McEntire suggested.

"That might do it, Sam Eddy. Okay, in half an hour, we'll change the guards, then get everyone else to the hotel for a few hours. Sam Eddy and Alex will handle the debriefing, which is scheduled for six in the morning. With luck, we can be wheels-up by 7:30 A.M."

Kimball dropped off the packing crate and sat on it.

"We've got one more snag," he said.

"What's one more, with all we've had?" Halek said.

"This one could be intense." He told them what he and Sam Eddy had learned from Wilcox. "I told the man from Washington we wanted to get your reaction before making a decision. He's waiting for it."

"So the sucker's a wannabe dictator, in addition to a druglord," Mabry said. "I move that we put him down for the count."

"And longer," Keeper added.

"You're missing the point," McEntire said. "We're going to land in Rangoon the day after their air force changes ownership. We may be cancelled out, or we may be talking to brand-new generals."

"Or we may land in the middle of a civil war," Kimball added.

"Or?" Soames asked. "There's got to be another choice. What have you and Sam Eddy cooked up?"

Kimball told them about it.

When he finished, Gander said, "Doesn't bother me. Go for it."

The reaction was unanimous, and Kimball broke up the meeting.

They climbed into the vans that had been loaned to them and headed for the hotel. Kimball was sitting next to Billingsly, who leaned over and said, "Your girlfriend called."

"Cathy?"

"Cathy? Who's Cathy?"

"You said. . . ."

"I know what I said. A.J.'s all screwed up."

"What in the hell are you talking about, Connie?"

"Susan called. I told her you'd call when we got back to the hotel."

Jesus. Now, Billingsly and Soames had him lined up with Susan McEntire. He eyed Billingsly under the light of passing street lamps, but the man stared straight ahead, maybe just a little embarrassed.

When he reached the hotel, and then the third floor room he shared with McEntire, he waited until Sam Eddy had crawled into the bathtub before calling Phoenix. It was noon there.

"Kimball Aero Tech."

"Hey, Andrea."

"Kim! God, am I glad to hear your voice. Let me get Susie."

232

She came on a few seconds later. "You son of a bitch! You didn't tell me."

"Tell you what?"

"It was in the papers."

"What was in the papers?"

"The crash. Who was flying? Sam Eddy?"

"No, it was me."

"Damn it, are you okay?"

"I'm fine, Susie. A couple bruises. What'd the papers have to say?"

"Nobody was mentioned by name, not even the company. But damn it! We can read between the lines, Kim. You should have told me, so I could call the wives."

Kimball sighed. He wasn't thinking very straight.

"You're right, Susie. I'm sorry."

"Sam Eddy's a son of a bitch, too. I talked to him right after the crash, and he didn't say a word."

"I said I'm sorry."

"Have you seen a doctor?"

He told her about the doctor. "My prognosis is so good I'll have insurance agents calling day and night."

"I'm relieved," she said. "How is Sam Eddy doing?"

"He's in the tub, splashing water all over hell, and singing, *We'll Sing in the Sunshine.*"

"That's his theme song, all right," Susan said. "But he looks all right?"

"I'm not going to go in and peek. He's fine."

"You call me immediately if there's any more problems. Especially a crash! Goddamn it!"

"I do apologize, Susie. I had too much on my mind, and I forgot the courtesies."

"To hell with the courtesies. There's people here who love you, Kim. Don't let them down again."

Dial tone.

Kimball replaced the phone as Sam Eddy came out of the bathroom wrapped in a fluffy white towel.

233

"Did you know," McEntire said, "that I kept the rest of that cough syrup?"

"No lie? The Johnnie Walker syrup?"

"You want a shot?"

"We flying in the morning?"

"Nope. We're passengers."

"Just one, then."

McEntire poured them each a shot.

Kimball took his glass and a sip of the liquor. The warm liquid slithered down his throat.

McEntire pulled back the covers on his bed and slipped into it.

"Sam Eddy, you understand women, right?"

"Wrong. I'm the first to admit it."

"But—"

"It's your dilemma, buddy," McEntire said, "but I figure you'll work it out."

Christ! Everyone knew more than Kimball did.

On the night of July 22, Crider reached his contact in Alexandria again.

"I'm here," the man said, his voice tinny on the phone.

"And I'm here," Crider said. "What did you find out?"

"You're in the right place. They'll be in New Delhi tomorrow morning."

"Shit. That doesn't give me any time at all."

"And then Dacca on the twenty-sixth."

Crider tried to think of contacts he might make in Bangladesh, but a first run through his memory was not encouraging. Maybe he could get the ordnance he needed out of Sri Lanka.

"And after that?"

The man read off a list that ended in Manila. "But you can't wait much longer, Crider."

"Don't use my name."

"Sorry. The contractor is expecting results, and damned soon."

Crider looked at his watch.

"We're too short of time here. It'll have to take place in Dacca."

"Do it right."

"Don't sweat it. All the world is going to hear about this one."

He had decided to be less subtle.

TURBULENCE

Fifteen

Kimball had been a little more relaxed in New Delhi, Jimmy Gander thought. He and Hamilton had handled the brass and delivered the product presentations. And Hamilton, in fact, was becoming pretty proficient at the public relations thing from the way Kimball had praised him afterward.

Which was all right with Gander. He didn't want to be pressed into service as a glad-hander; he wanted to fly the missions, even if he had to play mama in the Kappa Kat as he had in India.

From the post-demonstration briefings conducted by whoever had served in the presentation role in Chad, Pakistan, and India, it was apparent that the Alpha Kat/Kappa Kat combination had impressed the observers for the most part. They oohed and aahed over the stealth and propulsion technology. Many appreciated the maneuver specifications and the vertical combat ability. Still, there seemed to be some reservations on the part of old-time air force commanders in regard to the tactical requirements, just as there was back in the U.S.

People, whether they were military aviators or not, were always resistant to change. When the F-4 Phantom was introduced, pilots generally reacted negatively. They didn't like the thought of the guy in the back seat (GIB). Pilots wanted to do it all; particularly not share victories with some navigator, but the reality was that the increased sophistication of the radars and weapons systems meant that the pilot didn't have time to do it all. He needed someone else to handle radar and weapons. And after they acclimated to it, the pilots came to love McDonnell Douglas's F-4, the American fighter with the highest production record of any American strike aircraft.

For those accustomed to two-seat Phantoms and the Navy's F-14 Tomcats, however, no one seemed to appreciate the efficiency of having one backseater in the Kappa Kat serving six to twelve fighters.

What was more, as far as the Phantom was concerned, the F-4 was utilized by the United States Air Force, Navy, and Marines. That was almost unheard of; the three military services normally fought like bear cubs to have their own distinctive, mission-dedicated aircraft.

The Alpha Kat and the Kappa Kat had been designed to take the stress of shipboard catapult launches and arrested landings, though they had not yet built a naval prototype. The airplanes were intended, like the Phantom, to be tri-service. And that capability, because of the in-born interservice jealousies, was a negative.

Another negative, as far as the reviewing committees had fed back to them, was that the Alpha Kat could not stand alone. They liked the price, but they didn't like the lack of electronics. The Indian Air Force, a large one with forty-five squadrons, had experience with Sukhoi Su-7, French SEPECAT Jaguar, and MiG-21 fighters. Pilots and commanders who liked the idea of solo flight wouldn't take kindly to the Alpha Kat's reliance on an airborne control craft.

Hamilton had found one sympathetic ear in an Indian Navy admiral. India was the first country on the tour which operated an aircraft carrier, the INS *Vikrant,* with a current aircraft complement of Hawker Siddeley Sea Hawks and Harriers. While the admiral appeared excited, Kimball and McEntire had been less so. A sale of, say, two squadrons of Alpha Kats to the Navy might undermine any sales to the Indian Air Force if the normal interservice rivalries were maintained.

Kimball and McEntire, and all of them for that matter, were banking on the downsizing of defense forces and the shrinking of budgets to overcome tradition, rivalry, and customary operational tactics to sell the Alpha Kat concept. All of those traits of air defense organizations were deeply ingrained and would be difficult to combat.

"Bengals, Hawkeye," Soames called on Tac Two, jolting Gander into a quick scan of his panel and the autopilot.

The five Alpha Kats chanted their numbers.

"Let's take it down to angels six and make a right turn to one-three-five."

Gander clicked his mike twice, reduced his throttle setting, and eased the controller over. On his right, Keeper, as Bengal Four, matched his turn.

The Kappa Kat and the two C-141s were ahead of him and lower by a thousand feet.

He assumed that somewhere along the way, Soames had received permission to enter Bangladesh's air space because the wide expanse of the Brahmaputra River could be seen about five miles away. The sun reflected nicely off the water's surface, and the jungle along its banks was a deep green.

Hiding the real Bengal tigers, no doubt. They'd be calling for Bengals Six through Ninety-Nine.

The two squadrons of the Bangladesh Defense Force (Air Wing) were based at Tezgaon and Jessore, but the demonstrations were scheduled to be mounted out of Dacca. Gander figured the Air Wing didn't want the visitors to see anything supersecret, but doubted that Kimball would be shooting photos of ancient Shenyang F-4s or MiG-19s.

241

The letdown and approach into Dacca was uneventful, and by eleven o'clock, all of the tour aircraft were parked, as had become customary, in a separate section of the airport. There were some military brass on hand to greet them, and Kimball, McEntire, Soames, and Hamilton were whisked away. Gander didn't think they were going bar-hopping.

Everyone pitched in to tie down the airplanes and run post-flight checks.

Everyone was subdued. The normal horseplay and macho jokes were absent.

Everyone knew this was the twenty-sixth of July.

Combat night.

Even Jimmy Gander was nervous.

Henry Loh sat alone in his office in the Quonset hut. In the outer office, he could hear Jake Switzer talking to his pilots, laying out their patrols for tomorrow morning. They would take off at six o'clock. Arrangements had already been made for them to land for refueling in Mandalay.

He picked up the telephone and asked the switchboard to get a number in Rangoon.

It was Mauk's home telephone, and he answered on the third ring.

"Good day, Colonel."

"Yes, it is."

"Our preparations are complete."

"That is excellent," Mauk said. "And timely. The anticipation has created something of a morale problem. It will be rectified by action."

"At five o'clock in the morning," Loh said, "I will call you with the final signal."

"I will be waiting."

Loh depressed the cancel bar, then told the switchboard to get him the number in Bangkok.

Lon Pot, also, was waiting by the telephone.

"We are ready," Loh reported.

"I have talked to the other chiefs," Lon Pot said, "and they also are prepared. We will proceed."

"After so many months of preparation, I am relieved."

"As am I, my friend. I will be near this telephone if anything unexpected should arise. On the morning of the twenty-eighth, I will be at Don Muang Airport."

"And I will pick you up there," Loh promised.

He hung up and sighed deeply. He really did not know how well the operation would develop. Colonel Mauk was not to be trusted fully. If the man wanted the remaining four hundred thousand dollars committed to him, he would deliver the Union of Burma Air Force.

If Mauk betrayed Lon Pot, he would eventually die, and slowly. If Loh's squadrons were ambushed by UBAF fighters, Loh would simply disappear.

And arise in Australia, or perhaps Tahiti, taking his long-deserved vacation. Later, he would find additional action elsewhere in the world.

The telephone rang and he picked it up.

As ever, he did not identify himself. "Yes?"

"I thought of one more thing," Mauk said.

"What is that?"

"The defense ministry, purely without the consent of the air force, has scheduled a demonstration flight on the twenty-eighth."

"A demonstration of what?" Loh asked.

"An American fighter called the Alpha Kat."

"I have never heard of it."

"It is a stealth-technology airplane. I have seen the specifications."

"Why did you not tell me of this earlier?"

"It did not seem important," Mauk said. "The country cannot afford new aircraft anyway."

While Loh considered the timing, he asked, "How many aircraft are involved?"

"From the schedule I received from the ministry, six fighter planes and one AWACS aircraft."

"They are to arrive on the twenty-eighth?"

"In the morning, yes. In Rangoon."

"Very well," Loh said, "if they do not cancel after the news breaks, let them come. We can always nationalize them and add them to our inventory."

"Excellent," Mauk said. "That is excellent."

For the afternoon portion of the presentation, Kimball sat in the audience of air force officers and defense ministry officials and let Alex Hamilton carry the ball.

Hamilton had missed his calling, Kimball thought. His professorial air gave him a facade of competence and knowledge, and yet, he didn't flaunt it. No arrogance, there. He had lost nearly twelve pounds since leaving the states, probably from lack of donuts and Danish as much as the heat, and in New Delhi, had had to have his suit taken in.

He looked smooth, and he spoke with a quiet, assured voice. He maintained nice eye contact with the audience, and even Kimball felt like he was welcome to buy a couple Alpha Kats. No rush, though. No pressure.

They were several miles north of Dacca, transported to the site by buses. Their rows of folding chairs were lined up under the fringe of jungle canopy, facing an open field. Several stewards moved about, offering cold drinks.

Out in the field, Walt Hammond and Elliot Stott had inflated one of the weather balloons from a helium cylinder. As he watched, the balloon lifted away, trailing its target package and a thousand-foot, slim nylon tether. The foot-square box suspended from the balloon contained a simple radio that emitted signals on the radar K-band, giving the radar-guided missiles something to home on. Additionally, the box contained a remotely fired flare, providing heat for the infrared seekers.

Kimball's portable radio burped with static, then reported, "Lion, Hawkeye."

Kimball raised the radio as a couple of his neighbors watched and said, "Go, Papa."

"Any time you're ready."

"Stand by."

Kimball signalled Hamilton, who departed from the holding pattern he had maintained with his presentation.

"As I mentioned a little earlier, gentlemen, the price of the Alpha Kat is kept as low as it is as a result of moving all of the high-cost electronics to the Kappa Kat. The fighter is, if we get down to earth about it, nothing more than a very maneuverable weapons platform. All it does is deliver the weapons. In the ground attack role, it can aim and release on its own.

"In the aerial defense role, however, in order to maintain its stealthy characteristics, there are shortcomings designed into the performance. Those shortcomings are made up in the control craft.

"The purpose of the exercise this afternoon, gentlemen, is to prove to you that two Alpha Kats can deliver missiles against an aerial target, utilizing the data links from the Kappa Kat. The weapons system officer is aboard the command craft, and he will make the target acquisition. That data is then fed to the attack aircraft, which will deliver the ordnance.

"For reasons of our visibility, the first fighter in will launch the AIM-9L missile from two miles, although as you know, the range could be up to eleven miles."

Kimball watched Hammond and Stott preparing the second balloon for launch.

"The second strike aircraft will launch the AMRAAM

245

active radar-targeting missile, which has an effective range of seventy miles. Again, so that we may see the performance, the launch will be made from two miles out."

Hamilton raised a forefinger in Kimball's direction.

"Hawkeye, Lion. Send Bengal One."

"Roger that, Lion. I've already acquired the target."

Hamilton swung an arm toward the east. "Gentlemen, you'll have to watch closely since the Alpha Kat's coloring is difficult to see even in daylight. You will want to watch the area of sky to your two o'clock, and in perspective, about three meters above the top of the jungle."

Kimball spoke to Hammond on the radio. "Kickapoo, light the candle."

"Roger, Lion."

Out in the field, Hammond used his remote control to set off the flare. Abruptly, a bright white fluorescence blossomed below the balloon, which was high above them.

"Don't look directly at the flare, gentlemen," Hamilton cautioned. "It may affect your vision for a moment. There! We have visual on the incoming airplane."

"What? Where . . . I don't. . . ."

"Look slightly to the right, around two-thirty on our clock face," Hamilton said.

Kimball spotted the Alpha Kat and heard others speak up as they finally found it. It was low, two thousand feet off the ground, and moving slowly, at around four hundred knots. They had decided to keep the speed down, to give the audience more than a couple of seconds of visual contact.

"The aircraft is moving at four hundred knots, gentlemen. The altitude is two thousand feet above ground level."

The fighter was a pimple on the sky for several seconds, visible because she allowed herself to be backlit

246

against the clear sky, then she rapidly grew in size. At two miles of distance, her canted rudders became discernible.

And two missiles lanced away from her, streaking thin white plumes of vapor behind them.

Both missiles appeared to spiral for a moment, as if their heat-seeking heads had lost contact with the target, then they locked on and whistled straight across the sky, rapidly accelerating to their top end of Mach 3.

They didn't have to hit the target actually. The proximity detectors would detonate them within twenty feet of the objective if they didn't hit.

One struck the box, and the other went off a few yards away.

A thousand feet up, with thirty pairs of eyes watching, the Sidewinders exploded.

There was only six ounces of explosive in the plastic case of each warhead, and not much of the detonation sound reached the audience. The balloon absorbed a few thousand plastic splinters, lost its buoyancy, and took a dive toward the far side of the field.

The Alpha Kat passed over a second later, already beginning a vertical climb.

Damn, she's beautiful!

Hammond let go of the second balloon.

"Once again, gentlemen, if you'll look to the east, we'll find our second fighter."

"Hawkeye, Lion. Number two," Kimball said into the radio.

"Roger that, Lion. Bengal Two's on the way."

The launch of the radar-seeking AMRAAMs went off without a hitch, and Alex Hamilton pointed out to the audience the fact that, immediately on launch, the Alpha Kat turned off and headed north.

"The AMRAAM has an active radar-seeker," Hamilton explained, "rather than semi-active. The missile is

Fire-and-Forget. Our Alpha Kat is already looking for her next target while the AMRAAMs are taking care of this one."

The second balloon also took two hits.

As they headed back toward the buses, one general asked Kimball if he could take another close look at the Alpha Kat, to assure himself that it did not have targeting radar. Kimball promised him that he could poke all over the plane. And he would stay close beside the man.

Climbing the steps into the bus, Kimball told Hamilton, "Nicely done, Alex."

"Think so?"

"Damned right. You're a natural."

"That's good, because I'm considering going into a television ministry."

Kimball grinned at him. "Which one?"

"MLBM Club."

"What's that?"

"My Lord has Bigger Missiles."

Six-and-a-half miles north of Dacca Airport, Derek Crider, Wheeler, Del Gart, Corey O'Brian, and Alan Adage worked quietly in the dark.

Gart opened both of the back doors of the rented van, climbed inside, and pushed the elongated canvas bags out to his cohorts.

Crider took his bag, weighing thirty-two pounds, found the canvas handles, and carried it off the road, down through a drainage ditch, and into the trees. The undergrowth grabbed at his ankles as he trudged along.

He could not see much, and he banged into the boles of several trees before he reached the tiny clearing thirty yards from the road.

The clearing was less than twenty feet across, but the stars were visible, and that was all that mattered.

The rest of the team emerged from the trees, and as his night vision became better, Crider could see their outlines as they knelt in the mixed grass and weeds and dirt and opened the bags.

Crider went to his own knees, found the big zipper with his hand, and pulled it open the length of the oblong case. Reaching inside, he withdrew the Stinger carefully.

He heard jet engines approaching and looked up. The clearance and strobe warning lights of an airliner appeared suddenly over the clearing. The silhouette blocked out the stars. That made it a clear enough target.

Having a couple of days planning time made all the difference. He had been able to reach his contact in Sri Lanka, and by the time Lujan put the Lear down at Dacca, the shoulder-fired Stinger surface-to-air missiles were already in-country.

He had used them before, as had Wheeler, Gart, and Adage. The whole unit weighed thirty-one pounds, and the missile itself weighed only twenty-two pounds. It carried a smooth-cased fragmentation charge, and it was guided by passive infrared targeting. The effective range was three miles.

He removed the protective covers and pressed a button to test the battery circuit. A green light told him the weapon was ready.

"You're absolutely sure we're in the right place?" Wheeler asked.

"Wind's out of the north, and will be all night long," Crider said. "They'll take off right over us. You saw the commercial airliner."

"We don't want to shoot down anything with three hundred people on it," Wheeler said.

"Why not?" O'Brian asked. "The panic would help us disappear."

"I'll tell you when to fire," Crider said.

249

Crider spread them out in a long row, Adage on the far left, and they all sat down to wait. Crider took the right end of the row and cradled the Stinger across his lap.

"This sure as hell won't look like equipment failure," Gart said. "If we manage to hit all five of them."

"They'll take off the same way they did in New Delhi," Crider said. "The command craft will go first, and we let it go. The fighters will take off as a pair, followed by three more. Alan, you and Del take the first two. Wait as long as you can, so the second flight doesn't scramble on us."

"It's not going to look like an aircraft failure," Gart repeated.

"At this point, I don't give a shit. But to get down to it, Del, it's a system failure. The infrared radiation on these planes is supposed to be low. When we hit them, they've failed, and no one's going to buy a plane that can be taken out that easily."

"You sure we can hit them, Crider?"

"The wavelength on these babies is less than four-point-four microns," Crider said. "They track on an exhaust plume, rather than hot metal. The other thing to remember, they'll be taking off under full power, producing more heat than they would at cruise. Another thing, on takeoff, I'm pretty sure they won't have activated the infrared threat receivers. We'll hit them. I want at least three of them to feel good."

"That's it? We're getting paid to make you feel good?" O'Brian asked.

"Fuckin-A."

Plus, he'd come out of it nearly a million ahead. That had made him feel good already.

The Kappa Kat had disappeared by the time Kimball received his takeoff clearances from Dacca Control. He was lined up on Zero-One Right, with Halek on his right wing.

On Tac Two, he said, "Let's roll, Barnfire."

Two clicks in reply.

Kimball shoved the throttle to the forward stop, watched his RPMs come up, then released the brakes.

The fighter slammed him back in the seat and played tricks with his facial muscles as it shot forward.

The HUD airspeed readout climbed quickly, and though he was loaded to the max with fuel and ordnance, he still got off the ground way short of the runway's end.

Halek was right beside him, his left wingtip light less than twenty feet away.

Passing over the outer boundary markers, Kimball retracted his flaps and landing gear. The airspeed rose quickly to 350 knots.

"Bengal Three rolling," McEntire reported on Tac Two as he started his takeoff run with a flight of three.

Kimball kept his rate of climb nominal, reading 150 feet per minute, as the lights of Dacca fell behind.

"Kill the lights, Two," he ordered, and he and Halek shut down their running lights and anti-collision strobes. They would continue transmitting their IFF signals for the next five minutes.

Kimball was trimming his elevator and ailerons when Billingsly's deep voice calmly reported, "All Bengals, IR threat. Go passive."

Sixteen

"Son of a bitch!" Wheeler yelled.

Crider could not believe it.

He had seen the shadows of the first two planes blot out the stars. As soon as the next three appeared, he had soberly said, "Fire."

He had had the Stinger trained on the far right aircraft in the second flight. The earphones chimed a lock-on, and he squeezed the trigger. The missile had leaped from the launch tube, hesitated a microsecond, and then the solid rocket engine ignited.

It had zoomed away, homing on the invisible vapor trail of the fighter.

Then began an erratic dance.

Five red dots of Stinger exhausts whipped haphazardly around the sky, looking for something to home on.

Then, one by one, they had exploded harmlessly as their rocket motors were spent.

The Alpha Kats were no longer there.

The shadows had evaporated.

Gone.

He leaped to his feet and started running through the trees back toward the road and the van.

"Come on, goddamn it!" he yelled at the others. He heard feet pounding behind him.

And slammed into the trunk of a tree.

* * *

With Hawkeye's warning, Kimball had automatically pulled the throttle back, immediately reducing the turbofan's heat output to nearly nil.

He watched the airspeed readout and eased the controller forward, putting the nose down in an attempt to maintain airspeed.

Counting.

Losing altitude fast.

Flipped on the infrared threat receiver.

Heard nothing.

No blinking visual alarms on the HUD.

Counting.

No one saying anything.

Reached fifteen in his count and began to increase power.

His altitude was down to three hundred feet above the jungle canopy.

Slowly, the nose came up. He added more power.

"Bengals, Hawkeye. I read five explosions. Give me a count."

Kimball keyed the transmit button. "One."

"Two."

"Three."

"Four."

"Five."

The relief coursed through him.

"They were surface-to-air, infrared-tracking," Billingsly said. "Probably infantry weapons."

"One, Two here. I want to go back and plant a missile up their asses," Halek said.

"Negative," Kimball said. "You'd give us away."

"Shit."

"Maintain protocol, Two," Billingsly said. "Let's go hot mike."

Kimball locked in his transmit mode.

"What do you think, Cheetah?" McEntire asked.

253

"Same bunch that has been playing tag with us. They're getting more aggressive."

"Getting desperate, you think?" Billingsly asked.

"Looks that way," Kimball said, scanning the HUD to see that he was climbing through eight thousand feet. His speed was up to five hundred knots.

"One thing we know," McEntire said, "there's at least five of them."

"We want to do anything about it?" Billingsly asked.

"Not now, Papa. We've got an exercise to run."

"Roger that. Bengals, go to zero-eight-five, continue climbing to angels two-zero. At altitude, take it to Mach 1.5. I read you in close proximity to each other at this time. Now, kill the IFF."

Kimball checked both sides of his canopy, blinked his wingtip guidelights once, and saw four low-wattage blinks in reply. Halek was on his right wing, and McEntire had brought his flight, with Gander and Makura, up on the left side.

"Roger that, Papa." He shut down the IFF transponder.

"I'm taking my radar off the air," Billingsly said. "Dart, take it to angels three-zero. Bengals, maintain course, altitude, and speed."

The target was 435 miles away. At Mach 1.5, approximately 1,100 miles per hour at their altitude, the target was 23 minutes away. With a decrease in speed for the approach to the target, and a time on target of less than thirty seconds, the round trip was going to take them about fifty minutes.

Kimball checked his watch. A.J. Soames and Alex Hamilton would just now be headed to the Bangladesh target area to brief the observers. He could count on Hamilton to while away the time in an interesting fashion.

The strategy for this demonstration had been changed. They had taken off an hour before the planned strike on the dummy target in order to give the Bangladesh air force a large block of time to try and find them.

He could imagine the F-6s and MiG-19 Farmers taking off from Tezgaon and Jessore right now. They would blunder around the Bangladesh skies, hoping to bump into their adversaries, if only by accident.

The adversaries, however, were no longer in Bangladesh air space.

Kimball checked the fuel load. Fuel consumption was right on the money. They had much more fuel than necessary for the mission, but he liked to keep tabs on it.

"Bengals, go to one-one-five."

"Roger one-one-five, Papa." Kimball eased the controller over, and when the new heading came up on the HUD, locked in the autopilot.

The course change meant they were now over Indian territory once again.

Seventy miles to the south-south-west would be the Bay of Bengal. He checked over his shoulder, but it was too dark on a moonless night to make out water. There were clouds to the south, too, but he couldn't see them.

He checked the armaments panel. He had two Mk 84 five-hundred-pound bombs on the centerline hardpoints. On the inboard pylons were four Hellfire air-to-ground missiles, and on the outboard pylons were four Sidewinders.

The other four aircraft were armed identically.

With the panel selectors, he chose the aft bomb and Hellfires one and three. Carl Dent had very carefully loaded the simulator weapons labeled Mk 84B and System Two in those positions. Two of the Sidewinders on the outboard pylons were also live weapons, just in case they ran into opposition from interceptors.

"Bengals, we're at eight minutes and counting," Billingsly said.

"Bengals, One. Select weapons."

Kimball received four affirmative responses.

"Papa," he said, "I want weapons release."

"Bengals, weapons are released."

Kimball armed his selected weapons, then deployed the laser and infrared targeting lens. He selected both the night vision and infrared modes. At six minutes out, he pulled the infrared reader down over his visor. The irritating yellow square appeared in his vision.

"Bengals, One. Trail formation."

Kimball switched off the autopilot and turned on his wingtip guidelights for a minute, to allow the others to fall into a single line behind him.

Billingsly would be double-checking his navigation equipment now, feeding in the coordinates that Wilcox had given them. The supposedly hidden airfield that Lon Pot called Shan Base had at least four Maruts, one Mirage, two Aerospatiale choppers, and five or six transports in residence. According to Wilcox's sources, the commander was an American deserter named Switzer. His record as an Air Force pilot stateside and in Vietnam was dismal, and Kimball didn't give a damn whether the man survived the raid or not. He and Sam Eddy had discussed the advisability of telling the others they knew about Switzer, then decided against it.

"Bengals, Hawkeye. I'm giving you a data-link."

Kimball switched on his primary receiver and took a few seconds to orient himself with the display on the CRT. His blinking blue blip was centered on the screen. Near the top was the target, shown in orange.

They did not have map overlays for this part of the world, but Billingsly had programmed the target's coordinates into the computer and the GPS navigation data placed the target in the correct location on the screen.

Kimball turned slightly to the right, centering his path toward the target.

"Bengals, no airborne traffic to speak of."

A minute went by.

Very slowly.

"Bengal One, Hawkeye. Begin your approach. We want four-zero-zero knots. Start your dive."

Every step of the attack had been planned during the briefing, but Billingsly would keep them on track with a checklist.

"Roger, Papa. Initiating approach."

Kimball retarded his throttle, and when the airspeed indicator dropped out of the Mach numbers, eased the nose over and deployed the speed brakes.

A glance through the canopy gave him only the impression of jungle. He couldn't really see it.

"Bengals, Hawkeye. Select sequence."

On the armaments panel, he set up the sequence of weapons selection, the two Hellfires first and the bomb last.

The orange dot moved down the CRT.

"Bengals, one minute," Billingsly said. "I'm going active for two sweeps."

The air controller checked the immediate air space with his radar, then switched it back to passive.

"Two unidentifieds to the south, six-zero miles," he reported. "Nothing airborne in the immediate vicinity."

Kimball switched the screen to night vision.

His blip and the target blip disappeared, replaced by a green-hued image of the jungle top. He raised his head, moving the lens upward, seeking something.

He eased the controller backward, pulling slowly out of his dive.

Flashed his wingtip guidelights once.

There.

A rent in the jungle.

Lighter green on the screen.

Coming up fast.

Checked his rate of descent.

Jinked to the left.

257

Behind him, Halek would be going to the right a trifle, to attack the right side of the field.

With a thumb wheel on the control stick, he magnified the camera's image.

The clearing in the jungle leaped at him.

Aircraft parked along both sides of the pierced steel plank runway.

He dropped his head slightly. The yellow square found a fighter.

Marut.

Fingered the commit button.

LOCK-ON flashed on the HUD.

Raised his head.

C-123?

Commit.

LOCK-ON.

The first Hellfire leaped from its rail, trailing a white hot exhaust that would have dimmed his vision if he had been looking through the canopy.

He eased to the right, centering on the runway.

The second Hellfire whooshed away.

He centered the yellow square on the middle of the steel plank airstrip.

Commit the Mk 84.

Ease back on the control stick.

The clearing, the runway, everything disappeared from the screen.

"One's clear."

As he pulled the nose up and advanced the throttle, the jungle in his rearview mirror erupted.

Pinpricks of yellow-red light. Bright spouts of yellow-blue-orange. Very quiet. He couldn't hear the detonations.

"Two's clear."

He dropped his right wing and went into a shallow right turn, peering out the right side of the canopy.

There were more explosions shattering the deadly

darkness of the jungle.

"Three's clear."

Fires began to rage out of control. He saw streaks of white light as more Hellfires poured into the clearing.

"Four's clear."

A tremendous volcano of red and yellow spouted near the east end of the runway. Probably fuel storage.

"Five's clear."

The HUD compass reading came up on 280, the heading selected at the briefing for the climb out, and Kimball leveled his wings, then added more power.

"Let me have a light, One," Halek called out.

Kimball gave him two flashes, and he sensed, more than saw Halek closing up on his right wing.

"Well done, Bengals," Billingsly said. "Now, let's go see if we can't show our hosts what the Alpha Kat can do."

Jimmy Gander, as Bengal Five, had been the last one through. He pulled out of his turn, calling to Makura, "How about a hint, Falcon?"

As soon as Ito Makura flashed a light for him, he eased up behind and above Makura's wing, then jockeyed the throttle until his speed matched.

"Bengals, Hawkeye. Sitrep."

One by one, they reported fuel and weapons status. All of the planned ordnance had gotten off, and none of the five reported damage of any kind.

Gander couldn't wait. He rewound the video tape for the nightsight camera and played it back at half-speed. The CRT gave him his moment in history.

He didn't remember seeing half of what the camera said he saw. His adrenaline had been as high as the first time he had soloed.

"Hawkeye, Five."

"Go Five."

"You want a bomb damage report?"

"Damned right," Billingsly said. "It's tough being in the dark up here. First, everyone up to Mach 1.5?"

After they all checked off on the speed, Gander said, "I'm on the replay. Coming in. Freeze. Before I let go, I see . . . well hell, there's a lot of smoke, fire everywhere . . . a 123 with a wing blown off; one, no two Maruts in flames; a truck in pieces. Advancing tape."

The green tinted images were difficult to interpret with the thick haze of green smoke swirling around. He saw men running, some as if they were in panic. He hadn't noticed them at all on his run. After glancing ahead at the dim outline of Makura's Alpha Kat, he looked back to his CRT and continued, "There's a Mirage on the south side of the strip with its nose blown off, flaming. C-47 on fire. There's a DC-6 that looks okay, but I fired on it. My Hellfire's frozen just before impact. Jeep on its top. Big damned holes in the runway, debris still flying through the air. Advancing tape. The Hellfire hit the DC-6. Another Marut on fire. Small single engine, maybe an old Aeronica, in flames. Aerospatiale that I launched on. Another chopper in pieces. Jesus! They were shooting at us!"

"Who?" Kimball asked.

"Couple guys with rifles. Maybe they saw us in the light of the flames. I don't think I was hit. Coming on through. Whoo! That had to be a fuel depot. Nice shot, Falcon. I went through the flames, so they must have been a couple hundred feet high. That's it."

"I count three Maruts, a Mirage, two choppers, three transports," Billingsly said. "That's an expensive night for someone."

"Think we put a crimp in their plans, Cheetah?" McEntire asked.

"If I was in charge back there, Irish, I'd spend the rest of the night reevaluating."

"Bengals, Hawkeye. We're fifteen minutes away from

the target. I want everyone to pull the audio and video cassettes and store them. Insert fresh cassettes. Do it now."

After Billingsly received affirmative responses, he said, "Secure the two Mod-two Sidewinders now. I won't allow accidents."

Gander checked his armaments panel and de-selected the live AIM-9s.

"All right, Bengals. One, take your element to two-six-five. Three, go to three-one-zero."

"One, roger two-six-five."

"Three going three-one-zero."

Gander counted to two, then banked right into the new heading.

The excitation level of his blood had just about come back to normal. This was going to be a boring run.

A.J. Soames and Alex Hamilton were at the demonstration site with around twenty Bangladesh air force officers and two civilians. They were under a large canopy illuminated with red lights. Most of the observers were gathered around two large tables loaded with sandwiches.

Hamilton seemed to be at ease as he mingled in the crowd, talking to anyone who wanted to talk.

Soames was fidgety. The portable radio was slippery in his hands, coated with his own sweat.

The radio came to life. "Lion, Hawkeye."

He raised it to his face and said, "Lion."

"I think we've given them enough time to try and find us. We're commencing the exercise with five."

At the crackle of radio static, Hamilton had looked over at him.

Soames smiled and nodded.

"Gentlemen," Hamilton said, "I hate to disrupt the excellent meal, but I believe we're under attack."

He got some smiles in return.

"If you all would like to step outside and look toward the target, I can promise you that in a few minutes, there will not be a target."

The fires were out.

Except for the raging flames rising from the destroyed fuel tanks at the northeast end of the field.

Six hundred thousand imperial gallons would burn for a long time.

The thick, acrid smoke hung heavily in the windless clearing. Henry Loh had ordered the engines of the two undamaged aircraft, a Cessna 310 and a Douglas DC-4, started, and the planes had been turned in place in the attempt to fan the smoke with the propellers.

A dozen men toured the mounds of wreckage with fire extinguishers, searching out hot spots. At Shan Base, water was in short supply, and they did not have an effective fire control plan.

In fact, no plan had ever been developed for an attack on Shan Base. It was too well disguised. It would never happen. Henry Loh had known that.

Henry Loh was stunned.

He and Jean Franc, who served as his executive officer, walked the southern side of the strip, examining the remains of the First Squadron. As far as he could tell, less than ten percent would be salvageable as spare parts. No airplane that had been hit would fly again.

Halfway down the airstrip, they met Jake Switzer coming toward them. Like themselves, he was carrying a six-cell flashlight.

Switzer was chanting drawn-out repetitions of American obscenities.

"Jake?" he asked.

"I just cannot fucking believe this, Henry. We're wiped out."

Franc waved at the two aircraft whose engines were roaring at half-power settings. "Just the two left?"

"That's the sum of it," Switzer said. "You get a casualty count?"

"There are four dead and three wounded," Franc said. "One pilot lost, as well as three technicians."

"Fuck. Who's my pilot?"

"Lung. He was sleeping in a hammock under his Marut."

"Dumb shit."

"The ordnance dump?" Loh asked. It was located on the east end of the field, a half-kilometer to the south.

"It's all right. We've got more fucking missiles than we need. We can't deliver them anywhere."

He did not need to ask about the fuel stores. He thought of the endless trips they had made with the tankers, amassing their supply of aviation gasoline and JP-4 jet fuel.

Loh trained his light on the center of the runway. Pierced steel planking had been ripped out of the surface. Splinters and shards of bent steel were everywhere. A crater three meters deep and ten meters in diameter was carved almost exactly in the center of the runway.

"It'll take us two fucking days to repair the runway," Switzer said.

"We will recruit from the Hsong tribe," Loh told him. "It must be done in one day."

"Shit! Have you talked to Burov or Chung? If they got hit, too, we're done for."

"Not yet. The telephone lines are being repaired. I do not wish to use the radio."

The three pilots turned around and began walking to the west, crossing the runway between two craters. They entered the trees, trudging toward Loh's Quonset hut. Farther back in the jungle were hooches and tents utilized by the pilots and ground support people. None of them had been damaged.

As they entered the Quonset, their boots beating on the wooden floor, an Indian communications technician told Loh that the telephone line had been repaired.

He went straight back to his office, sat at the small wooden desk, and lifted the telephone.

He called Chung first.

The commander of the Third Squadron was not in bed.

"We are almost ready to launch aircraft, Henry."

"You may put them on standby, Kao." He briefly reported on the attack at Shan Base.

"No! It is impossible! Who?"

"I do not know, Kao. There were five aircraft. They fired ten missiles and dropped five bombs, probably five-hundred pound bombs. That would make them light ground assault craft. Two of my men saw the fifth airplane, but they describe it only as a delta-winged fighter. There were no markings that they recognized, or could see."

"Mauk? Would he have betrayed us?"

"He would be my first suspect," Loh said. "It is likely that he knows the location of Shan Base. I do not know where he would obtain the aircraft my men described."

"I will launch aircraft now and obliterate our fine Colonel Mauk," Chung said.

"No. Let me first make telephone calls. And send me one of your helicopters immediately."

Loh hung up, then called Burov. Their conversation was a copy of the one he had just held with Chung.

When he had finished with the ex-Soviet, he said, "Jake, you and Jean should start making calls around the province. Tell everyone to hold in place until they hear from me. Jake, call Micah Chao and Vol Soon, first."

"You will call the Prince?" Switzer asked.

"I will call the Prince," Loh said.

264

When the telephone rang, Lon Pot was sound asleep.

He awoke, but stayed warm on his side of the bed while Mai got up and went to the living room.

She came back quickly. "Master, it is Henry Loh."

Rubbing his eyes with the knuckles of his fists, Pot slipped out of the bed and walked naked into the living room. He picked up the receiver resting on the sideboard.

"There has been a setback, Prince."

That woke him up.

"Setback! What is this of a setback?"

"The First Squadron has been totally demolished."

"That is not true."

"It is unfortunately true, Prince." Loh quickly detailed the attack.

"Mauk. It must be Mauk." Pot felt the anger building deep in his stomach, spreading throughout his body. He would have heads impaled on poles. They would be carried through every village.

"That is possible, but not yet proven."

"Send Chung against him."

"We must not react just yet, Prince. A commander does not make decisions on impulse. We must have more information before deciding on a course of action."

"But we are to make the transition today," Pot insisted. He rubbed the center of his chest. His heart felt as if it were on fire.

"It must be delayed."

"I will not tolerate delay. Today is the day I become Prince of Burma."

He could hear Loh's sigh.

"Is that not so?" Pot demanded.

"If Mauk has betrayed us, then all of the Burmese army and air force may be waiting in ambush, Prince. I must go to Rangoon and learn what I can. I must meet with Micah Chao."

"How long must this delay take?" Pot asked, his aspirations sinking.

"At least two days, I think. The morning of the twenty-ninth."

"Make it so," Pot said and slammed the telephone down.

He turned toward the bedroom, feeling the heat suffusing his face.

Mai waited in the hallway for him.

"Master? Is—"

The flat of his palm caught her on the low side of her neck, and the blow smashed her against the wall.

"Goddamn it!" Wilcox shouted over the phone. "They were supposed to attack Chiang Base."

"They didn't," Simonson told him. "I've got the satellite photos on the desk right in front of me, Ben."

"That sonovabitching Kimball pulled a switch on me!"

"Tit for tat, I'd guess," Simonson said.

"Jesus!"

Wilcox was up and dressed. He had been waiting in the secure room of the American Embassy in New Delhi for Simonson's call. The Deputy Director of Operations was monitoring the action in Burma through the National Security Agency's overhead reconnaissance.

"What's the damage?" Wilcox asked.

"Damned near total, from what we can interpret of the photos. The jungle overhangs the area along the strip, and we don't get a clear view, but it looks as if there were a hell of a lot of airplanes on fire. That would be the whole First Squadron of the Dragon Wing, from what you told me. Almost a third of Pot's air force."

"You think that'll cancel his coup, Ted?"

"If it doesn't, it still buys us some time. I've told my people to get out and listen for rumors."

Wilcox couldn't get over Kimball's treachery. "Goddamn it. It was supposed to be Chiang Base."

"What the hell, Ben? He accomplished the purpose. Who gives a shit about Shan Base, anyway?"

"My source does."

"Why?"

"That's where he's supposed to be."

Seventeen

The Aerospatiale Gazelle five-seater was the helicopter assigned to Henry Loh by Lon Pot. It was painted in ivory with a twin band of red stripes running fore and aft. Lon Pot envisioned the twin red stripes on an ivory background as his eventual flag.

Kao Chung had sent it to Shan Base in the middle of the night, and Henry Loh had commandeered it for his trip to Rangoon, where he landed at four-fifteen in the morning.

Micah Chao was waiting for him.

The Police Chief was obviously not in good humor. In Rangoon, which was not yet officially Lon Pot's territory, of course, he was not allowed to wear his camouflage uniform and his Sam Browne belt. Without the belt and his huge Colt .45, he did not appear to carry the authority to which he felt he was entitled.

Loh slid out of the pilot's seat as the rotors ran down and ducked his head against the swirl of heated air. Despite the early morning, it was still sticky lukewarm in Rangoon, and once he left the rotor's downwash, the heat licked at him. He crossed the ramp with long strides to where Chao waited beside his Renault sedan.

The storm that covered Chao's face was reflected in his voice. "Tell me what happened."

Loh detailed the events quickly and then asked, "Have you suspended your operation?"

Chao nodded, somewhat miserably. "The snipers have all been pulled back."

Chao had his hand-picked sniper teams placed all over the city, ready to neutralize those high-level police, military, and government officials who did not favor a change in the status quo.

"This is not good for morale," Chao argued. "Any delay at all makes the men tense and more susceptible to error. We should have proceeded, despite the losses."

Henry Loh passed the blame to Lon Pot. "It was the Prince's decision. If Colonel Mauk has betrayed us, then we need to know what other surprises await."

"Mauk? Why Mauk?"

"Who else controls attack aircraft?"

"Perhaps the Thais. Mauk never left his quarters last night. Two regular patrols of SF.260MBs flew from here last night, nothing more."

"You are certain of this, Micah?"

"Absolutely. My intelligence network is utterly reliable," Chao boasted.

The policeman's certainty undermined Loh's confidence. He had been positive that Colonel Mauk had changed his mind, or had his mind changed for him, and initiated the surprise raid. In fact, Loh had looked forward to a confrontation with Burma's ragged air arm. He had always wanted to be an ace, and he had foreseen five or more slow 260MBs falling to the missiles and guns of his Mirage.

"We have a serious problem, Micah, if we do not know our aggressors."

"That is the first thing you have said with which I agree. Do we have a new date?"

"Yes, the twenty-ninth. But we must first determine the origin of the attack on Shan Base. If not, we may have to delay longer."

"Lon Pot would not agree," Chao said.

269

"If it meant the possible failure of the coup, he would be forced to agree."

Chao leaned back against the fender of the automobile and considered him with mean eyes.

"You have radar, antiaircraft guns, and surface-to-air units at each of the bases. . . ."

"As well as the Prince's compound and many of Vol Soon's army garrisons," Loh added.

"And yet, your elaborate defenses did not anticipate this attack. How is this possible?"

Loh did not like interrogations. They reminded him of the severe questioning he had once undergone at the hands of a Khmer Rouge maniac. He kept his voice steady, however, in response. "Squadron Commander Switzer is now interviewing the radar and missile crews, but it appears that they saw nothing. That is not impossible, Micah. The hostile aircraft could have flown low enough to evade radar contact."

"Across several hundred kilometers of Burmese territory? Without being spotted, or heard, by persons on the ground?"

"Difficult, yes. Impossible, no."

Chao pushed himself away from the fender. "Let us go see Mauk."

"We should not risk public contact with him," Loh protested.

"The risks have changed, have they not?"

Henry Loh nodded and crawled into the back of the car. Chao's driver started the engine and found his way to the airport gate, then into the labyrinth of streets that crisscrossed Rangoon.

Colonel Kun Mauk's residence was a narrow, two-story, French-styled villa cramped on a small lot overlooking the river. The driver spun the wheel and slid the car into the drive, startling the single guard standing nearly asleep against the trunk of a sugar palm.

He came to belated attention, but did not offer a

protest as Chao and Loh left the car and climbed the three short steps to the front door of the villa.

The ground floor windows were already illuminated. Mauk would have risen early on this important day.

When he opened the door readily at Chao's insistent banging, he was already dressed in his uniform. He eyed them both, then nodded them inside with his head.

"There is trouble, then?" Mauk asked.

"You will need to postpone your part of the operation," Loh said.

"For how long?"

"Two days."

"I will make a telephone call."

Loh and Chao followed him from the foyer into a small living room and waited while he made a single telephone call.

He replaced the receiver after issuing curt orders, then turned to Loh. "The nature of the problem?"

Loh explained it to him in detail.

"There were no radar contacts?"

"None. Would the Thais have intervened?"

"I think not," Mauk said.

"Who then?"

Mauk's eyes were opaque as he considered the possibilities. "The Americans."

"That is insane," Chao insisted.

"Not so," the colonel said. "They have long been concerned about stability in the region."

"Not to the point of armed interference," Chao said. "From where? An aircraft carrier?"

"From Dacca."

"Dacca! *You* are insane."

"There is a demonstration group of stealth aircraft on display there. I told you about them, Henry. The airplanes would be capable of making such a strike," Mauk said. "The distances are not long."

Loh was incensed. He had not known that the aircraft were nearby. His intelligence-gathering capabilities were limited.

"You told me they were due in Rangoon on the twenty-eighth, Colonel. You did not tell me they were poised to strike against us."

"And how would I have known that?" Mauk said. "I know only that this American, Bryce Kimball, will show his airplanes to us."

"What do they look like?"

Mauk's eyes focused on something else. "The brochure had a drawing. I think they are smaller than most interceptors. A delta wing, almost. Twin rudders. I remember that it uses a single jet engine."

Exactly what his man had seen, or thought he had seen. Loh could not understand the treachery. "It is the Americans!"

Micah Chao offered a twisted grin. "To whom will we complain? The United Nations?"

"We will assure that it does not happen again," Loh said. "I will order Chung's squadron to attack them in Dacca. The Bangladesh Air Force will not intercede."

"It is unnecessary," Mauk said. "They will be here in the morning. Why should we destroy the airplanes when we can use them?"

Both the afternoon aerial demonstration and the night ground attack exercise had gone smoothly, and Kimball was more than satisfied. He, A.J. Soames, and Alex Hamilton had conducted the post-demonstration briefing for three hours in the morning, and the Bangladesh defense establishment had appeared duly impressed. Kimball left the conference feeling that, if they could find the money, they would spring for enough aircraft to complete one or two squadrons.

For a change, their schedule gave them an afternoon

free. They weren't due to fly into Rangoon until morning, and as soon as his cab reached the hotel, Kimball headed for the room he shared with McEntire. Except for the guard contingent at the airport, most of the KAT employees were touring Dacca or sacking out.

Kimball intended to sack out.

Sam Eddy was already in the room, slouched in one of the two chairs at a small table. Two glasses and the bottle of Black Label were on the table in front of him.

Kimball shut the door. "Drinking without me?"

"Just looking at it, waiting for you to get back. How did it go?"

"If it weren't for the committees that have to get involved, we'd have had some signatures on the dotted line. Sometimes, I wish we were selling used cars."

"Too easy, Kim. You and me, we've always made it more difficult than it had to be. You want?"

"I want."

McEntire picked up the bottle and poured them each a couple inches of scotch.

Kimball flopped in the chair opposite him and took a sip from the glass. It went down smoothly despite its iceless warmth.

They had been so busy in the last couple of weeks that Kimball hadn't taken a good look at his best friend for awhile. He was conscious now of a subdued aspect to Sam Eddy that didn't seem usual.

"You doing all right, Sam Eddy?"

"Me? I'm doing Jim dandy, Kim-O."

"Any after-effects from the mission?"

McEntire thought about it and then shrugged. "Naw. It felt good. The airplanes did what we knew they'd do. And I'm damned glad everyone came through it clean."

"Me, too. I was sure the first attack would be a real surprise, and I didn't expect any ground fire. It looks

273

like there were a few potshots, but we didn't find any damage to Jimmy's plane."

"Next time," McEntire said, "I want to be the last one through."

"Next time, we'll change the tactics."

McEntire poured them each another half-inch. "Next thing you know, we'll be out of booze."

"We can stock up in Bangkok."

"Yeah, Bangkok. What about Rangoon? You think we can stretch enough time on the night flight to reach, what is it? . . . Chiang Base?"

"Shouldn't be a problem. Another half hour of flight time. And we want to put a little fear into that army garrison at Mawkmai."

"Too bad we don't have something nuclear with us," Sam Eddy said. "We could waste us a lot of poppies."

"Next year, on the next tour, we'll bring defoliants with us." Kimball wished that someone in world government had the courage to wipe out the production capability of the Golden Triangle.

"Next year, you bring defoliants with you."

"Retiring, are you?"

"Sure as hell thinking about it," McEntire said. "I'm getting too old for this shit."

Kimball sipped his scotch and studied McEntire, then finally decided the man was just tired. They all were. Adapting to a round-the-clock routine wasn't easy.

"What are you thinking now?" he asked.

"I'm thinking they'll be ready for us next time. We'll see some SAMs and some triple-A, whether they can track us or not."

"Probably. You getting worried?" Kimball asked.

"Not me, babe."

"I know who is. We should make a couple calls."

"Probably."

"It's after midnight in Phoenix. Let's get Susie out

274

of bed for a change. Go ahead and ring her up."

"You do it, Kim. She won't want to talk to me."

"Sam Eddy, what the hell? Are you—"

"No, Kim. It's not up for discussion."

"She still loves you," Kimball said.

"She's a beautiful lady," McEntire said, "in more ways than one. Let's just say I disappointed her, and now she's confused. My fault, and I admit it. End of discussion."

Kimball lifted the receiver from the set on the table, got the switchboard, and placed his transoceanic call. He had to wait six minutes before the call was completed and the operator rang him back.

"Sorry to get you out of bed," he said.

"I wasn't in bed," Susan said. "But I was thinking about it."

"First of all, everyone's in great shape."

"Sam Eddy?"

Kimball looked over at him. "Maybe a little tired. We all are."

"Did you. . . ."

"Yes. A-okay."

"It was earlier than planned," she said.

"Yes. There's a new situation, but we think we've delayed it."

"Just two to go," she said, and he knew she was talking about the extracurricular activities.

"That's all."

"Give my love to everyone."

"Everyone will be happy to hear that."

"And you be careful, Kim."

"That's me, thinking about number one."

"Why don't you let the others do the flying? You're the president, and we need . . ."

"Susie."

"Sorry. Call me tomorrow."

Kimball hung up. "The long-distance billing is going

to be higher than the fuel bill."

"She worries about you," Sam Eddy said.

"I don't know why."

"Someday, you'll have to sit down and think about it. What about Wilcox?"

"I don't think he's going to be happy with us."

"That'll improve my day," McEntire said. "I'll make this call."

Emilio Lujan landed the Learjet in Rangoon at eleven o'clock in the morning. The six of them cleared the Customs section and were checked into their hotel by 12:30 P.M. They had lunch in the dining room, then gathered in Crider's room.

"Suggestions?" Crider asked. He rubbed the side of his nose, which was still sore. He had damnéd near broken it when he ran into the tree. It was swollen and red.

Lujan opened the French doors to the balcony and stepped out onto it. Crider figured the pilot didn't want to hear, or know, more than it was necessary for him to know.

"The fucking missiles sure as hell didn't work," Del Gart said.

"There's too much we don't know about those planes," Wheeler said. "They obviously had some kind of infrared threat warning capability."

"I'll bet I could hit a tire or two on takeoff, if I had the right rifle," Alan Adage said.

"Tires go flat," Crider said. "That wouldn't look like a manufacturing problem unique to Kimball Aero."

"Shooting five planes down with Stingers isn't much of a manufacturing defect," Wheeler noted.

"It could have looked like one plane malfunctioning and colliding with the others," Crider said.

"Not bloody likely," O'Brian told him.

"Or terrorist hits, showing the planes aren't as

stealthy as Kimball Aero advertises," Crider added, which had been his scenario from the beginning.

"Let's get real," Wheeler said. "Rehashing history isn't doing the job."

Crider thought about it for a few minutes, then said, "Maybe we're going at this the wrong way. The contractor wanted us to make it look like a manufacturing problem, and that's the route I followed the first couple of times. But then I thought that the contractor may be a little shortsighted, so we tried it as a breakdown in infrared detection. Obviously, that didn't work either."

Wheeler licked his lips. With the napalm scars on his right cheek, his lips always looked dry. "What you're saying, Crider, is that you don't want the Kimball Aero planes to live up to their billing as stealth planes?"

"Right. Can we make them visible on radar? We could destroy their reputation right there, without having to plant any more explosives."

Del Gart, who had the most experience with electronics, got out of his chair and wandered around the room. The others watched him.

Finally, Gart said, "Yeah, if I can find the right components, we can rig up something. We could even arrange some other problems."

"Such as?" Crider asked.

"Missiles or bombs get hung up on the aircraft, for one. Landing gear doesn't deploy. Things like that."

"I like it," Crider said. "But let's keep it as simple as possible because we don't have a hell of a lot of time. You sit down, Del, and figure out what you need. When you've got a list, the rest of us will get out and find what you need."

Gart got himself a sheet of stationery and a ballpoint pen from the desk, then sprawled out on the bed.

When Ben Wilcox got back to the Embassy, there was a message for him. The message said, "Stay in your damned room."

He hadn't expected to hear from them so soon. He got a Seven-up and took it to the secure room.

He waited nearly an hour, sitting at a scarred table and reading Indian travel brochures, before the communications specialist signalled him and he picked up the phone.

"Yeah?"

"About time you got back," McEntire said.

"Where are you calling from?"

"My hotel. I'll play your game; no details."

"What in the hell were you two thinking about?" Wilcox asked.

"Life. Love. The pursuit of happiness."

"You picked the wrong place."

"No, it was delightful, old boy. In the middle of sleepy-time. No one was expecting us."

"Goddamn it! You're taking my orders."

"You get to see the pictures?" McEntire asked, ignoring him. "I'm sure you've got pictures."

Wilcox eyed the stack of satellite photos resting on the corner of the table. Simonson had transmitted them to him early in the morning.

"I saw them."

"What's it look like?" McEntire asked, with obvious enthusiasm.

"You levelled the place. There were four KIA."

"That's damned good camera resolution says this engineer. You actually saw the dead bodies?"

"I talked to my source."

"We read the papers this morning," McEntire said. "Nothing seems to have happened on the twenty-seventh in a certain Southeast Asian nation. Do you

278

think we scared them off, Mr. Washington?"

"It's been delayed," Wilcox agreed.

"So it's safe for us to fly in there tomorrow?"

"It's been delayed until the twenty-ninth."

"Hey, at least we had an effect!"

"Not a good one. You endangered my source."

"Better him than us, right?" McEntire asked with a clear lack of empathy.

"And as a result, the people that count have decided to call it off."

"Being in the line of fire, as we are, we tend to think of ourselves as the people who count."

"Forget it," Wilcox said. "It's over, and you fucked it up."

He couldn't help being bitter. He'd had it so well planned, and now Simonson and the DCI thought Kimball's people were rogues, uncontrollable. And they were right.

The echo on the line deadened as if McEntire had covered the mouthpiece.

"Hey!" Wilcox shouted.

No response for a second, then McEntire came back and said. "After a quick conversation with my colleague, we've decided that we disagree with you."

"I don't give a damn what you decide. You just stick to your primary schedule and forget the rest of it."

"I'm glad you don't care," McEntire said. "It makes it easier."

"Makes what easier?"

"We're talking in the abstract, remember?"

"You're not making any sense at all," Wilcox said.

"Now you're catching on," McEntire said. "I knew you could do it."

And hung up.

Wilcox replaced the receiver very deliberately, then crossed the room to where the communications technician sat at his console. The tech hit the eject button on the recorder and handed him the tape.

At least, Wilcox had his own ass covered.

A.J. Soames and Conrad Billingsly were passengers this trip, sharing a seat on the lower bunk in the crew compartment of the lead C-141. When he heard the engines throttled back, Soames checked his watch: 11:02 A.M.

"Magnificent Burma coming up, Connie."

"I'm ready for it. I hope it's ready for us."

Gander was flying in the left seat and had been bitching about it all the way. But he landed the giant transport as smoothly as if it had been a passenger-laden DC-10.

Soames felt the plane turn off the runway and stood up. He was ready to find his way to the hotel.

"A.J.! Come on up here!" Gander called.

Soames climbed the short ladder, edged past Keeper, who was serving as the flight engineer, and leaned over the control pedestal to peer through the windscreen.

A man on the ground was waving his arms, flagging them into a parking place.

And surrounding the parking area were about a hundred uniformed and armed soldiers.

"I don't like the looks of this at all, A.J." Gander told him.

Soames didn't like the looks of it either. "Think we should turn tail, Jimmy? Try to get back in the air?"

Mel Vrdlicka, riding as copilot, said, "It ain't going to happen, A.J. They've got a tanker truck traipsing along behind us."

Kimball, flying zero-eight as Bengal One, got the report from Soames on the clear channel.

On his Tac Two, he asked McEntire, "What do you think, Irish?"

After a moment's chewing of the oral report, Sam Eddy said, "I don't think they've figured out our real game. Not to the point where they could prove it, anyway."

"All they'd have to do is uncover a few missiles," Kimball reminded him.

"With the government as shaky as it is, they won't want an international incident. I don't think they're going to go digging up search warrants."

"I don't want an international incident either."

"I think we bluff it out, Cheetah. We're better off as a group, rather than heading back to Dacca and leaving the transports unprotected."

"I don't want to split us up, either. Go ahead and get our clearances, Hawkeye," Kimball said.

"Roger that, Bengal One," Contrarez said from the Kappa Kat.

Fifteen minutes later, they let down over the Gulf of Martaban, crossed the delta, and found the concrete of the runway. The five Alpha Kats, followed by the Kappa Kat, taxied behind a white pickup truck, paused to let a Thai Airways International Boeing 727 cross the taxiway, then moved on to parking places opposite the C-141s.

Kimball shut down the turbofan and auxiliary systems, then opened the canopy.

Soames was right.

Around a hundred armed soldiers spread out and made a perimeter around the KAT aircraft. The rifles were slung over their shoulders, but the sight was menacing nonetheless.

After he shrugged out of his equipment and slipped to the ground, Kimball headed for the transport where Soames and Billingsly were talking to several Burmese officers.

McEntire caught up with him, and they approached the group together.

A short man in an immaculately pressed uniform turned to them. His smile lit up the morning. Kimball likened the smile to that of a used car salesman and Nixon.

"Mr. Kimball! I am happy to meet you. I am Colonel Kun Mauk."

Kimball shook the proffered and calloused hand, then introduced McEntire.

With an upraised palm, he indicated the ring of soldiers. "To what do we owe the security, Colonel Mauk?"

"You are perhaps aware of some, shall we say, civil disturbances in the north? We merely wish to have you feel completely at ease during your short stay."

"I see, Colonel. I appreciate your concern."

"We are eager to see how well your airplanes perform, Mr. Kimball."

"And we're eager to show you."

They spent half-an-hour finalizing the times and locations for the aerial and ground demonstrations, then Mauk and his coterie of subordinates slipped through the cordon and disappeared.

Soames said, "This is a little uncomfortable, Kim."

"You're right."

"But we're creative, aren't we, gentlemen?" McEntire said. "At least, I am."

Jimmy Gander had his head stuck through the hatchway to the compartment. "Create something real quick, would you, Sam Eddy?"

"First of all, I suggest we call the hotel and cancel. Methinks it would be better if we all stayed with the planes today."

"What about my shower?" Soames said.

"You stand under that wing, A.J.," Gander said, "and I'll dump iced tea on you."

"We going to have to eat MREs?" Billingsly asked.

"We could always tour a Burmese prison," Kimball said.

Billingsly pushed Gander aside and climbed aboard the Starlifter. "I'm going to see if I can find some beans and franks."

Eighteen

The telephone this time was in an all-night drugstore on 23rd Street in the District, and the time was 1:20 A.M.

Brock Dixon picked up on the first ring.

"I don't know what's happening here," Derek Crider said, "but the damned Burmese have a security cordon around those planes like you wouldn't believe. We can't get within a mile of them."

Dixon had an idea about that, but held it for the moment. "You've got a plan?"

"We've got to figure out where the IFF transponder is located on the plane. One of my people is working on a way to alter it."

Dixon immediately saw the possibilities in that. "Good idea. It'll be in the cockpit, probably a slide-out unit, and probably small, like a car stereo. Kimball has miniaturized everything."

"We could slip into the cockpit and just pull it out?"

"Maybe. Depends on the power and antenna connections. But you know what? I'd give odds that they've got a couple replacement units with them somewhere."

"On one of the C-141s?" Crider asked.

"I don't know the set-up, but it seems likely."

"Good, that's great. We'll check it out."

"You have a backup plan?" Dixon asked.

"We've only got three more shots at them. One of

my people suggested putting a rocket into one of the transports. They've got enough simulated ordnance aboard to create a lot of fireworks. The way they park them, if a C-141's fuel went off, they'd lose the whole bunch."

"That's way too damned obvious," Dixon said. "It might look like a terrorist hit, yeah, but it still leaves them in business."

"If some of their personnel survive."

"Ease up on that scenario. Work on the transponders. And then there's something else."

"What else?" Crider demanded.

"I've got some pictures."

As a normal courtesy, the National Photographic Interpretation Center had provided Air Force Intelligence with a set of satellite photos showing a clandestine Burmese airfield in flames. Since it was not a normal event, Dixon's analyst had brought them to him. As soon as he saw the photos and read the background info, Dixon had deduced Ben Wilcox's intent. He was mad as hell that the CIA had not approached the National Security Council with the plan. The DCI had obviously gone around the NSC, directly to the President.

The Agency was getting out of hand again.

He had been thinking about leaking the information to one of the Congressional oversight committees and letting the political process weed out Wilcox, Simonson, and maybe the DCI. It would serve them right.

The problem, of course, was that Wilcox would be at arm's length with this operation. The General Accounting Office would never trace cash from the Agency's clandestine funds to Kimball Aero Tech. Even if they could prove Kimball made the raid on Lon Pot's operations, the civilian auditors would never connect it to the CIA.

285

Only by innuendo, and that was not enough.

But information was power, and right now, he could use the information in a better way.

"Pictures?" Crider asked.

"You know anything about a man named Lon Pot?"

"Yeah. Runs drugs."

"Anything else?"

"Not much."

Dixon briefed him on Pot's organization, including the names of his key advisors. "Pot moves around a lot. There's three or more clandestine airfields. He's got some hideaways in the jungle, up in the hills, and one place in Bangkok we know about, where his wife lives."

He gave Crider the address.

"Why are you telling me this?" Crider asked.

Dixon detailed the destruction of the airfield named Shan Base.

"I think Kimball's bunch conducted the air raid," Dixon said.

"No shit! He's trying to put the old fart out of business, huh?"

Dixon had also read the intelligence estimates that suggested Lon Pot was attempting to assume political power in the region, first in Burma, but he was not going to pass that on to Crider.

"I think Kimball's trying, yes. And I think there will be more attempts."

After a long silence, Crider asked, "So what do you want me to do? This isn't part of our contract."

"You're very creative," Dixon said. "I want you to use your imagination."

As soon as Dixon hung up, Crider used his imagination and began calling people he knew. He knew lots

286

of people in Southeast Asia.

By three o'clock, he had a list of weaponry in the region that he could get his hands on quickly, and he had a telephone number.

He called it, but the man was not available. He left his name and a note of urgency.

The telephone rang at 3:40 P.M.

"Mr. Crider?"

"That's me. You're Micah Chao?"

"I am. What can I do for you, Mr. Crider?"

"A couple of things, Mr. Chao. First, I'll give you some phone numbers and names to call, so you can check my background. Second, I want to get together with you and with a friend of yours named Henry Loh."

"To what purpose, Mr. Crider?"

"Mutual benefit. You wouldn't want to see a repeat of what happened at Shan Base, would you?"

"I will call you back in a half hour, Mr. Crider."

Lon Pot had arrived at Fragrant Flower in mid-afternoon. He had had to run down Kao Chung at Chiang Base and have him send one of the Third Squadron's Super Frelon helicopters to Bangkok to pick him up. Henry Loh had Lon Pot's personal helicopter somewhere in southern Burma.

Lon Pot did not appreciate that.

His assistants were telephoning all over the country, attempting to locate Henry Loh and Micah Chao, but with no success.

He had talked to Dao Van Luong who was in Mandalay. He had talked to Vol Soon, who complained that the army was becoming restive. The inaction was destroying their morale.

At five o'clock, Henry Loh called.

287

"Good afternoon, Prince. I had not known of your return to Fragrant Flower. Is that a good idea?"

"It seems that I must manage the operation myself, Air Force Chief," Pot said, without attempting to conceal his displeasure. "It all falls apart when I am gone."

"Still, your safety is my concern, Prince, and Bangkok would be a much safer place until after the transition."

Pot was mollified somewhat by Loh's concern.

"Where have you been all day? I have tried to find you numerous times."

"Micah Chao and I have learned many things today, Prince. We have learned, for example, the identity of the force that destroyed Shan Base, and—"

"Who!" Pot demanded.

"An American named Kimball."

"What! The Americans would not dare to intervene."

He was forced to keep his temper in check as Loh narrated the story of Bryce Kimball's aircraft and demonstrations. He interrupted frequently for details about stealth airplanes and capabilities.

"And these airplanes are now in Rangoon?"

"That is correct," Loh said. "There was a demonstration flight to show aerial capabilities a few hours ago. Colonel Mauk intends to commandeer them in the morning, after tonight's demonstration, on behalf of the Burmese government."

"So that they will become ours?"

"That is one possibility, Prince."

"What is another?"

"They will become Mauk's airplanes."

"Ah. And after all we have done for the man."

"I believe I can hold him in check, Prince, but it is a delicate situation."

"What do you need?"

"I need six Mirage aircraft that are currently in Sri Lanka, but which I can have here in two days. I have the pilots for them, and they will give us the balance of power we need over Mauk."

"Delays! Again, delays!"

"We want your transition to power to be successful, do we not, Prince?"

"What day are you suggesting, Henry Loh?"

"August first."

"It will not be suspended again."

"No, Prince, it will not."

"How much do these Mirages cost me?"

"They are used, but in immaculate condition. Sixty million dollars."

"Buy them. I will call Dao Van Luong."

Derek Crider watched Del Gart at work.

Gart was hunched over the table in Crider's hotel room, examining the three transponders that Corey O'Brian had, as O'Brian termed it, filched in the afternoon. As soon as the fighters and command aircraft had taken off for the afternoon demonstration, the Burmese soldiers around the aircraft had been given a rest break and had promptly disappeared. The Americans had gathered in one C-141 to listen to the radio reports of the demonstration, and O'Brian simply climbed into the other transport, spent seven minutes searching through the spare parts boxes, and walked out with three transponders.

They were small, about four inches wide by one inch high by nine inches deep. Gart said they were perfect for his purpose because they could be changed out so readily. On the back end of each were power and antenna connectors, and the whole unit slipped into a sleeve in the Alpha Kat's stack of communications components. Two screws held it in place. With a power screwdriver, Gart estimated that he could change one unit for another in less than a minute.

Blue smoke curled upward from the hot tip of a soldering iron resting in a wire holder next to Gart's hand. Alan Adage sat on the other side of the table handing small needle-nosed pliers, solder extractors, and components to Gart as he called for them.

Wheeler had obtained two bottles of Kentucky bourbon on the street somewhere, and everyone had a glass of well-watered whiskey. Crider wouldn't let them get stronger until the delicate work was done.

He was on the bed, leaning back against the wall, and he was pleased with the day's developments.

He sipped from his bourbon glass.

The phone rang at his elbow.

He picked it up.

"Mr. Crider," he said.

"We have a deal," the voice he recognized as belonging to Henry Loh told him.

"I think it's a good one."

"Did you obtain the transponders?" Loh asked.

"We've got them. There are only three, but that should be enough for you."

"Tell me again about the process."

Crider shifted the phone to his other ear. "The Alpha Kat takes off with the transponder operating, so that the control tower can track it. Before the exercise begins, the pilot shuts off the transponder, entering his stealth mode."

"Yes, I understand that."

Crider hoped that he himself did. He wasn't really sure of the procedures used by Kimball, but he spoke with as much authority as he could muster.

"We have modified the transponders by adding an

290

integrated circuit. As soon as the pilot turns off the power, the unit will wait ten minutes, then begin transmitting again. However, the indicator light on the unit will not warn the pilot. Your radars will see him, plain as day, but he won't know that."

"Excellent," Loh said.

Crider was certain that Loh didn't give a damn one way or another who was flying the Alpha Kats. If Mauk was successful in grabbing them, Mauk's pilots would go down. If Loh got hold of them, he could pull the transponders. If nothing else, Kimball's pilots would bite the dust, proving to the world's military that the aircraft were vulnerable and negating any sales Kimball might have lined up.

Everyone wins.

"The money?" Crider asked.

"The money will be transferred tonight."

"Sixty?"

"That is correct. And I am sending six pilots to Sri Lanka on the next flight out of Rangoon."

"The aircraft will be ready for them."

"And the other arrangements?"

"As soon as my bank in Grand Cayman receives the electronic funds transfer, I will order the wire transfer to pay for the aircraft. And I will order the other transfers."

"That is good," Henry Loh said and hung up.

Crider thought so, too. His commission from the weapons broke on the deal was two million, and he would clear eight hundred thousand. He had to spread a couple hundred thousand among his contacts in Southeast Asia, to keep them friendly contacts. And he had to transfer a half million each to Chao's and Loh's accounts.

* * *

Kimball walked among the pilots on the darkened ramp and handed out their passports. Keeper, Cadwell, Metger, and Greer stuffed the fake passports in the pockets of their flight suits. The three appeared subdued in an eager way, if that were possible.

Tonight, as he had done last night, Kimball had drawn names out of Tex Brabham's seven-gallon hat for the three open spots on the fighter roster. They all wanted to go, but there weren't enough seats. He and McEntire had decided early on that the two of them would take every mission flight, but tonight McEntire stepped aside and a fourth name was drawn, Greer's.

"Everybody got it down?" Kimball asked. "Any part of the briefing we need to go over again?"

The fighter pilots shook their heads.

He looked over to Conrad Billingsly who, along with Sam Miller, Fred Nackerman, and Speedy Contrarez, would be aboard the Kappa Kat.

Billingsly held up his clipboard with the checklist. "Got it all here, Kim."

"Let's fire them up."

Kimball turned and headed for ought-eight.

Twelve minutes later, they were lined up on the taxiway, waiting for takeoff clearance. While he waited, Kimball double-checked the coordinates of the target area.

Target areas, he corrected himself.

Jimmy Gander watched as the last three Alpha Kats left the runway, their anti-collision strobes pulsing in the night.

The rest of the group were still huddled around the ramp of the C-141. The ring of Burmese soldiers that had been attending them broke up at some officer's command and headed somewhere for a rest break.

Coffee, or tea, or opium, whatever they did on rest breaks.

McEntire said, "I need two volunteers. That's you, A.J., and you, Alex."

"I'd be happy to volunteer, Sam Eddy," Soames said.

"I've been hoping and praying for this chance to contribute," Hamilton told him.

"The three of us will go out to the target site for the demonstration, then come back here and sack out in the other Starlifter. In the morning, we'll conduct the post-demonstration briefing."

"A.J. and I can handle it," Hamilton said.

"No. I want the three of us to stick together. Jimmy, you load everyone else in this bird and be off the ground in ten minutes."

Gander straightened his back, suddenly alert. He wondered if he had missed something during the briefing.

"If the tower gives you any static," McEntire said, "you tell them you're part of the demo, monitoring the action. Hell, they don't know any different."

"Am I part of the demo?" Gander asked.

"Nah. You head straight for Bangkok. Kim and I want everyone . . . almost everyone . . . out of Burma tonight."

"Sam Eddy," Tex Brabham drawled, "I'm going to go over to the other transport and camp out in the back until the demonstration's done."

"No, Tex . . ."

"Got to keep the rifles oiled, you know?"

"Okay, Tex. Thanks," McEntire said. "Jimmy, you hit the road."

Gander was going to protest, thought about who outranked who, and started up the ramp.

He started barking out his own orders. "Mel, you're

293

in the right seat. Jay, you're flight engineer. Walt, pull the chocks and get us cranked up."

Everyone started moving.

As he pushed open the door into the crew compartment, Gander thought that training and discipline paid off every time.

Chiang Base, as identified on the satellite photographs provided by Wilcox, was located just over the border in northern Thailand, three hundred miles from Rangoon.

It was a mere excursion for the KAT airplanes, barely a thirty-minute round-trip detour from the exercise area at Mach 1.5.

The Golden Triangle was no longer simply the home of poppy growers. It had become a tourist mecca also. While the semiautonomous tribes that inhabited the area still operated under the governance of warlords, much as they had a century before, relationships between Bangkok and the north country had improved. Chiang Mai was essentially the capital of northern Thailand, and Chiang Rai, a hundred miles northeast of Chiang Mai, was the stepping stone into the Triangle for visitors. Deluxe resort hotels had blossomed in Chiang Rai, and another had been constructed in the heart of the Golden Triangle, overlooking Laos and Burma.

The tourists came for the moderate weather, to examine in detail the cultures of the hill tribes, to explore the beauty of the rivers and forests, and maybe to find cheap sources for other nirvanas.

The tourists hadn't deterred the poppy growers at all. Record productions of processed opium still flowed southward into southern Thailand for export to the United States and Europe.

Lon Pot's Chiang Base was due west of Chiang Rai, near the base of the 7500-foot mountain dubbed Doi Pha Hom Pak.

That was their only hot target tonight. Kimball had wanted to also hit a Lon Pot army post at Mawkmai, but the distances and extra time and ordnance loads couldn't be easily explained in their demonstration schedule.

Billingsly had a map overlay for Thailand on disk, and the Kappa Kat's data-link had displayed it on Kimball's CRT. Doi Pha Hom Pak was clearly designated. It was at the top of the screen, forty miles away from the blinking blue blip that was Alpha Kat zero-eight. The airspeed readout at the top of the HUD showed Mach 1.4. His altitude was 15,000 feet.

"Hawkeye, One. You want to paint me a target?"

"Coming up, One. Keying it in now."

Billingsly tapped the coordinates into his keyboard aboard the Kappa Kat, and a red cross suddenly appeared on Kimball's screen.

"Thanks, Frog."

"Anytime. Bengals, you'd better shed the speed. One, we've got hostiles on the other side of the mountain. Due north of the peak at angels twelve, heading zero-eight-four."

Kimball eased the throttle back and checked for the wingtip lights on either side of him. Everyone was in place. His altitude began to bleed off slowly.

"You're sure they're hostile, Frog?"

"Roger. The infrared signatures say Mirage 2000. Four of them. They're turning back toward me now."

"What's your situation, Hawkeye?"

"I'm at three-nine thousand, fifty-five miles to your northwest."

"Take one of mine as a CAP."

"Not just yet, Cheetah. We can go off the air and

dodge these puppies for a little while if we have to. If they take me as bait, we'll be able to pull them off you. You dump the ordnance first."

"Vector us in, Hawkeye. I'm showing six-zero-zero knots."

"Bengals Four and Five, go to zero-seven-zero and Tac Three."

"Four."

"Five, gone."

Contrarez took over control of Metger and Greer, who would make their ground attack from the east. The two fighters peeled off Kimball's right wing, diving hard, and their wingtip guidelights disappeared.

"Bengal One," Billingsly said, "In two minutes, go to zero-zero-five."

Kimball tapped two minutes into his instrument panel chronometer and said, "Roger that, two minutes and zero-zero-five."

In an interlaced pattern, Kimball and his flight of three intended to attack from the south, spaced between the attacks from the east, then climb abruptly to the right to avoid the peak.

"Bengal One, Hawkeye."

"Go," Kimball said.

"I just went to the two-two-oh radar scan and checked Muang Base. They're flying a four-plane formation there, too."

"Waiting for us, you think?"

"Roger, Cheetah. Ambush city. The hostiles here have turned back toward you, and they're ignoring me."

"They've been told to stay in contact with the airfield," Kimball guessed.

"That's the way I interpret it. They . . . hold one." After a few seconds, Billingsly said, "I just read some probes by SAM radars. They're expecting us."

"How many SAMs, Hawkeye?"

"Six. They shut down again. They're only radiating periodically."

"Let's hold up a minute, Frog."

Using his controller, Kimball eased into a right turn. Glancing out the canopy, he saw that Keeper and Cadwell were staying with him.

"Speedy, put Four and Five in a three-sixty," Billingsly told Contrarez. Kimball heard the order since Tac Two was locked open, hot.

"Frog," Kimball said, "you want to give me any odds that Chiang Base has any aircraft in residence?"

"I'd put up a buck says they do, Cheetah, if you put up ten thousand."

"Let's adapt then, Frog. Put Bengal Three on the ground to hole the runway. The minute that happens, we're bound to see SAM radars lighting up. Four and Five take out the SAM sites. One and Two jettison bombs and take on the Mirages."

"I'm thinking about it, Cheetah. Okay, I've got my mind wrapped around it. I can't let you jettison the dummy bombs, though."

They would have to have them for the run on the demonstration target.

"Gotcha, Hawkeye. We can manage the aerial with the dummy's intact."

"Roger that. Okey-dokey. Everybody give me a half-second squawk, so I'm sure my computer's still got you in the right place."

Kimball reached down for his transponder, flipped the toggle upward, counted to himself, "One thousand and," then snapped it off.

"Right on, Bengals. Speedy, split your two and station them northeast and southeast of the target, ready to hit SAMs. Three, go to angels four, heading three-five-four."

"Three."

Kimball checked over his left shoulder and saw Cadwell drop out of the formation. His lights went dark.

"Kill the lights, Two," Kimball ordered and shut down his own guidelights.

"All weapons are free," Billingsly said. "One and Two, jettison aft bombs."

Kimball raised the protective flap on the armaments panel, selected Center Line Two, and released the bomb. He selected his live Sidewinders and AMRAAMs and armed them.

"One, this is Two," Keeper said. "I'm armed and ready to kick ass."

"One, take heading zero-one-two. I'm going to hold you until the Mirages pounce."

"Roger that," Kimball said.

He eased out of his right turn and swung back to the left until the heading appeared on the HUD. The altitude held steady at 14,000 feet.

"Three," Billingsly said, "you're thirty seconds out. Commit when ready."

"Three."

Kimball scanned the skies. The stars were clear. The moon was dim and low in the west. Below, the landscape was blacked out. A few thin threads suggested waterways or possible roads. On his left, the peak of Doi Pha Hom Pak was a dark smear against the stars lining the horizon.

He watched the area he thought was the base of the mountain.

Abruptly, he saw tiny pricks of light blossom. They were nearly ten miles away.

"Three's clear. Got the runway and a couple trucks. No aircraft on the ground."

"SAMs lighting up," Billingsly warned.

"Triple-A, also," Bengal Three reported. "They're shooting blind."

Kimball saw the trail of a surface-to-air missile leap from the jungle. The tracers of antiaircraft rounds began to poke upwards, like the quills on a porcupine.

"They're firing SAMs without targets, too," he said. "Trying to hit something by accident."

"Speedy just sent Four and Five," Billingsly said. "Okay, One. Here come the Mirages. Diving hard from twelve thousand. You want three-four-zero."

"One. We're gone."

Kimball flashed his guidelights once for Keeper, then rolled over into a diving left turn. He pulled out on Billingsly's heading and eased in more power.

"Two, space it out."

"Roger, One."

"Hawkeye here. They're radiating to beat hell, looking for any kind of target."

"Paint 'em, Frog."

Kimball selected his AMRAAM radar seekers while Billingsly locked his computer onto the transmitting radars of the Mirages. Transmitted to the Alpha Kat by the data-link, four red blips appeared on the CRT.

"Two, I've got the right pair," Kimball said.

"Roger, One."

Locating the search stud on the controller, Kimball pressed it. The radar seeker of the first AMRAAM came to life and an orange target symbol appeared on the CRT. He pulled the nose up and to the right.

The target rose passed over the closest red blip. He depressed the stud.

LOCK-ON appeared on the screen.

Kimball squeezed the firing button.

The missile left the pylon with a blaze of fiery white trailing it.

He forgot about it, jinked the nose down and left.

LOCK-ON for the second target.

A missile screamed by on his left, departing Keeper's fighter.

Fired.

Second missile away.

Altitude 7,540 feet.

Kimball hauled the controller back and rotated upward.

Shoved the throttle to its forward stops.

"Scratch two SAMs," Billingsly reported.

"Two missiles gone," Kimball said.

"Make that four," Keeper added.

"I've got the tracks," Billingsly said. "Two more SAMs out."

Altitude 11,600.

Kimball pulled on over until he was inverted and looked up through the canopy.

He saw the tracers from the antiaircraft guns rising up toward him, but stopping thousands of feet too soon.

An orange and red and blue flower suddenly appeared against the earth.

Then a second flower.

And a third.

Seconds passed.

Only a three-flower bouquet tonight.

"Scratch three Mirages," Hawkeye reported. "The fourth one dodged out on us. Good damned work, guys. And Five got the last two SAMS."

"Where'd the fourth one go, Hawkeye?" Kimball asked. "I've still got Sidewinders."

"He's on the deck, headed for China. Let him go."

Kimball glanced at the chronometer. Billingsly was right. They couldn't waste more time and still get to the demonstration site as scheduled.

"Form us up, Frog."

After Billingsly gave each of them new headings and brought Four and Five back on Tac Two, Kimball asked, "Bengals, how you doing?"

"Four's A-one."

"Five. Do we get to do victory rolls?"

"Three. I'm a little pissed. What's it going to look like, two trucks painted under my canopy?"

"Two. Who cares? We kicked us some ass."

Nineteen

Lujan called from the airport at eleven o'clock.

"Hey, Emilio, what's up?" Crider asked.

"They ain't come back, man."

"Who?"

"The planes."

Crider spilled his bourbon sitting up on the bed so fast. "You're sure?"

"They're hard to miss, man. The honchos, they all come back twenty minutes ago. In two helicopters. But none of the KAT airplanes have shown up."

"None of the KAT people?"

"Oh, sure, there's a couple of them, and one of the Starlifters is still here, but everything else, gone."

"Goddamn! Get the plane ready to go, Emilio."

Crider slammed the phone down, crawled out of bed, and headed for the shower.

Jimmy Gander and Mel Vrdlicka had made all the arrangements with the Don Muang Airport operations people, who weren't unhappy about having the Kimball Aero Tech aircraft show up a day early. They liked the landing and parking fees as much as any fixed base operator.

They had been assigned space near the domestic terminal, which was the old airport terminal. The new international terminal next door was modern and bristling

302

with traffic. United Airlines had a large array of aircraft snugged up to the jetways, and there were planes sporting Singapore Airlines, British Airways, and Finnair logos as well.

Gander was happy they hadn't been shunted off to Ubom or U-Tapeo, the military airfields that had supported U.S. tactical and strategic units during the Vietnam debacle. He hadn't been to Thailand in ten years, but he could tell, just by breathing deeply, that the air pollution in Bangkok had gotten progressively worse.

After the American dollars started surfacing in Bangkok during the Vietnam era, flowing from military people either stationed nearby or R&R-ing in the city, Bangkok had grown from a million-and-a-half people to six million in twenty years. There wasn't room enough for them, but they packed themselves in anyway.

He longed for Phoenix.

The quiet serenity of the desert.

The smell of sage and mesquite.

In fact, he was thinking about hitting Mollie with the idea of selling their two-story off Indian School Road and looking for a small acreage much farther out of the city. Raise some horses, maybe. Timmy should learn to ride soon.

"You know what I heard?" Walt Hammond asked. They were all sitting around the opened ramp of the Starlifter. That ramp was getting old as a home, too.

"What'd you hear?" Wagers asked.

"I heard that that doc in Riyadh got Kim some scotch."

"He probably needed it," Wagers said.

"I'd like a shot of scotch. Or something."

A few heads turned toward the city. Many of them had been there before, but some had not. They had heard the stories, though, of Patpong Road and the live sex shows, young girls racked like pots and pans behind windows with numbers painted on their breasts, free-flowing booze and drugs. The VD clinics were almost as numerous as the bars named Miami and L.A. and Manhattan.

"Forget it," Vrdlicka said. "It's fifteen miles to town, but that's a ninety-minute taxi trip."

Warren Mabry stood up and moved out from under the tail.

"There they are. Lights off to the west."

Everyone clambered to their feet and moved to where they could watch the runway.

The Kappa Kat touched down.

Two Alpha Kats followed.

And three more.

They yelled and screamed.

The mood became more exuberant as the Kimball Aero aircraft turned off on the taxiway and crawled across the field toward them.

"About all we need now," Jimmy Gander said, "is four more people."

A.J. Soames woke to the smell of coffee.

He groaned and rolled over.

His back was bent out of shape, literally, and ached. With some trepidation, he pushed himself upright and rolled to his feet. The parachute packs he had been sleeping on were dented in all the wrong places.

Alex Hamilton, who had started the coffee on a hot plate, was digging through the box of MREs.

"You're not going to find any Danish in there," Soames told him.

"Hell, A.J., I'm just looking for American."

Tex Brabham pushed himself halfway out of his sleeping spot on the canvas sling seats and pushed his hat back on his head. He had his arms wrapped around an M-16.

When they had flipped coins last night, McEntire and

Hamilton had won the two bunks in the crew compartment. Getting to sleep, though, had been difficult. The Burmese troops had shown up again, prepared to guard, or detain, the KAT aircraft. When the aircraft didn't return, there had been some yelling and apparently some telephone conferences by the officer in charge with bigwigs.

A harried senior lieutenant demanded to know where the planes were.

Bangkok, McEntire told him.

That is not right, the lieutenant said.

McEntire had insisted that the flight to Thailand had been part of their plans all along. What's the big deal? he had asked the lieutenant, who didn't seem to know.

"Where's Sam Eddy?" Soames asked Hamilton.

"Still asleep."

Soames walked forward, skirting packing cases, passed through the hatch, and found McEntire sitting on the side of the lower bunk. He appeared fatigued. He sat with his chin in his hand. A black forest of stubble coated his cheeks.

"I don't sleep well on airplanes either, Sam Eddy."

McEntire looked up and grinned. "Hell, A.J., it'd be all right if the thing was moving, and I was at the controls. I sleep all right then."

"Alex has coffee brewing."

"Yeah, okay. I'll be with you in a minute."

Soames went back to join the others and take a cup of strong, strong coffee from Hamilton.

Brabham opened a tin of soda crackers and passed them around.

Soames looked at them for a second and decided he wasn't hungry.

Ten minutes later, after a session with an electric razor, McEntire came back.

He looked a hell of a lot better, but there were still dark rings under his eyes.

"Well," he said, "this may be interesting."

"You don't think our hosts are going to be ecstatic?" Soames asked.

"Doubt it. A.J., I want you to stay here with Tex. Have this hummer ready to roll by ten o'clock. Alex and I will cover the debriefing."

"And if they don't want us to roll?"

"We'll play it by ear. We've got a radio on our side, and we could raise Bangkok and get the Embassy involved. Without the airplanes here, though, I don't think Mauk's going to raise a lot of hell. They don't know anything they can prove, and if they say something about the attacks on Lon Pot's little retreats, the world's going to wonder who's protecting whom. I think we've got them aced."

Colonel Kun Mauk showed up at eight o'clock in a staff car to pick up McEntire and Hamilton. There was fire in his eyes and a dark suffusion covering his cheeks, but he struggled with, and achieved, civility.

Soames and Brabham spent the next two hours tying down cargo and getting the Starlifter ready for flight.

When those chores were done, Soames sat in the pilot's seat, and Brabham took the flight engineer's position. They ran through the checklist as far as they could.

And waited.

10:30 A.M. slid by.

At 10:45 A.M., Soames saw the staff car approaching. Except for the driver in front, McEntire and Hamilton were alone in the backseat.

They got out of the sedan, crossed to the entry hatch, and climbed aboard.

Brabham called down to them, "You guys all right?"

Hamilton crawled up the ladder. "Yeah. It was a little hairy there for awhile. Mauk wanted us to bring the planes back after the Bangkok demonstration, so he could take another look at them. He suggested strongly that we hang around here until that happened. I know damned well he was on the verge of ordering us detained."

"And?" Soames asked.

"And Sam Eddy was mercifully brief. Invited Mauk to Arizona, all expenses paid, for another look."

"And?"

"And the defense minister, who may or may not be able to overrule Mauk, said he'd think about it."

McEntire called up from the crew compartment. "You want to get us up a few thousand feet, A.J., so I can take a nap?"

Ben Wilcox hadn't been out of the U.S. Embassy in New Delhi for hours, and it felt like weeks. He needed a shave and a shower. He had stayed close to the secure room since talking to Simonson five hours before, when he had first learned of the attack on Chiang Base.

He had just stepped out into the corridor and used a wall-mounted house phone to order a roast beef sandwich for lunch when the communications technician called him. "Washington, Mr. Wilcox."

"Thanks."

He went back into the claustrophobic room and picked up a phone.

"Wilcox."

"We've confirmed that three Mirages were shot down, Ben. One pilot bailed out. The airfield was torn up a little and they lost six Samsong radar sites. We understand there were a dozen fatalities among the radar crews, but that's an iffy number."

"Kimball's goddamned airplanes work, don't they?"

"Yeah, it looks like they do."

"Maybe our brothers down the river are making a mistake, Ted."

Simonson wasn't going to comment on the military mind. "There's a new deadline date. The first of

August."

"And Kimball keeps shoving them back into a corner. Jesus, Ted, have you talked to the people upstairs?"

"Yeah, and they're still unhappy. They don't mind looking at the pictures and hearing the reports, but they don't like having somebody out there with lethal weaponry who won't follow their orders."

"Sounds like LBJ, Ted."

"Micromanagement, that's right. Still, we're supposed to abort the mission. Some of the civilians think that Lon Pot can't succeed at this point anyway."

"That's bullshit," Wilcox said.

"Maybe. Have you talked to Kimball?"

"He's not answering the phone. I believe he might be mad at us," Wilcox said.

"Then, there's something else. Donegal called."

"Damn it, I need to talk to him."

"He just left a message. Lon Pot got himself six new Mirages. Pot's also aware that Bryce Kimball is the man causing him problems. He's also rigged up some kind of trap for Kimball."

"Trap? What trap?"

"There's no detail, Ben. Just that the Alpha Kats have been tampered with, and every one will go down if they fly against Pot again. Sounds to me like a hint that we should stop interfering with Pot's life."

"Shit! It's not possible."

"Now you sound like Kimball."

"I'm going to have to stop him, Ted."

"Yeah, Ben. You've done very well at stopping him, haven't you? As I remember, you set up the scenario because you knew you couldn't stop him."

On his flight back to Fragrant Flower in Lon Pot's Aerospatiale, Henry Loh counted his blessings.

His blessings had just been enriched by another half

308

million American dollars, now residing in Singapore. Lon Pot's journey into politics was making Loh an even richer man.

And the latest deal had also made Micah Chao a close ally. That could never hurt.

No matter, which way it turned out, however, Loh thought that his future might best be served by resigning his title of Chief soon after the battle was won or lost. He could buy himself an airplane of some kind and tour Indonesia. Perhaps he would go on to South America.

He had never been to South America before.

There was just one niggling, irritating, little detail.

Henry Loh had never lost before, not if he did not count Vietnam, which he did not. He had bailed out of there long before the end.

In the past three days, he had lost seven very expensive fighter aircraft, in addition to transports and helicopters. Lon Pot might well bill him for the losses. He would not put it above the Prince to do such a thing.

Additionally, he felt betrayals closing in from all sides. Kun Mauk was definitely a concern. He sometimes wondered about Jake Switzer. Over time, he had learned that Americans could never be fully trusted.

It was a problem that he had with his entire pilot cadre. While a number of his pilots were of Southeast Asian heritage, the very experienced men came from America, France, Germany, China, and Russia. There were none that he could rely on totally.

This Crider, for instance. While the aircraft purchase had been sweet for all of them, he was not certain that Crider would carry out the final part of the deal: emplacing the doctored transponders in the Alpha Kat aircraft.

The outcome was in doubt. And yet most outcomes were in doubt, and he had survived. All he could do, he decided, was to move ahead with what he had.

He had six relatively new Mirages. He saw them on the ground at Fragrant Flower as he topped the ridge. He eased off the collective and allowed the helicopter to settle to a soft landing just off the runway.

The dust swirled around him, and he waited until the rotors had almost stopped turning and the dust had settled before stepping out.

Jake Switzer approached him.

"The airplanes?" he asked.

"They're fine, Henry. As advertised."

"Have you talked to Kao?"

"He's fine, too, but not very damned happy. He said he was lucky to have gotten away last night. He was nearly clipped by a missile. No one, and I mean no one, ever saw one of the attacking planes."

Loh told him what he had learned from Crider about the stealth aircraft.

"No shit! How in the hell are we going to fight that, Henry?"

Without mentioning Crider's name, Loh told him about Crider's plans for the transponders.

"Well. That might be all right. Yeah, I can deal with that."

"What is the state of repair at Shan Base?"

Switzer looked at his watch. "In another hour or so, we should be able to take the planes in there and get missiles loaded. Jean promised me a runway by then anyway."

"And Chung is at Muang?"

"Right. He's sending tankers with JP-4 for us."

"Very well, Jake. You call Burov and have him meet you with all of his aircraft at Shan Base. Then, tell Chung to move his squadron here, to Fragrant Flower. He is to get two of the new aircraft."

"We're abandoning Muang?"

"For the time being. I suspect that this American Kimball knows the location of Muang, just as he did

310

Shan and Chiang. We will give him an empty present, and we will stage from here and from Shan to wrap it for him."

Switzer grinned. "Good by me."

"Now, I must go talk to the Prince."

"Good luck. I went up there for a drink, and he wasn't in the best of moods, Henry."

Loh nodded, then climbed in a pickup truck, turned it around and drove up the twin ruts to the compound. A guard at the main gate peeked out at him, then opened the doors so he could drive inside. He parked the truck in a garage, then walked the gravelled path through Lon Pot's forest to the front door of the main house.

Dao Van Luong opened the door for him. His face said he had had a long afternoon.

Without speaking, Dao led him to the living room.

It was maybe ninety-five degrees Fahrenheit outside, but Pot had the air-conditioning at full race and a fire going in the fireplace. He was seated in front of it, reading from one of his leather-bound books.

"Good afternoon, Prince. You saw the new airplanes?"

"The Finance Chief went down to look at them. He assures me that we received excellent value."

"I think that is so," Loh agreed.

Lon Pot dog-eared a page and closed the book.

"Henry, this is not going well. I am dissatisfied."

"It is going to get much better, Prince." Loh detailed his plans once again.

"And then we will be rid of this . . . this Kimball?"

"That is true."

"And what of Mauk?"

"To be truthful, Prince, I am still uncertain of him. However, when he was unable to commandeer the American airplanes, it was a tremendous setback for him. I think that now he has no choice but to proceed

311

with his promise to us."

"And then he will die," Lon Pot said.

"Yes. We will make it so."

Pot smiled.

And Henry Loh smiled back. He was much happier when Lon Pot was happy.

Ben Wilcox made six calls to the United States. He talked to people at Commerce and the FAA who owed him favors. Then he called the Assistant Secretary of State for Asia.

"Ben? How's the spook business?"

"Very slow, Adrian."

"You watching what's happening in Burma?"

"We're watching that very closely, of course. The results are still up in the air, but as a matter of fact, that's why I'm calling."

"About Burma?"

"Actually, about a problem in Thailand. I think you could help me defuse a situation there with one phone call."

"I'd be glad to try, Ben."

Kimball didn't breathe well until the second Starlifter got in from Rangoon. When it did, and was parked with the rest of the Kimball Aero craft, he relaxed a bit.

Except for two guards, the whole KAT personnel complement moved into nearby Airport Hotel, which was a practical hotel and not very exotic. Andrea Deacon had chosen it for its moderate room rates, which, for the thirty of them, was still running $1500 a night.

They had an extra day in Bangkok now, and Kimball gave everyone who wasn't scheduled for a stint on guard duty permission to explore the city. He figured most of them would ignore the truly grand sights of the temples, the National Museum, the National Art Gallery, and the Temple of the Reclining Buddha and head right for Patpong Road.

He and Sam Eddy McEntire moved their duffle bags into their room.

"Your turn to call Susan," McEntire said.

"I called last time."

"Yeah, but only after I offered."

Shaking his head, Kimball reached for the phone. It tingled in his hand, and he picked it up.

"Kimball."

"Kim, this is Ito."

"Problem?"

"There seems to be. I think you should come over here right away."

"What is it?"

"They don't want me to talk on the telephone. Come now, please."

He related the conversation to Sam Eddy as they took the carpeted stairs two-at-a-time from their room on the second floor.

There was a taxi waiting at the entrance, and Kimball went quickly through the required negotiations before getting into the back.

When they arrived at their ramp space next to the domestic terminal, they found a half-dozen military vehicles parked among the aircraft.

Uniformed Thais were moving among the planes, placing yellow seals on the access doors and the hatches. It wasn't quite a repeat of the events in Rangoon, but it was more unnerving.

Kimball hopped out of the cab and ran across the tarmac toward a short man in an officer's uniform.

"What's going on here?" he demanded.

The officer turned to him and smiled. "You are Mr. Kimball?"

313

"That's right. What in hell are you doing?"

"Your aircraft have been grounded, Mr. Kimball."

"What the hell? What for?"

"The Thai government is impounding the airplanes at the request of the United States Department of State. Beyond that, sir, I know nothing."

Twenty

The United States Embassy was located at 95 Wireless Road. There was a new expressway running north and south, parallel to and east of Wireless Road, but that didn't help Kimball any. His cab driver took nearly two hours to navigate the Rama 6 Road south into the city and to wind his way through traffic-congested streets entertaining Kimball and McEntire by pointing out the entertaining and historical sights along the way, detailing their relative importance in nearly unintelligible Pidgin English.

Without warning, he snapped quick detours to point out Jim Thompson's House, the home of the American architect who came out of the OSS after World War II and revitalized the Thai silk industry; the National Stadium; and the *Wat Traimitr,* the Temple of the Golden Buddha where a chapel contained a nine-hundred-year-old solid gold Buddha weighing five-and-a-half tons.

Kimball yelled at the driver a number of times, attempting to get him back on track, but he was quite obviously unable to hear with his mouth open.

McEntire slumped back in his corner of the seat and seemed to accept his fate.

Buses, trucks, motor scooters, and tuk-tuks, three-wheeled minibuses which sounded like their names, surrounded them. Kimball thought of Kevin Costner, caught in the middle of a thundering herd of buffalo.

These buffalo didn't move, however.

They were almost to the Embassy, inching along in near gridlock, gagging on exhaust fumes, when McEntire said, "Wilcox."

"Wilcox?"

"Right, Wilcox."

Kimball sagged back in the seat and thought about it, but not for long.

"You're probably right. Why?"

"I think if Bennie had his own way, we wouldn't have a problem," McEntire said. "I'm betting the higher-ups got nervous about our antics. Whatever. Wilcox is the one with enough clout to get us grounded."

The horn of an old Anglia in the next lane began to bleat. A distinguished-looking, gray-haired old Englishman in a tweed cap was behind the wheel, and he kept bleating the horn even though it had absolutely no effect on the traffic ahead, beside, or behind him.

Kimball reached through his window and banged his fist on the Anglia's fender.

The Brit looked at him.

Kimball shook his hand at the man.

He smiled and quit bleating.

"Jesus, you're tough," Sam Eddy said.

"This whole damned thing is giving me a headache. Why would they want the operation shut down now? We've got Lon Pot on the run. He keeps backing off on his deadlines."

"I can think of a couple reasons. If you cool down some, Kim, you'll think of them, too."

"Okay. One, and this is a real contradiction, the stealth planes are too obvious."

"Right on. Anyone who's watching close, and we can be sure a number of very concerned intelligence agencies are, sees Lon Pot getting hit a couple times, but the hostile force is invisible. The KAT people just happen to be demonstrating invisible aircraft in the area. Hell, Kim, even I can put one and one together."

"We're obviously American, and we're obviously bought. Washington doesn't care to have the connection made," Kimball said.

"It might have been different if Pot wasn't making a play for his own country, with everybody watching him. We zip through, Pot loses a bunch of planes and product, and no one gives a damn. But with Pot on the political move, too many paid-up members of the UN are keeping an eye on him. They wouldn't cotton to a unilateral move by the U.S. in this new world order."

"The timing's wrong."

"Just like poor drama or bad comedy."

"Or wishful antiterrorism," Kimball said.

The taxi driver stomped the pedal, and they shot into a hole in the next lane, dashing ahead of the Anglia.

"I read it that way. If we were after the druggie . . ."

"Which we thought we were," Kimball said.

"Not to be playing Monday morning quarterback," McEntire said, "but I didn't quite buy Wilcox's drug theory back in Colorado. No, wait. I bought the money end. We needed money, and that's all my vote depended on. You were thinking about Randy, weren't you?"

Kimball sighed, the image of his brother, the impish grin stretching his mouth, rose in his mind. "I was thinking about Randy," he admitted.

"It's okay with me," Sam Eddy said. "I thought about him, too, but I figured Wilcox was using him

317

for the hook."

"I knew he was doing it," Kimball said, "and I didn't give a damn."

"But we both got snookered. Pot turns out to be a bigger prize than we planned on. He's got an international presence now, so we get shut down before we embarrass the people on the mall."

The driver swung hard into a gap on Rama 4 Road and accelerated.

"All right," Kimball said. "That's where we're at, shut down."

"Plus," added McEntire, "we didn't play Wilcox's game. The ball didn't go where it was supposed to go, and the 'tilt' sign came on."

Kimball grinned. "Neither of us have ever been good with orders."

"We going to play his game, now? Or maybe it's not his any more. We going to play the CIA's game?"

"If we shut up, Sam Eddy, and ask please, and promise to not stray from the righteous path, we can have those planes free in a couple hours."

"The problem with you, Kim, is you never make a promise you don't intend to keep."

"Same with you."

"I've slipped from time to time," McEntire said. "A couple times too many. Anyway, are you going to promise Wilcox that we'll forego another joyride over Burma?"

"If I do, we finish the tour and maybe sell some airplanes. That's got to be the first priority, Sam Eddy. People depend on us."

"We've still got this other little problem," Sam Eddy said. "The one where our airplanes blow up on someone else's schedule. Wilcox hasn't been very helpful with that one."

"He hasn't been very forthcoming, has he?" Kimball

318

agreed. "I suppose it's a case of 'he has his problems, and we have ours.' "

Both of them were shoved to the right as the cab made a hard left turn onto Wireless Road.

"I'll tell you what, Kim. You make a promise to Wilcox for everyone except me. I'll take one loaded Alpha Kat and make one run."

Kimball just looked at him.

"I mean it. For you and me and Randy and your folks."

"Shit!" Kimball said. He wouldn't let Sam Eddy assume his own, for lack of a better word, vengeance.

"Then don't make any goddamned promises at all. Not for you, not for me, and not for any one of the people back at Don Muang. We all came for the same reasons, Kim. And there's more than one priority."

Kimball stared hard at Sam Eddy. He could sometimes be extremely moody, but he rarely expressed his moods. This one was heated.

The cab bounced and squeaked to a stop in front of the Embassy. Kimball got out in relief, dug into his pocket, and came up with two red 100 *baht* notes, the amount he had negotiated before the ride began. He shoved them into the tour guide's hand.

The two of them marched past a couple Thai policemen, entered the Embassy, and showed their passports to the Marine on duty. He aimed them toward an information desk.

The pretty blonde at the desk asked, "How may we help you, gentlemen?"

"By hauling the ambassador out here right now," Kimball said.

Sam Eddy grabbed his arm. "Or better, Miss, by finding the political officer, or whatever the cover is for the CIA man. We'd certainly like to speak with

319

him. And we need to talk to the Deputy Director for Intelligence. He's at the American Embassy in New Delhi right now."

"What?" Alarm in her eyes.

"Ben Wilcox is his name," McEntire said and smiled. His smiles always achieved female cooperation. "Please."

"Excuse me for just one minute," she said. "I'll be right back."

They didn't get the ambassador, of course. He was at some very important function.

They got a roly-poly, smiley little man who insisted he was the commerce attaché, and maybe he was. He listened sympathetically to the problem, didn't suggest any solutions that might get him in trouble, and got them on a supposedly secure phone with Wilcox.

"What the hell are you doing?" Kimball demanded.

The DDI's voice was irritatingly controlled and only raised the level of Kimball's anger. "It seems that the FAA is double-checking your airworthiness certificates, after that accident in Saudi Arabia, Mr. Kimball. I'm sure it'll all be straightened out soon."

"Wilcox, goddamn it! I want those planes cleared for flight, and I want it taken care of now."

"These things take time, Mr. Kimball. Certainly, you understand that."

"I understand that I've got a damned good story for the *Washington Post*."

McEntire, on the other side of the table, shook his head. Kimball knew the threat was empty. They didn't have a shred of paper that pointed toward the CIA.

Wilcox knew it, too. "I'd bet, Mr. Kimball, that your aircraft will be released in a week or ten days. Why don't you just enjoy the city? You've earned a vacation."

Kimball slammed the phone down, but that didn't

320

help either.

Derek Crider, Alan Adage, and Del Gart left their rental car in the parking lot of the domestic terminal and carried their canvas carry-alls across the lot. They skirted the building to the south, walking along the chainlink fence toward an employee entrance.

"First time I ever did a job armed only with a power screwdriver," Adage said.

"The way things are going," Gart said, "my battery will be dead when I need it most."

Crider didn't say anything. They passed the corner of a building and the Kimball Aero airplanes came into view.

Crider slid to a stop. "Goddamn."

The aircraft were there, as expected.

But they were surrounded by a single stripe of yellow tape, draped in sagging intervals from one portable stanchion to another. Small yellow tags dotted the fighters and the command aircraft.

"What the hell?" Gart said.

One Thai in a police uniform sauntered among the aircraft, obviously bored.

The two C-141 transports were not within the cordoned-off zone. They were parked side-by-side sixty feet from the Alpha Kats and appeared to be all buttoned up. Crider couldn't see any Americans hanging around.

"It looks to me," Crider said, "as if they've been confiscated."

"Or impounded," Adage said. "Maybe they didn't pay their fees. Or take their shots."

"What now?" Gart asked.

Crider thought it over. "This may make it easier than we thought it was going to be. I don't see any-

321

one other than the local cop."

"Let's give it a try," Gart said. "We can always tell the cop we're here to correct the problem. He probably doesn't know shit about the problem."

Crider led the way to the employee entrance, manned by an employee of the airport security force.

He held up his clipboard for the guard to see a thick wad of red *baht* notes peeking from under the paper on the clipboard.

"What is this?"

"We've got some parts to deliver."

"Parts. What kind of parts?"

They opened the carry-alls and let him take a good look in each.

"Those are squawk-ident transponders," Crider explained patiently.

The guard reached inside Crider's valise and fingered the black box. He'd probably never seen anything like it before in his life.

He looked at the clipboard.

"Okay," he said.

He took the clipboard, initialed the bottom line, and gave the clipboard back.

Minus the *baht* notes.

The rest of it was even easier.

Jimmy Gander and Ito Makura, who had drawn the first six-hour stint of guard duty, had spent the first three hours of their tour confined to a small, drab room in the terminal building.

As soon as they had exited the Starlifter with their M-16s, a Thai policeman, one of two left to watch the aircraft, had yelled at them, drawn his pistol, confiscated the rifles, and led them away.

Gander protested all the way, but in vain. The cop

didn't understand English. And couldn't read it, either, when Gander forced his copy of the weapons permit on him.

The supervisor in the security office could speak English, but he had motioned them into the little room, said he must examine the permits and make some telephone calls, and locked the door.

Gander fumed, demanded the use of a telephone, and got nowhere.

Makura climbed on a chair to peer through the single small window, hut he couldn't see the aircraft from where they were confined.

After a mere two hours and fifty minutes, the supervisor came back, smiling. "All is in order."

"Jesus Christ!"

"Yes. But you may not carry the weapons more than twenty meters away from the airplanes."

"I knew that," Gander said.

"The officer will carry them back for you."

"Wonderful."

"You are free to go."

Smile.

Gander followed the policeman carrying their weapons down a maze of narrow corridors in the administrative section. When they reached a door onto the tarmac, he said, "Ito, go find a phone and tell Kim what happened."

"Got it, Jimmy."

As he and the cop neared the impounded planes, Gander scanned the area. It didn't look any different than when they'd been taken away from it. The Alpha Kats and the Kappa Kat were still buttoned up.

He walked alongside the yellow tape and took the assault rifles from the cop, who ducked under the tape and went to join his partner.

Gander rounded the corner stanchion and approached the Starlifter.

The hatch into the crew compartment was closed.

He distinctly remembered leaving it open, in the hopes that the heat wouldn't build up inside.

Gander stopped where he was and rotated.

The Americans exiting through the employee gate stood out like three sore thumbs. They were a full head taller than the Thais milling around near the gate.

Gander yelled, "Hey!"

The Thais all looked his way.

The Americans didn't. They slipped through the gate and began walking north.

Gander ran to the crew hatch, shoved the rifles inside, and then loped toward the gate.

The guard was only there to keep people out, not in, and he didn't give Gander a second glance.

His quarries were running now, headed for the parking lots, but they were tall enough for him to track.

Gander went to full gallop.

Except for Gander, all of the pilots and Tex Brabham were crammed into the room shared by Soames and Billingsly when Kimball got back. He had been using the telephone in his own room.

"All right," he said, "I've made some headway."

Soames hoped so. The atmosphere was definitely dampened by pessimism. There were no jokes today, off-color or not. He asked, "Did you find Jimmy?"

"No."

All they had heard from Gander was a phone message left at the desk saying that the airplanes might have been tampered with by three Americans. Gander had called it in at 4:15 P.M., three hours before.

"So what's the headway?" Vrdlicka asked. His depressed tone said he was worried about his friend.

Kimball leaned against the dresser. "The Thai cops insist that no one was allowed inside the tape. But you know the power of the *baht*. They apologized profusely for detaining Jimmy and Ito."

Makura said, "Jeez, now we are getting somewhere."

"What about the demonstration flights tomorrow?" Soames asked.

"Indefinitely suspended. I called Manila to delay our arrival, but they had already heard that our certificates had been withdrawn, and they postponed indefinitely. They'll call us."

McEntire was stretched out across the head of one bed shoved against the wall, his head and shoulders resting on a pair of pillows. He said, "Have we gotten to the part where we're making headway, Kim?"

"I got some concessions. As long as we don't start or move the planes, we can work on them. I pleaded the humidity here and the need to keep moisture out of the fuel bladders. We can refuel all of the planes, including the transports. We can do our normal maintenance."

"And we can see if anybody's been fucking around with them?" Brabham asked.

"Right, Tex."

"We can strip their seals?"

"Yes. Just leave the ribbon in place."

Brabham climbed out of his chair, and Tom Keeper was the quickest at anticipating the vacancy. He claimed it by rolling backwards over the arm.

"I'll get the boys up and go on out there, then," Brabham said.

Kimball grabbed Brabham's arm as he passed and leaned close to whisper in his ear.

325

Soames also leaned in close and heard, "Tex, tell Carl Dent to stay out of sight inside the Starlifter, but to prepare a full ordnance load for ought-eight. He's to be prepared to missile-up at any moment."

"Now wait just a goddamned minute!" Soames said.

The undercurrent murmur in the room died away.

"Stay out of it, A.J.," Kimball said.

McEntire came off the bed. "Who's doing what to whom, A.J.?"

Brabham started for the door, and Soames slipped in front of him and rested his shoulder against it.

"Move, A.J.," Brabham said.

"In a minute. Kim, you're not going anywhere without me. You'll need a controller, and I'm it."

"Fuck this," McEntire said. "No one's going anywhere, or doing anything, on the spur of the moment."

"It's my fight, Sam Eddy," Kimball said.

"You heard what I said, buddy. If we're sticking to Mr. Washington's plan, we're also sticking to our plan. Admittedly, given the current conditions, we'll need some alternative departure routes, but that's easy enough."

"Damn it, Sam Eddy, I'm the president!"

"Damn it, yourself. I think we can rustle up enough votes to oust you."

"Shut up a minute," Soames said, loud enough that everyone shut up.

The rifts were widening under the pressure, and he wasn't certain of some of the motives, but he wasn't going to stand by and watch it happen.

"We haven't got a quorum for a shareholder's meeting," Soames said, "but I guess we could call this the executive committee. I'm going to want to see enough hands in the air before I go along with anything that deviates from what we all agreed on in Phoenix. Any-

326

one object to that?"

All he saw were heads shaking negatively.

Except for Kimball's.

"Anyone want to try busting out of here?"

All of the hands went up.

Except for Kimball's.

"You're out-voted, Kim."

"You're out of line, A.J.," Brabham said.

"Hang on, Tex. I'm barely started. Next, I want to know just . . ."

The telephone rang.

"That'll be Susie," McEntire said, "wanting to know if we're all happy."

Keeper grabbed the phone, listened a second, and said, "It's Gander. He wants to talk to you, Kim."

It was after midnight before they beached the Oriental Hotel. Located on Oriental Avenue, the hotel overlooked the Chao Phraya River, and was spread over enough acreage to accommodate expansive gardens, two tennis courts, and a swimming pool. Until recently, the Oriental had been considered the best hotel in the world.

They came by the river route, using a long-tail boat, named for the absurdly long drive shaft turning the propeller, and disembarked near the Garden Wing of the hotel. Duplex rooms looking out on the river and the gardens made up the wing.

Kimball paid the boat's operator, then gave him another five hundred *baht* to wait for them. He stepped ashore, followed by McEntire, Cadwell, Mabry, and Halek, all of whom had drawn the short straws and professed to be happy about it.

The garden's paths were lit with small yellow lamps, but it only served to make the shadows darker. Gan-

der emerged from the blackness near one of the duplexes, identifiable by the outline of his Stetson.

Kimball left the path and met him in the middle of
a patch of grass that would have impressed the
greenskeepers at Pebble Beach or Rock Creek.

" 'Bout time, boss," Gander said.

"We had to go back to Don Muang to retrieve the
hardware," Kimball said. "You were right, Jimmy.
The gate guard didn't check us on the way out."

"What've you got?"

"The four pistols. We weren't about to hide an assault rifle."

"Okay. They've got six rooms. Three duplexes. They
travel better than we do. You know these suckers run
two hundred and fifty bucks a night?"

"We getting a tour, Jimmy?"

"No. I followed them back here, but didn't pinpoint
the rooms until late because they all got together for
dinner. I'm hungry, by the way."

"I'll buy you a cheeseburger later," Sam Eddy said.
"So, what do they look like?"

"Hard guys." Gander described each of the six
men. "All of them Americans, I think, except for the
Latino. He could be something else. And one of
them's got an Irish brogue that could be the real
thing."

"Any names?" Kimball asked.

"I heard Crider, Wheeler, and Gart mentioned, but
that's all. If I had to guess, Crider's in charge."

"Good work, Jimmy. Any suggestions?"

"We're short a couple guns. Let's try to take them
one at a time, starting with the Hispanic. He's the
smallest."

"If somebody yells, we lose a few," Halek said.

"Two at a time, then," Kimball said. "We want Crider, for sure."

328

Gander explained the layout of the rooms and who was occupying which room, and they split up. Kimball and Halek followed Gander across a sidewalk to another row of duplexes and they stepped into grass between two buildings.

As he studiously attempted to place his feet on soft ground, Kimball kept thinking about stealthy Indians. Hiawatha or somebody from his bookish youth.

Gander slowed as they reached the second building, sliding into the shadows next to it, putting his back to the wall. Kimball slipped around him and peeked around the corner. He saw sliding glass doors that opened on a small patio.

And they were open, the occupant taking advantage of the balmy night.

Kimball reached under his shirt and pulled the Browning nine millimeter from its perch in the small of his back. His thumb found the safety and clicked it off.

He heard the snick of Halek's pistol being armed.

He went first, tiptoeing across the patio to stand next to the open door. The pale white curtains were drawn, billowing outward between the open doors a little.

He couldn't hear any noises, any movement.

Reaching with his left hand, the pistol held muzzle-up in his right, he grabbed the fabric between his thumb and fingers and drew it back slightly.

As he leaned his head to peer through the gap, he realized his body was probably backlit through the curtains. He hesitated, considering his vulnerability, then pressed forward to see.

There was the bed, ghostly white.

One form in it, lying on its side, its back to him. He stepped through the curtain onto deep, sound-absorbing carpet.

Crossing quickly to the bed, he switched the gun to his left hand, reached over the man's head, and slapped his hand over his mouth.

Shoved the muzzle into the back of his neck as he came to life, struggling.

Then Gander was there, gripping the man's arms.

Kimball leaned down and whispered, "Move again, *hombre,* and I'm going to put your lights out."

He quit struggling.

Halek appeared, tucked his Browning into his belt, and began cutting the sheets into strips. The man was sleeping nude, and he wouldn't like being caught that way. In the thin light spilling outside, his eyes rolled wildly in their sockets. In four minutes, the captive was gagged and trussed like a rodeo calf. Gander had that experience.

Halek rapidly went through the man's suitcase and pants pockets.

"Looks like he's a pilot, Kim," he whispered. "Got a license and log. Passport says his name is Sanchez. There's lease papers and keys."

"Leave the money and bring the paperwork and the keys. Let's make it tough for him to get out of the country."

Halek stuffed his pockets with documents.

"Who's next door, Jimmy?"

"That'll be Crider."

"Let's go."

Crider was a more cautious man. His doors were closed and locked.

Kimball was considering his next move when all hell broke loose.

Two loud shots rang out from the next row of buildings.

People started yelling.

He grabbed a metal chair from next to a glass-topped table, rotated nearly a full turn, and slammed it as hard as he could into the glass door.

Glass exploded everywhere.

He danced through the doorframe, trying to stay away from the jagged edges.

Crider was sitting bolt upright in his bed, his hand scrambling beneath his pillow.

"If you find it, Crider, you're a dead man," Kimball said, holding the Browning steady on the man's forehead.

Crider pulled his hand out.

The use of his name didn't stop him from trying to bluff it out. "What the hell's going on? You want money? Take it."

Gander and Halek came through the broken door.

"We'd better move," Gander said.

"Out of the bed, Crider."

He slid out from under the sheet, wearing boxer shorts, and stood up slowly, keeping his hands out in front of him. Kimball had the feeling Crider had done this before.

Halek sliced sheets.

Gander slipped behind the man, pulled his arms behind him, and bound them tightly, from wrists to elbows.

"Get the paperwork, Jay."

Halek searched the slacks and jacket of a suit tossed over a chair and came up with the passport and wallet.

"Let's roll," Kimball said.

Gander shoved Crider barefooted through the broken glass and out the door.

The captive complained about the glass, but he complained quietly.

Kimball heard feet pounding on the sidewalk. More people were screaming for the police. Lights came on in most of the duplexes.

Somewhere to Kimball's right, and ahead of him, somebody yelled, "Derek?"

They ran for the river, passing the last duplex at a canter, Crider jerked along between Gander and Halek. Because of his bound arms, he couldn't run well, but the two pilots didn't let him lose his balance.

Four more shots rang out behind them.

And the more prudent hotel guests immediately shut off their room lights.

Ahead of him, Kimball saw a shadow prancing among deeper shadows.

And the shadow hollered, "Stop, or I'll shoot!"

Twenty-one

"There's three of 'em, Alan!" Crider yelled, diving for the ground and pulling Halek and Gander with him.

Kimball, with the awareness a fighter pilot has for his tactical situation, realized he was outlined by the lights still on in a few duplexes behind him. A stand of three palm trees ten feet away on the left was his closest cover, and as he made a cut off his right foot and headed for them, he heard the sharp crack of a pistol and a bullet whistled past his head. Its sonic trail concussed against his eardrums.

He saw the muzzle flash in the darkness ahead, and almost without thinking, squeezed off two shots in reply.

Then hit the ground.

Heard his shots tearing leaves.

Rolled wildly to his left.

Another bullet kicked dirt in his face.

The image of the muzzle flash hung on his retina. He whipped his Browning out in front of him, gripped it in both hands, aimed to the right of the flash memory, and squeezed the trigger.

The automatic bucked.

The bullet hit meat.

Deep groan.

He scrambled awkwardly to his feet, running toward the sound.

"Jay! Jimmy!"

Kimball heard them hauling Crider to his feet, chasing after him.

When he reached a thicket of shrubbery, he searched the ground rapidly and saw the dark form sprawled on the grass. It didn't move.

He knelt beside the man and tried to feel for a pulse on the side of the throat, but his hand came away slippery and wet with blood.

"Come on, Kim!" Gander yelled. "Forget him!"

Leaping to his feet, Kimball circled around the shrubbery, and then the river was before him, the quay softly lit by regularly spaced lampposts.

Among the dozen boats held against the dock, their boat was waiting. Thais had a strange kind of loyalty to strangers who had paid them.

He heard more feet running on a gravel path, and whipped around, raising the automatic.

"Me, Kim!" McEntire called.

They came trotting into the light, and Kimball saw that McEntire and Mabry were carrying Cadwell between them.

"Jesus!"

"In the boat," Sam Eddy urged.

They leaped from the quay into the longtail boat. Gander and Halek more or less threw Crider aboard, who tripped and fell heavily on his side, then followed him.

"Let's go," Kimball yelled to the driver.

His eyes were wide with fear, but he quickly took in all the guns, revved the ratty motor, and pulled out into the current, joining other boats on the move.

Mabry and McEntire helped Cadwell move forward, into the protection of the deck cabin, and Gander prodded Crider with the toe of his cowboy boot, forcing him to follow, scooting along on his knees.

Kimball dropped to the deck next to McEntire, who was examining Cadwell with a small flashlight.

The left shoulder, arm, and side of Cadwell's blue sport shirt turned a slick black under the light. McEntire ripped the sleeve away.

"Cardsharp?" Kimball asked.

"Not too bad, Kim. Hurts like hell, but I don't think the slug's in me."

"Roll over," Sam Eddy ordered.

Gritting his teeth, and assisted by Kimball and Mabry, Cadwell rolled onto his side.

McEntire probed with the light and his finger.

"No bullet, Howard," he said. "Took a chunk out of the back of your arm, and furrowed your back. Bleeding like a stuck hog, however."

"Damn, thanks, Doc," Cadwell said.

While Mabry cut up Cadwell's shirt and used it as a bandage, Kimball checked aft. Jay Halek was sitting next to their boatman, chatting with him, and keeping him on a course up the river.

"What the hell happened, Sam Eddy?"

"We were tying up the first guy, when the second guy popped over for a drink, I guess. He skipped the drink, shot Howard, and disappeared into the dark. I thought the prudent course might be to leave, but we ran into a third guy with a gun. We exchanged pleasantries."

"Shit."

"Yeah. I think I downed him for good."

"Kim got one of them, too," Gander said. "Probably the one who shot Howie. The one called Alan, right, Crider?"

Crider didn't respond. He was lodged against the cabin wall, his arms still bound behind him, and his boxer shorts bunched up.

Through the open front end of the deckhouse, Kimball could see the river curving to the left. The lights of dozens of watercraft moved with, and opposite, their course. More lights lined the river's shores.

There were sirens sounding behind them now, converging on the hotel.

Kimball moved over next to Crider.

"What's your first name, Crider?"

The man pursed his lips.

Kimball was certain that the man's passport and ID, which Halek had, wouldn't agree with the truth.

McEntire crawled over next to Kimball and turned his flashlight on the captive's face.

The close-cropped hair suggested military, and the taut skin of the face, along with the rippling shoulder and arm muscles, indicated a man who was fit and could be dangerous. The cold gray eyes confirmed the impression.

"I'll tell you what, Crider. I'm running out of both time and patience. I want quick and accurate answers to some questions."

Under the glare of Sam Eddy's light, Crider's lips tightened.

Jay Halek came forward with Crider's passport and handed it to Kimball. "Take a look at this, Kim. The entry and exit stamps match our stops except for Islamabad."

Kimball took the blue book, held it under Sam Eddy's light, and glanced at it. Just looking at the dates brought back the memory of the Alpha Kat exploding from under him. He took the wallet from Halek and scanned through it, found the slip of paper listing phone numbers and times. He shoved both the passport and the wallet in his pocket.

His anger rose proportionately to what he had read, and he didn't bother disguising it. "Well. Mr. Joseph Brooks, huh. Brooks or Crider, it puts you where I thought you were. You happen to have four million on you? You owe me for a plane."

"Go to hell," Crider said.

"That's all I need," McEntire said. "Let's ice him."

"Fine with me."

336

Crider didn't think they'd do it.

Kimball told him, "I was flying the plane you rigged, Crider. If you think I give a shit about you, think again. I'm going to make my own justice system."

The hard eyes stared back at him.

But they flickered.

Kimball looked at McEntire, nodded, and they each grabbed one of Crider's legs and dragged him across the splintery deck out of the deckhouse.

"Stick close to the driver, Jay," Kimball said.

Halek went aft.

Crider began to struggle, kicking his legs, rolling back and forth on his bound arms.

Kimball gripped the man's ankle with both hands.

McEntire had a firm grasp on the other ankle. He laughed and said, "Make a wish, Kim."

They stood up outside the deckhouse, raising Crider upside down, to where he rested on the back of his thick neck.

Spread his legs a little more.

Heaved upward.

Swung his torso outboard and lowered him headfirst into the polluted water of the Chao Phraya.

The leg bucked and fought in Kimball's hands. He tightened his grip.

"How long, Sam Eddy?"

"Ah, hell, Kim. You messed up my count. Now I'll have to start over."

The water tended to drag Crider back alongside the hull of the boat, and Kimball braced his feet against the pull.

The boatman, Halek, Mabry, Gander, and Cadwell, who was raised upward on his good arm, watched the action silently.

"Let's try now," McEntire said.

They hauled him inboard, dripping, gagging water.

"Crider?"

337

"Fuck you!"

Back in the water.

McEntire counted to three hundred this time.

Lifted him out.

Spitting, coughing. A stream of filthy water erupted from his mouth.

"Who you working for?" Kimball asked.

Hacking cough. More water gushing from his mouth.

"Who?"

"Goddamn it, I don't know."

"Back over the side," Sam Eddy said.

"I don't know, damn it!" There was an edge of hysteria in Crider's voice. "Hold on! I'd tell you if I knew."

"Tell me everything you know," Kimball said.

Crider told them.

It wasn't much. No names. Phone contacts only.

"How do you make contact?" McEntire asked.

"Numbers and times in my billfold." He coughed and spit more water.

"What else have you been doing?" Kimball asked.

"That's it! Nothing else!"

"Why don't I believe you?"

"Asshole! We weren't trying to hurt anyone. Just the planes."

Kimball and McEntire stood up, raised Crider's legs high (he wasn't fighting as hard now) and started swinging him.

"Goddamn it! Henry Loh!"

They dropped him headfirst on the deck, maybe a little harder than necessary.

Henry Loh, according to Wilcox's information, was the man heading Lon Pot's little air wing.

"Tell me about Henry Loh."

Crider told them about the deal for the six Mirages.

"What else did you learn from Henry Loh?"

"He works for Lon Pot."

"Where is Lon Pot?"

338

"Here. In Bangkok."

That was news.

"Got an address?"

Crider gave them one. "It's near Chinatown, his wife's place. Half block from Yawaraj Road."

Kimball left Sam Eddy kneeling over Crider and duck-walked back to where Gander waited with Mabry and Cadwell.

"How you doing, Cardsharp?"

"Hurts like hell, Kim, but as long as it's hurting, I know I'm all right."

Kimball handed Gander his Browning. "Jimmy, we're going to drop you off somewhere along here. All of you. Buy Howard a new shirt. Buy a bottle of whiskey," he looked back at Crider, "cheap whiskey, and start pouring it in our friend. When he's nice and drunk, take him back to the airport. Anybody asks, he's a fellow pilot that got rolled, okay?"

"Gotcha, Kim."

"If you don't think you can get through the gate with the guns, ditch them."

"Where are you going?"

"Sam Eddy and I are going to visit a lady."

Gander grinned at him. "You single guys just can't leave it alone, can you?"

A relieved boatman let them off on a dock near Mahachai Road and grinned nervously as Kimball gave him five thousand *baht*. It was much more than he might have expected, and enough that he wouldn't want to brag about it.

Kimball and McEntire, who still had one of the pistols, flagged a taxi, bargained a fare, and climbed in.

It took twenty minutes to find the address and another two hundred *baht* to keep the driver waiting.

The front door was made of steel, but it had a wrought-iron protected window in it. McEntire stood to one side of the door, out of sight, and Kimball, who couldn't find a doorbell, banged on the door with his fist.

After a few minutes a light came on inside, then a hardened and matured Oriental face appeared in the window and stared out at Kimball. He shook his head negatively, waving Kimball away with his hand.

McEntire stuck the muzzle of the automatic against the glass, aimed in the middle of the man's face.

He opened the door.

Kimball pushed in, shoving the man aside.

"Lon Pot?"

He knew the name, but he didn't know English. Shook his head madly.

"Lon Pot?"

More negatives.

"Mai Pot?"

The eyes clicked upward.

"Wait here, Sam Eddy."

"Happily," McEntire said, holding the pistol at the ready and roughly pushing the man back into the foyer. He closed the door.

Kimball took the stairs two at a time and reached the landing at the top.

He banged on that door several times.

When it finally opened wide, he was surprised to see a small boy.

Damn it. He didn't want to be faced by a small boy.

A woman appeared from a hallway, clutching a silken, embroidered robe around her. She moved up behind the boy and put her arm over his shoulder. There was real beauty in her face, despite the touch of fear in her eyes.

"What do you want?" she asked. Her English was stilted, but she obviously recognized him as American.

"I want Lon Pot."

"He no . . . is not here. You must go."

Kimball heard the sickly thunk of metal striking flesh

340

and bone and looked down to the foyer. McEntire had clubbed the Oriental, whose eyes rolled backward as he sagged to the tiles. Sam Eddy now had the gun trained on a second man, motioning him into the foyer from a doorway.

"Getting crowded, Kim," he called.

"Where is Lon Pot?" Kimball asked the woman. He kept his hands at his sides, trying to dispel her fright.

"Why you want Lon Pot?"

To hell with her fright. "I may kill the man."

Her hand rose to her mouth.

"Why kill?"

"He killed my parents and brother."

Her head sagged forward, her chin resting on her chest.

"Can you tell me where to find him?"

She said something to the boy, in what Kimball thought might be Vietnamese, and the boy slipped out from under her arm and ran back into the depths of the apartment.

She raised her head and looked directly into his eyes. There was no fear there, now, just a wicked gleam.

"I tell you where to find Lon Pot."

Kimball was amazed.

"You make me widow."

"I'll damned sure try."

In her halting English, she described to him a large compound called Fragrant Flower, and she graphically related its location relative to villages, rivers, and roads.

Kimball wondered if Wilcox had had this information.

He didn't think he'd have to leave Mai Pot and the boy bound and gagged. He thanked her and backed out of the room, closing the door behind him.

Back down in the entrance hall, just in case the other Asian could understand English, he told McEntire, "Pot's not here. Come on."

Together, they raced out the door and into the back of the cab.

McEntire told the driver, "Don Muang. You do it fast, and we'll double your fare."

Kimball was shoved off balance into the seat as the cab whipped a U-turn and headed out of the alley.

When he got himself upright, he leaned over the back of the front seat and told the driver, "We want to make a stop at the central post office."

The man nodded vigorously.

"Forget to mail your postcards?" Sam Eddy asked.

"Forgot to call home," Kimball said. "The international telecommunications center is next door."

It was nearly three in the morning when Kimball picked up a phone and got the AT&T operator. He used his credit card and long distance information to make his call.

"Central Intelligence Agency."

"I want the Deputy Director of Operations." Kimball didn't even know his name, but he was certain the man knew as much as Wilcox knew.

"I'm sorry, sir, but—"

"It's three o'clock in the afternoon there. You can find him somewhere. Just tell him it's Bryce Kimball."

It took nearly eight minutes to run him down.

At nine minutes after nine o'clock at night, Brock Dixon picked up the public telephone after its first ring.

He looked around the mall, but didn't see anything suspicious. He turned back to face the wall, pushing himself close between the short partitions separating the four telephones.

"Yeah, Crider?"

"Wrong party. This is Bryce Kimball."

Dixon nearly dropped the phone. What the hell?

"Who? What are you . . . ?"

"I don't know who you are, asshole, and I don't know where you are, but it doesn't matter."

"Listen, goddamn it!"

"You listen. Take a look around. I'm sure you'll see someone you recognize."

Kimball hung up on him.

Dixon was afraid to turn around. He replaced the receiver, took a deep breath, and rotated slowly.

In the sparse crowd moving along the central atrium of the mall, he didn't see anyone who . . .

There.

Ted Simonson.

He stood near a planter full of tall greenery, just looking at him, nodding slightly.

Dixon started walking in the opposite direction.

Two men rose from a bench and began to close on him.

He turned around and started the other way.

Two more men emerged from the entrance to Sears.

And Ted Simonson kept nodding.

Lon Pot emerged from the master suite, stood for a moment on the balcony, and then descended the stairs.

He tried so hard to appear regal, Henry Loh thought. He and Dao Van Luong stood as the Prince approached them across the soft plushness of the white carpet.

"Well," Pot demanded.

He thought he was managing the coup, but all he had done in the hours since he returned to Fragrant Flower was to ask questions of Dao or Loh, wanting to know if the orders they had formulated had been carried out.

Dao said, "I have just talked to Vol Soon. The army is prepared, Prince."

"Chao is ready, also," Loh said. "He has been in contact with Colonel Mauk. Beginning at four o'clock in the morning, the country is yours."

Pot almost smiled. "And this American? Kimball?"

"Their aircraft are quarantined at Don Muang. They are no longer a threat," Loh said. "We flew air defense last night, but there was no attack on any of your facilities, Prince."

"Suppose the airplanes are released. What then?"

Loh smiled. "They are no longer stealth aircraft, though their pilots do not know that. We will keep an air cover near Shan Base and here. If, by any chance, the Alpha Kats come, they will not last long."

"Who is flying this air cover?" Pot asked.

"Two of the pilots from Switzer's squadron."

"No. You will fly it. And you will use all of the Third Squadron's aircraft."

The man was becoming paranoid, Loh thought, but he would not argue. If the Americans came, he would achieve his goal of becoming an ace very easily.

"Very well, Prince. I will issue the necessary orders. At 3:30 A.M., Pyotr will launch his aircraft from here and fly the intimidation patrols to the south. At the same time, Switzer will take the new Mirages and fly the north and coast patrols. I will assume command of Kao Chung's squadron, and we will maintain a twenty-four-hour air defense of Shan Base and Fragrant Flower."

"Make it so," Lon Pot said.

His broken teeth marred his smile, but he was happy because he had finally made a decision.

Susan McEntire called at six o'clock.

Kimball and Sam Eddy were devouring a large platter of hamburgers and French fries in their room, chasing them with Classic Coke.

McEntire lifted the phone off its cradle and handed it

to Kimball.

" 'Lo," he said.

"Where have you been all day?"

"Busy. We're working on this end, Susie."

"I'll bet you are. You made the papers here."

"Ah, damn. What'd they say about us."

"That the airplanes are grounded, pending a review of the airworthiness certificates."

"Not good publicity, huh?"

"Damn it, Kim! You didn't call me yesterday, and I've tried a dozen times today."

"We really have been working. Sam Eddy and I have been to the Embassy three times. We've been hitting every Thai government office we can think of."

"At least," she said, "you can't . . . do the other."

"Don't worry about it, Susie."

"But I do."

"The guys are all fine."

"I worry about you."

Women! No. Susan. Kimball had an instantaneous image of her. He could smell the fine aroma of her dark red hair, see those big green eyes locked on his own. He remembered her tears when they left Phoenix.

As a test, he compared the image with that of Cathy Colby, but Cathy's features were blurred.

"You are a puzzle, Susie," he said.

"We'll have a long talk when you come home," she said. "Why don't you come home now?"

"It won't be long."

McEntire motioned for the phone.

"Sam Eddy wants to talk to you. I'll call tomorrow or the next day."

"No, I don't. . . ."

He passed the phone to McEntire.

"Susie, you still have the key to my apartment, right?"

Pause.

345

"Do me a big favor, will you? My plants are going to die if they don't get water. Yeah, thanks, hon."

McEntire hung up and went back to his hamburger. His mood had changed, and he didn't seem inclined to talk.

Kimball finished his Coke and got up from his chair. "It's about that time, Sam Eddy."

"I know. I'm a clock-watcher from way back. You sure you want to do it this way, Kim?"

"No, I don't. But I got out-voted, remember?"

They had put the plan to all of the Kimball Aero Tech employees in mid-morning. Kimball had offered an alternative that primarily affected himself alone, but that had been turned down when Soames and McEntire lobbied the voters.

Sam Eddy pulled himself out of his chair, and the two of them went through the room, stuffing paper and documents in their pockets. They were leaving their duffle bags.

They left the hotel together, certain that the desk clerk saw them, wandering slowly down the street. From time to time, they saw some of the others, out shopping for trinkets and souvenirs, ready for a good time.

The shadows got longer as the sun settled in the west.

To kill time, they stopped in a jewelry store and examined almost everything behind the glass counters.

McEntire asked to see an emerald ring. He held it up to the light, then handed it to Kimball.

"Look like the real thing to you, Kim?"

Kimball peered at it in the light. The deep yellowish-green appeared clear and cold.

"Looks good to me, Sam Eddy, but you're more of an expert than I am."

"I've bought a few, I guess. For too many women."

McEntire engaged the proprietor in a long barrage of

offers and counteroffers, switching back and forth between Thai *baht* and American dollars. He finally forked over nine hundred dollars American.

"Stateside," he said, "it'll be worth twice that."

They kept meandering around the streets, trying out the shops, buying a couple T-shirts, always moving toward the airport, and at nine o'clock, they entered the domestic terminal.

Airline traffic seemed normal, and the terminal was crowded with a couple dozen different nationalities, all of them going somewhere important.

Moving easily through the crowd, Kimball found the airport offices, and after showing their passports, they were allowed to pass through the employee-only corridors and go out on the tarmac. All of the KAT people were entering the airport grounds through different gates and doors.

Ahead of them, they saw the shadowy outlines of the Alpha Kats and Kappa Kat backed up by the soaring tails of the Starlifters.

There were no lights in the section, but the yellow tape surrounding the aircraft was clearly visible.

Approaching one of the Thai guards, Kimball said, "We're going to do some work, all right?" He pointed to the transports. "Over there?"

The guard nodded his acceptance.

Kimball saw Tex Brabham talking to the other guard.

And Kimball punched this one in the stomach.

The air went out of him, and his head whipped down. McEntire clipped him smartly behind the ear with the edge of his hand.

"Ow!" McEntire yelped. "That's not supposed to hurt me. James Bond doesn't get hurt."

Kimball caught the collapsing Thai, spun his body around, and got his hands under his arms.

"Bond has a stand-in," he said.

"Damn it. I knew there was a trick to it," McEntire

said as he lifted the guard's feet.

They hauled him across the tarmac to the darkest spot against the chainlink fence, meeting Brabham and Dent with the other guard.

Dent whipped nylon line out of his pocket and went to work tying them up.

Kimball and McEntire trotted to the first C-141, opened the hatch, and climbed into the crew compartment. Walt Hammond was seated on the raised flight deck, looking down on Crider, who was spread-eagled on the lower bunk, his wrists and ankles tied to the four corners. His mouth was stuffed with an oily rag, held in place by someone's tie wrapped around his head.

His eyes followed Kimball as he peeled off his shirt and slacks, shoving them into a locker. McEntire changed out of his civvies also, and a few minutes later, they were both in their flight suits and pressure suits.

"He been a good boy?" Kimball asked Hammond.

"The best. Any time he looks happy, I tell him about the joys of free-flying from ten thousand feet. Without a chute, of course."

"Of course," Kimball said, handing his helmet and mask to Hammond. "Don't let me forget these, Walt."

He slipped into the cargo bay and found most of the pilots and mechanics waiting for him.

"Anyone have a problem getting into the airport?"

No one had.

McEntire came through the doorway and joined them.

"Anyone have any questions about the sequence? Do we have it down pat?"

"Down pat," Soames said.

"We can always draw names again," Kimball said. "I don't want to force anybody into this."

Gander, Halek, and Vrdlicka, who had drawn the

positive numbers for the Alpha Kats, shook their heads violently.

Howard Cadwell, bare-backed and trussed in clean white bandages, said, "I think I got fucked over. Jimmy wouldn't let me draw."

"Next time, Howie."

Brabham and Dent pulled open the passage door and joined them in the hot cargo bay.

"How about the Kappa people?"

Soames, Hamilton, Mabry, and Keeper had drawn the seats on the Kappa Kat.

Soames said, "Kim, let's just get on with it."

"Roger, A.J."

He looked around the bay. Cardboard, slats, and chunks of crating were shoved against the far wall. Missiles were loaded on the dollies, ready to roll as soon as the ramp was dropped. More missiles were unpacked, resting on canvas beds, ready to be lifted onto the empty dollies as they came back. He was certain the floor of the other transport was similarly cluttered.

"Carl?" he asked.

"We figure we've got the time down to twenty minutes, Kim."

"Without lights?"

"We know our babies."

"Setup?"

"A Sidewinder and an AMRAAM each on the two outboard pylons. Four Hellfires on the inboard pylons. On the centerline, we're slinging a gun pod."

"Good. Jay, did you find the Lear?"

Among the personal effects they had lifted from the Hispanic pilot at the Oriental had been the lease papers and keys for a Lear business jet.

"It's about a quarter-mile north of us, Kim."

"Good. Give me the keys."

Halek tossed him the key ring. Kimball caught it, then checked his watch.

349

"The planes all check out, Tex?"

"They're clean, Kim. And we went over our entire inventory. I can't see where the asshole," he pointed a stubby forefinger toward the crew compartment, "got hold of anything."

"Okay. 9:35 P.M. all right with you, Tex?"

"Any time's all right with me, chief."

"I'll go at 9:35 P.M."

"We'll be waiting." Brabham gave him two coils of quarter-inch nylon rope.

McEntire punched him lightly on the shoulder as he left the bay. Kimball gave him a wink.

He stayed close to the fence, walking behind parked aircraft. There were several Thai International planes, a Boeing 737 from India Air, a large number of private light twins and business jets.

He found the Lear by its tail number, checked the immediate vicinity, and finding no one interested in him, walked up to the Lear and unlocked the door.

He let the door down and climbed inside. It took him five minutes to rig the ropes, one to the brake release, and one looped around the throttle handles. The line to the throttles was hooked around the console so that tugging it from the rear pulled the handles forward. He trailed both ropes along the floor and tossed their ends out the door.

He leaned down and looked through the windscreen at the runways that passed in front of the plane. He counted the planes taking off and compared them to the second hand on his watch. The interval was almost six minutes.

Then he sat in the pilot's seat, powered up the instruments, and went through the checklist as best he remembered it. He hadn't flown a Lear in years.

He waited, checking his watch occasionally.

At 9:33 P.M., he fired the port jet, then the starboard. They both spooled up quickly, but he didn't worry about temperatures and pressures.

He levered himself out of the seat, backed through the curtain into the cabin, then descended the steps.

Watched the runway and waited.

Waited.

A silvery DC-9 flashed past, its engines at full throttle. He waited until he saw it start to rotate, then backed away from the fuselage and pulled his throttle rope hard.

The twin engines immediately started to scream.

The plane bucked against the rope.

Kimball backed away a little farther, keeping a firm grip on the other rope.

When he was clear of the stabilizer and the engines were crying a moan that hurt his ears, he jerked the rope.

Then he started running.

Twenty-two

A.J. Soames was in the Hawkeye Three position, Alex Hamilton backing him up in the air controller's seat on his right. Warren Mabry was the aircraft commander, and Tom Keeper was in the right seat.

Soames was proud of the whole damned bunch of them. Pilots and techs working side-by-side in nearly pitch darkness, they had missiled-up in less than eighteen minutes. The start carts were positioned between aircraft, and all of the pilots were in their assigned seats, except for Kimball.

Kimball absolutely would not let anyone else take the risks with the Lear.

Kimball was very protective of his charges. From the information provided by the CIA man, Kimball, McEntire, Billingsly, and Soames knew the names and background of some of the pilots they might face: Loh, Switzer, Chung, Burov. Kimball had decided to not pass that data on to the other pilots. He thought it was much better if they confronted nameless adversaries, and Soames agreed with him.

He could see Tex Brabham's hat moving between the planes, as he checked on his mechanics and the start carts.

Mabry whistled through his teeth. The *Colonel Bogie March.*

Soames craned his neck to look north.

The Lear emerged from the line of parked aircraft,

appeared to hesitate, then rapidly picked up speed. The unmanned business jet zipped toward a ninety-degree intersection with the main runways.

With some trepidation, Soames quickly scanned the end of the runways. A civilian airliner was just turning onto it from the taxiway.

Hold on, mother.

The Lear bounced over a section of grass, then crossed a taxiway, still gathering speed. It lumbered through the depression of the median between the taxiway and the first runway. He figured it was doing at least fifty by the time it hit the first runway.

Tex Brabham shouted, "Light 'em up! Come on, fuckers! Move!"

The Kappa Kat's left turbofan started to spin.

The Lear bounced as it hit the next runway.

The jet engine ignited behind him with its pleasant whine, and Mabry started turning the right turbine.

The business jet struck a runway light standard and leaped a trifle as it went off the side of the second runway, attempting to launch itself, but the control surfaces were following their own whims. Soames could see the silver airplane clearly in the runway lights now. It was wavering wildly, shifting from side to side.

The left wing came up, and the nose went down. The jet began rolling in a careening, caterwauling fashion. It flipped and flopped, tearing itself apart, for nearly a quarter-mile before it exploded into flames.

The second turbojet fired, and Mabry released the brakes and began to roll even as he warmed the engines.

The Alpha Kats were firing up all around them. Soames saw Walt Hammond sitting in zero-eight, starting the engine for Kimball.

Mabry turned out behind the Starlifters, now designated Atlas One and Two, and headed for the taxiway. Both C-141s had their portside engines running.

"Leave the goddamned start carts!" Brabham yelled at someone. "Mount up! Come on!"

Soames closed the rear canopy so he could use the rearview mirror. When it sealed itself into place, he saw that two Alpha Kats had pulled in behind them.

Glancing at Alex Hamilton, he saw narrowed, squinting eyes that betrayed jangled nerves. Soames gave him a wide grin, and Hamilton smiled back, gave him a thumb's up, then snapped his oxygen mask in position.

Soames saw Kimball running back, circling around the first transport.

On the intercom, Mabry said, "Miner, you monitoring the tower?"

"Roger, Dingbat," Keeper told him.

The emergency trucks had started rolling. Blue pulsing strobes lit up the far end of the field and started down the far right runway. Sirens began to keen.

Keeper told them that, on Tac One, Bangkok Air Control was suspending all takeoffs and landings, citing an emergency on the field.

Switching to Tac Two, Soames said, "Bengals, let me hear from you."

"Three's right on your ass."

"Two in line."

"Five here."

"Four."

As Mabry turned right onto the taxiway, Soames peered across Hamilton to check the lineup. The first C-141 had drawn up behind Bengal Four. The second transport was just easing out of the parking line, Walt Hammond running alongside it, then being dragged inside.

Kimball was in zero-eight, just closing the cockpit. "One, you clear?"

"Got me, Hawkeye. I'll be the last one out."

That hadn't been part of the plan, but Soames said, "Roger, One. Remember, guys, no lights, no IFF. Hawkeye Four, go to Tac Four and remind Atlas."

"Gone Four, Papa," Hamilton said.

The transports didn't have the ability to scramble communications on the frequencies used by the KAT planes, and Tac Four had been set up as the common, unscrambled frequency for inter-craft dialogue with the Starlifters.

With their fuel and ordnance loads, and especially with the Starlifters, they needed most of the runway, so Mabry was leading them to the far end where the airliner sat in suspense. Her running lights, anti-collision strobe, and landing lights appeared bright.

Keeper, monitoring the air control frequency, reported, "The tower hasn't seen us yet."

"They're busy," Mabry said.

They were taxiing fast, almost thirty miles an hour, and they weren't showing any lights. At the tail end, Kimball reported that he had reached the taxiway.

On the intercom, Mabry said, "That 727's in our way, Papa. We're going to have to turn short and cross the median. It may be a little rough."

Soames passed the message to the Alphas, and Hamilton notified the Starlifters.

As Mabry braked and turned off the taxiway, dipping through the slight depression of the median, Keeper said, "They've seen us. I'm getting lots of babble. Who are we? Stop. Stop. Emergency on the field."

"No shit?" Mabry said.

"I only go by what I'm told, Dingbat. You want me to respond?"

"No response," Soames said.

As the Kappa Kat lurched back onto concrete, Mabry didn't hesitate for a second. He turned onto the runway ahead of the airliner, almost lined up with the center stripe, and slammed the twin throttles forward.

On the right, halfway down the strip, the blue emergency lights were gathering in the field around the wrecked Lear. Flames from its burning fuel climbed high into the sky and black smoke was beginning to drift over the runways.

Soames heard the fighter pilots making cryptic calls as they lined up in pairs and poured on the power.

The Kappa Kat accelerated smoothly, the main landing gear rumbling beneath them.

The runway lights flickered and went out.

The sudden loss of the guiding lights was almost blinding.

"Goddamn!" Mabry said. "Is it dark in here, or is it just me?"

"Our hosts don't want us to leave," Soames said.

"We've got one-ninety," Keeper said.

Mabry rotated, the wheels quit rumbling, and they were airborne.

"Flaps and gear, Miner."

"Coming up. Greens."

"Bengals, Hawkeye. I'll want to know."

As he went through two thousand feet, Mabry began a shallow turn to the left.

"Three's flying," Vrdlicka said.

"Two's off," Halek reported.

A few heartbeats later, Soames heard McEntire's voice. "Four."

"And Five," Gander said.

The monstrous transports took more time, and they had a greater interval because of the air turbulence they created. Two minutes went by, the Kappa Kat already at ten thousand feet, before Sam Miller reported in to Hamilton on Tac Four.

"Atlas One's clear, Papa," Hamilton said. "He's starting his turn."

"Roger, Flamethrower."

Both of the transports would turn to the right, heading for the sea and international airways.

"Atlas Two's wheels-up," Hamilton said.

"Roger that. Tell them to have a nice trip, Flamethrower."

Soames flicked on the radar, cutting back to a thirty-mile scan, and filtering out a lot of ground clutter. He immediately saw seven blips, five of them in what appeared to be normal airliner traffic lanes, and two of them flying as a pair. They were turning toward the transports, which they could see on their radars.

None of the KAT planes had squawked an ID, and none of them appeared on the screen.

"One's clear, Hawkeye."

Soames felt relief for the first time in three hours.

"Atlas has company coming, Cheetah. Pair of interceptors at Mach one."

"Vector me, Papa, then shut down."

"Go to one-nine-seven." Soames switched his radar set to passive.

For the next nine minutes, he longed to switch to active and see what was going on. Mabry continued to climb, settling in on a northerly course.

"Hawkeye, One. I think I surprised the hell out of these guys."

"Tell me, One."

"They're a couple of Royal Thai F-5s, and they thought they were in the driver's seat, coming up on the Starlifters. I snuck up behind them, hit my landing lights, and gave them a five-round burst of twenty

357

mike-mike above their heads. I think they're trying to clean up the cockpits now."

"What're they doing?"

"They got the message. They can't see me, now, but they know I'm here somewhere. They're diverting from the Atlases and heading in the direction of Ubom. I'll stay with them for a little bit, then catch up."

On Tac Four, Miller reported to Hamilton, who passed it on. "Papa, thank One for them and tell him they're feet wet. He can leave anytime."

On the primary tactical channel, Soames said, "One, Hawkeye. They're clear."

"Roger, Hawkeye. I'm saying bye-bye."

"All Bengals, form on me. I need a second's squawk from everyone to locate you."

One by one, the IFF transponders came on, and Soames locked their positions into his computer memory. As long as they maintained heading and speed, the computer could guess where they were.

Wilcox had been in Bangkok since early in the morning. Immediately after arrival, he had crossed from the international terminal to the domestic terminal to reassure himself that the KAT planes were still there. They were, nicely corralled by yellow tape.

He had then taxied into the Embassy, checked in, and called Langley only to have Ted Simonson ream him out.

"What the hell, Ted?"

"I've got a major general under lock and key. I don't know what the hell to do with him."

"Jesus. One of ours?"

"Hell, yes, one of ours." Simonson told him about Kimball's call and the predetermined set of telephone contacts Kimball had discovered between someone

358

named Crider and the head of Air Force Intelligence.

"I don't know what your man Kimball is doing, but I couldn't very well turn him down on this, Ben. If Crider's responsible for the sabotage of the airplanes, Dixon's in deep. Now, I don't know what to do."

"Is Dixon talking?"

"Hell, yes. He's talking about having my balls bouncing around his tennis court."

"Keep him quiet for a few more hours, and I'll run down Kimball."

Before he even had a chance to start making calls, though, the Thai police contacted the Embassy about dead Americans at the Oriental Hotel, and Wilcox got caught up in that.

He went to the morgue with a delegation from the Embassy, expecting to find Kimball and McEntire laid out on the slabs. He had never seen the faces on the bodies before. One had a full red beard, and the other had nasty burn scars covering his right cheek and temple.

Then the Thai police got him involved with the others they had arrested at the hotel. There were three of them, and they were all carrying false passports, and none of them were talking. They didn't know the dead men, and they didn't know anything. According to the hotel registrations, there had been a sixth American man, but he was nowhere to be found.

With the false passports and the refusal to cooperate, the State Department people found it difficult to assist them, and for the time being, they were left to the whims of the Thai prosecutors.

It was after 6:00 P.M. by the time he got back to the Embassy and began calling the Airport Hotel. No one was answering the room telephones there. The front desk reported that the Americans were probably shopping or taking in the nightlife. The clerk had seen them leaving by twos or threes.

For the next three hours, Wilcox had called Kimball's room at the hotel every twenty minutes. He was getting madder by the minute. He knew damned well Kimball was responsible for two dead men.

At 9:40 P.M., one of the communications specialists said, "They just shut down Don Muang. There's been some kind of accident."

Wilcox didn't think anything about it for twenty minutes. Then it slowly dawned on him that the KAT aircraft were at Don Muang. Kimball and accidents were never coincidences.

He ordered a technician to get the tower for him.

After a slightly heated discussion about his power to ask questions, the supervisor finally gave in and said, "No, Mr. Wilcox, they are not here."

"Not there?"

"They took off against orders. We turned the problem over to the Royal Thai Air Force."

Wilcox slammed the phone down, picked it up, and called Langley.

"Simonson."

"Get hold of somebody at the NSA and find out where the satellites are."

"What's going on, Ben?"

"Kimball's on the loose somewhere. I think we'll want to watch the Muang Base."

"Kimball's gone? With his airplanes?"

"With his airplanes."

"Shit. See if I ever let you run an operation again."

"Okay, Bengals, listen up."

Gander tightened his harness straps and shifted the oxygen mask to reseat it. He pulled his visor down.

"In a second, I'm going to go active and see what

we've got around. If we're clear, we follow plan A. Bengal One, with Two and Three will go after Shan Base again. If our information's correct, the Fragrant Flower compound and its airstrip is eleven miles southeast of Shan. Four and Five will take it out."

They had decided to pass on an attack against the Muang Base in Laos, the third target given to them by the man from Washington. Kimball and McEntire figured the aircraft would have been moved by now, just as they had been moved from Chiang Base. The Fragrant Flower target was a new one.

Gander looked ahead to see the guidelights of McEntire's plane ahead and to the left of him. A half-mile to the left were Kimball, Halek, and Vrdlicka. They were all at 12,000 feet, some twenty thousand feet below the Kappa Kat which had climbed away ten minutes before.

Below them, the hills weren't distinguishable from the blackness of the jungle. A few rivulets of water winked occasionally.

"Going active," Soames said.

A split second later, Soames said, "Hey, Jesus Christ! Flight of three closing on you. Eight miles dead ahead. Goddamn it! Three of you are radiating. Scramble! Scramble now!"

Gander took one glance at his transponder. It was off.

McEntire's guidelights went off, and he concentrated on trying to stay on his leader's wing, chasing a shadow.

McEntire climbed. Going almost vertical.

Gander hauled the stick back, eased in throttle, and stayed with him.

"Data feeds are in," Soames called. "Weapons free. Arm 'em up. Infrared says Mirages."

Keeping his eye on McEntire, and following him

361

through a roll to the right, Gander reached over with his left hand and armed all of his pylons.

"One. Got a lock on the lead hostile. Gone."

A flash of brilliant white on Gander's left evolved into a missile trail. Gander rolled upright, still behind McEntire, but apt to lose him at any moment. Every time the lead airplane went below the horizon, it disappeared from Gander's sight.

"Shut down those damned transponders," Soames ordered.

A chorus of negatives told Hawkeye that all the transponders indicated they were turned off.

"Something's fucked up," Soames said.

With the data feed from the Kappa Kat appearing on Gander's screen, he could see what it was. McEntire was radiating a blip. So were two of the aircraft in the other element.

To the north, three blips were spreading out as they approached.

One abruptly disappeared. Through the canopy, Gander saw the explosion, white and orange, maybe six miles away.

"Down one," Soames reported.

"Stay with me, Five," McEntire said, pulling his nose up and climbing again.

"Like snot on a doorknob, Irish."

They climbed high and fast, trying to get altitude on the aggressors.

And then, boom! They were into it. McEntire launched two missiles, but the Mirage dodged them, diving beneath them. Gander pushed his nose down and had him in the gunsight for a half second, and fired off thirty cannon rounds. The tracers all fell far behind the target.

McEntire rolled right and went into a tight right turn, coming back. Gander rolled hard, jockeyed the

362

stick back, and stayed with him.

"One, Hawkeye. You've got a Mirage tight on your six. Pull Gs!"

On his CRT, Gander saw the blip that must be Kimball. A second blip was a thousand yards behind him.

McEntire swung toward the blips and firewalled the throttle. Gander bounced in his turbulence for a second before he could find the spacing. He shoved his own throttle forward, but McEntire had gained a couple thousand yards on him. "He's got a radar lock on you, One," Soames said.

"Break left, Cheetah," McEntire ordered.

The blip on the screen hung there for an instant, then slipped sideways.

McEntire launched two Sidewinders.

The hot exhaust stung Gander's night vision as he followed the trails converging on the hot red exhaust of the Mirage, praying.

Wham!

Both missiles slammed into the Mirage, and it blew apart in streaks of yellow and blue.

"Thanks, Irish," Kimball called.

"Anytime, buddy."

And then from above and a thousand yards behind him, Gander saw the streak of a missile homing on McEntire.

"Hot one coming at you, Four," he called. "Break right."

McEntire broke right, but not soon enough.

The missile almost lost its heat source as Bengal Four turned her exhaust away from it, but it passed close enough for the proximity fuse to detonate the warhead.

Gander saw the missile's explosion, followed quickly by the eruption of the Alpha Kat's fuel cells as hot splinters of shrapnel penetrated the fuselage.

The Alpha Kat blew up in a thousand pieces.

Gander was still at full power, and he whipped the control stick back.

He felt the pieces of debris striking the wings.

And saw the Mirage directly above him.

Too close for a missile.

He triggered off a long burst of twenty millimeter rounds.

The tracers lanced out, reaching, stitching to the right, missing the fuselage, cutting a wide path in the wing.

The right wing peeled away from the Mirage, and the fuselage whipped hard to the left, then spiraled down into darkness, trailing a long blue flame behind it.

Gander retarded throttle and rolled to his right.

"There, you son of a bitch," Gander said to himself.

But it wasn't enough.

Not nearly enough.

Henry Loh had been scheduled for the next flight of fighters. He was in the main house with Lon Pot and Dao Van Luong, staying close to the radio in Pot's office, when Chung announced the intruders on his Mirage's radar screen.

Loh had grabbed the microphone and yelled, "Attack, attack, attack."

Then he leaped out of his chair and ran from the house. In the compound, he yelled for pilots and slid behind the wheel of a pickup.

Jean Franc and one of his countrymen dove into the back of the pickup.

The guards at the gate barely got them open before he shot through and started careening down the hill toward the airstrip. Loh nearly turned the truck over a couple of times when it tried to climb out of the ruts of the road.

Dao had alerted the mechanics at the strip, and the remaining three Mirages were being started as they arrived. He slid the pickup to a stop, hopped out, and ran toward his fighter.

Precious seconds were lost as he was helped into his pressure suit and parachute. He scrambled up the ladder and into the cockpit, strapping in and hooking up.

He dialed the radio to Shan Base's frequency.

"Rose One, Amber One."

"Rose, go Amber," Switzer called.

"We are under attack here."

"We'll scramble now. Rose out."

He switched to Chung's frequency.

"Jade One?"

There was no answer.

"Jade One."

Nothing.

"Jade Two or Three?"

Again, nothing.

Loh looked to his right and saw that Franc and the other pilot were in their cockpits, the canopies closing.

He closed his own, scanned his instruments, and released the brakes. The gyros were still coming up to speed. He turned on the radar set.

The Mirage eased forward, onto the asphalt of the runway, and he turned to line up with the center of it. He held the brakes and ran up the engines, watching the tailpipe temperatures.

The runway lights came on.

He could not help thinking that, though the money was nice, he was about to launch his reputation as a fighter aircraft ace, and that was much better.

* * *

365

Kimball was numb.

The Alpha Kat flew herself, an extension of his nerve endings. His mind felt absolutely clear, but his body was detached, off on its own, responding as directed, but unaware of heat, cold, pain, elation.

"One and Three, you're still radiating," Soames told them. "Get rid of the transponders."

"While we're waiting," Soames went on, his voice so steady it was deadly, "Five, you have the lead. Two, you're his wingman. You're off to Target Two. Go to heading three-one-five, angels one-one. Meet Hawkeye Four on Tac Three."

"Five," Gander replied.

"Two, gone," Halek said.

Kimball's mind told the aircraft to level its wings, enter a slight climb, and then begin a wide turn to the right.

Sam Eddy. Damn, buddy, I don't know if I can do it without you.

His body reacted to Soames's instructions. He pulled his flight gloves off and dropped them on the floor. His left hand found the leg pocket of his flight suit that contained the multipurpose knife. His right hand left the control stick in position and popped open the screwdriver blade of the knife. He had to loosen his harness in order to lean far enough forward to work on the transponder's face. He turned up the cockpit lighting enough to see the screws. It was an awkwardly shaped screwdriver, but within a minute, he had withdrawn the two screws.

He got his fingernails behind the faceplate and tugged. The transponder came out of its sleeve, and he dropped it between the seat and the fuselage side. Collapsed the knife and shoved it back into his leg pocket.

"Good, One. You went away," Soames said. "Come

on, Downhill, snap it up!"

Kimball's body dimmed the cockpit lights once again and retightened his harness straps.

"All right, Three! I lost you on the radar."

"Damned glad to hear it, Hawkeye," Vrdlicka said. "Cheetah, can I have a light?"

Kimball turned on his guidelights, and a few seconds later, Vrdlicka eased up beside him.

Where are you, my friend?

He scanned the HUD. His circle was bringing him up on due south. The speed was steady at 550 knots. Altitude 8,750 feet.

"Weapons status?" Soames asked.

"One. Four Hellfires, one Sidewinder, one AMRAAM. I've got six hundred rounds of twenty mike-mike."

"Three. Full load, less one Sidewinder and fifty rounds of twenty."

"All right, good. We're about to make our first pass at Target One. We are now northeast of the compound, and I am changing the pre-flight plan."

That was almost a surprise. The dogfight had carried them farther north than he had realized. Originally, the tactics had called for the first run on Target One by McEntire and Gander from the south.

McEntire.

Sam Eddy, my friend.

All the good ones leave me.

"Vector me," Kimball said as he double-checked his armaments panel.

"One-eight-five should be right, One. Go now."

Kimball eased out of his turn on the heading, pushed the nose over, and started down. He saw two strings of runway lights appear in the darkness.

"Three, trail formation. Give him a thousand yards."

"Roger that," Vrdlicka said.

367

Kimball deployed the night vision lens and activated the infrared sensor. Pulling his infrared reader down, he found three hot spots right away. The area around them was painted pale green. The asphalt runway, still carrying the heat of day, stood out against the landscape, and the runway lights were green pearls. On the left, higher up a hillside, was the large compound. There were a few lights on in its interior buildings.

Too close. Maybe six miles.

He eased the nose down some more and backed off on the throttle.

Kicked the speed brakes out.

"I put my boards out, Three," he warned.

"Three."

When he was down to four hundred knots, he pulled the brakes back in.

The first hot spot was moving now, racing along the runway, coming toward him.

"Hawkeye, I'm reading three hot aircraft on the ground. The first is on his takeoff run."

"Let's take the first one first, then," Soames said.

"Good idea, Hawkeye."

Henry Loh knew that his attack radar had to have some altitude before it worked effectively, but he had expected to see at least a few moving blips among the ground clutter as he started his takeoff roll.

Maybe Chung had gotten them all?

That would be disappointing.

Speed ninety-five knots.

The compound went by on his right.

Idiot Lon Pot. He should shut off the lights.

The adrenaline pumped into his veins. He felt high, ready to soar.

He hoped Chung had not hit any of Kimball's aircraft. He needed at least five of them to call himself an ace.

And he knew that he had the advantage.

Crider had made them visible for him.

And Wilcox had made him invulnerable.

Switzer, Chung, Burov—none of them knew that Loh was invulnerable. They did not know that the Americans had orders not to shoot at him.

But he did not have similar orders not to shoot at the Americans.

The airspeed indicator showed 122 knots.

His secondary radio was set to the American emergency frequency, 243.0. He pressed the transmit button. "Kimball, I am Henry Loh. Do you read me?"

There was no answer.

Surely, they were monitoring the emergency channel.

He began to have doubts.

They had to know which aircraft was his.

His airspeed reached takeoff velocity, and he rotated, immediately withdrawing the flaps and landing gear.

He climbed steeply, trading speed for altitude.

"Kimball, I am Henry Loh."

"Big fucking deal," the radio responded.

Loh peered forward through the windscreen.

And there was a slim, twin-ruddered shadow against the stars.

Coming directly at him.

No radar return.

His missiles were useless.

Worse, they were not even armed yet.

Suddenly, green tracers erupted out of the shadow.

Passing below him.

Rising.

He pulled back on the stick.

The stall warning buzzer went off.

369

Screaming at him.

The speed gone, his left wing dipped.

The Mirage rolled inverted.

Tumbled.

Henry Loh's last thought was that he would never be an ace.

Kimball wanted to save at least two of his Hellfires. He would use two of them on the runway, to stop the last two planes from taking off. Head-on, his air-to-air missiles weren't going to be as effective.

By the time the Kappa Kat determined the plane taking off was radiating, and illuminated him for the data-link to Bengal One, he was too close.

He heard the two radio calls coming in on his Tac Five receiver, and was mystified by them. Henry Loh meant nothing more to him than another drug runner, responsible for his brother Randy's and his parents' deaths.

And indirectly, the death of Sam Eddy.

He keyed Tac Five. "Big fucking deal."

The Mirage had just lifted off the runway when Kimball opened up with the gun.

The green tracers probed below the Mirage, and he lifted the nose.

But the big fighter, trying to evade, went into a stall, whipped a wing over, and plowed into the earth off the end of the runway.

"Nice shot," Vrdlicka called.

"Didn't even hit him," Kimball radioed back.

Leveled off, heading directly down the strip.

Used the yellow square to target the strip both left and right of center and launched two Hellfires.

They lanced away, slammed into the asphalt and erupted.

He jinked upward and left to dodge the debris.

Found a Mirage and two helicopters parked off the left side of the runway. Another Mirage was on the end of the runway, prepared for its takeoff run.

The parked Mirage was hot.

The infrared lens told him so, and he locked on, then launched the Sidewinder.

It streaked off the wing pylon.

He pulled up and missed seeing the hit.

But below him, the landscape illuminated white-hot.

"Two choppers and a Mirage, Three."

"See 'em," Vrdlicka said. "Launched."

Kimball rolled right, and as he came around in his circle, looked back at the airstrip. He couldn't see Bengal Three, but Vrdlicka had hit the remaining Mirage and both choppers. Four fires raged at the south end of the runway.

There were no flames on the north end, from the Mirage that had stalled out.

Henry Loh?

Kimball dipped the nose and slowed some more as he came back to the north end of the airfield.

If Loh had gotten out, he was going to rip him up with cannon rounds.

The image picked up by the night vision lens was quickly gone as he shot over the wreckage, but he would remember it.

Loh had ejected from the Mirage after it went inverted. The ejection seat had rocketed him headfirst into the ground. All he saw was the bottom of the seat and a pair of legs.

"Hawkeye, One. Any other aggressors around?"

"Negative, One. You're clear for your final pass."

Kimball rolled left to complete another 360-degree turn and get some distance from the compound.

He turned on his wingtip guidelights, and Vrdlicka

joined with him four miles north of the compound. Together, they turned back.

"One, Hawkeye. Bengals Five and Two report total destruction at Shan Base. They caught every damned one of them on the ground."

"Damn," Kimball said, "now they'll expect me to buy them a beer."

He lined up on the compound, which was easy to do. Lights were on in some of the houses within it. He guessed that a lot of people inside were in a state of panic.

As he closed in, he saw that, down by the airstrip, more figures were running around. The headlights of vehicles dashed about.

"We want to hit the trucks?" Vrdlicka asked.

"Skip them. Dump it all in the compound."

Two miles out, he lifted his head enough to aim the night vision lens. The wall of the compound came up.

Roof.

Garden?

A wall of windows, brightly lit.

Two figures behind the windows, peering out.

LOCK-ON.

Committed.

The Hellfires launched.

He fired his last AMRAAM also, just to get rid of it.

Kimball eased the stick back and nosed upward.

Both Hellfires had detonated inside the house by the time he went over it.

He went into another right turn, looking back.

Vrdlicka's missiles had gone into another house and probably a garage with stored gasoline. The flames reached for the stars, red and yellow and orange and spreading.

He hoped Mai Pot was a widow.

372

That's all I can do, Sam Eddy. Is it enough?

There would be some satisfaction in Mai Pot's becoming a widow, though it was not as great a satisfaction as he had thought it might be.

Kimball felt as if his body was becoming his own again as Soames called, "Bengals, form on me. Be tender with the throttles, please. We've got twenty-three hundred miles to go, and fuel may be tight by now."

Rolling into a westerly heading, Kimball began a climb, looking for Vrdlicka to join with him.

He was looking forward to seeing a real prince.

LANDING

Twenty-three

On the third of August, Ben Wilcox and Ted Simonson reviewed the damage.

"It's not as bad as it could have been," Simonson said.

"No. The objectives were met," Wilcox said. "We got rid of a drug kingpin and we suppressed a coup attempt. The anti-drug people and the State Department will both be happy, though not happy with us, since they don't know our role. But damn, Ted, there were a hell of a lot of collateral problems with this operation."

"First, there's Crider."

"He's in jail in Riyadh."

"Right, and though we've made overtures, it looks as if they're going to go ahead and try him for the sabotage of the Alpha Kat."

"The punishment can be brutal in Saudi Arabia."

"We can count on that, I think."

"Knowing how Dixon has worked in the past, though, I don't think Crider can name names," Wilcox said.

"I'm sure that's true. Still, the trial has scared the hell out of Dixon. He's afraid we may leak his telephone connection with Crider to the Saudis."

Wilcox was certain that Simonson had made that point clear to Dixon before he released the general from custody. "I'll bet he retires."

"He's already turned his papers in. Not unsurprisingly, a general named Ailesworth who has something to do with procurement is also retiring."

Wilcox grinned. "Kimball shot down some people he'll never know about. Still, I regret the loss of Henry Loh. He'd been on my payroll for twenty years."

"But, damn it, Ben, you knew he grabbed the bucks anywhere he could. He didn't care whether he was on the winning side or the losing side, as long as he came out of it unscathed, with a few more millions in his accounts."

"Yeah, but I understood him, Ted. And I'd promised him that his information wouldn't get him killed."

"Did you also tell that to Kimball?"

"No. I don't give out the names of my best sources. What's the current status in Burma?"

"Lon Pot's army kicked off its own coup attempt. Apparently, there was a major disruption of communications. My analysts don't think the army knew that their air support had evaporated. Colonel Mauk crushed the major advances with air-to-ground suppression, and all that's left is some mopping up."

"Mauk will come out of this a hero," Wilcox said. "We may have to get close to him."

"I think it's a good idea."

Susan McEntire arrived in Riyadh on the morning of the fourth of August, and Kimball met her at the airport. The short white skirt and print blouse had been left behind in favor of a smart blue traveling suit.

She was very subdued on the drive to the hotel. Since he had already taken a room for her, he carried her two pieces of luggage directly up to her suite.

He unlocked the door and ushered her inside.

Turning slowly, she surveyed the expansive and elegant sitting room, but he felt she wasn't really seeing it. She settled onto the sofa and lit a cigarette.

"I don't suppose a girl can get a drink?" she asked.

"No. Not unless it's soft."

"Seven-up?"

"Sure." He went to the small refrigerator and got it for her. He even poured it in a glass over ice cubes.

"Thanks. Do you want to hear about what's going on in Phoenix?"

"I do," he said, taking one of the chairs opposite her.

"As soon as the governor heard that the Saudis were buying sixty airplanes, and that they'd subsidize a new factory here if the U.S. wouldn't restore our airworthiness certificates, he and a contingent of congressmen began a blitz of Washington. He assured me that Kimball Aero would be staying in Arizona."

"Paying taxes there," Kimball added.

"Of course. No one in the state wants to lose a promising and substantial industry. There's employment, as well as a tax base, to think about."

Kimball retrieved the emerald ring from his pocket and handed it to her.

"Sam Eddy bought this for you."

"What?"

"He stuck it in the pocket of my slacks. I'd left them in a locker on the Starlifter and didn't find it until we landed here."

Susan stubbed out her cigarette in the ashtray on the coffee table and held the ring in her fingers, twisting it so that the light from the lamp reflected in brilliant green splatters on her hands.

He realized for the first time that the emerald was the exact shade of her eyes, something Sam Eddy probably knew when he bought it. The silver flecks around the irises seemed particularly intense. The tears were welling up in the corners.

"Sam Eddy didn't intend to return from this trip," she said.

It was Kimball's turn to say, "What? That's crazy, Susie."

"I went up to his apartment to water the plants. All of his plants were plastic."

"Uh—"

"There was a letter for me. Along with his will. He named you executor."

Kimball had known that.

"All of his KAT shares go into a trust administered by me," she said. "The income is to go to AIDS research."

Kimball hadn't been aware of that.

"He was HIV-positive, Kim."

"Oh, shit."

"That's why he divorced me."

"You . . . ?"

"I'm fine. He gave me up. He gave up all women. That was his problem. Always had been."

Kimball felt devastated. He wished he'd known, but he didn't know what he would have done about it.

"I never stopped loving him," she said.

"I know."

"And I was kind of like him."

Kimball didn't say anything.

"Because I loved the two of you."

And she started bawling.

Women.

He got up, went around the coffee table, and sat on the sofa beside her.

Put his arm around her shoulders.

And held her while she cried.

ZEBRA'S MASTER STORYTELLER—
LEWIS ORDE

THE EAGLE AND THE DOVE   (2832, $4.95/$5.95)
In this sweeping panorama of unbridled ambition that stretches across two continents—from the regal trappings of London's St. James's Square to the posh, limousine-lined streets of New York City's wealthy East Side—the vibrant heiress to Roland Eagles' vast newspaper empire loses her heart to the one man whose self-centered ambition may bring ruin to the very world she cherishes.

HERITAGE   (2397, $3.95/$4.95)
This is the magnificent saga of beautiful, innocent Leah Boruchowicz and her two brothers who were forced by the shadow of the Holocaust to flee their parents' home. They were poor but determined immigrants, each battling for happiness, success and survival, each hoping to fulfill a dream. And in a city where the streets teamed with temptation, and where ambition, money and violence challenged the very core of their beliefs, this courageous family would fight for love, power and their very lifeline—their heritage.

THE LION'S WAY   (2087, $4.50/$5.95)
This is the compelling saga of men and women torn between family and tradition, ambition and fame, passion and need . . . a story of the troubled and talented Daniel Kirschbaum, whose struggle to rise above his poor immigrant heritage becomes the driving force in his life. It is a tapestry of lives interwoven and intermingled, a world of glamor and ghettos, crime and passion, love and hate, war and peace, triumphs and tears—and above all, of one man's unrelenting determination to survive.

THE TIGER'S HEART   (3303, $4.95/$5.95)
A family held together by tradition—and torn apart by love! As beautiful and unique as the natural gem she was named for, Pearl Resnick always stood out in the crowded world of New York City's Lower East Side. And as she blossomed into womanhood, she caught the eye of more than one man—but she vowed to make a better life for herself. In a journey that would take her from the squalor of a ghetto to the elegance of Central Park West, Pearl triumphs over the challenges of life—until she must face the cruel twisted fate of passion and the betrayal of her own heart!

Available wherever paperbacks are sold, or order direct from the Publisher. Send cover price plus 50¢ per copy for mailing and handling to Zebra Books, Dept. 3958, 475 Park Avenue South, New York, N.Y. 10016. Residents of New York and Tennessee must include sales tax. DO NOT SEND CASH. For a free Zebra/Pinnacle catalog please write to the above address.